Praise for

The Summer Job

~~~

One of *Cosmopolitan*'s "New Books to Feed Your Wanderlust"

One of *Marie Claire*'s "Ultimate Summer Beach Reads"

One of the *New York Post*'s
"30 Best Books on Our Summer Reading List"

One of *Real Simple*'s "31 Best Beach Reads"

One of *Country Living*'s "30 Can't-Miss Beach Reads for This Summer"

One of *Parade*'s "25 Books You'll Want to Read This Sizzling Season"

One of *Fortune*'s "10 Entertaining New Books to Read This Summer"

~~~

"With a gorgeously picturesque setting, an utterly charming cast, and a hilarious protagonist, Lizzy Dent's *The Summer Job* is my perfect summer read! Sure to be one of the sweetest, funniest, and sexiest books of the year. As soon as I finished it, I wanted to read it again. Do not miss this one!"

—Emily Henry, author of *People We Meet on Vacation*

"This novel is what happens when you combine *Sweetbitter* with *The Princess Switch*, place it in the Scottish Highlands, and throw in a whole lot of wine." —*Entertainment Weekly*

"A rom-com-esque adventure in which a girl steals her best friend's identity to spend the season at a luxury Scottish Highland resort. Lol, same." —*Cosmopolitan*

"Funny, romantic, hilariously chaotic, and full to the brim with Scottish charm." —*Parade*

"The secluded Scotland setting makes it easy to immerse yourself in Birdy's world. . . . Plenty of bad decisions and dramatic disasters, a cast of supporting characters to love and hate, and a sweet and tender romance despite all odds. But through it all, you can't help but root for Birdy!" —*PopSugar*

"If you're a fan of *Outlander* but want an adventure in the Scottish Highlands with a little more Wi-Fi, this is the read for you." —Shondaland

"Dent hits a home run with her first novel. . . . This witty, banter-filled novel seems frothy at first, but aptly balances the humor with darker subjects. Lovely descriptions of Scotland, quirky supporting characters, and a thoroughly lovable heroine make this a sure bet for fans of Jenny Colgan." —*Library Journal* (starred review)

"Dent's debut is a frothy story reminiscent of late 1990s chick lit, complete with unexpected friendships, offbeat situations, and a re-latable protagonist whose inner journey will charm and delight readers. It's escapist fun with surprising emotional depth; fans of Emily Henry and Katie Fforde should add this to their summer-read list." —*Booklist*

ALSO BY LIZZY DENT

The Summer Job

The Setup

LIZZY DENT

G. P. PUTNAM'S SONS
NEW YORK

PUTNAM
— EST. 1838 —

G. P. Putnam's Sons
Publishers Since 1838
An imprint of Penguin Random House LLC
penguinrandomhouse.com

Library of Congress Cataloging-in-Publication Data

Names: Dent, Lizzy, author.
Title: The setup / Lizzy Dent.
Description: New York : G. P. Putnam's Sons, [2022] |
Identifiers: LCCN 2022011388 (print) | LCCN 2022011389 (ebook) |
ISBN 9780593422069 (trade paperback) | ISBN 9780593422076 (ebook)
Subjects: LCGFT: Novels.
Classification: LCC PR9639.4.D45 S48 2022 (print) |
LCC PR9639.4.D45 (ebook) | DDC 823/.92—dc23/eng/20220310
LC record available at https://lccn.loc.gov/2022011388
LC ebook record available at https://lccn.loc.gov/2022011389

Printed in the United States of America
1   3   5   7   9   10   8   6   4   2

Interior art: Crystal ball © anniebirdie / Shutterstock
Book design by Alison Cnockaert

To Me.
You be proud of yourself.

The
Setup

Prologue

~~~

THE LAST FRIDAY IN AUGUST . . .

THERE ARE TWO men in my life. But this is not a love triangle.

I put my hand on the cold metal of the door and I close my eyes.

This is it. This is the moment I've been building toward for the last three months. I take a big, deep breath in and contemplate everything that has happened to bring me here to this moment. To this decision.

Can I go in? Am I going to see if he's here?

I glance back down the street and I feel a strong pull along the waterfront in the other direction. Or—am I heading home, to him?

Trust your heart. Trust your gut. Trust your intuition.

I shake my head. Which one of these invisible threads in my internal tug-of-war is my heart? Is it the soft and gentle pull home? A strong thread, I note. Strong and solid. Or is it the wild and hopeful yank toward what may or may not be behind this door?

I feel my skirt blow against my thighs, the breeze whipping it up slightly. I look out toward the water, willing the ocean air to blow me in the right direction. But I know, deep down, that the only person who can make this decision is me. And after thirty-one years on this earth, I can say with absolute certainty, the person I do *not* trust to make this decision is me.

And yet, pushing this door open, even just to look, would *be* the decision.

Can I deny myself that?

Part One

JUNE

1

BUDAPEST

S ZIA," SAYS A WOMAN with a throaty Hungarian accent.

"Hiya," I say as I push the fringed bloodred velvet curtains aside. The room is dark, filled with strung beads, rich blue fairy lights, and candles. I feel a thrill coursing through my veins as I move toward the small wooden table in the center of the room. I can't believe I'm about to have my fortune read by a proper clairvoyant.

I touch the red velvet tablecloth and peer at the worn deck of tarot cards and an almost burned-out candle in one of those bronze candleholders with the finger hole.

"Tarot or palm?" my fortune-teller asks, her back to me as she lights another candle. The golden glow around her adds to the mystique.

"Umm . . . palm," I say hesitantly, "if that's okay? There's always a risk of death with the cards, isn't there."

"Death," she whispers, "death can sometimes mean rebirth."

And then she slowly turns to profile and I see the most, and I mean *the most*, enormous, bulging baby bump.

I gasp.

"Oh yes. I see! Rebirth, because . . . because you're . . ." I flap a hand in the direction of her belly and then I giggle, but it's a nervous giggle. "Do you need a hand?"

"No," she snaps as she struggles toward me. As I wait the long moments it takes for her to make her way to the table, I note the purple satin and gold lace enshrouding her, the thin gold chains around her neck, and wrists full of jangling bangles. Her face is obscured by the fall of a net veil, and I can just make out thick black eye makeup, the flash of gold hoop earrings, and not much else.

"Ten thousand forint for a full profile, which includes relationships, fortune, and . . . love."

"Yes! A full profile!" I nearly shout it, my heart thumping almost loudly enough for me to hear it over the Eastern European folk music plucking away in the background.

"Sit," she commands.

As I slide onto the little brown stool, she stops moving suddenly, her breath quickening. She is still for a moment, her shrouded face tilting up to the ceiling, then a moment later she seems to visibly relax. Is reading my fortune causing her discomfort? What does that mean? Is my energy strong? Am I vibrating? I look down at my trembling hands.

"Sit," she says even more sharply.

"I'm sitting, I'm sitting," I say as she finally breathes out and moves toward the table. "Are you . . . okay?"

"Full profile, you said? Pass me your hand."

I reach across and lay my hand in hers, palm facing up. Her fingers are clammy and warm.

"Are you ready?"

I feel almost giddy with excitement. "Oh yes," I say as I straighten myself up. "I should tell you, I'm kind of an amateur astrology enthusiast. I'm a Sagittarius, by the way, Aquarius rising." I cannot believe I stumbled upon this place. It feels like I was meant to be here.

Maybe after this the road ahead will no longer be an endless, nerve-racking mystery, but rather a future to be moved toward. A future I can believe in. Oh, my heart sighs, the quiet peace in that.

There is a moment of silence before she turns her head down to inspect my palm.

"What is your name?"

"Mara."

"And where are you from, Mara?"

"England," I say brightly, and then: "Technically I'm from a small town just north of Newcastle on the Scottish border, but I'd need to get out a map—"

"Well, Mara," she interrupts, "this is your lifeline. There is a very long line here, long and unbroken. Very general, nothing of note. Some signs of trauma here, but since then, very plain and unremarkable."

I hold my tongue. *Plain and unremarkable.* I already know that. I'd tried and failed to stand out from the crowd, and so I have found it safer to stay in the shadows. I don't need to hear where I am now; I want to know where I'm going to be next. I need her to confirm what I feel in my bones: that something big is coming.

"Are you here on holiday?"

"Yes," I say. "I was supposed to be here with my best friend. Her first 'post-baby' getaway, but she pulled out because, well . . . babies are a lot of work." And then I glance down at her belly and swiftly add, "I'm sure you'll be absolutely smashing at it, though. Nothing to worry about. I suppose you already know that, being a clairvoyant—"

"Shhh," she hisses. She seems uncomfortable, I notice, as she moves slightly in the seat.

"Sorry," I say meekly. *Shut up, Mara.*

"Although your life is small, you seek adventure," she continues.

I frown. This was true once, as an eighteen-year-old leaving home with two suitcases and a head full of dreams. Now? I am not so sure. If there's still a part of me that is adventurous, it's only a whisper. So quiet, I almost can't believe it was ever there.

This long weekend away with my best friend was *supposed* to be an adventure. Charlie, a seasoned globe-trotter, chose Budapest because it was the coolest destination on the planet. Hip new cafés, famous "ruin bars" built into the shells of crumbling buildings; it was the European creative, fashion, and art community's new industrious home. She sold it to me hard. Then Charlie pulled out abruptly. She was stressed about leaving baby Sophie, who'd had a fever two nights running, and she called me as I was trying to make every clothing possibility fit into a tiny suitcase. It was a mere sixteen hours before the flight. It wasn't the first time she'd canceled on me since becoming a mum, but I was so sure this trip was actually going to happen. Charlie and Mara: the Flirty Thirties. The brilliant sequel to our Tipsy Twenties. Charlie's return to the world. The long-anticipated reboot to our friendship. I was so deflated I cried. Then she cried and apologized, and I felt guilty for crying. And then, to alleviate my guilt, I put on the bravest brave face I could, and told her I would go anyway, have a fantastic time, and she shouldn't worry *at all.*

"It will be good for you, Mara," she'd said.

But I've struggled for two straight days. Charlie prepaid for this incredible hotel in the heart of Terézváros, the very coolest district in the city. The Stories Hotel has an enormous glass-ceilinged atrium filled with huge plants, trees, and hanging vines where you could sit for a cocktail or breakfast. My hotel room was also enormous, with dark-plum walls and mid-century styling, an actual record player, and a minibar with full 750-milliliter bottles of tequila, and there was a roaming bartender who could come to your door to shake you a margarita at 2 a.m., apparently. If ever a room was there to remind you that you were traveling alone, it was this room. Every time I looked across at the two ornate champagne coupes atop the bar, I plunged into a renewed sulk.

I'd ventured out only to eat, peruse a few shops, and scurry back to the comfort of my room and superfast Wi-Fi. On the second night I even messed up the sheets on the other bed just so I didn't feel so alone. I made one trip to a nearby hotel with a famous Turkish spa in the basement. When I emerged from the wellness elevator I saw a fully naked man in his eighties, casually leaning against a stone pillar, his squat penis just dangling there. I stayed perfectly still and waited for the doors to close before I breathed out. Screw that for a holiday activity. Besides, there *was* a bath in my room.

But I was here now, with this woman, this clairvoyant. I'd taken a wrong turn and, as fate would have it, stumbled upon this little shop. And, I hoped now, my future.

"I'd like to have more adventures," I offer my fortune-teller. At least that was true. "Just, like, *with someone*, you know?"

She nods.

"Here, your fate line; this break here means a change of career. Do you like your career?"

"Career?" I consider this. Would I call bookkeeping at a lido in coastal Kent a career? It felt more like retirement. I needed a change. I shake my head.

"You need change," she says, and my heart rate speeds up at the accuracy. It's almost like she can hear my thoughts. "Something with value. Ah, but here, your sun line."

"My sun line?"

"The sun line is for popularity and success. The longer and deeper and more parallel to your fate line, the more you will have of both. You have very little line at all."

"I see." I nod pitifully.

"You're struggling to make change. It holds you back. You think you should be somewhere else, and it makes you angry that you are only here. You feel average. Ordinary. Average job. Average house. Average car."

"Below average on the car front," I whisper to myself, picturing the former hearse that was the only thing I could afford before hastily leaving London.

"But you do not make the changes," she says. I feel like she's personally attacking me. "You are waiting for something, but life seems to move forward without you."

I nod slowly. I was waiting. Waiting for her to tell me when it would all get better.

"You are lonely . . . ," she says again.

"Yes. Lonely. Average. Ordinary. Got it," I say.

"Fine. Then, love," she says.

"Love," I breathe, biting my lip as I feel the heat rushing into my cheeks.

"You are searching for *someone* to make you feel whole," she says as I nod along, engrossed. "But what is really missing is *you*."

She flips my hand so she's looking at the side of my palm, below the small finger, and runs a thumb across the lines.

"But I feel children. And, yes, a great, romantic love."

"Really?"

"*Really*," she repeats.

"Does it say where? Or who?"

She closes her eyes now. I watch her head tilt slightly as she stares into my future, then looks back at me.

"I see great height. A tall man. Warm. Kind. I see the ocean. Someone who spends time with their passions. A lot of work with his hands. I see many people around him. You know him imminently."

"Imminently?"

"It means *very soon*."

"Yes." I yelp. "Really? Very soon?"

"But . . . ," she begins again.

"But?"

"There is something in the way," she says, tugging on my hand. "Somethings you need to fix before it all comes together."

"Fix?" I say, my heart quickening. The idea that I could, at last, have an action plan . . . thrilling. "What do I need to fix?"

"There are problems that need attention. When these are fixed, he will reveal himself to you."

"Does this mean I won't meet him until whatever it is, is fixed? I thought the meeting was imminent?" I can hear my voice rising in excitement, but I can't stop.

"He is—" Suddenly, her grip on my hand tightens as if she's squeezing the juice out of an orange. She throws her head back and yowls. It's a deep, long, guttural moan, much like the sound a transforming werewolf would make. Then she doubles forward, releases her grip on my hand, and clutches at her bump, her legs spreading wide as she breathes heavily out.

"Jesus fucking Christ!" she shouts.

I stand up, knocking the stool over as I do, shaking out my hand, which is aching from the firmness of her grip.

"Is it coming?" I say, panicked, taking another step back farther.

"Awwww," she says again, doing that fast, staccato breathing as she appears to calm. Her hands move to her stomach and she lets out another moan, this one less urgent, more like she's resigned to die from a stab wound.

"Shall I get help?" I say.

"It's time," she says.

She pulls the veil off and I see a woman who must be only a few years older than me. Across her forehead are dots of perspiration.

"Oh sweet baby Jesus," she says softly, her Hungarian accent more pronounced. "My phone? It's behind the large red candle."

I nod, move to the little shelf, and hand it to her.

"Can I do anything?" I ask, my voice weak and thin. I am hoping the answer is a clear *no* so I can get out of here, but the deeply ingrained need to be polite keeps me fixed firm in the spot.

"We need to go now," she says; then her eyes drop to her phone as she taps on the screen with great haste. I go to speak but she holds a finger up to me as she raises the phone to her ear, and I zip my mouth shut. A machine gun of Hungarian follows. Then she hangs up and removes her earrings and all of her necklaces and bracelets, rubbing at the skin on her wrists in relief. She looks at me, hard.

"Move. We have to go," she says.

"Um, okay, sure, I just need to call a taxi," I say quickly. I feel my heart start to thump. No, I do not want to wait on a street in a city I don't know as the dark begins to settle. *Alone.*

"The baby will not wait for you to call a taxi," she says.

"Please? I just . . . I don't really want to wait out there." I can hear my voice is high and strangled as I say it.

She tries to pull herself up from the table, and I swear the bump has dropped lower than it was. The harem pants are making it look even more precarious. She stands there staring at me, catching her breath from the exertion of standing, flush-faced and impatient.

"Then you need to lock up," she says between breaths.

"Um, okay. I can do that." I nod. "Is there a key, or . . ."

"Just blow out the candles and pull that plug, turn off the fan, and shut the door as you leave; it will lock behind you," she says, waving in several vague directions before she takes a deep breath, picks up an overnight bag in one hand and a money tin in the other, and heads to the door. I rush forward to hold it open for her, which involves a tricky, stretchy dance around her, and then she's out on the footpath.

As I reach into my handbag and pull out a handful of Hungarian forint, I can't help asking, "The guy? You know, the one? Were there any identifying features? How will I know? It's just that I've been single for like ten years and I've never been able to fully picture who he will be. I know what he won't be, for example, Scorpio, but—"

Her next contraction silences me. I meekly wave her off as she waddles toward a waiting car.

"Good luck," I say. "Leave everything with me. Don't even think about it. Everything is totally under control."

When her car speeds off, I sigh, gazing up the long avenue toward a massive construction site in one direction, and in the other the opera house. The sun is starting to go down, and I wonder what to do with my last night in this city. I feel giddy with excitement.

Perhaps I'll go for a cocktail at the hotel Párisi Udvar after all. Charlie had made the reservation for tonight, and it still stands. Perhaps if this meeting is truly imminent, I need to get myself out there and ready for it.

I go back inside and find the little card of the taxi company I'd been given by the hotel.

I dial the number and am told it will be a half hour before I can be picked up.

I look around and see the veil on the table alongside the fortune-teller's clip earrings and gold necklaces, and I glance up at the gilded mirror on the back wall. I wonder, for a moment, what it would feel like to wear them. I pick them all up and walk over to the mirror, fixing on the earrings, then the veil, and then draping over the seven chains. I look in the mirror and I feel a tingle make its way down my spine, imagining for a moment that I might have the powers she has. How does a clairvoyant know that they have the gift? I wonder.

What would it be like to see my future in front of me?

I close my eyes and try to make this imminent new love come alive in my imagination.

I can almost see the dark edges of his form as I conjure him in my mind—tall, passionate, working with his hands, with lots of people around him. I feel a jolt of excitement as I begin to picture his face . . . and then, I hear the creak of the door.

I spin around in a panic.

And in he walks.

2

~~~

"S ZIA," HE SAYS, placing an enormous cello gently on the ground by the entrance and removing a royal blue scarf. The first thing that I clock is his height—six foot at the very least—and then, as he slips off his dark wool jacket, it's the firm, round edges of his shoulders my eyes cannot be torn away from. Oh, he's impressive. And tall. *Tall.* I hear the echo of the fortune-teller in my head. The hairs on the back of my neck stand up, and I quietly gasp under the veil. What could be more imminent than right now?

"Hallo? Hello?" he says now, looking at me, confused. I need to speak.

"Ah . . . um . . . hallo," I say in my best attempt at a nondescriptive Central European accent. I don't want to tell him the shop is closed. He needs to stay.

"Are you closed? Your sign says open," he says. His voice is smooth and soft, though his accent is clipped staccato—German perhaps? I realize I am not speaking, and we are just staring at each other.

I look at the cello on the floor and then back up at him and then at the OPEN/CLOSED sign that is turned to face OPEN onto the street. I rush forward and spin it round and then turn back to him, seeing myself in the mirror over his shoulder. He thinks *I'm* the clairvoyant. Me. Of course he bloody does. Look at me.

"My sister came here and said I should come," he says, an explanation, apparently, for why he is here. He reminds me of a younger Alexander Skarsgård, but with the kind of awkward, slightly curved posture of someone who is leaning over something. Like a cello, for example. *Working with his hands.* I gasp again.

"You don't need an excuse to see a clairvoyant," I say, wondering if I sound more Russian than Hungarian or if it even matters. "There is no shame in seeking guidance." *There.* That's very fortune-teller-like, I think.

He frowns. I notice the strength in his jaw and the full head of sandy hair that is long at the front, floppy even, as if he's been too busy to get it cut.

His clothes tell me he's got time to shop. This is not a quickly-duck-into-M&S-for-a-wedding-shirt kind of guy. He has money and style. He is searching my face—or rather my veil—with his head cocked to the side, his thick eyebrows lowered, like an insecure art professor, unsure if the work is genius or crap.

"We can be quick?" he suggests. He takes a step closer to me, and I step back almost automatically, afraid that he'll see the eyes behind the veil. *Thank God for the veil.* He stoops to pick up the deck of cards on the little table, thumbing through them, and then places them down again, faceup so we can both see the two naked bodies of the Lovers card. I can feel myself blush. And then when I look up at him, I see he's also slightly mortified.

"I can do a palm reading," I say quickly.

"Do I sit here?" he asks, pointing at the little stool, which seems comically small against his size.

I nod, and as he lowers himself onto the tiny stool, my stomach flutters. *Am I doing this?* I don't know how else to keep him here. He has to move his long legs apart to reach his hand into the middle of the table. I imagine the cello resting in between his thighs, and the thought is inexplicably sexy.

I slide into the seat opposite him. When I look up, he's looking back at me. His eyes flicker a light caramel in the low light. I tip my head up to look into them, and when I do I feel everything inside me turn to hot wax, and I have to stop myself from melting right onto the burgundy carpet. I notice the left side of his mouth rises higher than the right as he smiles with a degree of apprehension or nerves. I see a sprinkle of freckles on the bridge of his nose, and thick, heavy eyebrows, which are dark in contrast to his sandy hair. I feel another tingle down my spine.

"You play the cello?"

"Since I was seven," he replies, "and of course I am lucky enough to play for a living."

"That sounds like a, um, a lot of work with your hands," I say.

"Yes," he says with a small laugh, looking back at his cello case, "it's definitely that."

Tall. And, of course, he's got many people around him. An *audience.* What else did she say? I stop for a moment and breathe out. I want to tear off the veil and explain everything to him, but I don't. Instead, I stare, thirstily—from his leather shoes and the dark wool trousers to the black polo neck and that strong jaw.

How did the fortune-teller start? My lifeline, I think. Okay, I'm going to do this. Here we go.

"Please give me your hand," I say, reaching forward, cursing my terribly bitten nails and flaked orange polish. As he leans forward and places his heavy hand in mine, I feel the warm sparkle as our skin touches. I catch my breath in my throat.

"What's your name?"

"Josef," he replies, "or Joe. Joe is fine. I only have ten minutes," he says, looking at a large silver watch on his other wrist, "so if we could make this fast."

I immediately think about sex and feel the heat rise in my cheeks. Fast and hungry. I wonder if that's what it would be like with him. I nod, unable to reply for a moment.

Under the light of the flickering candle his eyes move from our hands up to me, and I feel an undeniable twist in my stomach. I bite my lip.

He rubs his free palm along his trouser leg. He's nervous. "So, what can I ask you?"

I feel my heart beating in my chest a little, and then, panicked, I say, "It's fortune-teller, not fortune-*asker*."

"Oh. I see," he says, nodding, smiling wryly.

"You're at a crossroads," I say quickly, and he looks up at me and his lips tighten. It seemed like a safe opening gambit, but I'm not a clairvoyant. When he nods, I relax a little. I look down toward his hand, turning it over a couple of times to marvel at the length of his fingers and the small, calloused circle on the tip of each. I try not to think about that large hand curled around mine. I try not to picture his arm draped around my shoulders, protecting me from the world.

I try not to think of any of it until I realize I'm caressing his palm in a way that doesn't feel very fortune-teller-ish.

"You are traveling," I say next. It's a bit of a gamble, but then, I'm pretty sure that accent is not Hungarian.

He nods. "Concerts in Budapest, Prague, Frankfurt, Rome. Then we have the US most of the summer and the UK in late August. It's a lot. It's tiring."

He's going to be in the UK in August. My heart picks up to a gallop as I realize the predicament I'm in here. How can I meet him properly if he thinks I'm the fortune-teller? Was the emergency labor a twist of fate? Do I need to make a choice here—to take matters into my own hands? To give fate a nudge?

"You like traveling," I say, running my finger down the middle line. His fingers flex slightly and I struggle to stifle a moan. "But you want to feel more settled?"

"Yes," he confirms with a solitary nod, "that is correct."

"You want to find a reason to stay in one place?"

I realize I'm holding my breath and let it out as quietly as I can.

"Well, perhaps," he says, and I'm sure I see a very slight hint of something. Is he lonely? Lonely like me?

"Love," I say, slowly, carefully, studying his reaction to the word.

And there it is again. He *is* here because of love. He shifts in his seat awkwardly and nods. I think he's also quite embarrassed. "Love?" he says shyly, almost breathlessly, and it's all I can do to stop myself from climbing over the table and onto his lap.

"You are looking for love?" I say, squeezing his hand reassuringly, cursing myself for the little rise in intonation at the end of the sentence. I have to make predictions, not ask questions.

He shrugs and glances at the naked lovers on the cards just a few inches from our hands. I have to squish my thighs together.

"A deep, perfect love. A best friend. The kind of love where the world and the stars feel like they were made for you. The kind that leaves you breathless, but never, *ever* insecure?"

He looks up from the cards again, and I see the sides of his mouth curled slightly up in a smile.

"That sounds . . ." He pauses. "I mean . . ."

"But love is what you're ready for? Like now? You're single, right?"

And now he properly laughs, pulling his hand from mine, reaching into his side pocket and sliding out a small flask. I can see a redness in his cheeks as he takes a small swig of whatever there is in there. He looks back at me, his smile wide and full.

"Isn't everyone who comes here looking for love?"

"Not everyone. Some people want money."

"Money so they can find a better love," he says, sliding the flask back into his pocket.

I'm right. He's here because he wants a *partner* and he's too shy to admit it.

I start to feel worried. I have hardly any time here. What am I supposed to do?

"You want a big change in your life," I continue as he leans forward and offers me his enormous hand again. His smile now is shy, and he gives me permission to continue by a slight rise of the chin and a nod. The heat and damp from where our fingers touch is intoxicating, and I am no longer sure where to go with this. I probably have two minutes left.

"You are ready for a new love. A great love," I say, and then I take a huge, deep breath and say as confidently as I can, "an English girl."

"An English girl?" he says, his large brows coming together. "You can see that in my palm?"

I keep my voice steady. "An English girl. In a small town called Broadgate."

"Broadgate?"

"Yes, Broadgate," I say, as clearly as I can. "You can get the train there; there is a direct train from London Bridge. It's in Kent."

"Kent?"

"The South East of England. Maybe you should write this down?"

"Huh," he says, his amusement again drawing out a little dimple on his cheek, but he does reach into his coat and pull out a scrap of paper. There are a couple of awkward moments before he finds a pen in the breast pocket of his coat.

"Is Kent with a *K*?"

"Yes," I reply; then I wait in silence as he writes down *Kent*.

"And Broadgate?"

"Yes. You will find her there. In the summer—the last Friday in August."

"This seems rather unusual," he says. I feel relieved to see a flash of skepticism, and yet, I need him to believe. I can't stop now. I just need a venue, and in Broadgate there is only really one.

"A pub, down by the water. The Star and Anchor. Seven p.m. She will be there at the bar. Mara."

"Mara?" he asks.

"Mara," I repeat, as I close my eyes, slightly ashamed. "That is her name."

And then I hear someone knocking on the glass window. And then a shout. "Josef?" My eyes fly open. He is looking directly at me, and once again I am so thankful for the veil.

"Josef? Are you done?" the man's voice says again.

"That's the first violin," he says, "so now I have to go."

He stands, stretching both legs out in front of him as he does, and then shaking out his wrist. "How much?"

I tell him ten thousand forint, feeling my heart beating hard in my chest. As he fishes through his expensive, buttery leather wallet, I find myself desperately wanting him to stay.

"Can I take a picture?" I ask suddenly as he places the money on the table, my fake accent long forgotten. Perhaps he hasn't noticed since English isn't his first language. "A picture with the cello. For my friend. She likes the cello."

He looks perplexed but sort of shrugs, so I stand, my legs a little weak at first, and reach for my handbag. I hesitate before sliding up next to him. I try to ignore the stupid bright yellow Minions bumper case that Charlie gave me for Christmas, feeling utterly juvenile, and take a quick snap of the two of us together.

He stands perfectly tall and still and I move my head toward his shoulder, standing on tiptoes to bring our heads both in frame. The smell of whisky mixes with some kind of expensive cologne. It's intoxicating. Delicious.

I step back and look at him again. He must be around my age, and yet, I feel like a child.

"You're not going to take off the veil?" he asks, looking for my eyes behind the purple netting. And then I feel them almost connect. His eyes and mine. Everything falls away for a moment as I feel completely seen. It's like a punch to the stomach, as if I've been set on fire. My heart races. This was meant to happen.

"I want to see your face," he says.

"Oh no," I say, sliding my phone away. "It is better to have the barrier."

He smiles, defeated.

"Are you in town long?" I ask.

"We go tomorrow," he replies. Then he stops looking at me, and his body stiffens again. He lifts up his coat and slips it on. "This was . . . charming."

"Broadgate. August," I say, feeling desperate as he turns to leave. I wonder if I should rip the veil off. Tell him everything.

"Broadgate. August," he says, as that right dimple appears alongside his smile. "You never know, I might just be crazy enough to show up."

I drop my head and murmur, "I don't want to encourage you either way, but I would definitely go . . ." My voice trails off.

"Well. Thanks," he says, and then there is a twinkle of mischief in his eyes. "It was fun. I hope you have a nice evening." And with that, he picks up his cello and slips out between the red velvet curtains and then out the front door. My heart lurches. *No! This cannot be it.*

It is no coincidence that he walked in. It is no coincidence that I was here doing something I would never normally do. This is exactly what she predicted. *Who* she predicted. We were supposed to meet.

I tear off the veil and run out onto the street after him. But he is gone into the night.

3

~~~

KENT

THE BROADGATE LIDO was once fabulous. An incredible art deco building curved to mimic the bow of a ship overlooks a pool and a set of surf-beaten stairs that snake down a short, white cliff to the sea. The stone-and-concrete-clad facade looks sun-bleached white against the blue sky, reminiscent of something more at home in Mykonos and the Aegean Sea when the weather is just right. But the chalky white cliff face, rising right out of the sea, and tufts of green grasses below it make it feel distinctly southern English.

The pool overlooks a bay where seventy-three brightly colored beach huts sit like shards of rock candy along a promenade leading all the way to the only real night spot, the Star and Anchor pub, at the other headland.

The lido was built in the 1930s to draw the crowds away from Brighton and Ramsgate, but then the pool was swiftly shut during the Second World War and didn't reopen until the late fifties. It never really lived up to its potential and was now a crumbling relic of the past, almost too fragile to transform. *Almost.* To me, it was like the pearl in the oyster of this postcard-perfect town.

I push open the double doors, yawning from my late flight back from Hungary, the uncomfortable airport hotel bed, the early-morning train to Broadgate, and finally, the cab from the train station straight to work. The wheels of my suitcase make a loud grinding noise on the original black-and-white terrazzo tiled floor. I look up as I always do, at the huge and elaborate rounded roof, with the stained-glass circular center. It may not be the biggest lido on the English coast, but its original features are the best.

Today, though, I barely take notice. I'm floating on clouds because I cannot stop thinking about Joe. I've been reliving each moment of the night before in my head, my stomach fluttering deliciously, and I can't wait to tell another human.

As I approach the front desk, the fumes from the freshly chlorinated pool hit my nose first, then my eyes, followed by the lingering scent of stale sweat on plastic. Like the red stain of tomato soup on an old Tupperware container, this stench is permanent.

"You really notice it when you've been away," I say to Samira, screwing my nose up.

"Hi, Mara," Samira says, not looking up from her phone, "how was the trip, then?"

Samira is our receptionist, which involves taking money from, on average, fifty-two people a day, most of whom are discounted pensioners at one pound a dip. She is also indifferent toward me, since I had repeatedly turned down her offers to hang out when I'd first arrived. It wasn't *her.* It was me. I was not someone who made friends easily or readily anymore, and after a while, she stopped asking. But last week, Venus entered Cancer and I am embracing a period of compassion, empathy, and love for my fellow humans.

"It was truly incredible, Samira," I reply, smiling broadly.

That gets her attention.

"Budapest?" she says. "I always thought of Budapest as a sort of I've-done-everywhere-else destination. Like Finland. Or North Wales."

"Oh no," I say, "it's very cool. The Paris of the East."

"Is it, though?" she asks, her lip curling slightly, before she looks back at her phone.

I push the metal revolving gates and they turn with a heavy *thunk*, and then I make my way up the round staircase that snakes upward into our office space.

"Good morning, Nina!" says Gerry Walker, who joins me on the stairs but doesn't offer to help with my suitcase. Gerry is the general manager of the lido and three other council-owned properties in Broadgate and its surrounds. He is here at least one day a week, though, much to the irritation of the rest of us.

"Mara," I mutter to myself, tired of correcting him.

"Senior memberships are up zero point three percent," he says, slicking his thinning blond hair back. He adjusts his tie and then looks at me as if he's waiting for a response, activating a large, beaming, denture-filled smile. Gerry is the kind of man you feel is always one mouse click away from accidently exposing himself on a Zoom call.

"Oh really?" I reply as I lug my case up the final step and stop for a moment's rest, in the hope he leaves. Gerry gives me these little nuggets of so-called good news on occasion, since, as a bookkeeper, I'm the one who sees the (hardly any) money that comes into and goes out of this place. I'm also the one who questions the anomalies in the books. He knows I know there is something amiss. And I know he knows I know. But I've long since stopped commenting on the crisis. A zero-point-three percent increase in memberships wouldn't even fund a fix for the broken art deco tiles in the ladies' changing room.

"That's great news, Gerry," I say, forcing a smile and dragging my case off toward my desk.

When I was interviewed for the job as bookkeeper, Lynn, the duty manager, oversold the potential. I dreamed I would be part of the lido's transformation, arriving here with a bag full of energy and optimistic ideas. Fresh paint jobs, an alcohol license for events and functions, a Great Gatsby–style fundraising ball, a terrace café with sweeping views of the coast. But now I have fallen into line with everyone else who works here. Apathy and disillusion have firmly set in.

My desk sits next to the big windows overlooking the pool, its gleaming turquoise water rippling over white tiles, so inviting, so calm, compared to the dark and wild ocean it overlooks. The view is quite something. If a soul needed lifting, it could surely be done watching the greater black-backed gulls dive for fish behind the cresting waves on a warm summer's day.

"Hi, Lynn," I say as I slide into my desk.

Lynn is not just the duty manager, if anyone asks; she also oversees the local graffiti task force, the Mocha Mamas summer-fun playgroup, and the staff social club, among several other local community groups she's always encouraging me to join. She's broad and tall, with pink cheeks and short burgundy hair, and wears the same navy blue blazer every day. On her lapel, an ever-growing collection of pins—a St. George's Cross flag, *Girl Boss*, a raised solidarity fist, *Top Totty*, and a pride rainbow.

"Hey, Mara," she replies, unable to resist a brief glance at her watch. "You look happy as a clam. Nice weekend away, then?"

"Yes," I say, and then I take a deep breath. I could tell Lynn. She would do. "I met someone."

"You met someone?" she says. "Properly, though? Not one of these people on an app? You can never be sure of them. Could be a codfish. Could be anything these days. He's not Hungarian, is he?" To this she screws up her nose, and then with a flash of self-awareness insists, "You can't have a long-distance relationship, and we've left the EU now. I'm just thinking practically here."

"It's *catfish*, not codfish," I say, "and, no, I didn't meet him through an app. It was fate that drew us together." I can't help grinning, feeling the heat in my cheeks as I do.

"Well. Who is he, then?" she asks, folding her arms on her desk and tilting her head.

"His name is Josef, and he plays the cello," I say, feeling warmth rush over me as I recall him.

"The *cello*." She says *cello* as if it's very la-di-da and, clearly disinterested in hearing any more about Joe, swiftly changes the subject. "Before I forget, Mara, you need to sort the accounts for Gerry on the play area upgrade."

"I did that the Thursday before I left," I say, confused.

"Yes, well, on Friday he brought in a new supplier, and it all needs reviewing again."

"Great," I say, scoffing audibly.

"No rest for the wicked," Lynn quips. "I always say there's no point in going on holiday."

"Do you? You told me to go on holiday," I protest.

"Well, yes, but you're still relatively young and have no friends or interests. We all worry about it. Oh, don't look at me with that face—you said it yourself."

I realize I've told Lynn, a terrible gossip, far too much about my life.

"All right. All right," I say, logging on to my computer, then cursing as it asks me to update my password. "I just don't know why we're adding a children's climbing wall above a cliff."

"I know. I tried to fight it, but you know Gerry," Lynn says, slipping a box of Marlboro Lights into her jacket pocket and heading out for her hourly break and gossip.

I gaze out the window and sigh. I didn't mean to end up here.

Once upon a time, as a young and excitable Mara, I'd wanted to work in the movies. I'd been a video addict my whole childhood, dragging my parents to Blockbuster so often I'm sure I kept it afloat single-handedly in those last years. But things really ignited in me when Mum and Dad took us on holiday to the Peak District in 2003. As usual, my brother, Ben, and I were carted around between boring hikes and boring stately homes, dragging our feet and bickering the entire time. So, you can imagine our relief when hiking through the grounds of Chatsworth House, we came upon a man sitting in a camp chair, in a high-vis vest, informing us it was closed to visitors.

"Thank fuck," Ben said, and we'd fist-bumped.

Then the man said, "They're filming." When he saw my twelve-year-old face gasp with excitement, he smiled. "You can watch through those trees for a bit if you like. No cameras, though."

"Oh, God help us," said Dad, shaking his head at me, "we'll never get her home."

Across the lawn an adaptation of *Pride and Prejudice* was being filmed. I could just make out what turned out to be Keira Knightley in a pin-striped Georgian dress, bounding down the stairs in front of a massive camera on a long crane. I was mesmerized. I had never imagined what it looked like to make an actual movie. *These people did this for a job.*

Until that moment, making movies was a far-off magical mystery in a creative wonderland called Hollywood. I loved them. I obsessed about them. But I'd never considered the possibility *I* could *make* them.

Who were these people? Who was this crew of dozens, adjusting lighting, dusting on makeup, sitting in cranes with cameras? What did they all do? Could *I* do it?

And that was it. I knew I wanted to be a filmmaker.

But film school ended in a nuclear-level disaster. There was my first love, Noah, a cruel betrayal, a very public meltdown, and then a finals failure. I have never been able to recover from the emotional fallout.

Ashamed to go home, I'd headed to London to take a job at a cinema in East London and ended up doing their bookkeeping too. Free tickets, easy days, surrounded by my love of movies. Then I met Charlie through a flatmate-wanted ad, and we became instant best friends. Two northern girls in the Big Smoke. It was all I needed, and I settled into a small but secure life in London.

A few years later, I found I needed more money, so I took a bookkeeping job at Westminster Council. I was hoping for film premiers in Leicester Square, but I ended up dealing mostly with parking permits. Before I knew it, almost a decade had passed since I left film school. Charlie spent less and less time at the flat and more time on a sofa somewhere in Richmond with her boyfriend, Alex.

Then, eighteen months ago, Charlie left London for Kent with Alex, her now husband, and a baby on the way. I had stood on London Bridge one starry night wondering what the hell I was going to do next. I'd had enough of my dead-end job, where there was no progression because I was constantly outmaneuvered by savvy, educated Londoners. I didn't want a new person in my and Charlie's flat, and I was burning through my meager savings living there alone. I had had enough of London. I was sick of the smells of the city—the asphalt, the diesel fumes, the forked lines of urine that ran from buildings to the curb every morning on my way to the bus.

And so, the universe responded in haste. The very next day, I saw an ad for a bookkeeping job with Broadgate Council. Just twenty minutes from Charlie. A beautiful art deco building with so much potential, right by the sea. I had never lived on the edge of the earth before, and the idea was invigorating. My star sign that day sealed the deal:

> With the sun, Mars, and Mercury retrograde conjunct in Libra today, your ability to dream is felt tenfold. Use this moment to take a new professional step. Find a path with a great, expansive view ahead.

I think of that small paragraph a lot as I stare out onto the view, so wide, so filled with hope. And then I turn my head back to the electric glare of my PC, its outdated version of MS Office struggling to load up an Excel spreadsheet.

I think about calling Charlie, but just as I pull out the phone, senior lifeguard Ryan arrives at my desk.

"You went to Budapest, right? How was it?" He flicks his sandy hair back from his face, blowing upward at a curled lock that refuses to stay put.

"Very cultured," I say, making every effort not to look at his blue Crocs and regulation lifeguard board shorts as I say this. "And very historic. And fun. I went to see a proper fortune-teller."

"Really?" says Ryan. "What did the fortune-teller tell you?"

"That I was going to meet the one. *Imminently*. And I did." I cannot help sharing again, though it slightly embarrasses me. I am such a knob, but I can't be stopped. "But she said I have to fix some things before it all comes together."

"What do you need to fix? Your Tinder profile? 'Cos I can totally help with that."

"I don't do Tinder," I say. "Why would that be the first thing you think of, anyway?" I roll my eyes to the ceiling.

But then I worry slightly. I haven't really thought about the fixing part. Did I break something that I now need to address? Or is it more holistic than that? Do I need to fix myself? She said *many things*. What if Joe doesn't come to England unless I follow her advice?

I think of my front door's hinges, the curtain rail in my room, the toaster, the flashing light in the leisure center hallway, then the whole lido, my car's exhaust, my hair, my eyebrows, my nail polish, the wardrobe filled with mostly black clothes I picked up in the supermarket. Then my mind begins to wander. Perhaps it's bigger? My relationship with my family? Or bigger still? The flood barriers in the Thames Estuary, climate change, poverty, the way we live as a society contributing to our nation's poor mental health? Suddenly, I find I can't take a full, satisfying, deep breath.

"I'm fucked," I say, feeling dizzy, my palms on my desk as I try to slow my breathing.

I look up at Ryan, who looks fascinated and a bit scared, like he's poked a beehive with a stick and wants to watch the carnage for a bit before he runs.

Lynn returns to the desk in a waft of cigarette smoke.

"Mara's having some sort of episode," he says, bending down to take a closer look at my face.

"Are you looking for the keys, Ryan?" she asks while pulling them out of her top drawer. "They were found in one of the urinals this morning. I had to fish them out with a fork."

Ryan grabs the keys and saunters off, bumping the edge of the next desk as he goes.

"He's daft as a goose, but he *is* single," she says, slamming her drawer shut.

I stare hard at Lynn.

"What I'm saying is you should keep your limited options open. What are you, thirty-five?"

"I'm thirty-one," I say weakly.

"Oh really?" she says, cocking her head to the side. "You look older. It's not a wrinkle thing; it's more that you look . . . I don't know, worn-out."

I turn to stare down at the water below, watching an elderly lady breaststroke in the azure-blue of the pool. It's starting to warm up outside, and the early summer sunshine sparkles in the ripples of her wake.

My eyes move toward Ryan, who is high-fiving the on-duty lifeguard, and I long for their easy smiles of friendship.

You don't notice it when you're just moving through life—it's when something happens that means something to you. Something like fate connecting me with Joe. Something that big, and delicious and exciting, you want to tell people so you can live it over and over again. You need someone to squeeze your knee and tell you how excited they are for you. *I love this for you!*

I *need* to tell someone about Joe, and so, with Lynn zoned out on a Zoom call opposite me, I give Charlie a quick bell.

"Calling live with breaking news from Eastern Europe!" I say.

"Mara! Are you not back, then?! Has something happened?"

"No, I just meant I'm back. And I have news!"

She laughs loudly. A deep baritone cackle that is like a huge blanket being thrown over me. My spirits lift.

"Oh. Sorry. I missed the joke. It's baby brain. Constant anxiety," Charlie says. "It's *so* great that you went anyway. I've been thinking about you all weekend. I feel utterly wracked with guilt at bailing on you."

"Oh, forget it. I had a blast," I say. "It turned out to be quite fortuitous, as it happens."

"Ooh, exciting. Tell me the news!"

"I met someone," I swoon, wishing I was revealing this at our old flat, an empty bottle of wine between us as we lay on the floor with our legs up the wall, staring at the cracks in the ceiling plaster that I'd covered with glow-in-the-dark stars.

"What?" Then she gasps, "You met someone?"

I laugh. "I *did* meet someone. *The* someone, I think."

"Ooh! What? Really?" she says. "Mara!"

"Yeah, he's a cellist in an orchestra," I begin, eager to tell her everything while I have her attention. "I was walking through the Jewish Quarter and had gotten lost; then I saw this tiny shop, and inside this woman was doing readings. And just . . . *everything* she said . . ."

I hear Sophie start to wail in the background. "Damn it! Oh

God, this is so unfair. I really have to go and feed her, okay? Can I call you back?"

"It's almost like she can sense you're on the phone to me," I say, trying to sound jovial, but instantly regretting it.

"Sorry, Mar," she says. "Another time!?"

"I could just save it for Saturday?"

"What's happening Saturday?" she says.

"I'm coming up to see you, remember? You said I should come on Saturday and tell you all about the trip."

"Oh shit. Yes. Sorry. Great." I can hear the baby getting louder and the sound of Charlie heaving her up.

"Go. Go!" I say cheerily.

"Let's make sure we get together soon!"

And she's already forgotten about Saturday. She's like a goldfish at the moment—I'm never sure she's actually listening to anything I tell her. Losing Charlie to a baby is basically the adult version of when your best friend gets a boyfriend at school. All the pain, but you can't complain. I remind myself to be more patient; she's a new mum. She's tired. She's stressed. But it still hurts.

I moved here to be closer to Charlie, but I only really have the dregs of her left. She's been my only friend for the last decade. My only *close* friend. I'd met her right after my disastrous time at uni, when I was at my absolute lowest, and now, somehow, I only have her. But Charlie has Alex and Sophie—my person is somebody else's person.

And yet, fate sent me here. A council job. By the sea. At the world's most glorious pool. Like something out of a Wes Anderson film.

But in my six months here, I've never really found a way to fit in. It's like I pushed all my chips onto the Charlie square on a black-jack table and lost.

And now I'm alone.

In my deepest, most aching dreams, I thought I would be more.

My desk phone interrupts me with an almighty *ring*. I jump ten feet and grab it, pulling the receiver to my ear.

"Mara Williams," I say breathlessly.

"Mar," says Samira, "the turnstile is jammed again and Mrs. Cummings is stuck halfway. Can you bring the crowbar from the kitchen? Ryan is finding something to lubricate the arm."

"Why do you have to make it sound like a sex party?" shouts Lynn angrily in the background.

And then Ryan, apparently arriving at the scene, says cheerily, "All I have is Vaseline. Stay still, Mrs. Cummings."

4

I AM ALMOST COMATOSE with tiredness when I finally get to my front door and brace myself for interaction with my new flat-mate. Ashley Greene moved in while I was in Budapest, and except for one brief interview that turned quickly into a handing over of the keys, we've never really sat down and spoken.

Ashley, or "Ash" as she'd signed off her email, was busy with work and wanted to find "somewhere quiet." This suggested to me that she would not be home much, would not have many visitors, and would likely keep to herself in the evenings. It suggested tea, hot water bottles, and *Buffy* reruns in her bedroom. A nice, independent flatting situation, I thought.

Then I met Ash and was once again reminded that I should never trust my gut.

"Ash? Ashley?" I said, confused, to the dark-haired, dark-eyed *man* who was leaning against the Victorian-era lamppost outside the flat at the exact time we'd arranged to meet.

"Nice to meet you," he replied, stepping forward to offer a firm handshake.

"Aah," I replied. *"Ashley* is a woman."

"Oh no," he replied. "Oh shit."

I must have looked horrified, because he immediately threw his hands in the air and apologized profusely for the mistake.

"I'm really sorry, Mara," he said, "I didn't mean to . . . I can leave?"

He was so sincere, I ended up insisting that it didn't matter at all, and he should come on in and see the room. Besides, I had no specific reason *not* to live with a man, only that I'd never done it.

But right now, I don't want to live with anyone at all. All I want to do is be in my room, alone. Alone, googling, and fantasizing about Joe.

I look to the sky and pray to Jupiter as I slide the key into the little blue front door; hopefully Ash is not in, or maybe already in his room. Then I can avoid him altogether.

But no. He's the first thing I see when I swing the tiny front door open. Ash leaning over something that, admittedly, smells majestic.

"Mara Williams. Sagittarius," he says, raising both hands in delight. "I've made us some dinner!"

Ash is tall like Joe is tall. But where Joe is tall and lean, Ash is tall and bearlike. A great barrel of a chest, with large sloping shoulders. The next thing I notice is the splodges of plaster all over him; his job, I learned, was the same as my dad's. A plasterer. There is something so weirdly familiar about the cracked smear of paint on his forearm. Dulux emulsion in Cream Biscuit for halls and ceilings, I imagine.

Ash turns a bright smile toward me—one of those easy, full-face ones that appear on his boyish face with zero effort. A flick of the hair and a shrug of those big shoulders to tell me everything is all right in his world.

"Hi," I say, smiling back, dropping my keys into the bowl by the door. "Well. Welcome?"

"Welcome to you too," he says, raising his hands again, this time as if he is expecting to shake my hand or even hug me, but I am not sure which, so I just freeze on the spot and he drops them.

"Oh yes, but I already live here," I say, confused, "so it's me, welcoming you, to my house."

"Yes," he says, laughing, "welcome back, I mean. From the trip!"

"Ah, I see." I laugh a kind of skittish giggle and cringe at myself. *Loosen up, Mara. Relax. Everything is fine.*

When he motions for me to sit at my own dinner table like I am a guest, I prickle at the dynamic. He is clearly feeling rather more at home here than I am ready for. I spot my mail on the side table under a very large stone object. *That's new.* And there is a pile of books on the coffee table I don't recognize. I take a breath.

This is what it means to share your space with someone new, Mara. It's his space too. He is allowed to feel at home.

"Thank you," I say. I need friends, but I want to keep this relationship at arm's length; get too close too quickly and you risk them getting too comfortable. Like some kind of *Notting Hill* situation, where your flatmate is always walking around in his underpants, and you're just here trying to be normal and date Julia Roberts.

"I'm all moved in," he replies as he leans over to set the table. His face is flushed from the heat of the stove, and there's a shimmer of moisture on his forehead. It looks as though this has been a monster effort.

"Great," I say, "I hope you found some room in the bathroom. And somewhere to park."

"Oh yeah, sure," he says, nodding.

"You did? It took me ages to find somewhere, and I still have to walk eight minutes to get here."

"The church at the end of the street," he says.

I laugh at this. "Are you kidding?"

"No, tell Reggie that you're living on Sandhill Way, and he won't mind. Half the street parks there. Keeps it feeling popular, he says."

"Reggie?"

"The vicar," he says, as if everyone knows Reggie. "It's literally fifty meters up the road."

Ash is from Broadgate. He grew up here. His parents live here. That much I know from the flatmate interview. That means the only place in a twenty-mile radius that feels more mine than his is my bedroom. It dawns on me that he is at home already because this town *is* his home. So now, suddenly, I'm the new girl again.

He swings open the minuscule fridge and slides out two craft beers—Badger's Bottoms—and catches me staring at his tracksuit pant and chunky moss-green knit combination.

"Sorry, I've been working," he says, yanking his pants up.

"It's cool," I reply, "nineties student chic."

"Well then. It was a strategic choice?" he says with a laugh. Then he fills both our mismatched bowls with some kind of brown-red stew and slides them on the table. I take a subtle whiff and look at him, confused.

"It's goulash?" I say, my brows descending in confusion. "I've just . . . been in Hungary?"

"Yes, that's the point, silly," he replies.

"Oh," I say. It's quite sweet. "Thank you. It smells yum."

"Long day?" he asks.

"Yes," I sigh.

"Everything okay?"

Eyes to the cracked-plaster ceiling, I let out a long, dramatic moan and find that I do want to share everything about my day. Ash is looking at me with a bushy eyebrow raised and a wry grin. "Tell me," he says, a twinkle in his dark eyes. He leans forward and folds his arms on the small round dining table, invading my space immediately. "Go on. Let's get this flatmate show on the road. I've been looking forward to getting to know you. The new girl in town. Shoot."

Oh God. This is my worst nightmare. Actual, *purposeful*, getting to know me. I can already imagine myself sneaking in the side window to avoid him.

"Nothing. I just, one of those late-night flights. You know, you pay seventy quid for an airport hotel and get five hours' sleep at best," I say, sitting back to create some space. His eyes follow me moving, and after a moment, he takes the cue and moves back too.

"Nothing worse than a bad trip home after a great holiday," he says, picking up his fork again. "So, you didn't want to leave?"

"No, I didn't want to come back," I say. "There's a difference."

"Oh," he says, looking worried. His forehead is creased and his fork is still in his hand, hovering as he waits for me to elaborate. I take a bite of the beef and it's so chewy I have to hold my finger up and ask him to wait so I can explain. After about a minute of chewing, he starts to laugh. "A bit tough?"

"No, no," I say as I swallow hard and painfully, then smile. Ash laughs as if this is hilarious. He's not embarrassed by it.

"Room for improvement," he says and shrugs.

I want to explain that I shouldn't have moved here. That Broadgate was a mistake. That I imagined it would be something different. That I'd be saving a prewar relic and restoring the heart of the prettiest beachside town I'd ever seen. That I'd be spending lazy summer days swimming and eating ice cream with my best friend. That, as usual, I had foolishly imagined something more whimsical and romantic than the bleak reality I saw in front of me.

My mother called me a fantasist. She worried that all the movies I watched were warping my mind. "It's not normal," she'd say, slopping mashed potato on a pie, as though this *normal* was something to aspire to. It was hardly surprising I enjoyed the big, glossy world of romantic and comedic misadventure more than my drab life in small-town England.

"You've been in that room watching movies for five straight hours," she'd say.

"I'm sure I've heard this script before," I'd reply, rubbing my chin, tired of her jibes.

"Come and spend time back in reality, Mara. Prince Charming isn't coming to pick you up in his S-Class and whisk you off to Genovia," Dad would warn me.

"Cut!" I'd shout back at them, backing out of the room.

"You're becoming obsessed, Mara!" she'd insist.

"Take ninety-seven," I'd reply, yawning and snapping my hands at her like I was a human clapper.

"You're nuts," sensible Ben would say, shaking his head.

"End scene!" I'd retort as I slunk off upstairs to my bedroom, slammed my door, and sheepishly unpaused *Pretty Woman*.

The more they pushed me into a corner, the more I convinced

myself that I was destined for more. And yet, here I was. In the end, at a good, honest council job in a small town. Alone.

"Broadgate is not what I expected," I say. "That's all."

"Oh, it's a great place," he replies enthusiastically. "Sure, it's not as glamorous or cosmopolitan as Ramsgate—"

"Now, is that a high enough bar to set?" I ask, pointing my fork in his direction, and he laughs again. This guy laughs at everything. I wonder if it's nerves or if he really is this bright and happy.

"Most people find the place charming," he says, and I shrug.

"Well, it's definitely got its charms," I say.

It has an achingly cute seafront, wooden pier, and Georgian terraced houses, but in a way Broadgate feels like a glorious abandoned film set. No one is looking after it, not *really*. It's been left to flounder. The town, the lido, and at least sixty-five percent of its residents are old. Broadgate peaked early and kind of gave up. A bit like me, I think grimly.

"It's the lido," I say, channeling my frustration into that one thing. "It's falling apart at the seams, and my boss just doesn't seem to care."

"I patched up the hallway last winter. It has really good bones, you know. Everything that's wrong with that place is superficial."

"What do you mean?"

"It just needs some cash for a proper renovation. Maybe the pool needs redoing?" he says, thinking aloud now. "It was quite something back in the day, apparently. They say there were some epic parties."

I imagine the salt-eroded white cladding redone and sparkling in the summer sunshine. I imagine the pool filled with bathers, and the poolside littered with brightly colored umbrellas, people lazily sunning themselves, and I sigh.

"I'm sure there's a way. They just did up Saltdean in Sussex," he says, a face full of optimism that grates on me.

I sigh and shrug. "Sure, Ash. Maybe I just need to *try*."

"No! Do or do not. There is no try," he says in a gravelly voice.

"Did you just quote Yoda at me?"

He grins, and I can't help but return it. He quoted a movie. Sure, it was a quote everyone should know before the age of twelve, but it was a movie quote. This is a good sign. Perhaps this might just work.

"Broadgate is a great community; they'll back you right up."

"I don't really know anyone in the *community*," I say, a word that conjures up small-town apathy more than anything. "I'm not close to anyone here."

"Aw, Mara. You need to get yourself out there. There's plenty of people to meet, if you're feeling lonely. My mum has a book club," he says.

"That's kind," I say, although inside I'm quietly devastated. Has he really just suggested I join his mother at her book club as a way to meet people? My life is a disaster.

"Sure. Anytime. I know a bit of what it's like to be in a new place. You'll settle in if you make an effort."

"Everything is effort enough," I say, rubbing my temples as the last few days' events swirl around in my head, unstructured. Unfiled. Wild and confusing. "My brain hurts."

"You must be tired," he says.

There is a silence now and Ash moves the goulash around in his bowl and looks up at me. I catch his eye at the same time and sense a strange feeling coming from him. Is it pity? Does this man pity me? Is this what it's come to?

"Let me tell you about Budapest," I say, quickly breaking away from his gaze.

"Yes," he says, nodding.

"I met a man," I say, blushing as I do. Embarrassed to share it with this guy I hardly know. I'm that starved for people to tell.

"You did?" Ash replies, scratching at some plaster on his sleeve and flicking it off onto the floor.

"His name is Josef. He's a cellist."

"A cellist." He nods. "Impressive."

"It was pretty much *bam*. Like, here *he* is." After a thoughtful pause, I decide not to divulge the details just yet. I don't know if Ash will appreciate the delicate fabric of fate and destiny that will bring Joe to me in August. "I was waiting for something to happen. You know, that moment when you meet someone and they are meant for you and suddenly you feel your roots dig into the earth and there is a point to everything. I mean a point to *you*. Like, there is a point to Mara now. *I* exist for a reason. I'm not just white noise; I'm like an earthy part of the world. Do you know what I'm saying?"

Damn it, Mara. Too much.

But Ash looks at me thoughtfully. "I think I thought that once," he says at last. "But without grounding yourself *first*, it's fragile." He stands and drops his bowl into the sink and slides his empty beer bottle into the glass recycling bin. I'm surprised by his response.

"Sorry, that was a bit deep for a first date," I say, trying to make a joke of it.

He spins round and folds his arms, grinning. "Well, especially since you're talking about another dude."

I attempt to grin back. "The dinner was so kind," I say. Despite the nerves about sharing my space, I feel grateful that Ash has made such an effort. Like someone loosened the first eyelet on a corset, I breathe a little easier.

"Ah, had to earn some brownie points, first night and all," he replies, stretching and creaking his neck from side to side. His hands brush the ceiling as he reaches up, a giant in this tiny flat. "Well, see you in the morning?" And then he's off down the hallway, and I'm finally alone.

5

~~~

I FINISH THE GOULASH, saving the tough meat for the neighbor's cat, and I pull my phone out of my bag and check tomorrow's star sign. I've done it since I was thirteen, and my day never feels complete without a quick glance.

> You need a clear plan to bust out of this routine and unleash that wild and carefree you. It's time to test the limits of who you can truly be. Do not listen to the voices who try to minimize you. You're on a journey that will enrich your life and your belief in yourself. Change is ahead, and you know what to do next.

Change.

I glance at the broken hinge on the front door. At the dicky wheel on my suitcase. The roll of my gut protruding over the buckle of my jeans.

Fix many things.

It has to be *me* that needs fixing. Mara. This flat. My job. My car. My social circle, or lack thereof. My interests. If Joe is going to come in August—and he is, *I just know it*—everything will need to change.

It's time to test the limits of who you can truly be.

Maybe it's time? Time to try again? I take a very deep breath and feel a tingle in my stomach. I am reminded of that feeling when I left home at eighteen, my small-town life behind me, heading off to film school with dreams as big as the world felt. I was going to do big things. Be *someone*. Leaving home was a chance to meet *my people*, to meet my *person*. Finally be me without the limits my parents constantly put on me.

It's been hard to go back and face them with the brutal truth that it didn't work. That I came to nothing. That I left film school with a broken dream and a broken heart, and I have never recovered.

My mood sinks as I think about that broken heart. How cruel that it happened all at once.

His name was Noah. I met him during freshers' week and I fell hard. He was everything I'd imagined my first proper boyfriend would be. He read Bukowski and played guitar, and to my raging jealousy, his parents worked in film already. He talked about art and how to be a better feminist ally and was the first person I had met who had seen as many movies as I had—even if he liked some of the indulgent crap from navel gazers like Vincent Gallo, whereas I loved feel-good director John Hughes and sardonic Greta Gerwig. Regardless, I was his match, and he was mine. It was like we were made for each other.

"You're so fucking upbeat," he'd say to me, sucking back on his rolled-up cigarette. "You're like an art house Elle Woods."

And I'd laugh and we'd fight and banter and cook cheap student meals and drink cider.

I'd thought Noah was *the one*. Or at least, I hoped so hard that he was that I didn't see the reality of *who* he was.

I'd always gotten better grades than him. He used to call me a nerdy swat. I idolized him as the super-creative one. His scripts and his ideas were always so *out there* and I was always in awe, if a little confused by them. We often worked together, but on the final project our differences were starting to grate. Noah wanted to write one thing—a dark, broody (he called it gritty) short film, where very little happened, in my humble opinion. "A study in grief," he'd declared it, handing me the outline, which was scene after scene of grim man-thoughts inside a filthy basement apartment. I thought it was a bit indulgent. He told me that I was missing the whole point.

My idea was not going to win any awards either; it was a quirky tale of love and serendipity between a lonely taxi driver and his eccentric passenger. Initially, Noah had liked it, trying to find a way to merge the two until we had a messy outline that was neither idea and certainly not good.

With us at a desperate impasse, I went to see our professor to get some advice on what to do. But when I pushed through the heavy doors and stepped into the hall, I was surprised to see Noah walking into his office just ahead of me. He left the door just very slightly open behind him, and I couldn't help hearing everything as I waited on the little plastic seats outside our professor's office.

"How's your mum?" the professor said. It started to irritate me that they were connected through the industry.

"She's finally sold the studio," Noah replied.

"Good for her. What can I do for you, mate?" he said.

"I need a new partner."

"I see," said the professor coolly. "Has something happened with Mara? You two seemed to work well together."

"Yeah, she's cool," he says. And then I heard Noah sigh. "I don't want this to be a big deal, but we're kind of . . . not working out. I'm going to break up with her, and I feel like she's really suffocating me creatively. So, I wondered if there was a way we could be separated?" Noah's voice trailed off as I felt the sucker punch to my gut. *Break up with me? I was suffocating him creatively?*

"Oh dear," the professor said, and I heard him laugh lightly.

"I'm going for this internship at Scope Films. I don't want to be held back by her." I could picture his shoulders rise in a shrug as he casually tossed my reputation under a bus.

"Hmm," the professor muttered. "I've always wondered what you'd be capable of, on your own, Noah."

"I just know I could really nail this," he said excitedly.

"You *can* go it alone, of course, but we'd need to speak to Mara."

"Can I tell Mara?" he said. "She can get . . . emotional."

"Okay, but tell her to come and see me after."

"She hates my idea anyway. I'm sure she'll be relieved."

"The two of you are certainly born of different tastes."

"That's for sure," Noah replies. They both laugh.

"Want to share?"

And I sat there listening as he told *our* idea to the professor. But as he was telling it, he leaned into my idea more. A taxi driver falls for a feisty barista over many months as he takes her to and from work at the same time every day. A road accident upends their lives and reveals a series of strange connections. He'd made a couple of small changes. He'd made it more "art film." But still. My concept. My fucking idea.

I was crushed. They'd branded me a talentless, insecure girl with an obsession over Noah, and there was no way to plead my case. *I* was holding *him* back. Noah broke up with me that night, and I just sat there nodding, unable to find the words to fight back. We were separated for the project, and there was no way to write the story I'd wanted to without it looking like I'd copied him.

I turned up at his halls a few days later, drunk and distressed. The fight spilled out into the residence, to the amusement of the other students, and I can still feel that cold chill of realization that I was proving his story right. I handed in a hastily redrafted idea, but with only a few weeks to go, and my head awash with the confusion of it all, my script wasn't complete. I failed my finals.

The professor had tried to speak to me, but I'd shunned him. My heart couldn't bear to sit through a sanitized version of what I'd heard with my own ears. I was devastated. How had I misjudged Noah so badly? I thought he cared about me, wanted what was best for me. And worse—how had I dared to think that I could really make it?

I looked around my little flat as the memories washed over me, feeling still seasick from the waves of humiliation. But I also felt that small ball of anger in my stomach. I had never let that anger go; it remained like a buried fury. The white-hot injustice of it still seared me from the inside.

In the years that followed, I became extremely cautious of myself and of other people. I kept my circle small. I second-guessed myself all the time, and it ground my life to a halt. I had ceased trusting myself, my instincts, my decision-making. I tried therapy briefly. I did yoga breathing. I drilled further into astrology for answers. I leaned on Charlie to keep me upright.

And now, fate had taken me to Budapest. Forced me to go alone. Guided me to that small street. And into that shop. The reading was so spot-on. So real. And then in walked Joe. It had to mean even more than a chance at a happy ending. It had to be the push I needed to make all these changes. Pull my life together, and this is what is possible.

Enough is enough. It was time to learn to trust myself again. It was time to pull on some new clothes and a big smile and try to get out there again.

I am wiser now.

And then I glance down at my horoscope again.

You need a clear plan.

I *do* like a plan. And if there is one thing a planner loves, it's a list.

I reach into my notebook, turning the page to a fresh one. Then I peer across at the calendar on my phone. Eleven weeks and five days.

PROJECT MARA: ME, BUT BETTER
In Order of Urgency

1. Nails—ASAP

2. New job? Or make current one better?

3. New clothes—ASAP

4. Hair, possibly face. Look into some mild cosmetic interventions?

5. Upgrade flat, or at least have cracks in ceiling filled.

6. Get back into film somehow?

7. Learn classical music (basics only, no need to go nuts)

I look down at my list. That will do. And by the end of the summer—or in precisely eleven weeks and five days—I will be done. It's a makeover. A renovation. A restoration, even.

And then, when fate delivers Joe to me, I'll be ready. I bite my lip. I know I'm getting ahead of myself again, but I cannot help it. I take a deep, soothing breath and for the first time in a long time I feel something: the magic and sparkle that comes from hope. It's positively intoxicating. I close my eyes and soak in it.

6

~

I AM JOLTED AWAKE from a mildly exciting sex dream, which includes Joe, Ryan, and for some reason Gerry, by what sounds like concrete drilling, stopping and starting with anxiety-inducing irregularity. I sit up in bed, disorientated, trying to make sense of the noise. My phone is lying on the bed next to me. I fell asleep googling Joe again. I'd done it all week.

For a brief moment I remember a warm rush of intoxicating thrill, but then the almighty whirring starts again. It's the flatmate. In the kitchen. The entry into my life is now not just his size and his presence but also his noise.

I jump out of bed and take the four steps from my door to the kitchen and stare at him standing there in only some white underpants.

"I'm in *Notting Hill* already," I mutter as he feeds an enormous juicer with carrots, one at a time, staring intently. The clear difference between Ash and Hugh Grant's skinny, terminally underdressed flatmate, though, is that Ash is built. I mean really built. Broad across the chest, thick thighs, and hard stomach that hints at a six-pack, if he were to flex. I kind of want him to flex, if I'm honest.

"Oh shit!" he shouts as he sees me. Then, realizing he has nowhere to hide, he tries to cover his pants with his crossed arms while holding an insanely large carrot. "I thought you were at work."

"Right. No. It's Saturday." I smirk but feel the heat in my cheeks as I try not to look at the porn carrot, held tight in one fist, pointing upward.

"Yes. Sorry," he replies, glancing down at himself and looking mortified but unable to really move. "Excellent fucking work, Ash," he mutters to himself.

A laugh—it's like a large honk and snort combination that escapes my mouth—and I slink quickly away and back into my room.

"Won't happen again, Mara!" I hear him shout from the room as I close my door.

I jump back into bed and reopen Instagram.

Joe was fairly easy to find. I had a first name. I knew he was a cellist. I guessed he was probably touring in an orchestra, and the Vienna Philharmonic had been playing in Budapest that very weekend, and they had photos and short biographies of all their musicians. He was the first cellist, which meant he was the very best, and he lived in Vienna. And he had a public Instagram account. I stare now at his latest snap and remember the way he smiled at me when I asked for the photo. The way he asked if I would take my veil off—and our eyes connected. A small request that was so potently sexy when I recall it now, like he had asked me to remove my clothes. Oh God. I was deep in the vat of promise now.

I have less than three months to complete Project Mara, to be ready when fate brings him to my door. Or at least, to the Star and Anchor at 7 p.m. I glance around my bedroom with its muted neutral bedsheets, mushroom-colored curtains, IKEA dresser, and mirror smeared with sticky fingerprints and make a mental note to add "bedroom deep clean and revamp" to my list of upgrades. And then I actually look in my bedroom mirror. Noah once told me I was a "bootleg Anne Hathaway." It was said in jest, but it stuck with me.

I have big brown eyes that can make me look permanently startled, and long dark hair that has not seen a hairdresser in years, and my skin is so pale that it can look a little blue-toned in the winter. My eyebrows are beyond full—they are edging toward each other in the center, and I can do better than a smear of ChapStick on the makeup front.

Right now, *this* isn't a *look*. It is a *please don't look*.

At thirty-one. Lynn said I look older. Do I really? I have a deep line between my eyebrows from being in a constant state of mild vexation. I am wilting before I've ever bloomed.

I am going to change that. I have a plan. Project Mara, and I am hoping to tackle the first item on my list today: nails.

I open up my star sign for the day, an impulsive reaction to make sure I am on the right track.

Good news, Sagittarians! The universe is finally giving you the chance to expand again. Make it a priority right now to move and wander and dream. You were born to grow and to thrive. Get out there! The good stuff is coming.

I grin, holding my phone to my chest, a giddy rush through me, as I picture Joe's eyes as he spots me across the pub. The ultimate movie meet-cute (even if we've technically already met). That spotting of the girl across the room who you just know is the one. I am going to be *her*. *It's you . . . ?* he will say, just like Tom Hanks says to Meg Ryan on top of the Empire State Building. I am sitting in impossibly feminine strappy sandals and a willowy tea dress reading something literary but not too boring, like Elena Ferrante or Sally Rooney, and drinking something sophisticated like an old-fashioned or whisky neat. I will glance up, doe-eyed but sassy, flicking my hair back because it's fallen in front of my face—but in no way meaning to be sexy with it. But still. Sexy as.

"Do we know each other?" I'll ask.

My phone beeps, interrupting the moment, and it's my mother.

Have you been kidnapped? ☺

I glance at my watch. It is time to leave for Charlie's and I could call her when I was nearly there. That way there was a *Hi, Mum, I'm in the car* to signify the short time I would have for her, followed by the *I've just gotten to Charlie's house* to give the call a clear ending. There is only so much damage that can be done in ten minutes. By me, or by her.

A minute later, I slink through the house, hoping to avoid another interaction with Ash, but he sees me.

"I'm so sorry about the noise," he calls out, now fully clothed. "Could I make amends with a glass of mud-brown agricultural water?" He holds aloft his drink, stopping wearily to sniff it. "What an absolute carry-on for a single glass of tepid, earthy funk juice."

"Sounds inviting, but I know where that carrot has been," I say teasingly.

"This isn't going to escalate," he says quickly, looking extremely earnest. "You won't come home to find protein powder in the fridge, or kettlebells in the hall. My mum was throwing the juicer out and—"

"It's fine," I say, stepping backward toward the door. I throw him a bone so I can escape. "Juicing in your undies is not a crime, Ash. Not yet."

I shoot him a reassuring smile and pull open the door. A few steps up the road the sun hits my roll-neck sweater and I realize I have terribly misjudged the weather. I race up the cobblestoned streets to where I parked my car, stopping momentarily to notice the nearly empty car park at the church, which Ash mentioned. Could I really park there? With *my* car?

It's crappy. It's diesel. And it's a fucking vintage hearse. A death cart. With my long dark hair and pale face, I know how I look: like Wednesday Addams on a road trip.

Perhaps it isn't such a stretch to park at the church. I barrel up to the front door. I have this at least in common with Ash; I'm not much of a churchgoer myself.

I put my hand up to the cold wood at the front door.

Do you knock on a church door? Can anyone walk in? I think they can, and so I take a step in the door and peer inside. It does not look inviting. It looks dark and cold and a little scary. It doesn't smell inviting either. I stare up at the notice board pinned in the little entranceway. Choirs. Sunday schools. Soup kitchens. My eyes run across the sign for guitar lessons. Oil painting. Available nannies. Piano. Yoga. Tai chi. So many people putting themselves out there.

The notices all look a little sad. Lonely, untouched phone numbers remain untorn off so many of the posters that I feel a pang of sorrow. All those carefully snipped little tabs with mobile numbers and names like Jean and Helga and Moe. I suddenly can't bear the failed dreams permeating from the ink on those little sheets of paper.

And so I quickly tear off a bunch of numbers: guitar lessons, cross-stitch, choir, English tutorials, marching band, summer camp, and art classes. I keep going so that all the posters look like there has been keen interest.

I cannot get out of the church entrance hall quick enough. The parking request will have to wait. I get to my car and force open the door with a jiggle of the key and a precise yank upward. The car starts with a heavy diesel chug and rattles along the coastal road, the usual humiliating stares in my direction as my vintage hearse makes its way toward Margate.

When the satnav says I'm exactly ten minutes until Charlie's house, I call my mum.

"Mara! I've been worried! Did you get my messages yesterday?" Mum begins, her tone high, her voice tight.

I rest my mobile in my lap.

"Yes, sorry. I've been busy," I say. "Mum, I'm driving to Charlie's, okay?"

"I hope I'm on speaker."

"You are!"

"Are you using the phone mount that Dad sent you? Or is the phone in your lap again?"

I think about the unopened phone mount in the back.

"I'm using the phone mount, Elaine," I reply.

A huff at me for calling her by her first name, but the diversion works. "How was the big trip, then?"

"It was fine. I saw a bit of the city. It was very cool."

"Cool?" she repeats, confused.

"Yes, Budapest is very cool, very creative and cultured," I say.

"Oh lovely, Mara," she says. "It sounds like you've got the wanderlust."

"You should try it, Mum," I say. It's a dig. My mother doesn't like to travel and prefers to holiday in the north of England. She's barely noticed the pandemic, she's such a homebody.

I feel bad. I hate that I speak to my mother like this, and yet, I keep doing it. But it's easier to keep both parents at arm's length.

They are constant worriers and wing clippers, the pair of them. It was clear that when I left film school, without a degree and without an internship, I could never go back and face their *you should have had a plan B* tirade.

I hear a loud sigh and then she starts again. "And is everything good with work?"

"Fine," I say quickly. "Work is fine. My house is fine. My life is just fine."

"Ben got a new car; did you see the photos on Facebook?"

"No one is on Facebook anymore," I say, as the summer sun hits the windscreen and I'm almost blinded. "*Shit!*"

"Mara, I wish you wouldn't call me from the car," Mum says, sighing again. "I know you're very busy these days, but it would be nice to do a FaceTime so I can see you."

And just like that, I feel guilty. What my mother wants is more of me, I know it. But if she could see the reality of my life, it would be too much to bear. I have to give her something.

"I met someone, by the way."

"Ooh, Mara," she says, and then after a beat: "*Really?*"

"Yes, *really*, Mother."

"I just mean . . ." Her voice is silent for a moment as I hear her take a breath, and then more brightly, she continues. "Well, who is this lucky man?"

"He's a concert cellist. He lives in Vienna for now, but he's coming across in August, if not before," I say, "and his name is Josef. He's just perfect. Worldly. Handsome. Sophisticated."

"He certainly does sound intriguing," she says.

"He's perfect," I insist.

Silence on her end of the phone, before: "You can ask him to my birthday if you like."

"He lives in Vienna, Mother," I say quickly, trying to imagine all that dark, expensive wool and height moving around in my little childhood house, eating M&S party food from a disposable silver tray.

"Oh, that's a shame. What about Charlie?" she tries.

"I don't think she would be able to," I reply. "She's still breastfeeding."

"That doesn't mean she's dead, darling. Why don't you go and pick her up? I'd love to meet little Sophie. It would be great if you can bring someone. Otherwise, you'll spend the whole time in your room again."

"I won't this time."

"Ben's coming, and he misses you too," she says, sighing.

"Okay. Message received loud and clear. I'm pulling into Margate, Mum, have to go!"

Margate is a totally different beast from Broadgate. It's a big town, for one. Its regeneration is picking up steam. It's cool, fizzing with artistic buzz thanks to the new Turner Contemporary art gallery on the seafront, a myriad of little cafés and boutiques, and now, apparently, even a hotel owned by heroin-chic aughts rock band the Libertines. In comparison, Broadgate is like the quaint old nan who lives down the coast. I glance at my watch—I'm early, and I'm not allowed to be early, as Sophie will be sleeping. I pull up at the beachfront car park and decide to head onto the beach.

As I stand on the enormous sandy beach scattered with sun-bathers eager to make the most of the warming weather, my toes just touch the water and the midday sun feels so delicious on my bare arms and face. I take a photograph of the water lapping at my toes and post it to Instagram with the caption *#BeachVibes*.

Then I scroll through my Instagram. The night sky with Budapest, a steaming bowl of goulash, a big mug of beer, a sunflower, a loaf of bread, a cake fail. There is a shot of Charlie holding her baby, which I hilariously captioned *Charlie with the Other Woman*. I scroll back to before Charlie was pregnant, and there's the shot of me as a bridesmaid at her wedding, wearing lavender crepe. I was the only one in the wedding party who looked on the verge of tears. I scroll back farther and hit the London era. Me and Charlie about to see *Matilda*, the shining lights of the theater behind us. Me and Charlie outside *Hamilton*. Me and Charlie under a duvet watching a movie at our flat, the scene so familiar. Wine. Crisps. Our little movie-picking system of cards strewn across the table. Me and Charlie dressed up for Secret Cinema *Dirty Dancing*; it's a mid-motion shot of me falling forward, the watermelon tumbling out of my hands and Charlie mid–explosive laugh. Me and Charlie at the Tate Modern, where she got us thrown out for sticking her head in Duchamp's *Fountain* (which is actually a urinal). It was this Mara that I needed to be with more people. This laughing, joyous, happy Mara. I miss her and my heart aches.

It's after 1 p.m. now and time to head to Charlie's house. She was very specific about not knocking on the door before 1 p.m., as it could wake Sophie from her nap, *if she ever fucking has one*, and I try to do everything just as she asks. I'm apprehensive about seeing her. I can't deny I need to hear her say sorry again about missing our trip.

Charlie lives just two streets back from the old town in a gorgeous bright white and orange brick Victorian-era home. Her husband, Alex, a successful London upper-management type, had spotted a gap in the market and converted a small car park into a heated outdoor street-food area called MarGraze, with a side hustle of art events through the summer. Charlie was a graphic designer and so she created the "look." It's a clever venture, and something Broadgate could desperately do with. The car park at the lido is always half-empty, and what better way to attract some bathers away from the sea than with a low-key street-food hub. I should talk to the guy at the coffee-to-go cart.

Before I've had a chance to use her huge iron knocker, I hear the barking and the front door open as Charlie, ten-month-old on her hip, flings open the front door, smiling like mad.

"Look at your face!" she says, smiling warmly, if a little wearily.

"I'm melting, let me in," I say, grinning. "Oh wow, you're so grown, Sophie!" I shout over the noise of the dog, trying to elicit a smile out of the little thing. But she cries louder and buries her head in Charlie's neck.

Charlie looks gorgeous, if exhausted. Her dark curly hair is tossed back in a low ponytail, and her athleisure wear is fresh, hanging off her in a trail of muted-nude cottons and viscose.

"Shut the hell up!" she snaps at the dog as it leaps and yelps, and she opens the door, wedging herself between it and me so the dog can't escape. "Quick! Barney got out yesterday and nearly got run over by an Uber Eats."

"You have Uber here?" I marvel. "Hello, Barney," I say, patting him awkwardly on the head, as he leaps up, getting caught in my bag straps and almost yanking me over with his weight. "Yes, yes, we're very happy to see Mara."

"He's a very good but naughty boy," Charlie says, as she leans in for a kiss. She smells of perfume and breast milk, an overpowering cover-up of domestic scent. I instantly feel loss. "Alex will be back in twenty, and he's going to take her out in the pram so we can talk, uninterrupted, for an entire hour at least."

"The dog or the baby?"

"Both." She laughs.

"With respect, that would be great," I say, following her in the front door. "Hello, little one," I say in my best high voice, taking Sophie's little hand in my fingers, but once more she buries her head into Charlie's neck and squirms.

"She doesn't really know you. Give her time," Charlie says, waving me through to the open living area.

"I'm sorry we've not caught up more," I say. I want to add, *I have tried*, but I know the role I must play here: supportive, understanding, and definitely not in any way at all an added pressure to a new mum.

Moving in with Charlie had been so easy, it felt like fate brought me there. I needed a flat and Charlie needed a flatmate, and the rent was cheap and it was a short bus ride from my cinema job. I answered the ad and was the first person she met at her tiny Hackney Wick new build. I was early and she was watching the last fifteen minutes of *The Notebook* when I arrived.

"Shhh," she said, waving me in and motioning me toward the couch as she finished it, tissue in her hands.

I love to watch people watching things I love for the first time, and so Charlie watched the end of *The Notebook*, and I watched Charlie watching it. But, you know, subtly, so she didn't see me looking at her like a weirdo.

"Okay, I've fucking seen it now," she said, her eyes red and glassy, turning it off as the credits rolled. "The way people go on and on about it." She rolled her eyes.

"It's one of those movies," I said, nodding. "Hopelessly romantic or soppy shit?"

"Can I say soppy shit?" she said, standing up to get me a drink. "Do you think that movie has spoiled everyone's expectations about love?"

"Yes," I said, fresh from my humiliating breakup with my own Noah.

"I'm Charlie," she said, reaching out to shake my hand.

"Mara. Sagittarius."

"Ooh, snap!" she replied. "When's your birthday?"

"December thirteenth," I replied with a grin.

"Okay. No. Way," she said, both hands to her chest. "Me too."

"No way," I replied, and we both stared at each other, incredulous.

She opened a bottle of wine, then another, and we ended up lying on the floor listening to the highly underrated soundtrack from *Sleepless in Seattle*. I told her the universe brought us together, she agreed it was *really fucking weird we had the same birthday* and that she thought I was hilarious, and so I moved in right away. We were inseparable. People remarked on it. Charlie was the first person who enjoyed my musical movie nights. Who read me my horoscope over scrambled eggs and Earl Grey tea before work. My first real best friend. The kind you read about. She is mine and I am hers.

Her new house is a real work in progress, though she's done a great job of making it cozy. I spy her huge teapot, a relic from our London days, and some of the mismatched pottery on the open shelves. But my goodness, since Sophie came along it has become chaotic.

I try not to stare at the laundry piled high on one side of the cream sofa with its new darkened round milk stains, the pile of semi-broomed-up muck from the kitchen floor that hasn't made it to the bin yet.

"Don't look, for God's sake," Charlie says. "I've become a slob, Mara. There is no time to do anything except run around after this adorable little monster until eight p.m. Then after that all I can be fucked to do is sit on that couch and eat."

I laugh at this. "I can help?" I say, toying with the top of the wooden broom. "Let me at least do this."

"No. Alex's finally caved and got a cleaner, and he's coming tomorrow. I just want to sit with you and try to summon the feeling of Charlie from two years ago, please? I love the mothers' group and baby yoga and all the things I do with the local parents, but God I've missed the old me."

She puts Sophie down on the floor and she immediately crawls off at quite a pace. Charlie kicks shut a child gate on the door and rolls her eyes. "Alex will be back soon," she says. "What do you want to drink? Are you still partial to an old-fashioned?"

"No," I say, "my old-fashioned phase has been replaced by red wine and Celine Dion. Just like *Bridget Jones*." I sing "All by Myself" weakly, pretending to sob into my hands.

"You're not there yet, Mara. You're not Bridget Jones. She was thirty-two," she says, laughing.

"Then I have about six months," I reply. "Don't make me decide. I don't have time to consult my horoscope. Choose something for me."

"Same old Mara," she says, giggling. "I do actually have red wine. Alex opened it last night."

"Excellent."

"Oh, how is the new flatmate?" she says. I eye the fact that she's pouring *one* glass and not two. Not like Charlie.

"Ash? Oh, he's quite nice. He made me a goulash as a welcome home from Hungary," I say, raising both eyebrows.

"Oh, that's sweet," she says.

"Yeah, it was," I admit.

"Anything else? Is he cute?"

"Er? I guess? I haven't really thought about it," I say, pushing the vision of Ash and his bare thighs out of my mind. "I've been kind of sidetracked with my *trip*, as you know." I beam at her. I just want to get on to Joe.

"So that's all? Who is he?"

I sigh. "Oh, just some local guy. A painter-decorator like my dad. I mean, he's nice. He seems easygoing. I have barely seen him all week." I want to move on from Ash.

"O-kay," she says in a singsong voice, now raising both her eyebrows at me. "Oh, Mara" she says, quickly, "I'm so glad to see you. To see another adult whose life isn't all about children. You're just up the road, but it feels like you may as well be in London. I mean, it's twenty minutes away and look at us, catching up for the third time in six months. . . . It's hopeless."

"Forget it. You're a mum now. And I've been busy too. Not to mention us Sagittarians are feeling the effects of Mercury retrograde on our close relationships," I say, although I want to tell her that I wish she was more available too.

"That might explain my home life," she says wistfully. I want to pounce on the comment but suspect she won't want to talk about it. "Now, tell me all about Budapest," she says, grinning. "I'm so sorry, once again, for pulling out. Believe me, no one wants a weekend off all this more than me."

"It's okay, Charlie. Really," I say. "And in a way, maybe it was meant to happen. I mean, if you'd come, I don't think I would have met *him*."

"Oh yes. Go on. The man?"

"Yes. The man, Charlie. The *one*," I say. She smirks at me and briefly rolls her eyes.

"Well, I was wandering around these little streets, you know, just sort of aimlessly, and then I saw this little tarot shop and they did readings. You know I've always wanted to see a proper clairvoyant," I say, as Charlie nods in agreement. "She told me a lot of stuff, but the guts of it was that I was going to meet a man *imminently*. She said he was *tall. Warm*." I start to count on my fingers as I relay all his identifying features. "Worked with his hands. Had a lot of people around him. Was passionate. I think those were the key points."

"Oh, that's quite a bit more specific than I imagined it would be," Charlie says, frowning.

"Wait," I say, almost breathless with excitement now. "And then, she goes into labor. Like right in the middle of the reading. She's like, 'Get out now,' and 'Lock up for me.' And so, because, you know me, and I didn't want to wait outside on my own, I agreed to lock up for her. Then, while I waited for the taxi, I was, like, looking at her crystals and her old tarot decks, and then just for fun, I tried on her veil and all the jewelry, and then he walked in."

"Who?"

"Josef."

"Josef," she repeats, and I watch as she starts to weigh up exactly what I'm telling her.

"My God he was so fucking handsome. Tall, just like she said. And he was a cellist, so clearly he's passionate, working with his hands, and surrounded by people. An *audience*. Don't you see? He plays concerts." My eyes fly to the ceiling as I start to feel the dream enveloping me. "He looked a bit like Alexander Skarsgård. But he was also sort of old-fashioned and a bit kind of reserved. Very old-school romantic. Like he'd hold open the door but not expect me to stay at home with the baby."

As it tumbles out of my mouth I cringe. "Not that you are!" *Fuck, fuckity, fuck.*

"It's okay," she says, waving the comment away, "but what happened? Did you go for a drink, or . . . ?"

"Not exactly," I say, feeling giddy with nerves at how she'll take the rest of the story.

"I took fate by the shirt collar and read him his fortune. I told him that the love of his life was a woman called Mara and that he would find her at the Star and Anchor, in Broadgate, at seven p.m. on the last Friday of August. He's going to be in London anyway, so it wasn't too much of a stretch." I lift my fingers up to my face and cover my eyes before peeking out to see Charlie gasp.

"Oh God, Mara!"

"I know. Everything came together so perfectly. I have got three months to get myself ready to meet him," I say, grinning. I can feel my cheeks burning with the excitement of it. But then there is a long pause while Charlie looks at me, her mouth slightly ajar. Then I watch as she reaches her hands up to her face and rubs up and down, sighing.

"What?" I say.

"Mara," she says, laying her hands in her lap, twisting her engagement and wedding rings round in circles. "Slow down a minute."

"I know, I'm getting ahead of myself," I say, blowing out once in a show of calming my thoughts, which were, in fact, racing. *Please don't throw cold water on this. Please, Charlie.*

"It's a lot to take in, that's all," she says sharply. "So, the fortune-teller told you about this man. *The one.*"

"That's right," I say, nodding.

"And then she left, and you were standing there in her clothes and a man walked in."

"Not just a man," I say, biting my lip. But I can feel I haven't got Charlie on board. I'm hanging on to her by my fingertips.

"He came in, and you fake-read his fortune? And told him that *you* were *his the one.*"

"Yes," I say. "So, he's coming here in late August and I have to get myself ready because she also said I needed to fix a few things in my life. Which was frankly spot-on too."

"Oh, Mara, I don't know about this," she says now, and as she says it I feel all the sparkle seep out of the room. My shoulders slump forward and I shrug.

"I wish you were there; you would have seen . . ." My voice trails off.

"Mara, I have to say, as your friend—and I know that you don't like criticism . . . ," she begins.

"That's not true!" I raise my palms and shake my head.

"This all sounds pretty out-there. Can you hear yourself?"

Ouch.

She continues, grimacing momentarily before she does. "I just don't want to see . . . How are you going to feel if he doesn't come? Working yourself up like this."

"But he's going to. I just know it. Don't you think it's fate that all of that happened? You not coming. Then me being alone. Then the baby deciding to come at that exact moment. Then him walking in after she said I was going to meet him *imminently.*"

"Fate? That *you* told *him* that *you* were his destiny?" she says, shaking her head. "No, I think you've set it all up."

I sigh, irritated now. Charlie always enjoyed my talk of fate and destiny before. She always agreed that the universe was going to deliver my perfect guy at just the right time, and when he came, I'd know. And now here I am telling her that this is finally it, and she's gone cold.

"Mara," she says, "when you were dating in London, do you remember you would have one date, and then you'd come home and tell me all the reasons they weren't right for you? You are a chronic first dater. I used to think it was impressive how you knew exactly what you wanted and what he looked like and his star sign and all those things. But sometimes I wondered if it was just an excuse, so you didn't have to take a risk with someone."

"I don't think that's . . . ," I begin to protest, although I can feel the redness in my cheeks as I do.

"Remember Dan? That awesome, kind, creative guy you went on that date with? He was so great, Mara. And he *really* liked you. He looked like a young Leo DiCaprio. And, remember he had seen *Singin' in the Rain* with his grandmother a hundred times? I literally couldn't have summoned a better fit for you from the goddess Venus herself. And you wouldn't see him again because the heart said yes, but the horoscope said no?"

"Well . . . we all need boundaries," I say weakly.

"I love you," she says now, "but it feels like you rely on fate and all this external signposting so that you don't have to listen to what *you* really want."

"That didn't work out for me with Noah, as you know," I say, downing the last mouthful of my glass of wine, frustrated. "I followed my heart there and it was a disaster."

"That was ten years ago, Mara," she says quietly.

I don't reply for a moment, looking down at my fingers, picking at the paint on one of my nails. "It was fate," I say weakly. "Joe is my fate."

I fold my arms and force a grin. Keen to move on.

"Do you really think he's going to come, Mara. *Really?*"

"Well, no harm done if not," I say. "You said yourself I needed to get out there more."

"I meant you should go to an art class. Or get on Tinder."

Charlie sighs, glancing down at Sophie, who is smashing a colored block on the ground and gabbling away to herself. I frown. I have really misjudged this. I was sure Charlie would find this as extraordinary as I did.

"Bloody Tinder," I mutter.

"It's just worrying. You're going to work yourself up and I can't bear the thought of you there when he doesn't show," she says, shaking her head now, like she's frustrated with me. She sighs deeply, rubbing her face with her hands. "Mara. Your head's in the clouds on this stuff. Life doesn't work like that. You meet your life partner at work or through a friend."

It wounds me so deeply I can barely breathe for a moment.

"Well, those options are dead ends right now," I say and then regret it immediately. "Come on, Charlie, let me enjoy this? Please?"

"I'm sorry," she says after a long pause. "I just think it's not a good idea. I *really* don't want you to waste your summer waiting for this guy to show up. I can't watch it."

There is a silence in the room, and I think about Alex, who was supposed to come in twenty minutes to take the baby and the dog but isn't back. I look at Charlie, who is tired, who has never not had a drink with me unless she was pregnant, and I summon all my empathy for her. *Of course she's not going to get behind this,* I think. She's at the business end of romance; the meeting is done, the courtship, the wedding. Now she's at home with the baby and the breast milk and the mess. She doesn't want to hear about this.

"You're probably right," I say, as brightly as I can. "Still, it's a nice fantasy."

Charlie sighs too and tilts her head thoughtfully. "Did you know Oscar Wilde went to see a fortune-teller who predicted his early death?"

"No," I say.

"I read about it. It's weird, isn't it? How we feel like we need something to help guide us through life," she says. "My parents have Jesus. You have astrology. Alex currently has—brace yourself—Jordan fucking Peterson."

"Oh God."

"I just pray it's a phase," she says, rolling her eyes again.

"I've never understood how people can know themselves so well that they know exactly where they're going and what to do to get there. How to make clear decisions that truly come from just *them*. It's a mystery to me," I say.

"You do okay. You just need to trust yourself more, Mara. And try to connect more with other people. Not just men. Friends. Interests. You're never going to meet people stuck in front of a Coen brothers box set."

"Maybe. It's easier to trust what comes *to* me."

"Isn't that just absolving yourself of responsibility?"

"Or," I begin, dramatically raising my hands to the heavens, "it's leaving yourself open to all the universe can bring."

"Okay, loopy," she says, laughing at me.

"Do you ever worry that you'll never be happy?" I ask, looking at the broom in the corner of the kitchen.

"I *am* happy," she says, her eyes following mine to the broom, before she sighs and turns back to me. "Just, you know, trust yourself a bit, Mara. *Your* actual instincts. *Your* intuition."

"Never trust an Aquarius rising," I say, and we both laugh.

I am not going to give up on Joe. She's wrong. The clairvoyant confirmed it. *Fix lots of things and he will reveal himself.* I close my eyes and the picture of him coming into the pub is clearer than ever, his features so real I can almost touch them. I smile to myself.

"Where did you go?" Charlie says, a question she has asked me so many times over the last decade. A question I almost always answered. *I'm imagining that man from Whole Foods is chasing me down Carnaby Street to return the notebook I dropped. I'm trying to visualize the Underground guy as a protective Virgo, instead of a Pisces. I'm imagining what it would be like to receive flowers from someone who loves me. Just once.*

"Nowhere. Nothing. Anyway, tell me about you," I say. "Are you ever going to come and see me in Broadgate?"

7

THE SUN IS out over Broadgate today, and I decide to walk to work. I pull on my backpack, check for Ash as I emerge from my room—the coast is clear—and head out onto the street, my headphones playing Beethoven's Fifth. Christ, it's a fancy racket, all the aggressive strings jaunting away like a perpetual anxiety attack in D minor. I'll do ten minutes, and then I can sink into my guilty pleasure—the soundtrack to *Guardians of the Galaxy*.

Our little street, Sandhill Way, leads down toward the main street on the beachfront and is paved with cobblestones. It's a walking street, my street, once the small, bustling high street of medieval coastal Kent. Now some of the little stores are flats, but many shops still remain. A shoe-repair store, a fabric shop, an electrical goods store, a chemist, each of their storefronts painted a different pastel color. Someone has hung colorful bunting from one side to the other, and with the sun now firmly out, and us two weeks into June, I can finally start to see Broadgate in all its glory.

My day with Charlie has been on my mind. I have been brooding on it, like a lost lover, going through old photos and rewatching *Mamma Mia!* and crying to Meryl Streep singing "Slipping Through My Fingers" as she paints her daughter's toenails. Charlie used to paint my toenails. Now she doesn't have time to go to a nail bar. I really need to learn how to paint my own toenails.

If Charlie and I have been drifting this last year or so, it feels as though I can now barely see her on the horizon. In my less generous moments, I feel angry at her that I'm never invited around anymore, or that when I am, I feel like an interruption to her life, rather than a part of it.

"You must make new friends, Mara," I say to myself out loud, startling the lady who is walking just in front of me.

"Sorry," I say, blushing as she shakes her head and crosses the road.

At the end of my sweet, cobbled lane, I come out onto the wide, main street, a long promenade that winds around the bay in a half-moon. The promenade is dotted with small hotels, little seafood restaurants that bring oysters from Whitstable straight to the table, plus a few touristy shops and the local chipper. The stores selling beach paraphernalia have pushed their stands out on the sidewalk, so a bright plastic gauntlet of inflatables, Isle of Thanet and Broadgate fridge magnets, sunscreen, sandpit buckets and spades, and rolled-up beach towels greets me as I head to the zebra crossing and cross to the beach side.

The beachfront pedestrian promenade is broad, with traditional Victorian covered seating areas, grassy lawns for picnics, and several wide staircases that lead you down the ten steps or so onto the sand. To my left, the road meets a small fishing port with a long pier, where there are some huts selling whelks and cockles, and the Star and Anchor pub, with its dark Tudor beams and white cladding.

To the right, I see it: the Broadgate Lido, sitting on the headland, looking back at the town. Now the days are longer, I no longer get to see its white facade turn pinky-peach as the morning sun rises, but rather it flashes almost brilliant white in the bleaching summer sun.

Fired Up is a little café before the lido. Once the local fire station, it's a tiny redbrick building, not really much larger than a garage, with a sloped roof, a large red door, and a horse trough out the front. You could picture a wagon parked in there a hundred years ago, with the horses waiting lazily for the fire bell to ring. Above the door a plaque reads BROWN & SONS FIRE HOUSE 1831. I pop in to bag a Halloumi breakfast burger and a cup of sweet tea.

"You're Mara, right? You work at the lido?" says the woman behind the counter as she hands me my change.

"Yes," I reply, and pocket my change and head toward the door. But before I do, I stop myself and turn around, Charlie's advice to get out more ringing in my head. "Sorry. Um. And what's your name?"

"I'm Chrissie, love," she says, smiling a huge row of teeth in an enormous, generous mouth.

"Well, nice to meet you, Chrissie," I say, smiling back.

I walk out the door feeling proud of myself. *See, Mara, that wasn't so hard.*

I take a moment to gaze back down the bay, the Star and Anchor now far in the distance. From this vantage point, you can see all the cheerful little beach huts, which run along a wooden walkway on the sand. I marvel at the lido's position and potential, looking back down on this quintessential British seaside town, fretting for the hundredth time that it's been left to erode slowly away. I feel a gust of warm wind against my back, and I turn to see huge dark clouds on the horizon. Rain, damn it. And I didn't bring an umbrella.

By the time I arrive at work, the sun has completely disappeared, and the temperature has suddenly dropped. I push at the glass doors, but they don't budge, so I fish for my keys and let myself in, wondering if I'm weirdly early or I've forgotten about a bank holiday again. But that can't be it; it's Tuesday, and it was business as usual yesterday.

I get to my desk and am about to read my daily horoscope when Ryan appears like a tornado of energy, dragging one of the huge corduroy armchairs from Gerry's office up next to my desk, almost toppling a plant pot in the process.

"Easy, tiger," he says to the rubber plant, pushing it gently aside.

"Where is everyone? And what on earth are you doing?" I ask.

"Storm, innit," he says, nodding to the windows. Ahead, a distinct gray wall of cloud and rain is heading toward us menacingly. Ryan is off to get the second armchair as Samira arrives with popcorn.

"The pool is closed and Gerry's not here," she says to me curtly. "You can put down the work and back away slowly."

"You are both going to sit here with popcorn and watch the storm?" I ask, craning my neck to see if Gerry really isn't here.

"You bet," says Ryan, jumping into his armchair and swiping a fistful of the popcorn from Samira. "Front-row seats. Reckon we'll get ninety-kilometer gusts and the swell will be immense."

"Who doesn't love storms?" Samira asks. "Afterward we'll need to clear the pool and we get a couple of days off."

She and Ryan fist-bump.

"Why not invest in storm-surge protection?" I ask, although as I say it, I know the answer. It's the answer I always get. *Funding.* But when I ask how we apply for it, they say Gerry oversees it. But when I offered to help Gerry apply for funding he said it's under control. Yet here we are, watching the chalk cliffs melt into the ocean and take half the building with them, and everyone's acting like we're the *Titanic* band.

"It's a big job, but anything is possible," I say, shrugging.

"Mara has grand ideas for this place," Samira explains to Ryan.

"I did," I say, embarrassed by my initial enthusiasm.

"Gerry's on it, isn't he?" Ryan shouts while bending to retrieve loose popcorn from the floor.

"Gerry is not 'on' anything," Samira says wryly, "unless you count Viagra and Marlboro Reds."

"Viagra was invented in Kent," Ryan says proudly.

"Why am I not surprised?" I murmur.

"Why are you *here*, Mara?" Ryan asks now. "Why did you leave London to come *here*?"

I don't have an explanation that doesn't sound like I gave up on London and followed my best friend across the country, so I try for a deflection. "Who wouldn't leave London for all this?" I say, waving my arms around the office. It works: they both laugh.

Make new friends, I think to myself.

Samira and Ryan would be an easy start.

"So, how about I try to guess your star signs?" I say.

"I'm completely obvious, though," says Samira, tucking a loose tendril of hair behind her ear. "Where do you read yours?"

"Oh, *New York Mag*, and I follow some good Instagram accounts. Do you know Chani Nicholas? I like AstroTwins for my rising sign, and Love Lanyadoo too, but I don't follow them quite as much as I used to."

Too much, Mara. I laugh, a high-pitched strangled shrill to make it seem like I'm joking, but neither of them seems very fazed.

"She also sees fortune-tellers," Ryan says.

Samira is now nodding slowly at me. "You're a witch. I knew there was a reason you were so . . . um, weird and reclusive."

"Weird and reclusive. Put that in your Tinder bio!" shouts Ryan.

Weird and reclusive? I laugh. "No. No. No. Not a witch. I just find them so accurate and day-to-day helpful. But, like, if you ever need a ritualist sage burning to rid this place of its negative vibes, I could help." I can feel my heart beating faster as I press forth with the chitchat, desperate to keep it light. "So, Samira, I am definitely thinking air sign for you."

I see that she's half smirking at me, her perfectly colored plum lips curling up at one side.

"I *am* an air," says Samira.

"It's just, well, you're always so stylish," I say, feeling my cheeks redden, "and I'm wondering if . . . Libra?"

"My God," she says, "how in the hell?"

"It's a gift," I say, smiling.

"Do Ryan!" she says, eyes wide.

"Gemini," he says.

"I'm supposed to guess!" I protest, wondering whether I should mention that Samira and Ryan are astrological soul mates or whether that would be awkward. Without their rising signs, I can't be sure, so I say nothing.

"Can you guess me?" I say.

"Is there a star sign that doesn't accept invitations, go for coffee, or even, you know, talk to people?" Samira asks, and I wilt a little.

"Is there a star sign that takes itself too seriously?" says Ryan, and I force myself to laugh and thus disprove his jibe.

"I'm Sagittarius, actually. Although I never feel as outgoing as I'm supposed to be, but that's the sun sign for you. It's just a snapshot, really. I'm deep in my rising and moon signs."

"Okay, witch," says Samira.

"'Sagittarius. It's time to say *yes* . . . ,'" I say, reading my star sign aloud from *The Cut.* "'Reach out to broaden your circle but be wary of stretching yourself too thin and causing stress.'" Crushingly accurate.

"You can't be in danger of *that*," says Samira. She's being salty and I deserve it. She tried to get me out multiple times when I first arrived, and I said no to every invitation.

What people don't realize, but what I've come to understand, is this: I *do* want to get to know *her*, but I *don't* want *her* to get to know *me*. I disappoint. I start strong, and then after some time I cannot keep up with the bouncy, carefree Mara, and all the weird neuroses begin to leak out. And then I'm some other kind of Mara. I will do anything to avoid feeling like someone might get sick of me. Although I sure am sick of myself.

"Next time you ask me out, I promise to say yes," I say.

"Or *you* could make the effort?" she says, but before I have a chance to protest, I see that she's teasing me.

"Fair."

I'm feeling a tentative sense of connection with them both when a few moments later, Lynn walks in with a share bag of Maltesers and two coffees. She hands me one and I almost gasp.

"Thanks, Lynn," I say, truly touched. And then, to ram home the gratefulness, I add, "That's so kind of you, a coffee. Wow."

"Those kids don't drink it," she explains, nodding toward Samira and Ryan.

"Samira and I are around the same age," I say, feeling exasperated.

"I'm twenty-nine!" Samira says, nodding.

"Oh yes, and you're *thirty-one*," Lynn says, as if it's a joke we're all in on.

A huge gust causes a massive spray of water to hit the windows, and we all jump backward, and Ryan whoops with delight.

"I just realized, if you're Sagittarius, you haven't had a birthday with us yet," Samira says.

"No. But I don't like a fuss."

"Well, Ryan's nan makes cake."

"Black Forest gâteau," Ryan confirms.

"With the chocolate shavings on top," Lynn chimes in. "Make sure you tell us next time or we *all* miss out on cake."

"She's right," Ryan says. "Don't let us down, Mara."

"Sorry. Honestly, I find the attention of office birthdays a bit much. Everyone standing around singing out of tune and only there for the cake anyway."

I look around at them, each face a more confused and pitying picture than the last.

"Utterly tragic," Lynn says, under her breath but loud enough for everyone to hear.

"*Utterly tragic.* Put that in your Tinder bio!" shouts Ryan again.

"Oh, fuck off," I say, this time laughing.

I stare down at my chewed nails and pick at the flaking polish. "Samira, do you happen to have any nail polish remover?"

Samira stands up immediately and then shows me her nails. They are long, oblong, and shaped into near claws, painted a bluey, milky color with a single silver star on the tips of her ring fingers. "Wait here."

When she returns the storm is in full force, the weight of the gusts causing the building to groan as the huge waves engulf the edge of the pool below us. It is as exciting as it is scary. Samira pulls out what I think is her makeup but turns out to be a nail polish bag complete with nail-grooming kit, hand cream, and multiple shades of OPI color.

She grasps my hand, puts it on top of a cushion, and gets to work. "Choose a color," she commands as she dabs nail polish remover on each nail, rubbing down in a rhythmic motion.

I look through the different ones and hold up a bright pink.

"No," she says, pulling it out of my hand.

I try a pale pink.

"Absolutely not," she says, throwing that one straight in the trash bin.

"This?" I say, holding up a mustard yellow.

"Ugh," she replies, and picks out a dusky rose shade, holding it up to my face. "You've got that very English rose complexion. Pale with pinky undertones and natural pink-red lips."

"Oh, thanks," I say, instinctively trying to hide my face with my hand as I blush.

"You need more of these kinds of dusky tones. The black you're always wearing? You think it makes you disappear, but it ages you. I'd love to see you in some bold color with all that dark hair and pale skin."

"Samira has been trying to get me into cream linen blends for the last eighteen months," says Lynn. "You needn't be bullied."

"No, it's fine," I say, smiling at Samira. "It's helpful. I'm kind of embarking on a bit of a makeover, as it happens. A Mara 2.0, if you will."

"Oh, I will," she says, her eyes sparkling at the thought. "*Please* let me help."

She looks down at my nails and sighs. "It will be my greatest-ever achievement. I'll turn you from this into something less . . . depressing."

I laugh, but she isn't joking. "I'm serious, Mara. Can I do those eyebrows first, though? My God."

"Fine," I say, "you can be Stanley Tucci and I'll be Anne Hathaway."

"*Devil Wears Prada*," she says, grinning.

"The Michael Caine to my Sandra Bullock."

"*Miss Congeniality*?" she says, and I nod.

"*Pretty Woman*, without the sex work," I say.

"Or the credit card," she says grimly.

She looks back at my nails, and my eyes linger on the glossy black hair she has pulled back in a tortoiseshell grip, and I marvel at the easiness of her style.

"Where do you get your hair cut?" I ask.

"Happy Hair. Ask for Jackie," she says, glancing at my own hair, which is currently pulled back in a loose, messy bun and not in a fashionable way.

"So why *did* you move to Broadgate, then?" she whispers, leaning in to me so the others can't hear. She then begins a very brutal filing session, her headshaking and tutting intensifying as she makes her way through each broken and unkempt nail.

"Everyone left London. And my best friend is in Margate."

"Really?" Samira says, unscrewing the cap on the lovely dusty pink.

"Yes. Charlie," I say. "We used to do our nails together. I had a pretend spa that I would set up and there was a whole role-play thing we did together where I was the salon owner and she was the worn-out executive."

"Okay, so you were very close, then," she says, her perfectly manicured and powdered eyebrows raised in amusement.

"Yes, people sometimes thought we were in a relationship," I say with a self-deprecating chortle. This was a well-worn line I used to say proudly, but now that she has moved on and we are on the other side of thirty it sounds incredibly juvenile. I feel sad—and almost embarrassed—at the memory of us in our little Hackney Wick flat, with towels around our heads and cut-out slices of cucumber on our eyes and expensive Korean sheet masks.

Samira's eyes are fixed on mine as I pause to push away the tears that have been threatening since I left Charlie's house on Saturday. "She's married now," I say quietly.

"Is this the whole of May?" Lynn says, interrupting us. She's been counting out receipts that I've already counted out in the petty cash tin. I nod at her.

"Did you process those last two annual memberships I gave you?"

"I did," I say.

"We need more," she says, reaching up and patting her head. She looks at her fingers and then upward to the old stucco ceiling as another huge drop of water falls on her head. We all see it at the same time, and Ryan scrambles out of his armchair and rushes to the back of the office.

"*Leak!*" shouts Samira, and she yanks on my hand to let me know we're not moving.

Ryan returns with three big red plastic buckets and slides one onto Lynn's desk.

"We're really running out of time to save this place," Lynn says, as she tries to dry up the desk while thick drops of water fall from the ceiling into the bucket, in a loud and slightly depressing *plonk*. "Christ, all these receipts are soaked."

"Don't worry, Lynn, I've already logged them all. It's not the end of the world. None of it makes any dent in the bottom line."

"It has to," she mutters, her brows furrowed in distress.

"Nothing is going to change here without investment," I say. "Nothing."

"Well, the meeting next week will hopefully give us some sense of where they're at," says Lynn, and I nod. "Gerry is always promising. He needs to deliver."

My phone starts to vibrate, and I glance over at it, my nails still wet.

"Can you grab it?" I ask Samira, twinkling my gorgeous nails her way. "Just check who it is?"

"It's says *Mother*," she says.

"Oh God," I say, shaking my head. Samira frowns at this but puts my phone back on my desk.

"Are you seeing anyone?" she asks, in full beauty-therapist mode now.

"Well, sort of . . ." I begin, wondering if I can divulge the details to Samira.

"Mara's got a boyfriend in Europe," says Lynn, snatching the decision away.

"He's not quite my boyfriend," I say, correcting her. "It's only a new thing."

"European?" Samira says, her eyes shooting up. "Is *that* why you went to Budapest?"

"No. I met him on my holiday." I glare at Lynn, who is trying to dry out all the receipts from the petty cash tin.

"Isn't this fun, all of us here together?" says Lynn. "I'll miss it when we're all cast aside, unemployed. Samira takes a job fixing vending machines, Mara marries a cousin, and Ryan begins a life of light crime."

"Hello, operator, I'd like to report a murder?" says Ryan into his finger phone.

"Call the burns unit," says Samira.

I think for a moment about joining in on the joke. Saying something witty and off-the-cuff, but I don't. I hold back in case I misfire. And instead I just laugh.

Our jolly mood is interrupted by the slam of the office main doors.

"Fuck, it's Gerry," Samira whispers to me, as we hear the heavy footsteps climbing the stairs.

"Why is he here?" says Ryan, tutting but not moving. There is no point in trying to wriggle out of this situation. Ryan is lounging in an armchair holding the container of popcorn. Lynn is standing by the dripping bucket hanging up the wet receipts using paperclips and a length of dental floss as a washing line. And Samira looks like she's running a mobile nail bar.

Gerry looks from one face to the next, then sighs loudly and goes into his office and shuts his door.

"Well, that was a complete disaster," I say, panicking.

"*Complete disaster.* Put that in your Tinder bio!"

"Stop trying to put me on Tinder," I shout. "I'm not looking for a relationship."

"Oh, that's good. Put *that* in your Tinder—" he begins before I hurl a nail file at his head.

8

A FEW DAYS LATER, I'm sitting in the reception area of Happy Hair. Me, the only customer, and my new hairdresser, Jackie, who is nattering away on the phone at volume and seems to be waiting until my exact appointment time and not a moment before.

"I told him," she's almost shouting, "get yourself the hell out of Barcelona. Does he think he's twenty still? Not with that wrinkly ass."

I look over at Jackie, who rolls her eyes and gestures a chatty mouth with her hand to me as if she's trying to get off the phone, and yet, it's hard to believe there is anyone on the other end as she's talked without pause for the last ten minutes. I have learned that *Ivan had better do something about that neck if he's going to keep fucking around with Becky* and that *Jesse needs an OnlyFans account, as he's one tweet away from showing his hole on Twitter.* And then some endless cackling commences, and I can't help but join in.

I stare down at Joe's Instagram feed, which for a moment suddenly feels very dull and straight by comparison. I'm not absolutely convinced he would laugh at any gag that isn't triple layered and dipped in culture. Last night's post: a picture of his cello with a string missing and the caption *Das Ende einen langer Tour*. The end of a long tour. So, he's home in Vienna.

A new haircut and a revamp of my social media are definitely in order, and I plan to do both today.

"Sorry about that, darling," says my hairdresser, sliding next to me in her oversize black-and-white sweatshirt, her long silvery-blond hair wound up in braids around her head like a crown. "You're Ash's new flatmate, then?"

"Ash?" I reply. "Yes."

"Lucky you," she says, smirking.

"Yeah, he's very nice," I reply.

Jackie raises a single eyebrow, as if there is much to say on this subject. "And he's over *her*, is he?"

"Who?" I ask, craning my head to look at her instead of the reflection of her.

"I'm not one to gossip," she says, nodding, almost willing me to press her further. When I don't, she looks at me in the mirror and sort of winces, holds a comb to her cheek as if she's inspecting me.

"What *can't* I do you for today, then, lovely?" she says.

"I know. I know," I say, frowning. "I have had my hair like this for years."

"Years," she agrees, nodding.

"I need something fresh," I say, looking to face the mirror as she moves her head from side to side to take me all in. "It's just. Like, it says nothing. It just says . . ."

"Lonely thirty-something with no beans in the bank?"

"Um, I . . ."

"Do you have a cat?" she is now asking me.

"No."

"You want one, though, right?" she says, tapping my shoulder gently. For all intents and purposes, she's being rude, and yet, I feel myself grinning.

"I was thinking of something kind of dramatic. European perhaps?"

"Like a chic little French cut. Elfin?"

"Oh," I say, grabbing my hair by the ends and tugging them down in horror, "not that dramatic."

"What about bangs?"

"A fringe?" I say, as she holds the ends up over my face and parts them.

"Curtain bangs," she says, and when I "huh?" in confusion, she says, "a sort of middle parting, longer fringe, with a long shaggy bob."

I put both my hands up to my face and shake my head. "I don't know. I can't decide."

She leans in, pulling one of my hands from my face. "Lovely, would you like me to just make you look more gorgeous?"

"Yes, please," I say, "but what about the color?"

"The color?" She looks at the ends of my hair and then inspects my scalp with her comb. "Shall I sort of brighten you up with some foils around the face?"

"Nothing too dramatic," I say quickly.

"Don't worry, love, I'm not going to give you tiger stripes. I have actually been to the Big Smoke a few times. I did the hair on *Popworld* back in the day."

I sense that Jackie is finding me a bit annoying.

"Sorry," I say. "I actually haven't been to the hairdresser in four years, so I'm a bit unsure about all of it."

"Oh my God, what?" she says, clutching her chest and taking a seat on the stool next to me. "Four years?"

"Yes," I reply. "It's not you, it's me. It's a cost thing. And, if I'm honest, I find it a bit boring sitting here for an hour."

"This is going to take at least two hours, first of all," she says, "and second of all, it doesn't need to be boring. Did you know I can give you wine?"

My eyes widen as I quickly check my watch. "Well, I'm not going to say no to that."

She works like Edward Scissorhands, my long hair collecting in an over-dyed mass of black on the linoleum floor. Foils are applied. Hair is roughly washed and massaged with conditioner, then she blow-dries it to an incredible high gloss, finishing, finally, with her scissors to ensure the "perfect lines."

"Look at you," she says, as she snips away the final hairs around my fringe.

I bat my eyelids in the mirror and beam. I look transformed.

I have a shaggy brown bob and a long fringe parted in the middle, just as she suggested. It looks chic, a little bit *European*. I feel quite glamorous. I look down at my outfit, which, I agree, almost certainly needs work next. Jackie seems to sense my concern.

"Why don't you take this," she says, pulling a navy trench off the hanger by the door. "It's timeless and stylish and you won't see any of this." She wiggles her finger at my dungarees and wrinkles her nose.

"Oh really? Whose is it?"

"I have no idea. But obviously if someone comes up to you on the promenade and demands it back, we don't know each other. I'm joking!" she says, touching my arm. "My girl, you're far too serious. Some tourist left it here a year ago. They're not coming back."

"Thanks," I say, grinning. The trench is gorgeous.

"Eyebrows next, for the love of God," she mutters loud enough for me to hear.

When I emerge from the hairdresser, Jackie stands glassy-eyed waving me off. "Get on to the clothes next, right? And good luck with your boyfriend, darling. He's going to *love* the new you."

I may have once again overexaggerated my relationship with Joe.

Ash is standing outside the chipper exactly on time and does a double take when he sees me, which makes me instantly blush. *Please don't comment on the hair; let's pretend it's always been like this*, I think.

"Looking sharp," he says playfully.

"I've been to Happy Hair," I reply, and can't help shaking my head gently so the lighter crop sways slightly. "It's French. Well French style. Obviously, it was done in Kent."

"I didn't know we were making an effort for a battered cod?" Ash is wearing his steel-colored overalls.

"I'll pop in and get the dinner, and then I need a favor from you," I say quickly.

"A favor?" he repeats, grinning and stuffing his hands into his pockets like a teenager. "Well, that explains the out-of-the-blue dinner invitation. And here was me thinking you wanted to hang."

"Yes. A favor," I say, snappier than I mean to.

"Sorry, sure. I'm teasing. What do you need?" he says now, looking sheepish. "I just . . . I'm busy tonight."

"It will take no time at all," I say.

I pick up our order of fish and chips, and we wander down past the Star and Anchor and out onto the pier to find a bench. I look out to the sea and watch the swells rise and fall as the cackle of gulls pierces the rolling wall of ocean chorus. We sit quietly for a moment, engrossed in the smell of fatty battered fish and salt and vinegar.

"So, where are you off to tonight? Meeting friends?"

"You should really come out with us sometime," he says, as he flicks his hair out of his eyes and focuses on me. He didn't answer the question, exactly. I notice in the sunlight he has very small amber flecks in his deep brown eyes, and a small scar that runs through his left eyebrow. "Have you been in yet?"

I gaze at the old pub sitting there on the edge of the pier, the only bar in town, really, and where I will be meeting Josef. I shake my head.

"Actually, no," I say, frowning. It really is the only going-out place in Broadgate, and I think, not for the first time, that I should have sent Joe to somewhere like Gaucho in London.

"We'll have to take you for a night out. Best pub in Kent, if not England."

"Sure it is," I say, smiling wryly.

"It is! Built right on the edge of a pier, ten feet from the bar to the ocean. And it's pretty much as it's been for over three hundred years."

"Bit of typhoid with my tipple, then?"

"On a warm night when the stars are out . . . ," he says, suddenly lost in a daydream, "it's the best pub on earth."

"Everyone likes their local pub best," I say.

"No one has my local, though," he replies, his dark eyes fixed on mine like he's searching for something.

Occasionally, Ash has a way of looking at me that makes me feel very exposed. Like he's doing a live autopsy on my very spirit and can't find the cause of its death. Most of the time, however, he doesn't look directly at me for very long at all. Like he's thinking of something else entirely, making an actual effort to be looking elsewhere. I worry I've offended him.

"Yes, I think that would be nice. And hopefully one day you'll meet my best friend, Charlie. She's amazing. She lives in Margate."

"Really?" he says, head snapping back to look at me.

"What? I do have friends, you know," I say lightly. "And Charlie is my very best, even if I don't see her much since she had the baby."

He nods in understanding. But then, like a dog who's spotted a squirrel, he jolts straight up, pointing ahead to an older lady making her way up the pier to settle on a bench across from us.

"Hey! Isn't that Mrs. Watson?"

It was indeed my landlady. *Our* landlady.

"I think so?" I say, squinting through the golden light of the sun, which slightly silhouettes her fragile frame.

"She's here for the sunset," he says. "Come on, let's go ask her about doing up the flat."

She is perched with a perfectly straight back, her hair set in tight gray curls, wearing a two-piece suit with plaid slacks and matching single-breasted coat. Her makeup is flawless with that gorgeous, powdered finish that older ladies seem to go for. I smile at her. We've not really seen each other since I moved in, and I feel guilty about it.

"Mara, my dear," she says, turning her body stiffly to try to see me. I move farther round in front of her so she doesn't have to turn at all. "You look lovely."

"Thank you," I say, grimacing inwardly at the compliment.

"Maggie, would you have any issue with us doing the place up a bit?" Ash says, launching right in.

"Oh, I don't know anything about that sort of business, as you know, Ash," she says, waving a gloved hand away.

"You wouldn't have to do anything. I'm not talking about full *Grand Designs*–style make over," says Ash. "Just plug a few gaps, paint a few walls, that kind of thing."

"It's fine, Ash. I know you," she says, looking out to the sea now as if she's had enough of the conversation.

"Oh, that would be amazing, thank you," I say, as Ash motions me to move away from her.

"I'll be in touch, Maggie," he says, as he grabs my hand and pulls me toward the other side of the pier. His hand is warm and large and strong and covers mine almost completely. I pull it away.

"What's the hurry?"

"She wants to be alone," he says, as I sit back down on the bench and study Ash's face. He is more perceptive than he seems.

"Shouldn't we sign a contract or agreement about it?" I ask.

"It's okay; leave all those details with me."

"Um, I just think we should agree on what we're doing first," I say, as tactfully as I can. "Like, exactly what we're painting, and, um . . . the color?"

Ash laughs. "Relax, Mara. We'll get to all that."

I bristle. I *hate* being told to relax. But before I have a chance to probe further, he has changed the subject.

"So, what's this favor you want me to do, then?" he asks, breaking off a piece of crispy battered cod and shoveling it into his mouth. "The one I'm getting free dinner for."

"I thought with the haircut I'd get a profile pic for my socials," I say. Although I'm embarrassed to say it out loud, I do anyway. Besides, I've seen Ash in his underwear.

"Your socials?"

"Yes, that's what my workmate Samira calls them."

"I know Samira," he says, tossing a chip up into the sky and catching it in his mouth. "Up-leveling your personal brand. An *influencer*."

"Sort of," I say weakly, shoving my mouth full of chips so I don't need to elaborate further.

"Hot new profile pic with the new hair and the new coat for the hot new man to see?" he says, grinning, and now I feel so incredibly embarrassed the deep heat in my neck blossoms across my cheeks. *Fucking hell.*

"Hey, I'm just messing with you, Mara," he says quickly. "Of course I'll help."

"I feel like an idiot now," I say.

"Ignore me. I'm the big, dumb idiot. What do I know about love?" he says, taking a swig of his Coke. "Let's do this. What look are you going for?"

"Just this look. The Mara look," I say, looking as broodily as I can out toward the sea. "I can change the packaging, but the permanent look of deflation remains."

"Permanent? I've seen you smile," he says, with his eyebrows raised as if he's not going to let me get away with that. He rubs his hands down the pants of his boilersuit, stands up, and then grabs his iPhone from a zipped side pocket.

"You put yourself down too much," he says now; then he fiddles with his settings and before I have a chance to protest, he adds, "I'll use mine; it's newer and has a really good camera."

I slide my old phone in its big yellow bumper case into my handbag and sit with the greasy beige paper in my hands. And then I look up at Ash as the sun emerges from behind a cloud and the golden glow hits my eyes. He spins around and looks at the sun for a moment, and then back to me.

"Beautiful," he says, looking at me through the image on his phone. "The light, I mean."

I stare ahead toward the sun, the sky starting to turn pink as Ash moves around snapping me continuously, not really stopping to check what he's doing. Quantity over quality. Still, he's the only photographer I've got. "I kind of want wistful and arty. Like I didn't know anyone was photographing me."

He laughs and then bites his lip. "Sorry," he says, not looking very sorry. "Maybe stand up, then. Battered cod and a plastic bottle of water doesn't look wistful and arty."

Just then, a seagull dive-bombs me, its foot scratching right across my head before it steals in for a chip. I clutch the greasy paper to my chest, trying to hide it from the little bastard. But then he turns in the air and comes back for me, long, spindly yellow feet first.

"Oh my God, I'm being fucking attacked!" I scream, standing up clutching the food tighter to me and shaking my head furiously. The commotion and excitement seem to attract more of them, and suddenly I am overcome with gusts of wind and feathers.

"It's a massacre!" I scream again, losing all sense of my surroundings. "It's *The Birds*! I'm in *The Birds*!"

"Drop the food!" shouts Ash, but I can't focus, as the squawking sends my heart racing and I blindly run down the pier, gut first into a rubbish bin, winding myself. Then I feel another bastard zoom past me and I drop half the chips over the pier and hobble off as fast as I can, like a drunk burglar, stopping to look back only when I am safely under the awning of an ice cream stand.

"Cone or cup?" I hear behind me as I gasp and pant for breath, my hands trembling.

I look back down the pier to see Ash now jogging after me with my handbag, stopping momentarily to double over and laugh. "I'm sorry," he says as he arrives, handing me my bag, "that was just far too funny for words. The screaming—I couldn't tell if it was you or the birds."

I give him my best death stare.

"You're okay, right?" he says. "You're not hurt, Mara?"

"No," I say, ignoring the very real bruising of my ego.

"Cone or cup?" says the ice cream seller again behind me. I turn around and glare at him and his stupid candy-striped hat.

"I don't want ice cream," I snap.

"Then step aside," he says, nodding toward a gang of five-year-olds thundering toward us with much the same single-minded fervor as the seagulls. I feel like I might be having a panic attack.

Ash pulls me away from the stand. I feel the strength of his hand on my elbow as he squeezes me and then rubs my upper arm like I'm a child.

"Mara, that was so funny. Come on, you've got to find that funny. You're covered in bird shit, by the way."

I can't bear to touch my hair, so I fold my arms and shrug his hand away.

"You *were* like that lady from *The Birds*," he says.

"That lady was terrorized. Hitchcock actually terrorized her for that film."

His face turns serious as he pulls me in for a side-on squash. It's almost a hug and it's comforting. "Are you okay?"

"I'm humiliated," I say.

"They're just seagulls," he says.

"Horrible squawking beasts. Worse than cows."

"What's wrong with cows?"

"They stare," I reply.

"They stare," he says, nodding, trying desperately not to laugh now. "Come on, you're safe. They only wanted the chips."

I smile a little and shake my head at him. I look down at the smear of bird poo on Jackie's trench coat and tuck my bag under my arm in an attempt at dignity; then I look for a rubbish bin to toss what's left of dinner.

"This didn't go as planned, and now my hair is ruined."

"I got some good shots before the, erm, attack," he says, fishing for his phone in his pocket.

"Yes, but I wanted others. Of the pier and the water. Quaint English seaside photos. You know? Romantic and cozy. I was trying to build a perfect, quaint British seaside aesthetic, and now I'm just a pile of bird shit."

"We can still do that," he says, looking genuinely sorry for me. He pats his pockets and then tuts. "Shit, I must have dropped my phone. I'll just run back down the pier and get it. Wait here."

But while I am watching him dash back to get his phone, I feel an overwhelming shame at the ridiculousness of it all. At the ridiculousness of me. I feel embarrassed. And like a fool. And suddenly it is all too humiliating, and I want to be home in my room.

I seize the moment to escape back to the house. I will wee out the bedroom window if I have to, just to avoid him. Typical. I put myself out there, even just a little, and the world literally shits on me. This is why I don't want to go back for my mother's sixtieth. I open the browser on my phone, hastily checking three different sites for my star sign. Desperate for some reassurance—for a virtual, spiritual, soothing arm around my shoulders telling me I'm doing the right thing. And after a few different sites, I find the reading I need:

THE SETUP

Some days it feels like you can't move forward. Your ability to adapt and get things done is what will get you over the line, Sagittarius. You have time. Just steer the course and the rewards will be worth it.

An hour later I hear the front door open, and after fifteen minutes of creaking floorboards, as he moves around the house, I get a message from Ash.

Don't be embarrassed. Happens to tourists all summer long. I got you some snaps. You look great.

Twenty-four snaps, to be exact. Of the pier, an ice cream cone, the sand, a dog running along the waterfront. The candy-cane beach huts, all in a row. A guilty-looking seagull atop the pier railings with a chip in its mouth. And then me.

Me looking shyly at the camera, the golden sunlight catching the honey color of my eyes. It isn't quite the wistful off-duty artist look I'd hoped for, but it is very nice. Pretty, even. I upload it to Instagram, apply a light filter, and inspect it. I look good. I make it my profile picture, too, and my latest post. It feels like a first, tentative step toward the new me, and I like it.

A moment later there is a *ping*. A notification. My heart picks up. Someone has liked it already.

And it's Ash.

9

~~~~

THE CANTEEN AREA has been transformed for a meeting between the council and the lido members. Gerry and a couple of stiff suits are ready to talk to a group of about twenty locals, who are seated sparingly across the clearly ambitious fifty-odd seats I'd helped lay out.

While I wait for the latecomers to sit, I look down at my phone.

Joe has posted a photo of a violin in a velvet case, and when I swipe left, the other is a photo of his back as he looks out over a huge garden. The caption is in German and is brief, as is his style. Sometimes he only writes a single word, like *Hallo*.

"Hello to you, my handsome future husband," I whisper. "Oh, I know Charlie doesn't believe it, but just wait until we're double-dating at some fancy restaurant, and Joe is charming and secretly gets the bill." I grin at the thought. Last night at home, Ash asked me about Joe, somewhat out of the blue as he was making tea.

"When do you think we'll meet him, then?" he asked, squeezing the bag out with a teaspoon and dropping it into the compost.

"He's touring," I replied, a bit ashamed, as I pretended to be distracted by Netflix film listings. "So, um, late summer."

"Well. Nothing like a bit of delayed gratification," he replied.

I disliked the duplicitousness of it, but Ash didn't flinch, handing me a cup of tea, exactly as I liked it, and heading back to his room to do whatever it was he did in there all night. Joe had to come. He would come.

I scroll back over the dozens of photos I already know by heart. There are only twelve that are of him in his entire feed; all of them are gorgeous.

Could I comment on his post? Would it be weird? If he saw a like from someone called Mara, would it reinforce the fortune-telling? Help gently push this whole thing along? Or would that be a step too far in tinkering with fate? While I'm musing the pros and cons of interacting with him, my phone buzzes with a message from Charlie.

> When can we catch up again? I've been
> feeling bad about your last visit. I was so
> tired and feeling unwell. ☹

She must be alluding to her yet-to-be-disclosed pregnancy. I'm sure of it. It's the only explanation for the not drinking at her house that day, and I've been wondering if it's the real reason she pulled out of our trip to Budapest. I wish she would just tell me so we didn't have to do this dance.

It's fine! I'm all drama! I really shouldn't
leave the house! Which is why you should
come and visit?

I wait for her to read the message and then see she's typing a reply. But the reply never comes.

"What a warm welcome," says Gerry to very minimal scattered applause, two throaty coughs, and an ancient Nokia ringtone from an old dear in a floral swimming cap.

"I think that's you, Mildred," Gerry says, as she fumbles with the phone. "Hot date?" To this Gerry snort-laughs and then looks sideways to make sure everyone else is in on his joke. They are not. There is another cough. Good God, this is painful.

"As you may or may not know, the lido has the attention of developers," he begins.

I look straightaway to Lynn, whose eyes have dropped to the floor. She looks pained as she fiddles with the lapel of her navy blazer, her finger stroking the *Don't Worry Be Happy* badge. *Developers already?* No, I did not know that. Gerry was supposed to be applying for grants for improvements. I shuffle closer to her and whisper, "Did he just say this place is being sold to developers?"

"Shhh, just listen." Lynn frowns and then nods toward the front, where Gerry is now reading from a prepared speech.

"It was agreed that if we could see signs of a return to profitability by the end of the summer," he continues, looking shifty as hell, "then we could commence with renovations applications. But, if that looks unlikely, then unfortunately our lovely community lido will likely be sold to a private vendor."

There are no surprised gasps. Only a sneeze, and the cranking whirr of a fax machine I didn't know we had, coming from reception.

"This is our pool," comes a ragged voice from the back.

"Hear, hear!" shouts another.

"Who would ever buy this place?" I say to Lynn. "It can't turn a profit in its current state. And the prices, as I constantly tell everyone, are ridiculous! Swimming costs a pound."

"I don't know what more I can do," Lynn replies, a sadness in her eyes as she glances around at our regulars, a group so pale-skinned and wrinkled we could be at the casting of *Cocoon 3*.

"Well, if it gets sold they'll put a wanky seafood restaurant in the canteen, solar panels on the roof, and suddenly Shirley over there is paying fifteen quid a dip. Or worse, you have to become a private member."

"I think they are actually considering luxury apartments," Lynn replies sheepishly. "I've tried, love. I really have." I stifle my gasp. She knew!

"Obviously, revenue is continuing to fall," Gerry says, looking directly at me while making this salty point as if I, a bookkeeper, could have any sway over profitability. I can see the books, but I cannot do much to improve them, and especially not when Gerry has shot down every one of my ideas.

"This is really bloody upsetting," I say now, looking over at Ryan, who is mostly looking at his biceps in the reflection in the glass doors. When he sees me looking at him, he maneuvers his arm so it looks like he was scratching the back of his head. I wonder if he understands what is happening here.

"Next week, under the suggestion of our friends here at Broadgate Council, we are going to try to drum up business with a 'friends and family' introduction week, and so, as regular users of our facilities, we'd like volunteers to door-knock, bring a friend. That kind of thing."

I raise my hand and hear Lynn tutting as she shifts her weight slightly away from me.

"Two things, Gerry," I say.

"Yes, Nina. Everyone! This is Nina, who does our office accounts and knows better than anyone what we need to get back on our feet."

"It's Mara," I say, as I feel the slow crank of elderly heads turn my way. I look at the sea of faces and take a deep breath, feeling my skin heat and the sweat start to prickle on my neck. "Wouldn't a fundraiser to, say, replace the old sea steps, or bring in some new catering for the canteen, be beneficial?"

"A fundraiser?" Lynn says in a loud whisper.

"Can't we look at the activities we do? I know aqua aerobics is fun, but do we need four classes a day? No one came to the three fifteen class yesterday, or the five fifteen, for that matter. The soft play area would make a great place for deck loungers. I'm not saying turf out the toddlers, but perhaps a small baby pool would make more sense than a plastic ball pit seven feet from the sea?"

"Mara has a point," says Lynn. "She has a point, Gerry."

"I'm just saying that without a decent investment in the facilities, some new, exciting events to get the locals engaged—as well as the summer tourists—you're unlikely to pull new people in. An alcohol license for the canteen would reel in the younger people too. A floating cinema is an absolute slam dunk. Can't you just imagine it?"

Gerry's eyes narrow as he takes a moment to collect himself.

"This session is for our customers," says Gerry, "a sort of heads-up, a chance for them to chip in. We can discuss official ideas upstairs later, thank you."

"Sure," I say, feeling a bit embarrassed. And also a bit angry. I've pointed out our dismal deficit to Gerry month after month. I've offered to draw up funding applications. I think about Lynn and the paper receipts the day of that storm, *and* the fact that she keeps appearing with new membership forms when it's Samira's job to sign them up. She knew and didn't tell me. Why?

An hour later and Gerry is sitting on the edge of my desk, the crotch of his polyester navy trousers bunching in the most inappropriate manner. He's smiling, his yellowing teeth making me queasy.

"I understand you're upset, love," he says, nodding at me.

Ryan and Samira are both here too. Ryan is drinking a protein shake and kicking the back of the desk partition repeatedly. I can tell he's stressed. But it's Samira I'm most surprised about; her eyes look glassy. I catch her gaze and she looks away from me swiftly, pulling herself together with a deep breath and a sigh.

"I can't be the only one feeling blindsided," I say, my brows knotted together, arms folded. I take a moment to examine my feelings. Am I angry about the threat to my job? Or is my anger more to do with the threat to the lido itself?

"Blindsided," Gerry says, shaking his head. "There is no need to be dramatic. If the worst happens I'm sure you'll be snapped up by someone, somewhere. Everyone needs a bookkeeper, at least until you're all replaced with artificial intelligence machines." He chuckles, and then when I respond only with a blank face, he sighs. "Why don't we all go out for a nice pub lunch and talk about our options. How does that sound? A brainstorm over a pint of ale?"

"I just can't believe you're giving up. This membership drive is going to fail. You need so much more than Mildred bringing her friend Dotty one time." I realize, with some clarity, that I'm really upset about the possibility of this building becoming private. What a tragedy that would be.

"Look, *Mara*," he says sharply. Then his eyes flicker to the skies and he folds his arms, changes tack. "You know that we *all* love this place. But you must see that everyone is abandoning hope to save this as a council-funded enterprise. When I came in the other day, none of you were working. If you really cared . . ."

"There was a storm," I protest weakly.

"It will take millions in investment to turn it around, and the council are only talking about grants to make a few improvements." He looks through the glass windows down to the empty pool below. "This place has been here since 1932. It's old. Do you know how much has happened since 1932?"

"I don't see how that—" I begin, but he holds up a hand to stop me from speaking.

"World War II. Elvis. The moon landing and the miners' strike. Thatcher and 9/11. Grunge," he says, glancing so pointedly at me, I tug on my black-cardigan-and-plaid-shirt combo. *Must get on to the clothes.* And then as he looks to the square-paneled office ceiling, with its random lighting, he squeezes his eyes shut. "The London Olympics *and* the London bombings; that funny beetle that has been killing ash trees."

He appears to be straining for some more major events, so I chime in:

"The financial crash of 2007?"

"The Boxing Day tsunami," Ryan says with inappropriate glee, as Gerry nods along approvingly.

"Bryan Adams's record-breaking number one record for '(Everything I Do) I Do It for You,'" says Lynn.

"Oh, my mum loves that song," says Samira, nodding. "The *Robin Hood* one?"

"You should do this for your next quiz night, Lynn," says Gerry, eyes now wide with excitement. "Newsworthy things that have happened since Broadgate Lido was built."

I put my head in my hands for a moment, letting out a deep, pained groan.

This is not the fabulous seaside doer-upper that I created in my head. This is an off-the-rack council gig in a failing community leisure facility, and the boss doesn't care or have any future vision for it. I look at Lynn. Did she purposefully mislead me? I've bowled up to Gerry regularly with ideas, and he's said, *Things are in hand, Mara.* And *Just give me a few months.* And *I'm speaking with the council tomorrow.* After some time, I just stopped.

I take a deep breath and feel the creep of realization that none of us are going to have a job in three months. I think of Joe and feel my cheeks flush as though he were standing at the back of the room watching this unfold. I cannot be unemployed when Joe comes.

"It's hard to hear, Gerry," I say. "I am surprised, that's all, to discover the place I took a job at and moved all the way down from London for might be shutting down. I signed a one-year lease on my house."

"It's really more of a flat," mutters Lynn.

"Well, look. It's a lot of work to try and get this place going again, and do we really want that?" asks Gerry, pulling on the edge of his nose. "I've tried for funding, but you really need an ally in the council. And you'd need the community to be behind it. They're just not."

"But have we tried to rally them?" I say, my voice rising slightly.

Gerry waves the notion away with a flick of his hands. "It's just an enormous job, Mara. And is it really worth it? Let's do our little membership drive and then we can see if the town is even bothered."

"Oh my God," I say under my breath. *It's Gerry who can't be bothered.* He never took my ideas seriously. He was never going to help.

If this place is going to be saved, it will need to be by the four of us.

• • •

LATER, AS I'M sitting on one of the old benches overlooking the sea, and ignoring a stress headache, Samira comes over and perches at the other end. She adjusts her top around her neck and then tugs at the sleeves.

I admire the sharp white edge of that sleeve and wonder if it's a good time to ask her again for help with my style overhaul. She seemed so enthusiastic last week but hasn't mentioned it since. This is the part in making friendships where I worry that people suggest you hang out but don't really mean it. The classic British *We should catch up sometime*, which really means *Don't ever call me again.* And it's too pathetic and neurotic to say, *Did you really mean it when you said we should hang out?* No one wants to hang out with someone who is constantly giving off *thanks for being my friend* vibes. But then, she did try to ask me out a few times. Oh God. I'm overthinking this.

"I like your top," I say, trying gently to test the waters.

Samira says nothing and then looks out to the sea.

"Your hair is excellent, by the way. Jackie?"

"Yes. It feels so light," I say, shaking it out, and Samira smiles weakly.

"My mum comes here," Samira says quietly.

"She does?"

"Yes. She swims twice a week because she has bad knees and can't walk far," she says, shrugging, "and she can't go to a proper gym or Pilates class 'cos they cost about twenty quid a go."

"No one could accuse this place of being overpriced," I say glumly, as I move the bench seat slightly and my fingers emerge from the underside with white chewing gum attached to them.

"And my brother—he's the one in the walking frame—they think the salt water helps him sleep. And, you know, it gives Mum something to do with him every week. He struggles with most everyday tasks."

I think about my own mum and brother, and my heart squeezes in my chest a little. So far away. Mum's sixtieth is in just over a month's time. I have to go, I think. I have to turn up feeling good about myself and get through it as best I can.

I turn to Samira. She looks downcast and strokes the bright gel polish on her nails. "I know we haven't all put our best foot forward at work, but this is a really important place in the community for so many people. All those ideas you kept mentioning. Do you think we could do any of them? Do you think it would help? I'd be absolutely gutted if it closed."

"We need money. Sounds like we'll need an 'in' at the council to get any grants for that," I say glumly. "But in the meantime, I suppose, some fun events to draw younger people here, and try to get them to join? A better canteen with a coffee machine. Maybe coffee-cart guy wants to expand."

"Ugh. It feels like a mountain to climb," Samira says.

I nod. I care. I can feel the care in my stomach, and right now I can feel it radiating off Samira, whom I have made hardly any effort to get to know; I certainly did not know her mum and brother used and needed this pool.

"When I first got here I *was* full of ideas," I say, "but it feels like we'd really need a monster effort from everyone to put them into place. Including Gerry."

She remains silent. And all I can do is sigh. I admit to myself now that I didn't try very hard. Not *really*. Gerry said no a few times, and then I gave up. Classic Mara: the mere hint that I might be somehow annoying, and I pull away.

Samira sighs too, and looks at me. "The community needs this place. And I like working here."

The last part is a surprise.

"What do you think about trying to find some way to raise money? Shall we get Ryan and maybe even Lynn and come up with some ideas?"

"Um . . ."

"I'm very good on social media," she says, liberating her iPhone from her pocket and showing me her TikTok feed again. She really is extraordinarily photogenic, and her makeup skills are exceptional.

"We'd have to raise an awful lot of money, or start shagging a councilor," I say, scrunching up the wrapper of my sandwich, then fondling my brownie, wondering if I need to tone down the sugar intake as part of Project Mara.

"Sure, but imagine how great it would be to sort this place out," she says. "And imagine what it would do for the community if we could fix it."

"Fix it?" I say, turning my head to her again.

"Yeah. You know?" she says. "Wouldn't you feel good if you'd been responsible for fixing this place, restoring it to its former glory? And fixing up a huge part of the community. *Your* community."

I feel the chill up my back, down my forearms, and the hairs standing on end, goose bumps appearing like a little celestially charged rash up my arms. *Fix something.*

"Okay, I'm in."

"Oh, thank you so much, Mara," she says.

"But in exchange can you take me clothes shopping?" I say quickly. "I need something to wear to my mum's sixtieth and . . . basically . . . just . . . a new look?"

"That seems fair," she replies. "You help me, I'll help you."

"It's not really fair. One project is a fading thirties relic, in need of a total makeover, inside and out, and the other is—" I glance sideways at Samira. "Well, the lido."

"You knob," Samira says, laughing, shoving me sideways.

10

〜〜〜

PROJECT MARA IS moving along. Hair done. Shopping date with Samira on the calendar. And now I am going to expand my hobbies to include oil painting. Of all the little numbers I'd torn off the church notice board, this is the one that I most wanted to try out, and so it's my first. And besides, it's far more enticing than the other Saturday morning activity on offer—singles' wild swimming with someone called Sergeant Major Hooligan.

I imagine myself curiously brilliant at art, despite no prior experience. A new discovery in the art world, perhaps. The art teacher gasping with disbelief as he stands over my canvas, his admiration blossoming into a romantic obsession. Art is something that makes me insecure, and so, in the spirit of self-improvement and facing one's fears, here I am.

I knock on the wooden door of the little thatched cottage and adjust the beret I've worn to get into character. I am beaming like an overexcited child waiting to see Santa.

Lee opens the door in brightly splattered painter's overalls and Wellington boots, his tight black curls starting to gray around his face, which is mostly covered by a long, unkempt dove-gray beard. *Art Santa*, I think, looking at the length of it.

"You're late," he says in a thick East London accent.

"Sorry," I say, feeling thrown. "It's my car. I had to jump-start it. I need a new one, although I've been thinking about getting a bike."

"I don't need the whole backstory, baby," he replies.

"Right. Show, don't tell," I say.

Lee runs art classes in his atelier at a whopping one hundred quid for three hours.

"Mara, right?" he asks.

"I am," I say. "Mara Williams. Here to try to combat Jupiter retrograde."

We are a week into Jupiter retrograde and this could prove to be a problem. It is here, apparently, to slow my personal growth. But not today, Jupiter. *Not today.*

"Hello, fellow fire," he says, dipping his head. "Aries."

Thrilled, I clap my hands together excitedly, and when Lee reacts with muted amusement, I calm myself immediately. *Must not get carried away. Must stay cool. Must not be weird in front of people from same small town.*

He opens the door to the next room and I'm surprised to see three other painters all setting up their easels to hold the large blank canvas frames that cost an extra thirty pounds on top of the fee. "Your easel is there at the front. Within spitting distance of our subject," he says with a naughty wink, "so keep your coat on."

I take my place in the long, low-ceilinged room, which has a small raised platform at one end, paints and brushes filling the little shelving area at the back. Not a space on the floor is wasted, piled high with drop sheets and larger canvases leaning against window frames, obscuring what little light there is to begin with. Above me, from the ceiling, hang herbs and dried flowers bunched together with string. It's quite something.

"Where is the subject?" I whisper to the lady next to me, who is mixing skin tones on her palette with turpentine and linseed. She flicks her long ginger curls over her shoulder and rolls her beady eyes.

"He's later than you," she says, looking at my shoes, then my dungarees, then all the way up to my beret. She smirks, and when she turns away, I quickly take the beret off and pop it in my backpack.

The main door opens in a blinding light, reminding us that it is a bright summer's day we're all missing out on, and I squint for a moment before I make out a familiar shape. My heart starts to quicken as my eyes adjust.

Oh, hell no. I'm not painting *him* naked.

"Oh my God," I say under my breath, my eyes darting to Lee and then back to the figure, wrapped in a too-short terry toweling robe in baby blue.

"Nina!" booms the voice. "Fancy seeing you here."

"Hi, Gerry," I say, the heat in my cheeks instant and ferocious.

Lee guides Gerry to the front area of the stage, and while wrestling a thick smoothie and a bacon sandwich, he disrobes and perches on the edge of a stool, maneuvering the straw into his mouth as his whole naked body settles into position.

"Uh, Lee," I whisper, trying to get his attention, but he's already across with another painter, whispering quietly and intensely.

"How are you, Nina?" Gerry says. "Recovered from your little frustrations at work the other day?" He sucks hard on his straw and makes the most disgusting sound as he works hard to get the thick yogurt drink through.

"Yeah, sure," I say, looking at the ceiling and then the floor and then settling on a candelabra to the side of the stage. "Um, why are you doing this?"

It's a fair question. He manages four local council facilities in Broadgate, he has plenty of money, I presume, so why on earth is he here at this little local life-drawing class, naked on a stage, posing like he's a buxom, pert-breasted vixen in a Botticelli?

"Lee painted me and my third wife for the wedding, last year, and this is how I'm paying him." He glances down at his pectorals, attempting, I think, to make them move up and down. Then he looks up at me looking at him and I look away in horror.

"You've not made a start," Lee says, finally arriving, his hands clasped behind his back as he bobs up and down, observing my blank canvas.

"I . . . aah." I lean into Lee and lower my voice to a whisper. "This is my boss. And, um, I just think it's a bit inappropriate to be here, looking at him, you know . . . um, naked?"

Lee nods as if he's heard this a hundred times before.

"That's Gerry's daughter there at the back," he replies, and I swing my head around to see a girl of maybe twenty-five with her tongue jutting out the side of her mouth making huge circular strokes. She glares at me, irritated that we've broken her concentration. *What?* she mouths.

"Ew," I say, unable to hold it in. "I'm sorry. I can't."

I turn to Gerry, who is licking the tomato sauce from his bacon sandwich off his wrist, and my eyes drift down to his penis and balls, which, I note, appear to have undergone some kind of hair removal.

"Nope," I say, putting down my palette and shaking my head. "Can't do it."

"Why on earth are you so touchy, Nina? Is it the bad news from the other day?"

He says it so completely coolly.

"Obviously that was all very unexpected," I say, hiding my face behind the canvas and muttering swear words to myself. I am trapped.

"Well, it's had its heyday. Better for everyone if we just let the good ship progress roll on in," he says.

"Yes, but before we, um, abandon the lifeboats, we're still going to try to raise memberships and brainstorm other ways to keep it from being sold," I reply slowly, thinking of Samira and her family, my mood turning from embarrassment to anger.

Gerry laughs at this. "Sure."

I pick up the palette again. "You know what? I am going to paint," I say to Lee, who nods happily and wanders off, hands still clasped behind him.

I dip the brush in a mixture of browns and feel a slight thrill as my brush hits the canvas, the color bursting out into a thick brown splodge in the center. A creative awakening of some kind. I look back at Gerry and he suddenly looks smaller, less significant. Thoroughly, imperfectly human.

There is something here that Gerry isn't revealing. Does he have something to do with the sell-off? Is it in his interest? Is there some kind of corporate kickback behind his complete disinterest in helping the community? I'm going to suffer through this painting while I milk him about his bloody plans.

"In many ways, I think it's a good idea to convert the place," I say to him now, trying to hold my voice steady as I smear the paint in small strokes. "Imagine the apartments they could put in the old main building. Floor-to-ceiling windows with views down the bay. It's a million-pound dream. I guess it would bring a lot of money to the area. Like the Turner Contemporary did to Margate, but without, you know, public access."

"Precisely," he says. "The plans I've seen are hard to argue with. Six apartments in total. Although we've got issues with the nesting areas on the far side of the lido, but honestly, we could do with a few less seagulls on the coast. They're birds. They fly places. Who gives a toss about bloody birds?"

I nod accidentally, remembering my run-in with the seabirds last week.

"See? You get it," he says.

I swallow, hard. And then I lick my lips and keep going. "So why are we bothering going through this process of trying to get new people in and whatever, if all of this is a done deal?"

"I'm not a total monster, Nina," he says. I watch his Adam's apple bob up and down in his throat. "I do want to give everyone some warning and the feeling that they *can* put a stop to it if they care enough."

"The feeling?" I say, incredulous.

"I just mean that we can all shoulder the responsibility," he says, "like a team."

I shake my head wildly, behind the canvas so he can't see.

Then, after a beat, I poke my head back out and pretend to smile at him as he chews on the last of his bacon roll and shrugs, all the skin on his upper body moving up and down with the motion. "It's just business, love. Everyone will be looked after."

He means redundancies, I think.

I keep moving my paintbrush in tiny strokes, mixing browns

with taupes in circular sweeps of my brush, standing back momentarily to look at the image as it starts to gain texture. "It's a shame no one at the main council had more vision," I say. "The place could have used a champion."

"Well, that's why the developers are pushing to get it through ahead of the August election," he says, and then his face freezes slightly, as though something major has occurred to him, or he's said something he shouldn't. An August election? My mind starts to whirl with possibilities.

"Right," I say, as Lee reappears beside me and furrows his brows.

"Excellent brushstrokes, Mara," he says, "if not exactly the subject."

"Thank you." I can feel my insides bubbling with rage as I glance around my canvas, back toward Gerry. "Sounds like there's no point in us all sweating it, then. I'll tell the others."

He appears suddenly nervous about our interaction, and then, leaning forward so his penis slides off the stool and into a full, sagging dangle between his spread legs, he says, "Mara, I have no real horse in the race."

I'm *Mara* now, I notice with some irritation.

"Dad, can you put your tackle back on the seat?" shouts Gerry's daughter from the back, and he scoops himself up and settles back into his original position.

I feel ill.

"I mean, I love the old place too. I don't want you to think I haven't tried. It's business. It's progress. It's the best thing for the community; it will bring in a lot of money."

"I get it," I say.

He looks satisfied by that and relaxes. But I am furious. I cannot believe the blatant cheek of him. It's a done deal, this. The lido is going to go, and this sack of shriveled prunes is going to be the one to take it down. I think about how I'm going to walk into the office on Monday and let them all know. I picture myself marching in like Erin Brockovich, determined to fight for justice against all the odds, as Samira throws her arms around me and squeezes me tight. Then Lynn breaks down in tears as I explain my incredible out-of-left-field plan that *just might work*. I need to call an emergency meeting on Monday morning. I need to get them all together and see who has the will, and if there is a way.

I turn to Lee and say, "I'm finished," and I pick up my trench and my bag and leave him standing there staring at the huge turd I've painted perfectly, sitting right on a stool where Gerry should be.

WHEN I GET to work Monday morning, Lynn and Samira are both sitting on the edge of the pool, their toes lazily moving in the water, an intimate conversation going on.

I walk straight over to them, shielding my eyes from the morning sun as I approach. It's the first proper hot day of the year.

"Mara!" Lynn says, giddy with delight when she sees me.

"Hi, guys," I say, kicking my shoes off and joining them at the edge of the water. I slide my toes in, and for the first time since I arrived, it is blissful to feel the cooling water against my hot feet.

"We thought we could have our meeting here, with our toes in the pool. Gerry is in Canterbury again—another urgent council meeting," Lynn says conspiratorially. "And Ryan is on his way with cream buns and tea."

"Okay, great," I say. "He's very good with the snacks, isn't he?"

"He's a stupid sweetheart," says Samira, making ripples in the water with her toes. I look over at her, and her face is slightly dreamy at the talk of Ryan. She glances up and catches my eye, and the stoic face returns like a blind is being hastily drawn.

"So, um, I called you guys because I painted Gerry on the weekend, and it was both eye-opening and eye-closing."

Samira laughs, but Lynn is confused. "You painted Gerry?"

"Yes, he does nude modeling," I say, shuddering at the memory. "I went to an art class. His daughter was also there painting him. *Nude.*"

"You must be traumatized," says Lynn, eyes wide with a look of amusement she cannot hide.

"Art classes? You're really getting out there," says Samira. "New hair, new interests. You must get on to those eyebrows, though. They're extraordinary, Mara. You know, I can thread?"

I reach up to my eyebrows and imagine the feeling of a hundred tiny pins pricking my face until a thin, shapely brow emerges from the bushes. Perhaps I also need to get my eyelashes tinted. Or— gasp!—extensions.

"We still need to do the shopping," I say. "But yes, we should talk eyebrows."

Ryan rocks up with a box of cream buns and three mugs of tea. He looks like a model in reflector aviators, with his sandy hair still damp from a morning dip.

He sets the teas down on a little bench behind us, flicking back the lid on the cream buns and unceremoniously shoving half of one into his mouth.

"Just to get you up to speed, I did some digging on the plans for the lido," I say.

"Yeah?" he says.

"It is clear that the plans to sell the lido to developers are pretty far along, and that Gerry has no interest in stopping them. And perhaps even wants them to go ahead."

"It hurts to hear it said out loud," says Lynn, sighing, and Samira puts her arm around her and squeezes her in. It's the first affection I've seen between them, but it seems completely natural as Lynn leans into Samira, accepting the comfort before they both pull apart again. I get a longing, suddenly, for a hug too.

"You suspected, Lynn, didn't you?"

"I didn't want to scare any of you, but, yes, I have had some suspicions," she says, jutting her chin up to let me know she didn't want to speak about it.

"Well, I did a bit of digging myself, and I have all the meager options I can think of," I say. "But first, guys, I need to know. Are you all in?"

"What?" says Lynn, almost spitting her second cream bun into the pool. "Excuse me, Mara, we've been *all in* for years."

"Have we?" Ryan asks, dubious.

"We're in, Mara," says Samira, shaking her head and rolling her eyes.

Lynn has now folded her arms and is muttering out toward the English Channel. She takes a deep breath and nods at me. "Go on, Mara."

"Okay. I think the action needs to be twofold. We need to make some improvements around here. Just a few. A fundraiser. A cool event of some kind. To give people in the community a vision of what this place could be. There is also an election in around eight weeks, August twenty-first. And I think we should run someone against the current councilor, who clearly doesn't have the interests of the lido at heart. And if our person wins, then we could potentially halt the sale, or at least stall it for enough time to launch a proper *save the lido* campaign." I was around enough election hustle at Westminster Council when I worked in London. I know some of what it will take.

"But who?" Lynn says. "We need to find a candidate, and which of us knows anything about politics? Don't we need manifestos? Experience? A team? A political party?"

"The person can run as an independent," says Samira. "I know that because my cousin ran in Ramsgate a few years ago. He ran as a man in a cat costume. Called himself the Political Pussy Party."

"Yikes," I say.

"He was microdosing at the time," she explains.

"It has to be you, Lynn," I say, nodding to the pins all over her lapel. "No one knows this town and the community better than you. And from my very limited council election experience—you don't really need an entire manifesto. You just need a kind of catchphrase. Like, *Keep Broadgate Brilliant* or *Isn't Broad-great!*"

"Ooh, I like that. *Broad-great Is Really Great,*" Lynn says, as if it's settled.

"It's just a first idea," I say, wondering how to be diplomatic about her slogan. "Let's leave it to percolate."

A huge splash soaks all three of us as Ryan suddenly jumps into the pool and emerges shirtless in the waist-deep water. He flicks his head around and the spray hits us all across the face. "I think better when I'm wet," he says, folding his arms and nodding for us to continue.

"I'll do it," says Lynn suddenly. "I'll bloody well do it."

"Honestly, Lynn, you were kind of made for it," I say.

"You'd make a great politician, Lynn. You already have that kind of look with the trouser suits," Ryan says. "Samira can do all the social media. She's hot on TikTok. She has fourteen thousand followers."

"None of them are from Broadgate," Samira says quickly, blushing, I think, at being called *hot*. "But the point stands. I can do the socials."

"Perfect. You're the press secretary," I say. Seriously, I couldn't think of a better job for Samira. "What about Ryan? Can you hit the phones? Drum up support?"

"Of course. We can door-knock. Lifeguards for Lynn. I'll get the others to help. But what are you going to do?" Ryan asks. Then he looks to Lynn and to Samira. "What is Mara good at?"

There is a long silence.

"I'm thinking," Samira says after a while.

"She's good with money," says Ryan.

"Is she?" Samira asks, eyeing me.

"Yes, to be fair, that's why we're in this mess," says Lynn, raising an eyebrow my way.

"For the hundredth time, it's not my fault that we're losing money. I am just a bookkeeper. I can't control anything except a spreadsheet!" I say. "Bloody hell. There are so many inconsistencies in the finances, though. Donations. Duplicate sign-ups. It's strange. It's like Gerry is trying to run us into the ground, but at the same time, there is some unaccounted-for money keeping us afloat. I don't know what his game is."

"Yes, yes, yes, but what can *you* do to help?" Lynn pesters.

My phone beeps and I stand, apologizing to the team. "Why don't you all have a think about my value while I check this message."

I skulk over to the edge of the pool, staring across at the incredible view as I go. It really is breathtaking. I look over at the office space and imagine a local art gallery or a venue space up there. I imagine adding solar heating to the pool—just enough to take the edge off the chill so it can be enjoyed in winter. I envisage new sea stairs climbing down to the sand, and when that sun sets across the bay, fairy lights pick up the edge of the space, and a large projector beaming *The Great Gatsby* plays to a clientele of guests in floating flamingos. It really could be something, this place. I'm all in.

I look down at my phone.

It's Ash.

I signed for a package for you.

I smile at the message. So far, he's proving to be quite a good flatmate, after all my concerns. The endless cups of tea he makes for me. He's very quiet; in fact, he's in his room all the time. Gaming or something, probably. He doesn't want or expect anything from me. He just co-lives with me. I jump as my phone starts to ring in my hand, and this time it's Charlie.

I feel a small sense of being *wanted*, which makes me feel almost bloated with happiness.

"Charlie?" I say.

"Mara, how are you? I wanted to hear your voice," she says.

"Oh, all good here. Just in a work meeting," I say, looking over at my three colleagues, who are in various states of undress by the pool, sipping tea and gorging on cream buns. It *is* a work meeting of sorts.

"Oh good. Great. How *is* work?" says Charlie, sounding more relaxed.

"It's gotten interesting, at last." I feel a big sense of excitement as I start to imagine all the possibilities that lie ahead.

"Oh, that sounds . . . well . . . like a good project," Charlie says, and so I explain to her all about my ideas and the election, and she says things like *wow* and *cool* and *good for you, Mara*.

"I'm so happy to hear you thriving in a . . . you know, healthy way," she says.

"Yes. I've realized that this is my Saturn return, Charlie. It came late, but it's here. My upheaval. My big change. I am on the path."

"You've been waiting for it," she says lightly.

"I cut all my hair off, by the way," I say now, "and I'm going to get eyelash extensions and my brows waxed, and I'm going to fix this lido and fix my life, and then—and I know you don't believe me, but Joe is going to come. I can feel everything coming together. You're going to be so proud of me."

There is a pause on the other end of the phone.

"Okay, Mara," she says, weakly now.

"But listen to me going on. How are *you*?"

"I'm fine. Same old," she says.

"Mara!" Lynn shouts and waves excitedly in my direction.

"I have to go," I say to Charlie. "Don't worry about me. I'm cool as a cucumber. It's all falling into place."

And then I hang up before she has a chance to say anything else.

"Samira has been googling the US presidential election to see what kind of jobs people have . . . and we all agree you can be the campaign manager since you came up with the plan. What do you think?"

I look at Samira, Lynn, and Ryan smiling giddily at me, and we all stare wistfully out to the English Channel.

"I think let's bloody well do this!" I say, finding myself beaming with unbridled delight. "I'm so up for it."

"Put that in your—" Ryan begins.

"No," I snap, holding up a finger. "Don't sully this moment."

Part Two

JULY

12

~~~

"ASH, I NEED help," I say, holding my hand over my face as I speak.

"What's wrong, Mara?" he says, his voice tight with concern.

It was partially to avoid Samira's comment and subsequent offer to thread my eyebrows that I booked a wax and a dye for as soon as possible, with very little research. And then, when I was on the phone to the only available beauty therapist in nearby Faversham, I'd spontaneously asked for eyelash extensions too. *The thick, bushy kind*, I'd said. *So I look like Zooey Deschanel from* New Girl, I'd said. And something has happened—some kind of reaction—because I can barely see.

"My eyes are swollen from a . . . thing, and I can't really see very well," I explain.

"You can't see?" Ash says, his voice rising with immediate concern.

"Not really. I'm not sure I can catch a bus or walk. Can you come pick me up? I'm at the train station car park. Please, Ash."

"Of course, of course," he says.

I'm cowering behind the timetable so no one can see my face. It's stormy, mercifully, so most people are focused on the sky—holding newspapers, wrestling with umbrellas, darting across the road to waiting cars.

I've given up trying to keep dry myself.

"Excuse me?" I hear a very sharp voice behind me.

I spin around and there is a tutting office worker, irritated that she cannot read the timetable.

"Sorry," I say, stepping back when I catch her gawping at my face.

"Ash, please can you hurry?" I shout into the phone.

"I'm already on my way."

Five minutes later, Ash pulls up in a white van, leaning across and wrestling the passenger door open so I can climb in.

"Are you okay? Is it your eyes? Can you see?" he asks, his voice hurried, concerned. Perhaps also very slightly amused by the sight of me. Drenched, my chic, shaggy French bob with fringe now definitely lost to the weather, hand across my forehead like a visor so he can't see the full extent of this latest Project Mara misadventure.

"What happened?" he asks as I shake the rain off my hair, keeping my face turned away from him.

"It's a catastrophe," I say.

"What is?" He crunches the gears as he rounds the corner away from the station.

"I'm too embarrassed," I say, shaking my head slowly.

Ash nods, cutting down a back street, and even takes someone's private drive to get me home in record time.

"I have to go back to work," he says, as we pull up at the end of the street.

I can picture Ash, even if I can't see him that well, in his gray boilersuit, with ASH emblazoned across the left breast. A pen sticking out of his pocket. His hair pushed back under a cap with a yellow BONDS PLASTERS logo across the front. Ash so far seems to be the least judgmental person I've ever met, and he is going to find out anyway.

I slowly turn around and look at him.

"Oh shit," he says, his face completely still.

"Apparently some people can have a reaction," I say.

"*I'm* definitely having a reaction," he says.

"Everyone is going to have one," I reply, nodding. "I should have known when I walked in to find the Faversham Beauty Barn is also a veterinary clinic."

"It's in the name," he says, biting both his lips to stop himself from smiling. I can see he's now looking at my eyebrows, which, although beautifully shaped, did come out a little too dark. But then his eyes drop back to the real stars of the beauty shit show. The full-bodied Russian flutter eyelash extensions that look something like two tiny brooms affixed to my upper and lower lids. Both of which caused some kind of reaction, making my eyelids swell to the point that it is almost impossible to see.

There is a loud honk behind us, and I gather up the bags and go to head inside. "I have to wait until the swelling goes down, and then they will decide on a remedy."

"How long do you have to wait?"

"Forty-eight long, humiliating hours. So, until Monday. I was supposed to have my first day out with Samira tomorrow. She was taking me shopping," I say glumly.

"Say you're sick," he says. "Stomach flu."

"She's never gonna believe me," I reply. "Ugh. We were just starting to be friends."

The car behind him honks again, and Ash puts his arm outside the window and waves the driver on.

"Go. Go. I'm going to lie on the sofa with some frozen peas on my face," I say. "Thank you for picking me up and trying very hard not to laugh at me."

"Are you going to be able to see the front door?"

"I just have to tilt my head this way," I reply, hitting my head on the car doorframe as I do.

"Careful!" he yelps.

"I'll be fine. *Fine.* Just fine."

I close the door of the van and haul myself down Sandhill Way toward the house. It takes a minute to line the key up in the lock, and then I almost trip over a backpack on the floor. I make my way to the bathroom to inspect the view.

It's bad. Even with my sight line so tightly obscured, there is no missing this mess. My eyes look like the worst three-day bender you could imagine. They are swollen and red both on the upper and the lower lids. Like a bee has stung both, if you imagine the bee is an entire swarm of bees or maybe even a family of Japanese hornets.

I am almost too shocked to cry. Plus I'm not sure my tear ducts still work.

I pull my phone out of my back pocket and I call Charlie, who for the first time this year answers on the first ring.

"Charlie?"

"Hi, Mara! I thought you were Alex with the shopping list. I'm just at Tesco; what's going on?"

"I . . ." I am not sure how to tell her, I realize. Just a few days ago I had laid out all the amazing things I was going to do, and now here I am, a disaster at the first turn.

"Have you ever had Botox or anything?" I try wearily. "Are you against it? I can't remember. Is Botox feminist? I think you said it was, but I'm not sure if it is anymore."

"Botox? Hang on! Excuse me!" Charlie starts a conversation in the background. "Do you have a shoulder of lamb? No? What about chops? Oh great, can I have four, please? Fuck's sake, I hate this shit. No, sorry, I was speaking to my friend about something else. Mara?" she whispers into the phone. "I just offended the lady at the meat counter."

I look back into the mirror and marvel at the size of my swollen eyes again. I look like a lamb chop.

"It's okay," I say, prodding the skin around my eyes.

"So, what about Botox? I've not had it. Not yet anyway. You could call my friend Jenna. She's been doing it since she was twenty-three, although she *claims* it was to help with migraines, but whatever." Charlie laughs at this. "Wait. Did *you* get Botox?"

There is a pause, where I know I should say something, but suddenly I'm not sure I can handle telling Charlie.

"Did you get Botox, Mara?"

"Um. No. The real issue here is what I did to my eyes."

"Oh my God, what's happened?" she says, and I can hear her trolley stop rolling, her voice pitching down to deep concern. I have all her attention.

"I decided to get eyelash extensions. Nothing major, just a little subtle extra pop, as they say. A sort of Zooey Deschanel in *New Girl* thing. And, well. I've had a major reaction. I look like I've got a bad case of pinkeye. Or I'm really stoned. And I've been beaten up. A combination of all three?"

"So, it went wrong?" Charlie says, rather too excitedly.

"Yes," I say flatly.

"Oh, Mara." She is proper laughing now. Maybe I need to find this funny. Can I possibly find this funny? I look at my reflection in the mirror and imagine Joe's face when he walks into the Star and Anchor and sees me looking like this.

"Mara, you've gone all quiet—it will all be *okay*. They'll go down after a bit, I'm sure."

"Do you think so? They look like they're getting worse." I prod the top lid and wince. "I'll call the doctor again in a bit."

"You'll be fine. I promise you'll be laughing about it in a few days."

"Are you sure about that?"

"One hundred percent. But take it easy on yourself, Mara," she says gently, the tension returning to her voice. "Don't go crazy for this guy."

"I'm not. It's a good thing to have a bit of a revamp whether he comes or not," I say, not wanting to get into a conversation about Joe with her again. I don't need Charlie on board at this point. The universe is really testing me here, but the universe does not understand that I am completely committed and will not be put off. Joe is coming.

"Of course it is," she says now. "I really don't want you to think I'm not supportive. But don't put all your eggs in his basket, is what I'm saying."

"Let's not bring my eggs into it yet," I say, and this makes Charlie laugh lightly, more relaxed.

After we hang up, I feel flat again. It's becoming a recurring theme with my interactions with Charlie.

I walk to the fridge, open it, and look around for a beer. Nothing.

Then I check the cupboard in case there is some wine that was miraculously left there for some reason I don't know about, but I only find a quarter bottle of black sambuca. Better than nothing, I suppose. I pour out a small shot and knock it back. Then I take another.

When the warm fuzz kicks in, I wander blindly around the house, banging into a wall here and a sideboard there, halfheartedly cleaning up, and I end up outside Ash's room, hand hovering on the door handle for a moment. I have wondered for a while what he does in there every day. *Is* he a secret gamer? Does he watch sports? Who actually is he beyond this easygoing guy who never cleans the butter off his knife before shoving it into the jam jar but always remembers to put the bins out?

"You're going to snoop," I say out loud. "The question is, do you feel okay about that?"

"Yes," I answer myself. "Besides, you can hardly see."

I open the door wide and have to look around in all directions to take the full picture in through my partially obscured view.

Clothes everywhere. Boilersuit, jeans, socks, boxer shorts, strewn across the bed, an empty laundry basket on the floor, two coffee cups on his desk. I recoil momentarily, and then, my fascination outweighing my shame, I keep looking. There are folders and large academic-looking books piled up next to his computer, which is blinking with a screen saver of a rocket ship launching into space. I laugh. It reminds me of my brother's obsession with space when we were kids. I edge closer to see what he's doing at his desk, but my eyes are too swollen and my head too sore to really focus. I need to lie down for a bit.

His bed looks as though the covers were thrown back and he literally jumped out and ran. His plaid pj's are still sitting up stiffly with the underpants visible, like they were dumped and stepped out of. I'm surprised. Ash is even more untidy than I am.

But the room isn't dirty. It screams stress. It's someone who is juggling too much and hanging on by a thread, just focusing on the finish line. Would it be an invasion of privacy to clear it up for him? I wonder how on earth he can hear himself think in here.

I feel a rush of guilt and make my way quickly back out of his room.

Then I turn on the TV and open various streaming services until I find the largest selection of musicals I can. My happy place. My safe place. I decide to rewatch *Calamity Jane* for the hundredth time, mostly for the makeover scene. Then I grab some peas out of the freezer and lie on the couch with the bottle of sambuca.

As the music plays, I pull out my phone and look at Joe's Instagram. There's nothing new, and I find that I'm somewhat angry at him for my eyelash extensions. As if it's his fault. Him and his stupidly high beauty standards that I have imagined upon him.

I scroll through his feed again. A plush red-and-gold concert hall. A cello in its case. A view of mountains. A mushroom. His sexy long fingers caressing the neck of the cello. A street busker playing the violin. A train. Another grand, gilded concert hall. A Siamese cat. The view out of a plane. I feel suddenly frustrated that I have to wait as long as I do to see him again. I look again at his latest photo—it's a shot of a glass of something—brandy? Whisky? And then, because I've had two more shots of sambuca, I comment:

Yum and then add a drink emoji.

Then, before I hit Post, I stop myself and dissolve into self-hatred. Jesus Christ, what was I thinking? I toss my phone on the ground.

I think about Samira and how I'm going to have to cancel on her after months of saying no and then making a big fuss to organize a day out with her.

Three hours later, I wake from a drooling sofa sleep to the sound of Ash's key in the lock. I feel a huge wet patch next to me from where the peas have fallen off my face and onto the couch, and then I feel the throbbing in my eyes.

"Mara," Ash says, wincing when he sees me, the wet couch, the sambuca. And, most likely, the state of my eyes.

"Hi," I say glumly.

Ash moves slowly toward the armchair and perches on the edge.

"Are you . . . okay? I mean, have you spoken to the doctor?"

"No. But I spoke to the receptionist, who said eye drops, wash with a warm, clean hand towel, unless I'm in severe pain, which I'm not in, not really, so it's hurry up and wait, I suppose. She didn't seem very concerned. But then, she's not a doctor."

"Do you have anything you need to do this weekend?"

"No, I just have to cancel my plans with Samira."

"Okay, well, do it now. And then you can just chill here. I'll get food; you can watch movies and do whatever. I have a bit of work to do this weekend, so I'll be here to keep you company."

I remember the books in his room. *Work*. Is he actually studying? He hasn't told me, so I'm not supposed to know.

"First, though, I'm going to open that window because it smells of sambuca and self-pity in here." He stands and walks toward the small sash window that looks out onto the street.

"It's painted shut," I say pointedly.

"Well, the boys have a few clear days, so we can start the renos next week."

"Really?"

"*Really,*" he says, and then, as if he's formulating a plan, he nods. "Okay, you relax. I'll order dinner in. What do you fancy? Or would you like someone to take all the decisions off you?"

"Take all the decisions off me."

"Got it."

He looks at me for a moment. "I just have to say it. You don't need that shit done to your face," he says, shaking his head at me.

"It's nothing. Loads of people do it. Don't shame me."

He shrugs. "I'm just saying, maybe this Joe guy will think you're already just fine the way you are."

"It's no different to buying a new pair of shoes," I say.

"You know what I mean," he says, picking up a heavy book on the side table, and then putting it down again, and then playing with the keys in the bowl.

"I'm going to go and pick up a pizza," he says after a moment. "Can you find a film that isn't from 1950?"

"How dare you," I say, grinning. "But fine. This is nearly done anyway."

When Ash heads out, I send Samira an apologetic text.

> I need to cancel tomorrow, Samira, I'm so
> sorry! Can we try next week?

She replies right away: Why am I not surprised? ;-)

I sigh. I know it looks like me being evasive again. I'll need to explain on Monday.

I clean myself up, change into some comfy leggings and a *Hamilton* T-shirt, and ready myself on the sofa before I restart *Calamity Jane.* I fast-forward to the bit where she humiliates herself post-makeover in front of the whole town by throwing herself at Lieutenant Danny Gilmartin, all while the gorgeous and protective Wild Bill Hickok is standing *right there.*

"I have one pepperoni pizza and one mushroom pizza," Ash says as he returns, the smell of garlic wafting through the house as soon as he shuts the door.

I am ravenous.

"I also have Haribo, Maltesers, microwave popcorn, and a liter of cola, although I also have wine."

"Astonishing," I say. "Absolutely perfect."

He pours me a glass of wine, then himself one, and then drops the two pizzas on the coffee table and flops onto the sofa next to me. I immediately make myself smaller to compensate for his size.

"What are we watching?" he asks, flicking open the pizza box.

"Well, if it isn't weird . . . I have a method," I say, producing a little box I retrieved from my bedroom. I open the lid.

"There are about fifty cards in here, with all the movies I've ever five-starred. All you need to do is shuffle and then pick a card, and that's the one we watch. We leave it to fate."

Ash looks at the little box and picks up the first handmade white card, turning it over. It says *AVIATOR.*

"That's not your choice," I say quickly, taking it out of his hand. "I rewatched that last week. The five stars is for Cate Blanchett's outfits, mostly."

"So you can overrule fate when necessary. Got it," he says teasingly. And then he looks at me with such a genuinely tender smile I find myself shrinking further into the sofa. He touches the next card with his fingers.

"But . . ." He looks at me again, half frowning and half smiling. Then he winces again. "Shit, Mara, every time I look at you I'm reminded of *Rocky.*"

"Well, thank you, Ash," I say playfully. And then I nod at the cards in the box, encouraging him. "*Rocky* is there too, you know."

"But . . . you've seen them all?"

"I know, but I get to rewatch," I say, grinning. "If you've already seen it, we can pass, okay? But I love it when I've seen a film and the other person hasn't. Don't you? It's almost like I get to see it again through their eyes. Also, when I feel down, rewatching a favorite movie is literally the best thing ever. It's like hanging out with an old friend."

Rewatching a movie with Charlie is even better. A favorite film *and* a best friend. I feel a stab of sadness as I think of her and the gulf that is growing between us. Ash will have to do.

"This is kind of nuts," he says, and then he shakes his head. "I'll do it."

He leans forward and takes the homemade deck out of the box and shuffles. He does it with some skill and then lays the pack on the table next to the pizza box.

"It's very endearing, this," he says.

"What did you pick?" I reply, feeling myself blush at the compliment.

He slides the top card off and holds it to his chest; then he peeks at it, chuckling as he does. "Oh no," he says.

"What is it?"

"*The Wedding Singer*," he says, laughing, turning the card to face me.

"Perfect," I say, clasping my hands together. "Oh God, what a perfect choice. Comedy. Drew. Steve. The eighties. You see? The cards know. They *know*. Fate always knows how to deliver."

I quickly find it on one of my dozen streaming services and hit

Play. Then I settle back into the sofa, pulling the throw up to my neck and grabbing a slice of pizza.

"You have a lot of streaming services," Ash says, slipping his shoes off, and then thoughtfully moving them around to the side of the sofa out of my gaze.

"I get a Netflix login from Mum and Dad. Disney, I pay for. Amazon Prime was a thirtieth birthday present from my brother that I let run over onto another year and he hasn't noticed yet. Charlie and I share two others."

"Well, this is good news for me, your flatmate," he says, laughing.

"Steve Buscemi cameo incoming," I say, as "You Spin Me Round" in all its eighties glory is sung by Adam Sandler in a mullet.

As the film progresses, I find myself watching Ash more and more. He is one of those people who expresses all emotions exactly as he feels them, just like Charlie. This means he laughs hard at jokes, gasps during plot twists, and feels genuinely upset when Drew Barrymore is disrespected by her on-screen fiancé, Glenn.

"He doesn't deserve her," he says, shaking his head and tipping the last of the wine into my glass before he stands and clears away the pizza boxes and replaces them with two bowls of Haribo—one for each of us.

"It's a hangover from my childhood," he explains. "Mum couldn't just put a bag out in front of us kids; there would be bloodshed," he says, laughing. "They had to be shared. Exact same shapes and colors. Then the trade wars began. A gummy ring is worth two bears, for example. And I always wanted the rings and the cola bottles."

I giggle. I relate. I can so imagine this same scene unfolding at home with me and my brother, ending with Dad confiscating all the Haribo and sending us to bed early if we didn't "sort it out without all the unnecessary drama, *Mara*."

He sits down again, and this time his arm lands on my foot, which is sticking out of the end of the throw. I feel myself stiffen and look across at him. I move my foot quickly back, and he lifts his arm immediately as if only just realizing we touched. Or maybe he didn't mind the contact.

"Sorry," he says.

"No, no. I'm sorry."

The credits start to roll and he flicks on the side light. I find myself aware now of how I might look to Ash, slobbed out on the sofa, full of pizza and red wine and my *Rocky* eyes. I push my hair behind my ears and move the throw around to try to create a less slovenly figure.

"You look better," he says.

"What?"

"The eyes," he says, motioning to them with a wave of a large hand.

"Oh yeah, I think I can see more than a letterbox now. I'm seeing in four by three instead of sixteen by nine."

"More wine? Cup of tea? And can I pick another card?" he says. "Although it's a bit annoying you've seen them all. As much as I enjoyed that, I did find the commentary a bit distracting." He looks quickly to me with a broad grin, to ensure I know he's having a laugh.

"I can't help it," I say. Then I pause for a moment to consider something. "I do have another deck with films I've *not* seen. Can you make tea, though? I've had enough to drink."

I feel his eyes on me as I squeeze past him between the coffee table and the sofa. He has to move his knees to make room, and yet they still brush. I am finding sharing such intimate space with a man I don't really know strange to navigate. The intimacy feels like a prelude, although it isn't. It's like there needs to be a clear statement at some point that this is not something more than it is so I can stop reading into potential signals. As I push open the door, I decide that at some point, I'll make clear my intentions about Joe. Just to clear the vague air of unknowing that I'm feeling.

In my room, I reach into my cupboard and pull out the second small box of cards. It has been almost two years since I've looked inside it, and I run my fingers across the edge of the red cardboard. Do I want to share this with Ash? I'm not sure. It feels like holding on to it is holding on to a piece of Charlie, and like sharing it is giving part of her away. Still. Charlie isn't going to use this box anymore. Oh, fuck it, I'm going to share it with Ash.

"Another box?" he says, as I return to the lounge.

"It's full of all the films me and my best friend wanted to see. We started this whole dumb thing because after hours of scrolling we could never decide on a film, and she was sick of me rewatching my favorites. I have to say, though, it's got more additions from Charlie than me, because I worked at a cinema for years. Now, Ash, I feel a bit like sharing this is a betrayal. But I'm sure she and Alex have their own movie selection process now."

Ash laughs. "I'm sure they do, Mara."

"What?"

"Nothing," he says. "It's the idea that everyone has a movie selection process. It's funny."

"It's weird. Weird and reclusive, my workmate called me the other day." I laugh once. "Perhaps she's right."

"You're just new here," he says, and then he looks me in the eye with a teasing grin. "Although you're not *that* new. You must let me take you to the Star and Anchor for a proper drink and some scampi fries. Once you're feeling up to it, of course."

"Fine. Fine," I say. "Fine."

"Fine?" he teases.

"Yes, I'd love to, thanks," I say, throwing a cushion at him. "Have you always lived in Broadgate?"

"Mostly. Had a stint at uni, but that didn't work out."

"Ha," I say.

"What?"

"Same as me. I went to film school. But I . . . I failed my final year." I shrug.

"Oh yeah?" he questions, his eyebrows furrowing in disbelief.

"There was a whole thing with a final group project," I say, trying to keep it light. "And I had this idea, but my partner, who was also my boyfriend, sort of stole it, but not in a way I could prove. And then we broke up. He also told our professor that I was suffocating him. And I was just basically a mess. It was humiliating."

I feel my cheeks burn red-hot while I recount the memory, knowing I probably shouldn't share it. I don't come off looking very good in this story, even if Noah comes off looking worse.

"Oh my God," Ash says, turning to face me. "That's fucking . . . well, appalling."

"Yes. But in a weird way, I feel sort of like I ignored the signs and so I have to shoulder a bit of the blame."

"I can't imagine you ignoring *signs*," he says.

"Oh, not those kinds of signs. Now, *those* I would have listened to," I say, laughing. "I mean like, like, my actual feelings. I sort of knew deep down he wasn't completely honest or, you know, credible, or, like, faithful. I mean, you wouldn't point at Noah across a street and say, 'That man is built from blood and integrity.' If I look back now, most of the embarrassment is that I didn't stand up for myself sooner," I say, sighing. "But then, I've never been good at intuiting things. I don't really trust myself."

Ash doesn't respond right away. He looks like he might say something, but he doesn't.

"Why did *you* leave?" I say now.

"Missed home," he replies, shrugging, and I can't say I'm surprised. He turns his whole body around so we are both leaning back on opposite sofa arms, his legs on the floor and mine tucked out of the way. Neither of us crossing the center line.

"Where did you study?"

"Cambridge," he replies. "What? You look surprised."

"No. I'm not surprised you went to Cambridge," I say, unable to hide my stammering. "My dad is a plasterer and I just assumed you would have done an apprenticeship young. What did you study?"

"Physics," he says, grabbing a handful of Haribo. "Helps with keeping a house upright. So where are you from, then, Mara? You said Corbridge? Where's that?"

"Northumberland."

"A good northern lass, then," he says, and I resist the urge to toss another cushion at him.

I smile. "Come on now. Choose a card."

He reaches across the sofa, takes the pack, expertly shuffles it again, splits the deck, and picks the top card. I feel a small thrill of delight that he's not only indulging me, but apparently enjoying it. It feels so comforting to have that back in my life again, albeit tentatively. I smile at him and he smiles back, my range of vision almost full again as our eyes connect across the low light. I am reminded again of my best friend, even if this is different. Right now, in the moment, there is a sense of belonging and of home that

I haven't felt since I was with Charlie. And I've missed it. I smile at Ash again.

"What is it?" he says.

"Nothing," I say. "Go on, what does the card say?"

He looks down. "Hang on," he says, looking at back at me, stunned. "You've not seen *Lord of the Rings*?"

13

~~~

I'S 7 P.M. the following Saturday, and I'm going to meet Ash for a night at the famous Star and Anchor. He finally convinced me to go out after a week of evenings in front of the TV, and although I jumped at what felt like a cool, natural flatmate invitation out, I'm feeling that strange jittery anticipation you get before a date. I try to calm myself. *It's only Ash,* I say to myself in the mirror by the door. Is a dress too much to meet a flatmate for a drink? I rush back into my bedroom, fishing through all the various dark clothing for something more low-key, and decide on a navy off-the-shoulder blouse and trusty black Levi's. I pull them on and stop by the mirror again, fiddling with my new hair. I stand on tiptoes to see more of myself in the mirror. I am too short to ever be properly glamorous in that willowy way. Too much boob. Hair better, eyebrows neater. I have outlined my lips to give the impression they're a little fuller.

"Makeovers really *do* give a sense of control in a chaotic world,"

I say, thinking of Cher from *Clueless*, momentarily wishing that Joe looked a bit more like Paul Rudd.

I look at my watch. Time to go. *He's just your flatmate, Mara. This is totally normal, meeting a flatmate for a drink on a Saturday night. It checks off the make-new-friends part of Project Mara and you actually enjoy his company. Chill.* Be chill.

But I am not at all chill.

I wonder, in a panic, if I can get anyone to join us.

I think about Samira, who was so breezy about my cancellation this week at work but didn't make any mention of a reschedule, and I was too shy to ask.

I dial her number. "Hello," I say in my best light, singsongy voice. "You don't fancy a trip to the Star and Anchor with me and my flatmate, do you?"

"Hey, Mara. I'm afraid I have other plans," she says. "You need to give a bit more notice or you make a girl feel like an afterthought."

"Sorry," I say. "I'm a bit all over the place."

"It's fine," she says with a sigh. "If you still want to go clothes shopping, we have plenty of time before your mum's birthday. So, let's just find *and stick to* another time, okay?"

I apologize again. "Shit," I say, as I hang up and dial Ryan.

"Hi, Ryan?"

"Is that Mara?" he asks, and then I hear a large grunt and a heaving noise and immediately fear what I may have interrupted. "You picked a bad time, mate."

"Do you want to come for a drink with me and my flatmate, Ash?" I am trying. *Lord*, I'm trying.

"Can't," Ryan says, panting and grunting. "Got CrossFit, then band."

"Oh," I say, relieved he's just at the gym. And then afterward, I feel put out. Why do people have so many activities? Don't they get tired? I just want to be on my sofa. It occurs to me that in my haste to get some hobbies, I have actually signed up for pottery next week, and I grimace.

I decide it is better to probe no further. "Okay, enjoy cross-stitching," I say and hang up before he can correct me.

Oh well. I *tried* to make it a gang-of-friends-type thing, but it isn't to be. I'll just drop Joe into the conversation tonight and make a clear line in the sand.

As I come out onto the promenade, the Star and Anchor is at the other end of our bay, looking back across toward the lido in the late evening light. Where the lido sits atop a small chalky cliff, the Star and Anchor sits at the edge of the pier. You can just imagine small fishing boats pulling right up by the inn to stop for a warming bowl of stew and a glass of mead.

Inside, it feels weather-beaten but cozy. I slide onto a wooden stool at the far end of the bar so I can see everyone, but I'm tucked away nearly enough so no one can see me, and I look around and wait for Ash to come from wherever he's been.

It has dark blue and dark wood interiors, with cozy nooks and board games and books everywhere you turn. All around on the walls are framed constellations—Virgo, Orion, the Big Dipper, the Southern Cross—and there are various antique telescopes nailed to the walls. My God! What is this place? It's like my spiritual home.

The bartender holds himself with resigned indifference to everything. I wave him over and he slowly puts down the pint glass he is polishing and slings the damp towel over his shoulder.

"White wine," I say, and he shakes his head. "Vodka tonic? With lots of ice?"

One small nod. Then he unceremoniously tips a huge serving of vodka into a glass, tosses in two cubes of ice and some soggy lemon, and tops it with tonic before sliding it to me across the bar. It's about ninety percent vodka.

"Where you from?" he asks as he takes my ten-pound note with his fingertips as if I might be infectious.

"My name is Mara Williams and I live on Sandhill Way," I reply, and he seems to find this amusing. "Sagittarius," I add with a knowing wink.

His gray, wiry eyebrows knot together in confusion.

"The constellations on the wall?" I say. "I thought as a fellow astrology buff, you might want to know."

"Right," he says, looking up at the walls as if he's never noticed.

Fifteen minutes later, Ash strides through the pub doors, and I catch him doing a double take at me. The surprise at seeing me outside our home for the first time, I guess, sitting here in makeup and a nice off-the-shoulder blouse instead of a sweatshirt. I'm also a little surprised by the effort he's made. He looks handsome and tall. And big. And broad.

"You look very blue," I say, as he tips his head back and offers a tight-lipped smile. He looks, for the first time, a little stressed. "Even your socks and shoes. Like a big blue Teletubby."

"Well, thank you," he replies, amused, giving a little eye roll and a slightly shy smile too, which is something I've never seen on Ash. He *is* all in blue. A midnight-blue wool jumper that looks expensive and some fairly new-looking jeans. His dark hair is freshly cut—he's obviously been at the hairdresser—and I realize I have to make an effort to tear my eyes away from him.

"You look . . ." He stops, seeming to lose confidence in his comment, and I can feel his eyes drop to my bare collarbone. Before he looks over to the bartender, he says in a raspy voice, "Very nice too."

Mercifully the bartender arrives to divert attention from the awkwardness. It is just as I feared it might feel to be at a pub with just Ash. A bit awkward, with the boundaries unclear. We've both dressed up. I'm in no-man's-land. *Must bring up Joe.*

"Hey," the barman says, pushing back his shirt to reveal a sleeve of shipping tattoos.

"A pint of Busted Balls pale," says Ash, with a lift of the brows and hint of a smile.

Ash catches me staring at the bartender with my lip curled, as he fixes the pint and slides it onto the bar with an audible grunt.

"Take no notice of Eddie. He's a softie," Ash says, his voice lowered.

"Eddie," I repeat back.

"Eddie," says Ash, taking a sip of his beer. "And that guy over there playing darts is Dave. The girl wiping down the table by the toilets is Sasha. And in about"—he looks at his watch to assess the time—"thirty minutes you'll get Mrs. Chapman with the purple hair from the bookstore and Leon from the chemist in here for a quick one." Then he nods to two different tables, both with knackered parents and wriggling children bright red from a day in the sun. "They are tourists. And so are they." I can almost smell the sunscreen from here.

"Who's Mrs. Chapman?"

"She was my English teacher. I can't call her Jill," he says, pulling an awkward face.

"Is it weird to know absolutely everyone everywhere you go?" It makes me feel claustrophobic and perhaps agoraphobic just thinking about it.

"Weird? No. It's nice, isn't it?" he says, shrugging. "I couldn't get away quick enough when I was eighteen, but I'm happy to be home. It's like comfy trainers. Sasha and I used to play naked in my mother's backyard paddling pool." With this he waves at Sasha, who tosses her long blond hair extensions over her shoulder and grins at him flirtatiously, her eyes flickering across to me.

I marvel at the thought. I could never go home. I hated it there. But just as I think that, a flash of a different, parallel universe comes over me. What if I *didn't* hate it there? What if I found it comforting to go home, like Ash did? The fantasy was oddly appealing. I play with the hem of my shirt.

"So, what do you think of it?"

"The pub? I like it. I'm in heaven with all the constellations on the walls."

"Sagittarius," he says, grinning.

"Your man Eddie wasn't interested."

"Oh, well, it's a sailors' pub. This is all navigational paraphernalia."

"I see," I reply, laughing. "That makes more sense. The coast. Fishing. The Star and *Anchor*."

"Exactly," he says. "We'll make a local out of you yet."

I look at his hand, resting on the bar, less than an inch from my elbow. His fingers are thick but long, and the ever-present paint still clings to the edges of his nails. I can feel his energy through his fingertips, and it feels too intimate. I move my arms back.

"Well, it's nice to be out with you," I say cheerfully, raising my glass, and he clinks his with mine. "To flatmates."

"Flatmates," he says, nodding.

"So, thanks for the help last weekend," I say.

"It's no stress," he says. "I enjoyed it. I need my own box of cards, though."

"You can make a box," I reply, grinning. "No one is stopping you."

"How's things going with the lido? My folks were talking about it at home. It's definitely hit the Broadgate grapevine that it might be sold."

"Well, as it happens, we've got a plan to save it."

"Have you, now?" He smiles at me. "I can't wait to hear it."

"A ragtag bunch of misfits try to save the lido from sale to a hostile developer," I say, in my best movie-trailer voice. "We're basically going to do it up a bit and put on some fundraisers. And get Lynn elected to council to try to halt the sale."

"Give me a shout if you want help with the renos; I'm always happy to pitch in," he says, "if I have time." He adds this last comment as if he's reminding himself to plan his time better. I think of the books in his room again and wonder what it is he's up to.

"The guys would be so grateful," I say.

"Look at you making friends and having adventures," he says teasingly.

"I wouldn't call them friends yet." I've finished my drink already and feel a little woozy after such a massive serving of vodka. "It's still tentative. It's hard to let anyone *new* in."

I laugh, blushing as I do, but Ash doesn't. Instead he looks concerned, and my laughter descends into silence so all we can hear is the whir of the glass washer, the thud of darts hitting a dartboard, and the faint music, so low you have to strain to make out the tune.

"I am happy to get to know *you*," I clarify.

"Well, good. You can't be an island," he says.

"I know, I know," I reply, "I'm getting out there. It's all part of Project Mara."

"Oh. Project Mara?"

This feels like the time to talk about Joe. I need him to understand that meeting Joe was fate and that I'm focused on that.

"Project Mara is my self-improvement plan to get me ready for August. For when Joe gets here."

"Oh yes. Joe." Ash says this as if he's tugged a discarded memory loose in his brain.

"Yes," I say, nodding.

"So, what is he, then?" he says, staring intently at his beer. "How serious is it?"

"The most serious kind of serious. Buckle up, Ash," I say, grinning broadly. "I didn't tell you the whole story before." I take a large mouthful of my fresh glass of vodka, which has appeared without my ordering it. I cringe at the strength of it. I'm going to be drunk after just two drinks at this rate.

"O-kay," Ash says slowly.

"I had this amazing reading with a fortune-teller. And she was like, 'You're about to meet *the one*.' And she described him, quite clearly. She said it was imminent. And then I'm locking up for her, because she went into labor. And while I was waiting for my taxi, *boom*, in he walked. And he was exactly as she described. Like, Ash, it was so clear. And he thought I was the fortune-teller. And so I told him his fortune. Obviously, I'm not trained or gifted or whatever. I'm not clairvoyant. I'm just Mara," I say, ramming the point home.

"You *are* Mara," he agrees, nodding. I like the way he says it, my name. With a long emphasis on the first *a*. *Maaara*.

"And so, I just thought, I could tell him anything, you know? So

I said someone called Mara was his destiny and he's coming here in August. In seven weeks. Seven weeks yesterday, in fact!"

"I have to say I can't imagine you doing any of that," he says, shaking his head.

"I can't believe I did it either. What do you think?" I ask, turning myself on the stool to face him, our legs brushing together, and I rub at my knees awkwardly, as if trying to get rid of the lingering imprint.

"Sorry," I say, pushing the stool back slightly.

"What, about the guy? Joe? You have faith that he's going to come and find you."

"I'm not . . . what?" This irritates me. "It's not *faith*."

"Well, you believe it. You have *faith* in it."

I roll my eyes and sigh. "I don't expect people to get it. I can feel it inside me, that he's going to come here. I know it with every fiber of myself. I believe I was supposed to tell him to come. You don't think the universe has plans for you?"

He looks at me now, his eyes searching mine for a moment before he tears them away and looks back across the bar.

"If this Joe guy was meant to come into your life, then why not right then in that room? Why didn't you just take the veil off and ask him out for a beer?"

"Because I'm not ready!" I say, exasperated. "Look at the state of me. Plus the fortune-teller was pretty clear I needed to fix up my life before it would all come together."

Ash shakes his head from side to side and then scratches the back of his head. "I don't think like you do about this stuff."

"I get it, you went to Cambridge and did science and you believe in reason and you're probably an atheist," I say, "and life has no magic or soul or spirit or wonder."

"I disagree with that assessment," he says bluntly, but I'm on a slightly drunken roll now.

"And romantic love is just a series of hormones and brain chemicals, and we may as well just all do a test for it when we turn eighteen and find a match that way."

"I don't . . ." He frowns at this, and I feel his eyes down at my collarbone again. It makes me shift in my seat and tug at my top. "I definitely am not *that* clinical."

I felt the heat in his look that time. Or is it the vodka? Ash raises his hands as if he's been caught out. "Look, it's romantic and sweet that you believe Joe is coming here, and honestly, whatever you need to do. I get it. I really get it. Don't listen to my cynical old ass."

"You're just saying that," I say, leaning closer to him, looking him directly in the eye, my confidence growing with the vodka in my veins.

"You know better than anyone if there was a connection and what that might mean. You were there." He looks down at his beer and nods to the bartender to get him another.

"I know it could all be wrong," I say, shrugging, and for the first time I begin feeling uneasy. Could I be completely wrong? I've now told Charlie and Ash, and both of them have reacted—not with the dreamy excitement I'd hoped, but with unease. "It doesn't feel that way."

We sit for a moment in silence, and then I get that creeping realization that this visit to the pub has been all about me, and I'd better ask him some questions because humans are supposed to do that. But I'm also feeling the effects of the booze, my anxiety drinking now firmly affecting my vision and balance.

"Where did you get your haircut?" I ask, going for an easy conversation starter.

"Everyone under forty goes to Jackie or you end up with a purple wash and a perm," he says.

"Ash?" I say, leaning into him now, partially for stability, his warm shoulder brushing mine. "I'm not some woo-woo weirdo witch or anything. I'm a bookkeeper. From Corbridge."

Ash rolls his eyes to the ceiling and shakes his head. "You're funny. Charming, really."

"I'm charming?" I say, downing the last of my drink. I can hear myself slurring slightly. *Must stop drinking.* "Well, I hope so, because when Joe gets here and he sees me, he needs to find me charming too. And hot. Hair. Clothes. I really need new underwear also. Can you believe I bought my bra at M&S in 2011?" I am amused and slightly endeared to see Ash turning fire-engine red.

Ash shakes his head and puts a hand on the bar. "You know, you only need to be yourself. Otherwise, life will become really tiring really quickly."

"It's just a makeover. Don't *you* want to improve your life?" This comes out with rather more of an accusatory tone than I intend.

"Well, Mara, since you asked, I *am* actually making some changes."

"Like what?" I ask, my eyes narrowing. I glance at his hands again, the plaster on his thumb. "What are you doing to improve your life?"

"Well . . ." Ash pauses and looks thoughtfully at his drink before downing the last of it. We are both now without a drink, and I can feel that I'm starting to lose myself a bit. I suddenly just want to be transported to my bed.

"Well?" I ask, suddenly urgently wanting him to say something spectacular. Wanting him to be more. "What are your plans? What big thing do you want?"

Ash looks up to a framed picture of the solar system that sits just above the bar. It's oil on wood, twee but very precisely painted.

"I *want* to be an astronaut," he says, and then looks down at me, smiling. For the first time since Ash moved in, I notice it: a wistful dreaminess. Like he's holding something close to himself. Something special.

"Well, I really did mean a grown-up dream," I reply. "I wanted to be Audrey Hepburn, but that Vespa has driven off."

"*Roman Holiday*," he says. "My mum loves that movie."

"You know you keep comparing me to your mum?" I say, as I feel a yawn coming and cannot obscure it.

"Shall I walk you home?" he says.

"*Us* home you mean," I say, standing, a little unsteadily, on my feet.

Ash glances out the window. "I'm actually going to head out for a couple of hours."

"Where?"

"I have to meet someone tonight," he says, glancing at his watch, which is a very old silver watch, with one of those click-and-pull-back fasteners. Big and heavy.

"Who?"

Ash pauses for enough time that I realize what is going on, and then the outfit makes sense and I feel silly as the heat rises in my cheeks. A date. That's why he looks like a tall, handsome blue Tele-tubby.

"It's okay, you don't need to say," I reply as we stand at the entrance to the pub. I glance over his shoulder toward the direction home. It's been raining, and the stiff sea breeze makes it feel colder than it is. I take a step to go around him, but he does too, and then there is an awkward dance between us, where he ends up laughing and standing right out of the way with his arms out so I have the whole footpath to myself. And then I look up at him and for a fleeting moment wish he didn't have a date and we could walk home together.

"Let me know when you need help with any other parts of Project Mara," he says, putting his hands deep into his jeans pockets, making him look smaller and more boyish. "I'll get onto the flat in the next weeks when I've finished . . . some work."

"Really?" I say, wishing I could take back everything I've told him tonight. I'll wake up with regret tomorrow, I just know it. But it's too late to put it back. It's out, like a jack-in-the-box. Out for him to find silly, or charming, or whatever other thing he might think that I have zero control over.

"Yeah. And come and meet my mates sometime, Mara. They're nice. There's a couple of girls too. You don't have to hang out with my mum at her book club. Sorry about suggesting it."

I feel a smile creeping across my face. "I'd probably enjoy it, but don't tell anyone."

The golden light from the pub catches his eyes, and the murmur of the crowd can be heard through the inch of open sash window. I glance up at the sky beyond the awnings and see a slash of night stars. I look back at Ash, who has a look I can't place. Frustration, perhaps? His eyes flicker down toward me, and I feel time pause as we both collect ourselves.

"You look like you need to be home," he says.

"Yep," I say, probably too abruptly, taking off before I say anything else I'll regret. I concentrate only on the sound of my boots on the wet footpath. And this is why I never make new friends. It's the little steps that you need to take to move closer—the tiny bits you have to give away, and the parts of yourself the other person needs to be able to forgive. The risk they might not like what they see is a risk too big to dare.

14

Today you'll finally see some things that were hiding in plain sight. You'll connect with someone in an authentic way. And you'll refocus your waning attention on the project that needs you. Time is not on your side, Sagittarius. Eyes on the prize.

EVERY SINGLE TIME I start to question astrology, I'm hit with a daily reading like that. I close my phone and look for Samira, whom I'm meeting outside Fired Up café. I wave through the window at Chrissie behind the counter, who waves a hand back at me, lazily, without really looking up. Like we're neighbors. I've become something of a regular here lately, and it's comforting to be known, but at a distance.

The air is starting to get hot now, with July having firmly brought in the summer sun. The trees are green; the gardens outside the waterfront hotels are a symphony of scent and color. I gaze out across the bay. Gone is the dark, peaty water, the high sun bringing out all the shades of green against the shore. On this gorgeously sunny Saturday morning, I can see groups setting up on the beach for the day. Children being rubbed with sunscreen, parents erecting sun umbrellas, the beach huts open, bright patterned towels flung over their doors. Cars drive at a crawl along the promenade. There is music, too, coming out of a new ice cream store with a striped-pink-and-white awning. Everyone is sinking into this gloriously hot summer; the huddled, solitary tone of winter has given way to color and sound and people. So many people. I spot Samira as she makes her way across the road to me.

"It really comes alive, doesn't it," I say, my mouth starting to water at the thought of a vanilla cone.

"What? Broadgate?" She laughs as she says it. "Nightmare, mate. It's like an invasion. Still, we make hay, my friend." She clutches a clipboard and waves me back down the main street. She looks so understated in her maxi-skirt and a blouse with an oversize collar.

"How the hell do you put this stuff together?" I say in awe, motioning to her earrings, which pick out the blue in the skirt.

"Come, my little goth," she says, raising an arm toward the main street. "Signatures before signature look."

Our first stop is a small video store, tucked completely out of view in an alley that I thought was a private drive. On the front, a sign—*Now with Blu-ray!*—blinks lazily against the bright sun. I stop for a moment outside and turn to Samira. "What is this place?" I say, eyeing the fringed multicolored screen door. "It looks like a front for a meth lab. Is it a video store?"

"Of course it is."

"How did I not know? How did Ash not tell me?"

"What?" she says, "are you kidding? Have you not been in here? It's a bloody treasure trove. I can't believe you of all people haven't been in!"

We enter, and the first thing I see is floor-to-ceiling pine shelving rammed to the rafters with DVDs, and in front of us, rows of chest-level shelving, sorted into genres like NICOLAS CAGE and WANKY ART HOUSE CRAP and YOUR MUM'S ACCEPTABLE FAVORITES and FILMS FOR UPTIGHT WHITE PEOPLE. I burst out laughing.

"Oh my God, who runs this place?" I whisper to Samira.

"Hey," says a voice in the corner, a cloud of vape smoke clearing to reveal a middled-aged, potbellied man in a BAD TASTE T-shirt.

"This is Sanka," she says. "Sanka, this is Mara."

"Cool," he says, sucking back on his vape again.

"This store is amazing," I say, walking down the aisle, the section called HORRORS FOR HORNY TEENS making me chuckle. "You have so many incredible films here. You know, the problem with streaming is all the bloody rights issues. For example, *Cocoon* . . ."

"Ron Howard," says Sanka, turning slightly in his chair. I have his attention now.

"You can't actually watch that anywhere in the UK. Not even Amazon Prime. The rights are tied up, and without video stores there's simply no way to watch them. And you have it! Right here." I hold it up, grinning with delight. "And by the way, Steve Guttenberg was basically the eighties Paul Rudd and people are totally missing out."

"I have every *Police Academy* too," he says, nodding to the section titled VERY PROBLEMATIC EIGHTIES COMEDIES.

"We're trying to get Lynn nominated to run for the election," Samira says, as I ask Sanka for a membership sign-up form. "And wondered if you'd help a girl out?"

"I don't vote," he says.

"Well, do you nominate?" Samira says cheerily.

"I don't nominate," he replies, as he pulls out a plastic membership card from below the cash register and begins to enter my details into the computer.

"Oh, fuck's sake, Sanka," she says, irritated now. "We're not going to have a lot of options here. We have to keep this on the down low, because if our boss finds out she's running for council, he might make things difficult."

"So, this is a conspiracy?" he says, spinning his baseball cap backward so he can get his face closer to the form Samira is holding. "Why?"

Samira sighs and glances at her phone. "Please just sign the fucking form without all the carry-on."

I return from the shelves with seven films, including *Cocoon*, and plonk them on the countertop. "Sanka, is it?" I say. "I'm about to be the best damn customer you've ever had. Sign the form, or I'll go back home and give my money to Amazon."

He laughs, pulling out a pen, and scribbles his name across the form at the bottom.

"Fine, fine. You women," he says, shaking his head as he scans my pile of films, nodding in approval at each choice.

"Does anyone actually use that?" I say, nodding to the staircase leading down with an ADULTS ONLY sign above. "What with all the online porn, I'd have thought it was a bit redundant, no?"

Samira laughs, and I catch them both looking at each other knowingly.

"Have you heard of Secret Cinema?" he says.

"Yes, of course. I went to all of them when I lived in London."

"Well, that is an *actual* Secret Cinema."

I look at him, my mouth dropping to the floor, then I turn to Samira, who shrugs. I rush across to the staircase, ducking under the ADULTS ONLY sign, and tumble down the stairs two at a time. There I find rows of old sofas and armchairs, in a black-painted room, with a projector set up to a huge white screen on the wall at the front. There is a vintage popcorn machine, and even an old, seated gamer with *Donkey Kong.* It *is* a secret cinema. *Broadgate* has a cinema.

"You don't tell anyone," says Sanka as he joins me at the foot of the stairs. "It's a rights issue."

I turn to him and grin.

"Honey, I'm home," I say, clasping my hands together. "Sanka, I have a proposition for you."

"A proposition? I'm listening."

"Does that screen move easily? And do you think I could borrow it for one night, next Friday?"

"So, it's a *favor*, then," he says wearily, and I beam back at him, hopeful. "Still, we can talk."

By lunchtime, we've managed to get seven signatures. Samira has taken us to every dark corner of Broadgate, including the wholesale tourist souvenir shop by the motorway turn-off, and we even go to see Lee at his atelier, where he hands me the canvas painting of the turd I did a few weeks back.

"Gerry wasn't impressed," he says, "but I was. He is a real shit."

Samira helps me load the turd canvas into my car, and we head back down the main street, a couple of nuns crossing themselves as they see my hearse roll past.

"It happens a lot," I explain to Samira. "I need a new car, but I don't think anyone is desperate enough to buy this one."

As we cruise past Happy Hair, I point to Jackie, who is rolling an older lady underneath a large egg-shaped hair dryer. "What about Jackie? She's a friend, isn't she?"

"We can only go places where I can be sure people won't talk," she says. "It means we're severely limited, of course, this being Broadgate."

"It's a beachfront dark web," I marvel, feeling the heat in the sun now as I peel off my cardigan to reveal a black T-shirt underneath. Samira makes an audible gasp and shakes her head as though she's reached the end of her tether. "Let's get you to Joan's and get this all sorted," she says, pointing directly at me. "Besides, Joan is on the potential signature list, and I just can't look at those spindly arms sticking out of another oversize black mess."

Joan's is a vintage clothing store, tucked so far away from the main street that I'm surprised she does any business. It's got the same overstocked vibe as the video store, and Joan herself is the tiniest octogenarian I've ever seen. She must be under five foot, and she moves like a dancer, slightly on her toes, and with grace.

Samira ties up the signature quickly and then moves around the racks, pulling out dresses in varying arrays of cuts, colors, and patterns, but absolutely no black.

"It's like a toddler threw up a rainbow," I mutter as she shovels me into the dressing room. "And dresses. I don't really do dresses."

"Just . . . in." She waves at the changing room.

The first dress is pale pink, like cotton candy, with a skater skirt and a bodice so tight I can barely breathe when I emerge from behind the curtain.

"No," I say, looking at her with disdain.

"No," agrees Samira.

I huff and retreat behind the curtain to pull on a bright blue maxidress in a scratchy poly-cotton, its halter neck giving excellent side boob.

"No," she says again. "Try the red."

"*The red*" is a skintight red dress with padded shoulders and a skirt that I have to tug down with each step forward.

"That cut is better on you," she says. "But no."

I frown as she looks down at her phone and scrolls away on it idly.

"What?" she says, when she realizes I haven't moved. "This is a vintage store. You just have to keep trying, I'm afraid. Unless you can afford Selfridges, this is the best I can do."

"What's wrong with H&M?" I say. "We could have driven to Faversham."

Samira clutches her chest and sucks in half the air in the shop. "Fast fashion is not the answer. It's *never* the answer."

Shame-faced, I head back behind the curtain and tug on a fourth dress, this time a balloon-sleeved monstrosity in green silk that sits quite nicely across my neck but hangs far too long. I'm literally swimming in it.

As I emerge from the changing room, expecting a swift no, Samira jumps up. "Okay, now we're talking."

"This? Look at the sleeves! I'll have them in Mum's trifle."

"Mara, Mara, Mara," she says. "This is emerald green silk. Look at the way it hangs on you. *Joan!*"

Samira shouts for Joan, who arrives with a tape measure and a case of pins and begins nipping and tucking to Samira's instructions. Joan pushes me and pulls me in all directions until I feel like a pincushion who can barely breathe without a jab to the fanny.

"Oh my God," says Samira when Joan steps back and they survey the finished dress.

"Well done, dear," says Joan to Samira, spinning me around to face the mirror.

The sleeves have been pinned up to a little cap, and the drop waist raised to my true waist, the long flowing silk now hitting just below my knees. The higher neckline remains, with the original button work around the neck at the back, and a large round cutaway circle sits across my shoulder blades. It feels extremely special, even pinned up like this.

"Goodness," I say, turning myself in all directions. "I feel like Keira Knightley in *Atonement*."

I feel a flush of excitement. This is how I could look for Joe. Beautiful and sophisticated and oh so feminine. I think of him walking into the pub: this time I sparkle in shimmering green silk, my hair delicately curled around my face. In this new fantasy he walks straight up to me, pulling me up off my chair and kissing me hard on the mouth. Visions of the library sex scene in *Atonement* flash through my mind, my heart picking up with the excitement of it all. I want to be desired. I want to be desired in this dress.

"I'm nearly ready," I say under my breath.

"Is it too much for your mum's sixtieth?" Samira asks. "I think you could tone it down with flats and a little denim jacket if so. Otherwise, some silver heels? I dunno what the tone is." Then she grins, holding her phone up to take a photo. "You look amazing in that green. Amazing."

"I feel really good in it," I say, reaching my hands up to my waist, the pulled fabric making me conscious of every curve. "It's amazing. But it will be a road test at Mum's birthday, before the big day."

"What big day?" Samira asks.

"Nothing. Well, not nothing," I say. "The guy I met in Budapest, he's coming. And I'm going to wear this."

"He's coming to Broadgate?"

"He is," I say with renewed confidence.

"Well, you look stunning," she says, turning her phone around to show me a photo of myself, like the several dress mirrors are not enough. "You're enough to make a guy emigrate."

"Shall I do it, then?"

"Yes," say Samira and Joan at the same time.

"What will the total cost be with the dress and all the alterations, Joan? Approximately?"

"Let's see," she says. "I think we're looking at around a hundred and fifty? Maybe less. It depends on the stitching around the back here."

"A hundred and fifty?" I reply, gulping.

"It's a total one-off dress for life," says Samira. "You can't think of it in terms of one party. But also, I think you should get this dress too, this top, and these pants as your new non-black basics." She holds up an armful of clothes.

"Heavens," I reply, "I already spent thirty quid at the video store." I carefully unzip the side of my dress and shake it down, trying not to disrupt any of the pins. "And, like, now I need to go and buy a DVD player."

15

~~~

THE SHOPPING TRIP with Samira has made me a little braver. I have paired my own black leggings with an oversize white shirt. It's an attempt to wear something non-black and not feel excruciatingly visible. Unfortunately, though, the first person I see when I enter the office is incapable of passing by without commentary.

"Mara!" Lynn says, pulling her whole head back into her neck, her eyes wide in surprise. "What are you wearing?"

There is nothing positive to find in the way she's posed this question, as she has managed to emphasize both the *what* and the *you*.

"I'm wearing a white oversize shirt," I reply, pulling down the front hem as if I might be able to disappear inside it like it's a gigantic recycled cotton tent.

"You need a belt," she says, sighing. "Come with me."

I follow her to the lost-property box, which Samira refers to as "our box of norm-core accessories."

"Here," she says, thrusting a plain brown leather suit belt into my hand. "Otherwise you look like a tea cozy."

"Thanks, Lynn," I say, threading the belt around my waist.

"There, look," she says, pointing into the full-length mirror behind the swimming trophy chest. I maneuver myself so I can see better, and I have to admit the look is mildly better.

"You're looking very lovely these days, Mara," says Lynn. "Everyone has noticed."

"Thanks, Lynn," I say, feeling my heart swell at the compliment.

"I mean it. Even Gerry commented on your looks one afternoon, and you know how picky he is."

The compliment swiftly plummets in value.

"So, Campaign Manager, where are you at with the nominations, then?"

I nod. "We're all done. Ten signatures, and the paperwork is filled. I'll get it down to the office later today, and then you're officially in the running. Is it time to tell Gerry?"

"No," Lynn says, darting her eyes up from the paperwork and then swiftly back down again. "Ooh, Carole Langley. About bloody time she did something useful. There's Sanka from the video store. Joan is in there too, and Graham Piper. Quite an endorsement from him, Mara; he's Billie Piper's second cousin."

"You know we have to tell Gerry at some point? Once we submit, there's no turning back. Ryan's father has donated the billboard space outside his landscape gardening business. Your face is going to be right there for the whole town to see, with all the election information."

"I know, Mara. I sort of did tell him," she says, now looking up at me, perching her butt on the edge of my desk.

"Go on," I say.

"Well, I asked him, hypothetically, what would happen if a staff member ran for elected office, and he said that was a conflict of interest—"

"I'm not sure that's right, actually—"

Lynn holds up a hand. "Well, maybe not, but in any case, the general response I got was not an encouraging one. It's clear to me what I've been ignoring for too long. Gerry has not been trying to help this lido; he's been running it into the ground."

"Well, yes," I say, "I've been trying to tell you—"

"I know we've discussed it, but I couldn't truly accept it. But, Mara, everything is so obvious to me now. Did you know that he tried to cancel my mothers' group? He also told Eddie Sharp, the old boy who does the water jogging on Fridays, that he ought to join the leisure center in Whitstable. Eddie drives a mobility scooter! How's he going to get to Whitstable? Swim?"

"Lynn, we've got a plan—" I begin gently.

"Mara, I am acutely aware that when I hired you, I talked up the lido's potential. And I am sorry about that. The truth is, I'd hoped with your council experience in London you might have come with some ideas. And eventually, you came through. I just hope it's not too late."

I do something I can't remember doing for many years. I put my hand on her shoulder and squeeze it slightly.

"What are you doing?" she says, looking at my hand.

"I'm comforting you," I reply.

"Are you?" she replies, looking at my hand.

"Yes," I say, taking it away and then hiding it deep behind my back. But the tension in her face breaks and she smiles. "Well, it was very nice of you to try."

"There is something else. I thought we could do an event here to get younger people in. A floating cinema night."

"Go on," she says.

"Ryan could order in some extra rubber rings. Sanka can lend us his projector and screen, and Ash agreed to come and fit it. So far, not much in the way of cost. Samira has some source for LED fairy lights to string up around the pool. Lighting is going to be important, you see."

"Gosh, Mara, this is amazing."

"And then we charge ten pounds a ticket. We can get a temporary alcohol license—I've already looked into it; it will take five days—and then we can make a lot more on the bar," I say. "And I thought, whatever we raised, we could put toward new sun loungers. And I wondered—and, now, this really is a long shot—but I wondered about approaching the coffee-cart guy about moving his business out of our car park and into the canteen for the rest of the summer. Most of our regulars are his regulars anyway. He might sell even more coffee while people are here lounging about. We need more vibe here. Less cold community exercise space and more hip summer hangout. Well, a balance of both."

At that moment, Samira comes in holding a laptop, beaming and bouncy. She briefly looks out at the view of the pool and beams some more.

"Did you speak to Ryan about printing tickets?" I ask her, eyeing her from top to toe with suspicion. "And what are you so happy about?"

"Yes. And can't a girl be happy about a community project?" she replies.

"Yes, of course," I say, tugging at my shirt dress.

"I've noticed the shirt," Samira says, "and it's a five out of ten. We need to go out again. You should clear out your wardrobe too. If that's the best non-black outfit you've got on offer, we need to do more. Have you checked your email? I sent you a very easy system for clearing it out."

I want to sulk, but Samira makes her bossy instructions so devoid of emotion it's hard to feel offended. It's like she's ordering eggs. "Okay," I say.

"Lynn, I'll submit this later today"—I wave the election application at her—"and you need to get down to Snappy Snaps and get more photos taken."

"More photos?"

"Something Ryan is organizing with his disreputable gang of lifeguards," Samira says, chuckling away to herself at mention of Ryan. "We need them for the social media as well. I can't use the photo you provided; for God's sake, you're in a bikini."

"Fatphobic," says Lynn under her breath.

"No, it isn't that. You just need to look kind of . . ." Samira sighs, unable to find a way to present it without offending.

"Lynn, I think the point is that you need to look like you mean business. Not pleasure," I say, grinning. "Have you seen the current guy? The conservative candidate? He'll eat you alive. He's right up there on the church notice board, you know. *Keeping Broadgate Open for Business.*"

"Ooh, that's good," says Samira, nodding. "Sounds so sensible."

"All right," Lynn says, "I'll do the publicity shots."

After Lynn flounces out of the room, Samira turns to me and folds her arms. "I didn't know you went to church."

"I don't go to church. I just went in there once to ask about parking and there was this notice board, which was . . . oh, it was just so sweet and sad."

"A community board?"

"Yes. It had all these posters up, for things like pottery and life drawing and whatnot. That's how I ended up seeing Gerry naked as a life-drawing model."

"Oh God," she replies.

"I'm almost too scared to go to this pottery class next week," I say warily. "I have images of *Ghost*, and like, what if instead of Patrick Swayze, Gerry crouches at the wheel behind me."

"My ears are burning, ladies . . . ," says Gerry from behind, and I literally jump. *Did he hear me?* Samira shakes her head at me.

"Gerry! Yes, we were talking about you. We need you to approve something. We're going to hold a cinema screening in the pool to try to encourage younger folk to join the lido," I say, feeling my voice waver slightly as I do. I look across at Samira for support.

"Fine," he says, digging in his pockets for his keys.

"Fine?" I say. I was expecting a small degree of pushback. Something. Anything.

"Fine. I'm heading up to London and I'll be away for most of next week. Business planning," he says, smiling his wide yellow smile. "I really want you guys to enjoy the rest of the summer here."

I frown and Samira and I side-eye each other again.

"A last hurrah, as they say," he says now, fishing his keys out and looking us both in the eyes, darting from Samira to me as if he's searching for something. "Where is Lynn?"

"She's, um . . . she's gone for a smear," says Samira.

"Right," says Gerry, turning an acute shade of cherry red. "Right. Good. Well. Good. Cheerio, girls. I'll see you next week."

When we hear the front doors slam, Samira turns to me. "Do you think he understood what he was saying yes to?"

"No, he's far too wrapped up in whatever he's cooking. We're no threat."

Samira nods at me and then straightens slightly. "Oh shit, by the way, your flatmate, Ash, is downstairs."

"Ash is here?" I reply, mouth ajar.

"Yes, he said you asked for help and he has time right now," she says. "He's literally standing in the canteen right now making notes."

I tear down the spiral staircase and rush through the canteen and out onto the pool area, where Ash, in a pair of navy shorts and a white shirt, is eyeing up the walls of the canteen, notebook in hand.

"Hey, Mara," he says, grinning my way as he scribbles something down.

"You're helping?"

"I said I could," he says. "Besides, I am pretty intrigued by the idea of a floating cinema. Samira told me we were getting it from Sanka? I spoke to him already and he's agreed we can take the sound system too. I can hang it up against that wall." He points to the cliff face that sits at the far end of the pool area.

"That's exactly where I thought it could go," I yelp, unable to hide my delight.

"He also said to tell you he got the film-screening license and a new Blu-ray copy of the film in."

"Oh brilliant!"

"And I'll just put a lick of paint here on the front of the canteen. It's just a patch job, though, Mara, until you get funds to make a better job of it."

"Anything you can do," I say. "I just want her to look her best under the sparkle of fairy lights."

"I have a bit more time now that—" he says, pausing to stop himself mid-sentence. "Well, it's summer."

"How can I repay you?" I say, biting my lip, as the sun emerges from behind a wispy white cloud and hits me right in the eyes. I raise my hands to cover them.

"Cup of tea would be great," he says, his eyes intent on me. "I'm happy to help you, Mara. What's the film, by the way?"

I laugh. I may as well let him in on it. Samira and Ryan know now, having organized the tickets. "What's the best film we could show while the customers are dangling around in dark water?"

"*No*," he says, gasping and then shaking his head, his dark eyes solid.

"Yes," I reply. "It's a floating cinema classic, Ash."

16

~~~~~

BY THE WEEKEND, all the plans are underway, and I head home. For the first time in a very long time, I feel light. My spirit feels light. As I make my way home, I look up at the bright bunting that hangs high across my little road and then I turn back to the sea, grinning. The sun is on my face, and the air is warm with a refreshing sea breeze.

I become acutely aware of the feeling.

"I *am* a Sagittarius," I say aloud. This is the first time in so, so long I've felt my sun sign in me.

I burst through the front door and feel thrilled to find Ash curled up on the sofa with a beer and a film on.

"Yay! You're home!" I say.

"Hey, smiley," he says, grinning back at me.

"It's all coming together! It's going to be so amazing. Thanks for your help too! I'm totally buzzing," I say, a hundred miles an hour, and then I see him frowning at my chaotic interruption.

"Ooh? What are you watching?" I toss my bag on the floor and almost leap into place beside him on the sofa. I look down at my phone; it's 7:23 p.m., a little early to start, but I'm here for it.

"Oh God," he says, "pressure." He waves toward the screen, and I immediately recognize *Parasite*. "I never got to see it," he explains. "I dread to even ask, but have you seen it?"

"Oh, I see *every* Oscars best picture nomination," I say, adopting a very posh voice, "and have done since 2005. Bit easier then when it was only five films. Now you have to see around ten. Still, it's a glorious hobby."

He laughs at me, looking back to the screen and then to me. "I have to concentrate, Mara," he says. "Subtitles?"

"Okay, sure. I'll um . . . Friday night curry?"

"Lamb biryani, raita, and rice. Popadams. And a garlic naan," he says without looking at me.

I laugh. "Are you up for an all-night movie marathon?"

"Yes," he says, "I can't think of anything better. My brain is hurting and I need to decompress."

Ash has been doing other *things* all week. I realize I don't really know what a workweek looks like for him. I've assumed like my father's, but is it? I recall the books in his room for a moment, wondering if he does project planning or some kind of administrative work. Maybe that's why his brain hurts.

"Okay, I need to clear out my clothes drawers, so this is basically a perfect Friday night otherwise. Samira has sent me a step-by-step guide to streamline my wardrobe."

"Project Mara?" he says, raising an eyebrow.

"I just want to open my cupboard to the perfect capsule wardrobe in more shades than black."

"I always think black looks quite smart," says Ash, who usually wears a boilersuit.

For the rest of the evening, we are full to the brim with curry, and having finished *Parasite*, I'm forcing Ash through back-to-back romantic comedies that feature a makeover or a self-improvement scene. My secret happy place, which Ash is now fully abreast of. And, remarkably, enjoying.

While we watch, I have tipped the contents of my drawers on the floor and am going through each item one at a time.

"Is that another black hoodie?" he says, laughing loudly, on his fourth beer.

"Shhh . . . ," I say, holding my hand up. "They're just about to spot each other by the fountain." We are watching *Moonstruck*. A gorgeous, quirky romantic comedy starring the legend that is Cher. We watch her spin around in her red sparkly heels as Nicolas Cage finally spots her and she spots him.

"Oh God, it's just so romantic," I swoon.

Ash puts his hands deep into his tracksuit bottoms and cocks his head to the side. "Why on earth do you not work in movies?"

"Ha," I say, shrugging. "I do adore movies. I don't know. Maybe I'll go back one day and finish?"

"You should," he says, looking like he wants to elaborate, but doesn't.

I hold up an old black T-shirt with I'VE GOT A SAG VAG emblazoned across the front. A Sagittarius vagina, but no one ever got the joke but us. A gift from Charlie. I'll keep that one.

"Have you ever started to spring-clean and then at some point everything is much worse than before you started and you can't be bothered anymore? That's where I am."

"You have a lot of black clothes," he says, stretching his arm up high, the edge of his biceps reaching through his sleeve. I must work hard not to look, except that I fail and he catches me.

"Show-off," I say, feeling the heat in my cheeks.

"It's good to have a clear-out," he says, smirking.

"I thought so four hours ago. This is the pile that sparks joy, this is the pile that sparks *some* joy, and this is the pile that sparked joy a decade ago, were not cheap, and I think I'd better hang on to in case they come back into fashion and spark joy again. I tell you what; they can peel black skinny jeans off my old dead corpse."

"What's that pile?" he says, pointing to the mountain in a bag by the door.

"They all spark despair," I say. "Mostly because they don't fit."

He laughs before walking to the fridge, staring into the abyss, and then closing it again before he turns back to me. "Out of beer. Do you fancy getting some air? I want to stretch my legs."

"Oh yes, please. I want ice cream." I look up at him, touching my hair, which is a right bird's nest. "I guess no one will see any of this in the dark."

"You look fine," he says.

"Wow. *Fine*," I reply, nudging him as he passes me to get his jacket.

"Nice. Good. Normal?" he says now, laughing.

An hour later and we're spread out on the mossy grass above the beach, on a picnic blanket, having devoured another beer each and half a large tub of Ben and Jerry's cookie dough ice cream. I groan as I rub my belly, pushing it out to emphasize how full it feels. We both stare up at the night sky. Ash cracks open another can of beer, and we lie, side by side, talking. He is slightly tipsy now, and more relaxed and open because of it.

"So, the thing with *Moonstruck* is that Cher has kind of taken her foot off the gas. Her husband died and she thinks she's cursed, so she's going to do everything different this time with her new, very nice, but very dull, partner she admits she doesn't love. But when he proposes, up pops the estranged, one-armed brother—Nicolas Cage—with his white vests and his fire-baked bread and muscles and tortured sexiness."

"Who could resist?" he says, putting his arm behind his head.

"Exactly. And she finally looks at herself and thinks, *I need to put some time into* me. So, she makes herself over. That's what I'm doing. It's not like Sandy from *Grease*. I'm not going to be a different person and mold myself for the dude. Project Mara is not going quite that far. There's only so much mileage you can get out of this anyway." I motion down my body. It's a throwaway comment. I've said some version of it a hundred times, and yet, right now, it lands differently. Heavily.

"Don't say shit like that," he says.

"It's just a joke," I reply.

"Still."

For a moment there is a silence between us, and in the darkness, I can feel his head turn very slightly and then turn back. As if there is something else to be said but he decides not to.

"So, what's after *Moonstruck*?"

"I'm running out of ideas. BuzzFeed suggested *Mrs. Doubtfire*, but, like, would you call that a makeover film?"

"I would not," he says.

The silence returns. I pull myself up on my elbows and look out into the darkness of the ocean ahead.

"So, you're absolutely sure he's going to come?" Ash says.

"Yes," I say, closing my eyes tight to bring the picture of Joe's face, his eyes, his smile, into perfect focus in my mind. "I really do.

I *know* it. This is a bit embarrassing. But I haven't had a boyfriend since that guy from university," I say. "Noah."

There is always an issue. The way they administer sugar into a mug of tea could be analyzed with the obsessive detail of Stanley Kubrick. What does that slight tilt of the spoon and the too-slow spill of the uniform white grains mean? What does it reveal about his character, to leave sugar dissolving in the base of a floral cup without a single stir? And why do I even accept a date with a Scorpio? I know, though, I am just plain scared to get close.

"Really?" he says. "I mean, I only had two, but still."

"Yep," I say, laughing a little. "I really thought he was the one. Like, we met on my first week. He was loading camera equipment into the back of his car—a beaten-up gold eighties Datsun. A very cool car. Anyway, I helped him and we got talking because I'd just been to see *The Dark Knight*, and he hadn't seen it yet, and then we got talking about Christopher Nolan . . . and, I don't know. We were a good fit.

"Anyway, it ended so badly. So badly." I stop for a moment as I feel the very slight sting of tears in my eyes. I cannot believe it still affects me as it does. I shrug. "It's just too much of a risk, isn't it? To just throw your heart out there without some kind of confirmation you're going in the right direction."

"I guess so," he says. "But, Mara, everyone is someone else's heartache."

"Did you have yours broken?" I ask, cringing as I say it. *Too dramatic.* "It's just, a while ago Jackie said something and it sounded like—"

"I was engaged to a girl I saw for six years. Kate," he says. "And yes, she broke up with me and it sucked. But I'm open to meet someone now."

He's so clear about things, I think. We lie in silence for a bit, as the sound of cicadas fills the air, and the sky begins to reveal the starry night above us. I can hear the gentle crash of the waves on the shore below us as the breeze begins to cool. I rub my arms, deciding not to probe Ash anymore on whoever this Kate woman is.

"I have another question for you," I say. "You don't only paint houses, do you."

"No, Mara, there's more to my job than that. And that didn't sound like a question," he says, laughing.

I roll onto my side and look at him. He turns back and grins at me.

"Fine. I have another thing going on, yes," he says. "I may as well tell you; it's going to get pretty busy again come September."

"What is it?" I reply.

"This," he says, pulling my arm back down so we are both on our backs looking up at the night sky. "*This*."

"The stars or the red-eye out of Southend Airport?" I say, pointing at a moving flashing light above us.

"Exactly," he says, turning his head to me.

"Your pilot's license?" I say, confused.

"No. The night sky. The stars. You know when I said I wanted to be an astronaut?"

I laugh, elbowing him in the ribs, and he grabs my elbow and pushes me away playfully.

"Oh right. You're moonlighting for some secret NASA program."

"I wish. But no. I went to Cambridge to do physics because I wanted to ultimately do cosmology. They have this bachelor of natural sciences there, and then I was going to go on and do cosmology somewhere, maybe in Dorset."

"That's so cool," I say, turning my face to his.

"I dropped out and I've just always regretted not doing it," he says. "It was Cambridge really. It was competitive and full of posh kids called George and Rupert and Freddie. I got embarrassed of stupid things like my accent."

"Oh, I get that; I'm a Geordie," I say.

"But, you know, I got older and a bit tougher and in the end I wanted to finish the study. It always chewed away at me. Anyway, when I turned twenty-nine, I thought fuck it. So, I found a course at King's College in London and applied. I've been traveling up and back for the last few years, living with my parents. Wanted my own space in the end, though; that's why I moved in with you."

"I'm impressed," I say. And I am. This revelation about Ash has really surprised me. "But why all the secrecy? You should tell people; then they might stop calling you to go and help change their light bulbs," I say, blushing now at the help he offered at the lido.

"I like my job," he says, and then he laughs. "It's dumb, but when I left for Cambridge I felt so much pressure from everyone. My parents wouldn't shut up about it. You know what this town is like. I just want to keep this close to my chest until it's done. So it's just mine, you know? Then if I decide to do nothing with it, I can also feel cool about it."

"Would you do *nothing* with it?"

"Maybe. I like what I do. It's possible to just do something because it's interesting. Not every hobby or whatever has to be a career. Truth be told, though, I'd love to get funding for a telescope for the town. A proper one, you know?"

"Mm-hmm," I say, my mind whirring as if someone has lifted it up and shaken it like a snow globe. I am waiting for all my thoughts to settle, but they do not. Returning to study? Finishing something because you love it. Something just for you?

"I see you in a whole new starlight," I say. "*Nerd.*"

He smiles upward, not turning to face me, and then says, "It's been so full on, but I'm loving it, really. I have to force myself out of my room sometimes."

"Makes me nearly want to go back and chase my dreams," I say whimsically.

"Nothing stopping you," he says.

I stare back up at the fan of stars reaching from one end of the bay across to the other. My eyes move across the visible constellations toward the moon, which is large and milky yellow.

"I have a question for you. With all that we don't know, and with all that we can't prove, do you not leave any room at all for, like, magic or celestial influence of any kind?"

"You can't say either way one hundred percent for sure." He shrugs. "But no. Astrology, gods, whatever your belief structure. It's just a framework, isn't it? To make sense of our insignificance."

Now he turns to face me, and I breathe out.

"I think that's really kind of sad."

"There's magic enough up there in what we *do* know," he says, his eyes on the grass beside me as he speaks. "There's plenty of magic all around me."

My phone buzzes in my pocket and I fish around for it, the light bright in my eyes in the darkness. It's a WhatsApp from my dad. He famously hates technology, so this has to be important.

> I hope we're seeing you for your mother's
> birthday? Your brother's got some news to
> share and we'd all like to see you there
> Mara.

I grimace.

"What is it?" Ash says.

"It's my mum's birthday in a couple of weeks and *Mara you have to make an effort please*," I say, mimicking my dad's deep voice. "I've been avoiding them."

There is a silence, and I look at Ash, who is studying my face. I feel the heat in my neck begin to crawl up my cheeks at sharing the information. "You don't want to go home?" he asks.

"No," I say quietly.

"Why?"

"My parents and I kind of clash. They're not weird or horrible or anything. They're super nice, really. But I left home with all these big dreams of working in the movies. I went to film school. And they were like, *Mara, you need a plan B*.

"And then, you know, it didn't work out. And I had to call my dad for money a few times, and it was really excruciating. And it was easier to just stay away. I do go home, but I always feel like such a loser when I'm there. I can almost hear the *I told you so* ringing in my ears when I so much as think of Corbridge."

"You could be wrong," he says.

"Nah, I'm not," I reply. "I left them in no doubt I thought I was going to *make it*. And that I was embarrassed of them. I was a bit of a stupid teenage asshole."

"Hey, why don't I come?" he says.

"To Corbridge? Are you high?"

"Hear me out. There is a dark park in Northumberland, right? We could camp and drink whisky and look at Andromeda? You could go to your mum's birthday, and I'll come too, and then we can do that."

"You don't *really* want to come, do you?"

"A weekend away would be . . ." He sighs and then kind of moans. "It would be kind of amazing. What do you think?"

"I dunno, Ash," I say. "Plus it's high summer; you're not going to get the best out of the dark park."

"It will still be better than what we can see here. Come on." He's excited now, sitting up, staring out across the black ocean in front of us. "I could bring a telescope so we can at least see more than with the naked eye."

"Speaking of naked, there is a famous dogging spot right next to the car park," I say.

"Well, two birds," he says, grinning.

"As many birds as you like," I reply. And we both laugh as I stand up and rub the grass off my pants and reach out to help him up too. The blanket, the grass, it triggers a strong vision of Ash alone in the darkness. A small tent, the proximity of sleeping so close to him. I see the stars, feel the cool air and a warming whisky. I get a rush of pleasure at the thought of it, which is replaced almost as quickly by worry.

This idea is tempting the wrong fate.

And yet, I want to do it.

"Don't overthink it," Ash says, his eyes trying to catch mine. "If you like the idea, let's just go."

Don't overthink it. The words hum around in my mind, and I bristle. That's the very problem, of course. I already am overthinking it. And so now it's become a decision I have to somehow make.

17

'VE BEEN FRANTIC. It's only three days until our cinema event and it has been a herculean effort from everyone; the days feel short, and my thoughts chaotic. The trip to Corbridge and my mother's birthday is next weekend, and while work is proving a welcome distraction, I have a dreadful sense that things around me are starting to spin out of control.

It doesn't help that when I get home that evening, desperate for wine and a calming movie, I find Ash with a bucket of plain biscuit-colored paint in his hand, naked from the pants up, his boilersuit arms tied round his waist and his broad, sweaty, very fit chest bare. I have to duck under him to get through the door, immediately getting that smell of fresh sweat and newly sanded wood as I brush past him. And then I get a whiff of the paint.

"What are you doing?" I ask, feeling my cheeks burn from being within a whisper of his naked chest. I look down at the paint on the floor to avoid eye contact while the embarrassment subsides.

"Surprise!" he says. "I'm making a start on the entrance area."

"But what about—I thought we'd do it together, like, and plan the colors and whatnot," I say, and then I brush on a huge smile. "Don't get me wrong. It's . . . brilliant."

He raises an eyebrow, immediately clocking my fake smile. "You don't like Almost Oyster?"

"Is that the name of the color?"

"Yes."

"Is it an undercoat or something?"

"You're not a fan, Mara?" he says, his lip curling into a smile.

"Um. Not especially," I say, cursing my inability to lie about it. "But I'm still very grateful you're doing it. I'm worried about color choices. How will we choose them? Can we discuss it properly before it's finalized?"

All these upgrades in my life are starting to feel like upheaval. *It's too much.*

"We can. You've been so flat-out with work and the election, I did wonder if you would prefer we just went ahead and took the decision away from you," he says. "This is just a testing patch anyway. There's swatches on the floor by the TV for you to look through. But at any stage, you just tell me if you want me to make the decision for you."

"What if we put all the colors into a jar and pick one out?" I say, the stress starting to overwhelm me. "Leave it to fate?"

Ash finds this hilarious.

Just then, two other men in boilersuits emerge from the bathroom, carrying the toilet. Mercifully neither is showing as much skin as Ash is.

"What are you doing with the toilet?" I ask the two men, both of whom are staring at me and then across to Ash, almost identical wry smiles on their faces. I shift slightly in my place.

"You must be the lovely Mara," says one, a large potbellied man with a bald head and a pink, glowing, sweaty face. "Beautiful day for it." The other nods between heavy grunts as they carry it out and toss it in a trailer outside.

"What's going on in the bathroom?" I ask nervously, turning to Ash, frowning.

"The toilet had a crack in the bowl, so it needs replacing, and we have a spare at the shop," he says, tucking his hand under his armpit and across his chest as he speaks, as though he's just realized he's half-naked. "There was a break in the books, and the boys were happy to jump in. Don't look so freaked out, it's only the toilet and the bath we're replacing. Everything else is a lick of paint or varnish."

I stare at him hard, my heart leaping to a gallop as I try to find a way to communicate that I'm grateful, but the lack of warning and consultation and the number of people in my space have made me extraordinarily anxious. I worry they've gone in my room, which I have been forgetting to lock of late.

"Is it too hard to find a thank-you in there?" he says, grinning and waving the paintbrush in my direction, before turning back to continue with short, feathered strokes along the edge of the door.

When I don't respond, Ash stops and turns to me, his head sideways. He frowns. "Sorry, Mara. I should have warned you."

"Asked you," I say, correcting him.

"Asked you," he replies, nodding in agreement. "Trade habit, I'm afraid. I get asked and I do it. I thought you'd appreciate me just getting on with it."

"Of course, yes," I say, holding both my hands up and shaking my head. "I'm really grateful. I am. I'm just . . . I feel . . ."

I want to say I feel invaded, but I know it makes me sound even more ungrateful. Ash is looking at me, his face more pity now than frustration. And perhaps he also looks apologetic.

"It's your space. I get it," he says. "Next time we'll do a coin toss to decide what to do, right?"

He's teasing, but I cringe. After six weeks of easiness with Ash, there it is. The first full-on Mara-ism, the first neurotic thing, the first spark of crazy beginning to show itself. I look nervously across to my room. I hope they haven't been in there too.

The two other builders return and Ash nods at the bald one. "Gummy can talk you through everything we're doing. And then later tonight I can give you a rough estimate of timings so you know what's going on. I'll make sure you're across it all. Can you show Mara what's happening, Gummy?"

"Sure!" Gummy says, beaming at me. "Let's do the grand tour. We haven't touched your room. Ash said we had to ask you about that first."

"Oh, it's good to know he has some boundaries," I say, trying to make light of things.

Gummy laughs, but I'm not sure he knows why he's laughing, as he flings open the bathroom door. "New bath, new paint, new toilet. That's the lion's share of the heavy work, really. The rest is just surface stuff."

"But how will I shower?" I ask. "It's amazing, of course, but how long until—"

"Oh, right!" he butts in. "Ash got an old one from a house we just renovated down in Margate. Ash—you didn't tell her about the bathtub?" he calls into the other room, and Ash answers with a simple "No, it was supposed to be a surprise."

"Ash didn't tell me any of this," I say.

"Classic Ash," he replies.

"So, I can't actually have a shower?"

"Not for a couple of weeks, I imagine," Gummy replies, opening the door to Ash's room, which is a hideous tip, with everything pushed into the center of the room, large white streaks where they've filled cracks in the plaster, and tape around every skirting board and the window frame.

"Walls fixed, and we're going to strip the window back to the wood and stain it."

"Okay," I reply, nodding. Nothing too major here, but then Ash's little bedroom is in the best shape.

"As I said, we haven't touched your room," he says, pointing to my bedroom door. "Ash said we had to wait until you got home. Do you want us to fix any cracks and prep the paint?"

"God, this is some pressure," I say.

"We can do it next time," he says, laughing at my ill ease. "Give you some time to think. And we'll paint those cabinets in the kitchen, I thought. We'll take this top cupboard out, too, so you can get a bigger fridge if you want. This wood countertop here, it used to be the counter for the old shop. It's gorgeous, isn't it? A couple of hundred years old it is, by my reckoning. You can see all the old indentations from the hammers."

I look down at the wood, at what was just a few hours ago an old shaggy slab of oak and is now a dented thing of historic wonder. I feel my heart soften at the thought. *This is all good, Mara. Let go.*

"Place was a key cutter I think," Gummy continues, and I nod.

"Yes," I reply. "I think the woman who owns it, her husband ran it as one."

"Sure, but this is from even further back—must have been a shoemaker back before that. A Georgian shoemaker. Those grooves? See them? Ash said we should sand it, oil it, and see if we can find a couple of stools so you've got a breakfast bar. All in all, she's going to look pretty sweet."

I'm all in, by the end. I'm overwhelmed, but also, a small part of me is thrilled to bits by all the suggestions and at how it all might come together.

"When do you think you'll be done?" I ask. "Not to hurry you, of course."

"Depends. We should get quite a bit done today; then, it's when we're free, really. We're spending most of Friday at the lido, getting it ready for the cinema. But we'll have it finished in the next few weeks. I'm sure before the summer's over."

Before the last Friday in August? I wonder.

We head back into the main lounge, where Ash is finishing up his undercoat and the third guy seems to have managed to unstick the front window.

"Oh my God, fresh air," I say, and Ash turns around and grins at me.

"There's that smile," he teases. "Hey, look, Mara. Sorry again. It was just an impulsive decision 'cos we had time and Mrs. Watson said we could, and nothing here can't be changed or halted. Except the toilet. And maybe the bath."

I realize that all three of them are looking at me now, big smiling faces, proud of their surprise home makeover.

"I'm so grateful I could cry," I say, my voice cracking slightly. "No one has ever done anything like this for me."

Gummy comes over and throws a huge arm around my shoulders, which I cannot shrink away from.

I look over at Ash, who has turned away from me, and I feel tears coming. "I just need to make a call and do some other . . . things. And then if you're still here I'll make you all a cup of tea," I say quickly. And then: "Thank you."

But once I've closed the door of my room I don't come out. I sit there begging and praying no one knocks as I change into some slouchy pants and an old T-shirt.

I need someone to talk me down, so I check the time. It's 6:34, and I know Charlie will be in the middle of bedtime. I can't call, but I message her instead.

Can you talk? I need a talking to. x

Then I wait for a reply. Two minutes. Ten minutes. Twenty minutes. Nothing.

And so I call Samira.

"Hi, Samira," I say when she answers, before launching right into it.

"Two things. Can you take me shopping again?"

"You need to do your clear-out first."

"Yes, it's done. And now Ash is renovating the house, so it feels like I'm in the middle of a full-scale life makeover."

"Isn't that what you wanted?"

"I guess. It's just Ash arranged it all, and I'm kind of . . ."

"Mara. You are someone who has to check her star sign to see what to have for lunch. Isn't it better he just swooped in and did it?"

"I am doing all the arranging for the lido cinema event," I protest. "You make me sound completely useless."

"You're doing amazing. I just mean that it isn't ever an efficient use of time waiting for Mara to make a decision about things that affect her."

"Fine," I say. "I'm getting better, though. I guess. Also, it's just a big thing to do for me."

"It is," she says. "But it's his flat too, Mara. Aren't you both on the lease?"

"Yes," I reply, genuinely not having thought of that. And, of course, he knows Mrs. Watson. I am relieved. But, curiously, I feel slightly disappointed too. As *too much* as it was to believe that Ash was doing all this for me, it was a surprising letdown to think it was for him. "You're right. I really went and made it all about me," I say.

"That's kind of your thing," she says, laughing.

"What? Being a neurotic, self-centered egomaniac?"

"Put that in your Tinder bio," she says, laughing.

18

~~~

T IS THE Friday afternoon before our great cinema event and everything at the lido is abuzz. Ryan has been hitting the streets selling tickets, his team of three topless lifeguards proving a hit with the young women of Broadgate. Lynn has been spreading the word through all her community groups. Sanka has been hard selling at the video store. There are only a handful of tickets left, and yet, I'm still flapping around, an anxious mess, terrified no one will show up.

Samira is working with Ryan to help string up the lights all around the front of the canteen and in straight lines up the roof to the top of the dome.

"Oh God, please be careful, Samira!" I shout from the safety of the poolside, looking up at her as she maneuvers the heavy rig into Ryan's hands and he fixes it to the little point at the top, completing the task and sliding down the curved edge of the dome to meet Samira, whose arms he almost slides right into.

"What about *please be careful, Ryan?*" he shouts back at me. "Don't you care if I fall?"

I leave them to finish up, tingling with nervous excitement about how everything is coming together. Bunting has been hung across the entrance area, and helium balloons on long strings are tied on either side of the reception desk. Lynn has just arrived with the ticket sales totals. She looks at me with a pursed-lipped smile.

"What is it?" I say.

"It's worked," she replies, shaking her head in disbelief.

"Not completely. We need to convert this event into memberships. That's the goal," I say. I smile at her, genuinely so thrilled to play a part in making her this happy.

"Come on, let me show you what we've done with the canteen." I grab her hand and pull her through the turnstiles, past the spiral staircase into the canteen.

"In the daylight it looks a bit naff, but wait until the sun sets," I say.

The canteen has been transformed into a faux beachfront with blown-up air mattresses, big beach blankets and towels, and colorful lanterns dotted everywhere. Along the walls are a few old surfboards, sourced by Ryan. The canteen counter itself is decorated like a boat, the anchor and the wooden steering wheel borrowed from the Star and Anchor.

The centerpiece, though, is something Ryan found: a huge inflatable shark with its mouth open.

"Picture it when it's just the lanterns and the fairy lights and it's filled with people drinking cocktails," I say, looking to Lynn for confirmation that she likes it. "Cheap and cheerful, but it's the fun that counts."

"It's something else, Mara," she says, turning to me and grabbing both my hands. "I'm not staying for the films, though. I couldn't do it. *Jaws* and then *Open Water*? A double bill of water horror? I'm too old for that kind of gore."

"It's fine—just be here when we turn the lights on," I say.

We walk out onto the pool area and are hit by a wave of heat. The temperature couldn't be better. Any colder and the unheated pool would start to get too cold for people to float around in. We've cleared away the loungers to make space for people to sit on blankets around the pool area.

A regular is pulling himself up the ladder, while Ryan and Samira giggle together as they blow up the rings. I turn to find Ash fitting the final corner of the screen while Sanka watches nervously.

"How are you getting on?" I say, as Ash looks down at me grinning.

"Hey, Mara," he says. "Couldn't have picked a better day, could you?"

"What are you doing now?" Sanka snaps at Ash. I can see they are at the bickering end of this new relationship. Two complete opposites.

"I'm just drilling a small hole so we can pull the screen tighter," Ash replies with utmost patience. "See?" he says, yanking on the edge of the screen so the whole large, heavy fabric sits flat.

"Stop pulling on it," says Sanka, reaching for his vape in anxious concern.

By 8 p.m. the sun is finally heading down, the sky is beginning to turn from bright blue to deep blue, and I gaze out toward the cottony clouds that will form another spectacular sunset across the sky.

I turn to Ash, who has already opened a beer and is wiping the sweat from his brow. "Ninety-five fucking degrees is not a temperature for outdoor work," he says.

"I'm grateful as hell, if that helps?" I say.

"How can you be so chilled about all of this, and so stressed about the color shade for your house?" he says, reaching behind the bar to pull out a beer from an ice bucket and handing it to me. Eddie, also borrowed from the Star and Anchor, and taking a wholesale cut, rolls his eyes and throws his hands in the air, as if to say *Take them all.*

"I don't know. I am stressed. But it's kind of a happy, excited stress. It's not about me, I suppose," I say, shrugging. "Oh God, look, here's the first people. We have to get the lights on."

We turn to see a group of twentysomethings, the girls with their long hair and colorful bikinis with cut-off jeans and flippy skirts. The guys in their beach clothes, one wearing a sailor's cap. We move quickly away from the bar to make room and I delight in watching them peel notes out of their wallets to buy popcorn in paper bags and beers in reusable bamboo cups.

Ash takes a swig of his beer. "You go out and sit by the edge there and I'll turn them on, okay?"

"Thanks, Ash," I say. "I'm going to go take a minute."

I head over to the other side of the pool, looking back at the lido as I wait for the lights to come on. In this quiet moment of pleasure, I marvel at what I've managed to achieve with this amazing group of people around me. The canteen lights go down first, and each little lantern is turned on by Samira and Ryan as they make their way through the room. The bar lights up with all its little pindot fairy lights and the large search-and-rescue spotlight fixed overhead.

The sunset breaks into full pink-and-orange glory and I hold my breath as Ash finds the main switch and the lights suddenly burst on. It is absolutely magical. A twinkling, sparkling dream.

"Yes," I gasp, as Ash emerges from the side of the building and shoots me a thumbs-up.

Within a few minutes Samira appears with Ryan, and then Ash joins us just as the projector starts up. "Five minutes!" I say, looking at my watch.

The crowd is filling out and some start to make their way into the water, holding on to the floating rings and air mattresses, and someone has even brought a tiny blow-up boat for one. A young man wearing a shark mask dives into the water. Another shouts, "We're going to need bigger balls," and cannonballs in next to him.

Then I see Lynn, coming toward me with a bottle of champagne in her hand.

"Lynn," I hiss as she slips off the wrapper around the cork and starts to twist off the metal fixture. "No glass by the pool!"

"Who on earth is going to stop us?" says Lynn as the cork pops high into the air and right over the cliff into the sea. "It's cork," she says when she sees my face.

I spot Ash lingering back a little, giving us our moment together, and I wave him over to join us. Lynn pours a small serving into four bamboo tumblers and hands them to everyone but Samira, who is happy with her water.

"Look at you. What a success," Ash says, grinning. "Only you could have pulled something like this off, Mara."

"Thanks," I say, blushing.

"I guess you're working in the movies after all," he says, nudging me in the arm.

"I guess," I say, unable to hide my smile. I wonder if this is something I could share with my parents next weekend. *Next week-end*. I breathe out. Maybe I can do this?

"Now, don't forget," Lynn is saying now, "we're looking for memberships. Try to get them before they're too drunk."

"Why?" says Ryan.

"I'm trying to be slightly ethical," says Lynn.

Then the projector falls to black and *Jaws* begins to the whoop of tipsy voices around us.

19

～～～

WITH THE FLOATING cinema behind me, I have work, sneaky election-related tasks, a pottery class, and a re-watch of the entire seven seasons of *Downton Abbey* to distract me from the impending trip to see my family. But, as the hour draws closer, I am becoming increasingly manic.

It doesn't help my nerves at all when midweek Joe posts an image of the Royal Albert Hall with the caption *Destiny Awaits in England*. Like a crash zoom, there is suddenly nothing else in view.

As Ash handed me a cup of tea, he noted that Joe could have been talking about the Royal Albert Hall. "His destiny to play there?" Ash said, lifting his shoulders in a dismissive shrug. But I just *knew* he was thinking of me. I imagined him, like me, overcome with curiosity and the wait. Frantically looking up Maras in Kent, over and over, and seeing the picture of me on the pier and wondering if that was *the* Mara. And he can't resist the urge to find out. I know he can't.

On Friday, I get home and find Ash in the lounge, his feet up, with the new DVD player on. I look around the place, still in a state of half-finished renovation, the walls filled with plaster and prepped for paint, and the floor covered in cardboard tracks between all the rooms.

"This DVD player was a really good idea," says Ash.

"I can't believe you never used the video store," I say, plonking down on the couch next to him.

"Like most normal people, I stopped renting DVDs over a decade ago," he says. "Plus, to be honest, Sanka was always a bit unfriendly."

"He's really nice when you get to know him," I say, grinning at the change-up in dynamic. "You just need to make the effort, Ash, if you want to fit in."

Ash throws a cushion at me. "I tried at your bloody cinema night, didn't I? I think he can smell an amateur film watcher a mile off."

I lean forward and place my pottery disaster on the coffee table, and it sags in the middle. "I just picked it up," I say.

"Nice . . . beaker?" he says.

"I think so," I say, pointing to the rim, which has folded almost completely inward. "I couldn't bear to let the guy fire it because then I'd have to go back and do another class. I think my hobby is films, Ash. All this other stuff is just keeping me away from watching that television. Is that sad?"

"Only if you're always alone," he says, as he unpauses *An Officer and a Gentleman*, shrugging when I raise an eyebrow at his choice. "What? It's got the army in it. It's manly."

"I love it," I say. "The final scene when he picks her up and whisks her out of the factory, it's—"

"Spoiler!" he says, throwing a second cushion at me and hitting Pause again. "I can't believe you spoiled the ending!"

"It's one of the most iconic endings in any movie ever!" I reply. "It's even been spoofed on *The Simpsons.*"

"I just have other things in life going on, Mara," he says, and I throw the cushion back at him.

We sit for a moment in the quiet and I rub my hands on my jeans, still flecked with clay. "I've been thinking about my mum's birthday tomorrow," I say. "If you still want to come, I'd be really grateful for the company."

"Ah," he says, nodding. "When you didn't mention it again, I thought it was off the radar."

"I just think if you're with me, you can deflect some of the attention. Sorry."

"That's the point. I'll borrow a car off Mum and Dad, though. We can't go in my white van or that hearse."

"Thanks, Ash," I say, breathing out, relieved. "*Really.*"

"It's great. Honestly, I needed an excuse to visit the dark park, and now at last I have one."

He stands up and flicks the TV off. "I need some fresh air. I might pop out and get some beers. Do you want to come for a walk?"

"Sure. Let me have a quick shower . . ." As soon as I say it, I remember and groan. We still don't have a bloody shower. "Fuck," I say, "I've only washed myself at the lido or over the sink for a whole week. I stink."

"Why not the showers?"

"They're communal and open and cold," I say. Ash laughs at this.

"Not long, I promise."

"It's fine, really. I just"—I sniff my pits—"yeah. I stink."

"There is always the sea," says Ash, shrugging. "If you're desperate. Though it will be colder than those showers at the lido. Still, beer and a dip?"

I look at my phone to check the time. "Lynn is on the radio at nine. We could go and drink some beers and wait for her interview? That way I can build up a bit of Dutch courage?"

We take our place on the grassy bank overlooking the bay and drink beers out of cans as I ravage a portion of hot chips dipped into little pots of mayonnaise.

"These tiny portions are ridiculous," I say, scraping the last of a pot clean with the edge of a chip.

"Ridiculous," he says, as he reaches in to steal one and our hands touch. And there it is. That jolt I've been feeling. That electric pulse every time we touch, however incidentally.

I pick up a third beer and pull back the ring, feeling a little warmth spreading through me.

"Lynn!" I say, as a reminder pops up on my phone, lighting up on the grass in the darkness. I notice a missed call from Charlie as I open the app that has the local station and fiddle about until I find it and then lay it before me on speaker. I will message her tomorrow, I decide.

"Shhh, that's her, it's already started," I say to Ash.

"Yes, it was a great success, of course. We took in a lot of money and it just goes to show you how with a little bit of creativity, the Broadgate Lido, and indeed all of our neglected community buildings, can really have a new lease on life," says Lynn.

"And how do you feel about the criticism leveled at you? Running as an independent, potentially splitting the vote?" asks the old, croaky DJ. "Are you worried about the split?"

"Listen, Mark, I haven't done the splits since 1987. I don't intend to start now."

"Evasive," says Ash, laughing.

"Political," I reply.

Lynn does a great job of remaining upbeat and optimistic about the future of Broadgate, remembering to focus on things like health, education, and other matters that she called "irritating" during Samira's media briefing.

"She did well," I say, switching my phone off. "Good old Lynn. She agreed almost right away to run for the council. She just jumped right into the deep water without a thought about it."

I look out toward the sea. "I've hardly been in there, you know."

"Really?" says Ash.

"Yes. Nuts. I moved to the ocean, but I am not very at one with the ocean. It always seems like there's something lurking underneath the surface."

"Too much *Jaws*," he says. "You're more likely to get nipped on the toe by a crab."

"Well, now I'm never going in!" I protest. But then a moment later, as his laughter subsides, I think on it again. "These are those moments, aren't they Ash, where people who are brave and wild and carefree just fucking do it. They just jump in, right?"

"I think it might be," he replies.

"Well then," I reply, pulling myself up. "I'd better live a little."

A minute later we are standing on the edge of the stony bay, the blackness of the sea stretching out before us, with nothing but the twinkling lights of the night sky reflecting on its rippling surface.

"Look over there toward your pub," I say, stripping down to my underwear. And then there is a sudden rush through me. Something

I want to do. Something I've never done before. I don't second-guess it.

I glance over at Ash, and when I'm convinced he's not looking, I yank off everything else and rush for the sea. I plunge deep into the water with a sharp gasp, but it isn't as cold now. The sun is beginning to gently warm the shallows, and although I emerge breathless, I can stand it.

"Come on!" I shout into the darkness of the shore ahead. "Get your ass in."

I turn back out to watch the lights of the fishing boats trolling along the horizon. The stars stretch their scattered lights from the horizon up. As I hear the splash of Ash joining me, I turn, but I cannot see him. I wait for him to speak, to spill out from the depths next to me. Then, I feel a hand on my calf and yelp in surprise as Ash rises out of the sea, laughing.

But I am not laughing. I step back as he settles his face on me, his bare chest visible in the spill of the streetlights that just reaches us, like a distant glow, caressing the shallows.

"Mara," he says, as he takes a step forward. But I stand completely still, feeling the water roll off my skin, my body naked in front of him. I fold my arms over myself to cover my breasts. I can just see it, his arousal below the water surface. I feel the prickle of power and desire course through me. It has been so long since I've felt desired. For a moment, I want to reach out and touch him and feel his body hard against mine.

I see his eyes make their way down my neck to my collarbone, and then along the curve of my breasts to the water, just above my hips, rippling along my skin. It is cold, and I feel every follicle, every part of my skin tightening against the chill. I see his eyes, hungry and longing; in our silence I feel the question he's asking. The question I've known was coming.

And then the full light from a small fishing boat hits us, blinding me, so I turn away.

"They're going for squid," he says quietly as I crouch down again, spinning my face away. "The light attracts them. They swim straight into the danger."

I don't reply. I am breathless. And as the light passes over us and begins to make its way out to the sea, I find my voice.

"That's really sad," I say, feeling my body begin to shiver.

"What is?"

"The squid," I reply. "Swimming right into the danger. All following their instincts, happy and hoping for the best."

I turn back to Ash, who is looking at me, his lips pursed, willing me not to overthink this moment. But it's too late for that. I'm not going to swim into the light. No matter how much I want to.

"Can you look away while I get out?"

20

~

"YOU'RE NOT GOING *to let us down again, are you Mara?"* My dad's words swirl around in my mind and I roll my eyes to the heavens. I think I could be out of the will if I miss this family occasion. The last one—Easter—I claimed to be sick. I have invented and killed off a dog to get out of a Christmas. And who can forget bumping into my aunt at a gas station on my way through Northumberland to Edinburgh without telling my parents I was passing through. I have to go.

And yet, when I think about seeing them it makes me feel nearly sick with anxiety. The whole last decade—my twenties—I was burrowing down in my flat in London with Charlie and ignoring the distance that was growing. Pretending I was busy. Pretending I only had one night because they really needed me back at work. I had exaggerated my jobs. Made up boyfriends. Used any excuse I could to avoid going home and telling them the truth. That it didn't work out. That I had my heart broken. That I had my dream crushed. That I failed. That recovering from that kind of betrayal was impossible.

That I had moved to a small town on the coast of England because it was near my only friend. That without my family she was my everything and that she didn't have room for me anymore. I am so grateful Ash is going to come with me. The strange almost-moment in the water last night aside, he is my friend and my flat-mate and he will be a welcome distraction while we are there.

As I'm packing my bag, I pull up a video of the Viennese Philharmonic Orchestra playing in the grounds of a castle on a summer's evening. My eyes flicker back regularly to the screen to catch the moments when the camera is pointing toward the string section. There he is. His arms move the bow in strong, lingering strokes, his face focused and serious. It is good to remind myself of the plan. To also stay focused.

I try to imagine what it would be like to be led around those gardens by those strong hands, stopping for coffee or wine before he heads back to rehearsal and I take a sketchbook to a quiet corner of the rose garden to do some earnest but terrible drawing. I try to fantasize about the new life, a European life full of travel and coffee and little crisp pastries. Perhaps I could return to film school after all? I fall back on the bed and will myself to dissolve into the delicious fantasy.

My phone beeps. Another message from Charlie. *Shit*, I forgot to reply to her.

> **CHARLIE:** You've gone quiet? Did you get
> my message?

> **MARA:** Sorry, I've been super busy with
> work. How are you doing?
>
> **CHARLIE:** Can you talk?
>
> **MARA:** I can talk for a bit? Packing for
> Corbridge.
>
> **CHARLIE:** No worries, call me when you
> get some time, or when you're back. Love
> you xx

I stare at the exchange for a moment. Am I missing something here? I realize for the first time in as long as I've known her, I haven't been thinking of her. It's a strange, dislocated feeling now that I think about it. I message her again.

> Why don't you come visit? Say next
> weekend? ☺

But this time, I see the little colored ticks that show she has read it, but she doesn't reply right away.

I haul on jeans as black as my mood, but now, I pull on an electric-blue T-shirt and a pair of small leather saddle shoes—both new, both from Samira's and my shopping trip. I carefully take my new green dress out of the cupboard and lay it over the back of my chair. Then I pack knickers. A toothbrush. A plunging push-up bra I can wear for approximately four hours before it feels like I'm being sliced through the underarms by an elastic guillotine. And then, just in case, I pack some high-heeled sandals. I look in the mirror and see a new Mara looking back. Jackie has freshly cut my hair, and I've put on a little makeup, including a red lipstick. Everything about me says that I'm doing great. Now I just need to convince my parents.

Ash pulls up in a silver Mini convertible, looking every inch as though it might be his. I see his face from last night, looking across at me in the darkness. *He was drinking*, I tell myself. *It's fine. Just act like nothing happened.* Ash looks good, though. He's wearing a white T-shirt and faded jeans, and with his sun-kissed forehead it all kind of works with the car.

"Is it too much?" he asks, pulling a concerned face.

For a moment I wonder if he's talking about the whole trip. *Is it too much?* Probably. Everyone knows you never go on a road trip as "just friends." I cannot imagine a single film where it didn't end in death or sex. But then I see he's patting the side of the car door and I realize he's talking about the car.

"It's totally adorable," I reply, tossing my pack in the back seat unceremoniously, but then taking some care with my green dress, which I drape across the seat. Then I jump into the passenger side.

"It's Dad's baby, but he let me borrow it," he says.

I pull out my phone and plug it into the stereo. "I hope you don't mind Vivaldi?"

"Vi—what?"

"Vivaldi? I'm trying to expand my classical music repertoire. I recognized a Mozart track on a chocolate advert last night."

"I see," he says, with the very faintest of eye rolls.

As one of the *Four Seasons* blares out of the speakers and we take the coast road toward the motorway, I start to cringe. Ash is smirking as the jaunty music turns more than one head.

"And now we're in a car advert," I say, flicking quickly through my phone again to put us both out of our misery. "Why is all this music in adverts? Way to cheapen the classics, Saatchi and fucking Saatchi."

"Well, no one's going to pay for Beyoncé to help sell a Ford fucking Fiesta."

We both laugh, as Ash takes the A299 on-ramp toward London, the car moving effortlessly around corners and up to speed.

As I dither around, creating the perfect road trip playlist, Ash turns the Vivaldi off in a flash of irritation. "I can't take it anymore," he says. "God help me, can we have something with a guitar in it? I'm just a working-class guy from Kent, for God's sake. Put on Ed Sheeran."

"Sorry," I say, feeling sheepish. "If I'm honest, I'm sort of relieved you turned it off. I've had it up to my tits with Tchaikovsky."

"My balls with Brahms," he says, laughing.

"It's enough to give you a migraine," I say, "but at least I'll have an opinion on it, if Joe comes."

He laughs. "*If* he comes?"

"When," I say firmly.

As the rain threatens, we stop to raise the roof. Then we near Dartford and have to head for the M25, a route that should be very straightforward, but that Ash is turning into a complete catastrophe. The GPS navigation narration should have helped, but Ash seemed to have an innate distrust of it, shouting, "Can you check this is really the turn?" and "Isn't that a one-way?" and "There is no way I'm taking that on-ramp!"

"Why do you not trust the GPS?" I argue, as we round another enormous roundabout and Ash starts to sweat. "Look, we've already been past that McDonald's twice now. Shall we just stop for some nuggets?"

"No," says Ash sharply.

"If you'd just listen to the GPS," I say again.

"You know, Mara, that GPS doesn't think several roads in Broadgate exist. And one time, I had to help fish a Danish tourist out of the sea because he'd followed his GPS down a boat ramp and into the water."

"Oh," I say.

"I'm sure it's accurate in London or whatever, but I don't trust it."

I try not to laugh but I can't help myself. "Ash is afraid of machines. I'm not calling on you when the computers rise up."

"I'll be in Greenland," he snaps.

As we near the midway point and we're just about to stop for refreshments, our conversation has moved on to dating.

"So, you're telling me that you never—*never*—saw anyone after the first date?"

"No. Except Noah. And there weren't that many first dates anyway. My shortest date was thirty-seven minutes, and to be honest I should never have gone. Scorpio with Venus in Gemini."

Ash laughs. "You're a nightmare."

"Well, I just figured that when I saw someone and had one martini or latte, or whatever, I'd know. There would be a feeling or a moment where I would just *know*. But it never really happened again after Noah."

"It doesn't sound like he was really *the one*," Ash says. "He sounds like an asshole."

"He was," I say, "but I was so convinced he was the one. Like, utterly convinced of it. And to be fair, the good stuff was good. We both loved films. I kind of idolized him in a way; he had the upbringing I'd dreamed of. His parents worked in film, so he'd been around it a lot. He was on the set of *GoldenEye* when he was four, for example. You'd have thought he was the director the way he carried on, not a kid in an on-set crèche."

I laugh weakly and Ash gives that tender smile that makes me feel completely *seen*. "The clincher, though, was that his mother had done something on the *Pride and Prejudice* film, and when I found that out, I just thought the universe had put us together."

I tell Ash about the day with my parents and how we stumbled upon the filming and how transfixed I was, that that was the day I knew what I wanted to do with my life. "And I just thought, my *God*. He could have been there on set when I was there watching them. Like it was meant to be."

"Okay, so what was the bad stuff?" Ash asks.

"The bad stuff was kind of less obvious. Like he'd make little comments about what I was doing and I just found myself second-guessing everything."

"Example?"

"One time there was a party and most of our class were going and I sent him a text asking if he wanted to go together and meet there, and he replied, 'Are you coming, then?' It sounds innocuous when I say it, but it would send me into a tailspin. And he knew it. I'd reply, 'Yes, is that okay?' even though it wasn't his party to invite me to. And he'd reply, 'Up to you.' It was so confusing. I'd say to him, 'Why are you being weird?' and he would shrug his stupid narrow shoulders and roll a cigarette and tell me to chill out."

Ash glances across at me. "What the fuck?"

"I was younger then," I say, frowning. "Looking back, I was extremely naïve. I arrived ready to be with my people at last. To be

220

full Mara. Mara Unleashed. And, well . . . in movie terms, I bombed."

Ash laughs. "I bet that's not true."

"Well, I failed, without an internship, and without a boyfriend and made a fool of myself in front of half my year."

"I'm so sorry," Ash says. "Don't you want to try again?"

"I am," I say. "Joe."

"I mean with university," he replies, sighing.

I consider it for a moment. "I'm sure the course is different now. The technology moves so quickly. The theory I'd be okay with. I don't know." I shrug. "It's too late."

"I'm *literally* back at university now and I'm a year older than you," says Ash.

"Yeah, but no offense, you can be an old scientist, but I'm not sure I can be an old film-set intern. It's so complicated. I'd have to start again."

I try to push the picture of eighteen-year-old Mara out of my head. God, I feel sorry for my younger self. I was desperate to find my place and fit in. I threw everything at it until that day I heard the way Noah spoke about me to the professor. And then the cheating. It was a dark year, that following year. Dark and difficult to climb back from. I sometimes feel like only the skin and bones escaped, but my real self is still somewhere in the darkness.

Except I don't feel that way right now.

Lately it's started to grate on me that I left myself behind. Why did I think I couldn't try again? Like Ash is. Why did I let that whole experience completely crush me? I spent that whole decade in London scared of being myself except when I was with Charlie. Scared to try anything new, with anyone new. I'd never imagined a decade could pass where I had done almost nothing. Nothing that I *really* wanted.

"Tell me your story," I say. "Kate?"

"Kate," he repeats with a sigh. "My story is far less interesting, I'm afraid. Six years together. Engagement. Then I told her I wanted to go back to university, and she dumped me."

"Supportive," I say, stunned.

"She wanted to get married and buy a house, and I was like, I'm not ready, I want to be a student again," he says. "I get it. I feel bad. I feel like I wasted her time."

"You're not even a little bit bitter?"

"Sure. In my darkest hours and all that . . . ," he says. "But I feel like I've moved on now."

By noon, we're at a truck stop somewhere near Coventry. Ash is eating a greasy-looking sausage roll, which he claims is "the same temperature as foot fungus," and I am calling Lynn to make sure all the election preparations are done for the weekend.

"Don't say a word," I whisper to Ash as she answers, her tone brisk.

"Samira already told me you were going on a mini-break with Ash," she says, "and I said, for someone who claims to have no life, she has an awful lot of pottery and art classes and mini-breaks."

"Is nothing private—" I begin, but she jumps straight in.

"Then Samira said you were the best help we had on this election and that 'beggars can't be choosers.' Then Ryan said that *beggars can't be choosers* should be your new Tinder bio. He gave us all doughnuts again this morning. Really, he brings in a lot of doughnuts. Samira's favorites too, I notice. I don't want to gossip, but do you get the feeling that those two—"

"Yes," I say, interrupting. "But let's not say it out loud and make it a thing until they're ready."

"Just when I thought you were fitting in," she says wistfully.

"I'll be back on Monday. And don't forget to talk to Gerry. I mean it!"

"Yes, yes," she says. "Fine, fine."

I hang up and look at Ash, who is trying to remove the film of grease on his face and fingers with a tiny paper towel.

"Was it worth it?" I ask.

"Hell yes," he says.

I tip the last of my coffee into my mouth and then lean forward, lowering my voice. "I actually really like my workmates," I say. "They've grown on me. When I first arrived, I thought I would have nothing in common with any of them. And as it turns out, I like them. All three of them."

"You seem to be settling in," he says, pulling back the tab on his Coke, which makes that refreshing hiss. "I've noticed a change, at least. You hardly spoke that first night we hung out. And now you don't shut up."

He's teasing, and I return his wry, cheeky smile, eyes sending the message that I will seek revenge at some point. If I could shove him over from across this Formica table I would. I picture it, pushing him to the ground and then engaging in a playful wrestling match that is just a front for the hard-to-ignore sexual tension that is building between us. It's becoming a problem. The skinny-dipping night was so tantalizingly close to crossing some kind of line, and I am grateful that it didn't.

"Yeah, I am settling in," I say, shaking the image from my mind. "I love their directness. It's so refreshing. My friend Charlie, since she got married, she's been so hard to read. And now that she has Alex and the baby, I've started second-guessing her. I hate it."

"Maybe she's struggling," Ash says, tipping the last of his Coke down his throat.

"Who?"

"Your friend Charlie," he says. "My sister really struggled with loneliness and isolation when she had her baby. She took medication for it."

"Oh," I say. "I don't think so. Not Charlie. She's never been short on friends. She has mummy groups and all sorts of weird baby activities she's always going to with her new friend Ella or Bella or Stella or Daniella."

But as I'm saying it, I think about our exchange this morning. Did she want to talk? As in *talk*?

"My sister put on a pretty brave face too," he says, shrugging. "Don't underestimate how hard it can be is all I'm saying, Mara."

"All right, Mum," I say, rolling my eyes, trying to ignore a niggling worry about Charlie.

"Are we going to talk about that?" he says.

"What?" I say absently, my mind still on Charlie.

"Your parents. Your dad. Your mum. Your brother? Any of it? I'd like to know what I'm walking into."

"Sure. I mean. Okay."

It's my turn to drive, and I slide into the driver's seat while Ash directs me toward the motorway on-ramp with a lazy wave of his hand.

"There," he says.

"Can you give me more bloody notice?" I say, turning too swiftly and nearly taking out a traffic cone. "I need clear, precise instructions. Like the satnav."

He nods and fixes the satnav to the hands-free mount.

"Stay on the M11 for one hundred sixty-nine miles," says the satnav lady.

"A hundred and sixty-nine miles? At least you won't need directions anytime soon," says Ash, sinking back into his seat.

I grin as I squeeze the accelerator and it responds with a powerful purr and eases quickly forward. "The thing about my car is that it doesn't really break fifty. This is literally the fastest I've driven. You might die."

After a minute or so of him watching me like an eagle, hands gripping the seat as I overtake a car, he begins to relax.

"So, about your parents?"

"Oh boy," I say. "Well, you should know that they are very nice and they will love you. My dad especially because you have a *real* job. And my mum because she's never seen me with a boy, even if she knows you're my flatmate."

"So why are you so nervous about seeing them? That all sounds normal to me."

"Arghhhh," I say. "I don't know. Ash, I left home a bit of an asshole. I thought I was going to be somebody. I was a total country mouse heading for the big city. Like Christina Aguilera in *Burlesque* or something. I was going to make it in . . . *Hollywood*. But, you know, Pinewood, because it's England."

"Uh-ha," Ash says, looking down at my hand on the gearshift. The feel of his stare makes me feel the need to flex my fingers, so I do.

"And then I *failed*. I just hate seeing them. It reminds me of all the big dreams I had, how hard I fought for them to happen. And how they didn't."

"I'm sure they don't judge you," he says. "My parents were kind of relieved when I came back from Cambridge. I mean, don't get me wrong, they bragged to the whole town when I went, but then they bragged that I missed home even more." He laughs at the memory, which I find crushingly tender, and I'm surprised to feel longing for the same relationship with my mother.

"Maybe," I say. "The problem is, I've not really been honest with them about how bad it was."

"But they know you didn't pass or whatever?" he says.

"Um . . . not exactly," I say, side-eying him in abject humiliation.

"Oh boy," says Ash. "Well, I'll just nod along and do whatever you need me to do, okay?"

He reaches across and puts his hand on my thigh, patting it slightly, and it distracts me so much, the car juts hard to the right.

21

~~~

S IX HOURS AND thirty-five minutes after we left Broadgate, we turn onto my street.

The house I grew up in is on a postwar terraced street. Someone had the foresight to plant trees, but not to make room for car parking, so there is a constant planning battle with those who want to preserve fifty-year-old silver birch and those who want room for their second car.

The Mini inches slowly up the road, and I sneak a look at Ash, his hair blowing now in the cool northern wind and his Ray-Bans pushed up on his forehead. He looks cool. Hot, even. Maybe bringing him was a stroke of genius after all.

"Look, a sign," says Ash, pointing at an A4 page stuck to the garage door of the neighbor. "It says RESERVED 4 MARA. That's sweet." *It is*, I think, but don't say it.

"My old bedroom," I say, as I stop the car and point to the

top-floor bedroom window, the garish purple curtains still drawn. I get a visceral wave of déjà vu as I see them.

OPEN YOUR BLOODY CURTAINS AND COME AND JOIN US FOR DINNER, MARA would be etched onto my mother's gravestone, I swear to God.

"We so should have got the train," I say, as we pull up and stop. I stretch my legs as much as I can in the cramped space and rub at my sore back.

"Agreed," he says. "I want a nana nap."

"Same. But game face on, okay? Heads down, polite hellos, then tomorrow we leave. Okay, you have to look away while I put this new dress on," I say.

"New dress?" he says, looking down at his own outfit.

"You look fine," I say quickly. "The outfit is my armor, if you know what I mean."

"It's going to be fine, Mara," he says. "They're your parents. They sound normal and like they love you, no matter what."

"I'm not telling them anything, okay? We don't go into details," I say, feeling my cheeks burn red.

"Okay, okay," he says. "Like I said, I'll do whatever you want."

"Good. Otherwise they'll do the thing they do all the time."

"What thing?"

"Are you sure you're happy, Mara?" I say with a shrug.

"You're not happy?" he asks.

I consider this. Ordinarily I would have said no, but lately . . . "I guess I am kind of happy?" I say. "Maybe? For the first time in ages, I don't feel *unhappy*."

I hand him a T-shirt to hold up as a screen between us, and then wriggle out of my shirt and jeans, changing into the push-up bra.

I hear Ash clear his throat slightly, and I quickly pull the green silk over my head.

"Nothing you haven't already seen," I quip, but when Ash doesn't reply, the comment feels heavy and loaded.

I touch up my makeup and redo the red lip in the exact way that Samira showed me: pencil first, fill it in later.

I look down at the beautiful vintage silk and then pull on the strappy sandals. Finally, I grab the trench Jackie gave me.

Then, while Ash is still waiting behind the T-shirt, I slide out of the car.

"You can look now," I say.

He drops the T-shirt without looking up and climbs out of the car, rounds the back, opens the boot, and grabs his overnight bag. Then he looks up at me, stopping in his place.

I do a little curtsy and then a twirl, and he stares at me like I've reached inside and squeezed his heart with my bare hands.

"Okay, we're good to go in," I say, looking to the door.

"It's going to be fine."

"I don't feel fine. I don't feel happy," I say. "I feel nervous as hell."

"My mum says happiness is a journey, not a destination."

"Not this journey. This journey is going to be excruciating." I jut my thumb toward the front door so he's sure I mean the seeing-my-parents part of this journey, and not the traveling-with-Ash part.

He stops just before we get to the door and turns to me. "Anything I need to know before we ring the bell?"

"What do you mean?"

"I don't know. Homophobic aunt. Sleazy uncle. Aggressive brother?"

"No, no," I say, shaking my head. "Everything behind this door is painfully average. You'll see."

"Jesus, Mara," Ash says, frowning at me.

"Sorry," I say, tugging on my trench coat. "It's how I feel. Or felt. I'm not sure how I feel. I honestly hardly see them anymore. You'll see," I say, flapping about with my hair again. "What am I projecting with this look? Does it say *successful and together woman?*"

He moves his whole mouth to one side and then looks at the garage door. "Honestly?"

"Honestly," I reply, wanting him to lie, obviously.

"You look incredible," he says, turning to the door and knocking three times.

Mum throws open the door and looks like she might burst into tears when she claps eyes on me, and I feel claustrophobic almost instantly. Then she leans forward and gives me a half hug, with some awkward back patting, as I side-eye Ash.

"Mara. Look at you," she says, pulling back. Her eyes dart from my eyes to my red lips, to the trench with the skirt of the dress poking through. Then she looks at the shoes. "You look so different. So grown-up. I barely recognized you. Look at your hair! You've finally cut it! Her brother used to call her Cousin It," she explains to Ash, and then covers her mouth and says, "Whoops." The first embarrassment.

"Nice to meet you, Mrs. Williams. I'm Mara's flatmate, Ash," he says, and I mutter apologies for not introducing them.

"Oh, it's Elaine, darling," she says, beaming at him. "Is that your car?"

"It's hardly going to be mine, is it?" I mutter, and Mum does that uncomfortable laugh she always does when we're in company and *I* embarrass *her.*

"Oh, Mara," she says, looking between me and Ash, her cheeks turning red, "you're so funny."

Mum looks different. Thinner. And her long hair is pinned back in an elaborate plaited bun. We have the same hair color, the same eyes, the same round face, and while I feel my chubby cheeks make me look immature and girlish, they keep mum looking utterly youthful. "Well. It's wonderful that you're here. Come in, come in."

We both take a tentative step in the door. Ash looks around, and I am watching everything through his eyes. One of the things about having a builder for a father is that every damn thing in our house is custom-made. From the TV stand to the dining table, every single piece of furniture—except for the sofa—has been built, altered, or at the very least installed by my dad. The only problem is that Dad has no cohesive style. So whereas there is some quite nice delicate woodwork around the kitchen island, it is totally overwhelmed by the hefty wooden cabinets he made from scratch using someone's old staircase.

I dreamed so hard of having an IKEA dresser when I was fifteen.

"I like that," Ash says, pointing to the pergola in the garden that Dad made when we were kids.

"Sure, because what this mid-century terrace house in Northumberland needs is a Spanish-style pergola," I mutter to him. "But yes, it's gorgeous. My cousin got married under it."

Dad strolls over, tall and strapping, kisses me on the forehead, and shakes Ash's hand with his thick workman's fingers. He's got skinny jeans on. The kind that funnel too tightly up his body and explode into a massive paunch and broad shoulders, giving him the look of an inverted triangle.

"A builder?" Dad says, nodding in approval. "Good honest work, that."

"He's not *just* a builder," I interrupt, and then, when I see Dad's crushed expression, I quickly clarify, "I mean he's not *only* a builder. It's not the only thing he does."

"You know, before Mara got fed up with me, she had a real thing about builders," my dad is now saying.

"What are you talking about?" I snap, and feel a gentle press on my arm from Ash. Telling me not to worry, I suppose. To let him go on.

Then my mother says, "Oh, they're just flatmates, Neil. You've got that new boyfriend now anyway, don't you, Mara? The one from Europe?"

"Vienna," says Ash without skipping a beat. "He's a cellist."

I feel my cheeks redden. The first lie. Ash knows very well that Joe is not my boyfriend.

"Yes." Mum nods, a sort of veil of relief washing across her face, which I am sure is because someone has confirmed it as not being the fantasy it actually is. I look over at Ash and mouth *thank you.* And he raises a shoulder like it's no problem at all.

The barbecue is set up in the garden. Everywhere, Dad's and Mum's friends—most of whom I've known since I was a kid—are drinking under bunting and silver balloons. Someone has made one of those rectangle frosted cakes with Mum's face on it. M&S party food is laid out across two trestle tables. Two young girls are playing a dancing game on my old Nintendo Wii. An elderly neighbor watches on from the TV armchair, sipping on tea from Mum's best china. Every time I look over at Ash, he seems a mixture of delighted and amused.

"Shall I introduce you to my brother?" I ask. "May as well get that out of the way."

"Yeah," he says. "Also, if you don't mind, I'd like a drink."

"Shit, sorry," I say, motioning with my head to the chiller filled with beer, wine, and plenty of vodka. Once we're *with drink*, I take Ash over to see my brother, Ben, who is gesticulating wildly at a group of people—his audience—while his wife watches on with pride. I get a wave of joy when I see him. My big brother.

"My brother is very much your salt-of-the-earth northerner. Very straight down the line," I whisper to Ash. And then I take a deep breath. "Hi, Ben!"

Ben spins around and beams at me, throwing his arms around me and tugging me in for a hug. He smells of beer and sweat and Lynx Africa. "Mara! The prodigal daughter returns. How's things in the Big Smoke? Oh, wait. Didn't you move to Brighton?"

"Broadgate," I say.

"You look . . . different," he says. "Nice to meet you. You're the flatmate, right?"

Ash nods and they shake hands. "Ash," he says. I watch with curiosity as Ben looks Ash up and down, apparently confused that this normal-looking guy would be on a weekend away with his kooky sister. I find myself moving slightly closer to Ash, as if he provides some kind of force field against Ben and his presumptions about me.

"So, what's been going on, Mara?" Ben says. "We've not seen each other since Aunt Jenny's funeral. Bloody hopeless, aren't we?"

I nod. "Not much. Working. I went on holiday to Hungary."

"Mum says you're working at an art gallery or something? Mum!" he shouts out across the deck. "Where did you say Mara was working?"

"A museum or an art gallery," she says, raising her hands as if it's some kind of mystery.

I feel the heat creeping up my neck as I send aggressive *do not blow my cover* messages to Ash.

"Well, it's just a council-run property on the coast, really. Nothing fancy. It's more of a community center," I say, stammering, as I feel the weight of Ash's confusion radiating from him.

"It's a gem," Ash chimes in, before swiftly changing the subject. "We're going to take a drive up to Hadrian's Wall, and maybe see Holy Island on the way back. But I really came to see the dark park."

I want to hug him for changing the subject.

"I'm ashamed to say I've not been in ages," Ben says. "Dad says he's waiting for grandkids to resume the camping trips. Remember our trips, Mara? You were always spotting shit that wasn't there. So cute."

I groan and avert my eyes from his teasing grin.

Dad arrives with the face cake of my mother sliced up into finger-size pieces. I grab a piece and feel slightly weird seeing a single brown fondant left eye beaming up at me.

"An eye," I say.

"I can't believe you're eating my mother," Ben says to Ash as he tosses a slice into his mouth, and Ash almost gags.

"Just messing with you, bro," says Ben.

"Oh my God, Ben! Don't be gross," I say, hitting him on the arm. "Come on, Ash, I'll show you my room."

But it takes a good hour to get there. There are aunts to hug, kids to cuddle, and Dad hovering around interjecting every five minutes to say things like, "No, you're not hallucinating, Mara's finally home! Can you believe it? Doesn't she look like a princess? Whatever happened to that job you got at the film studio?"

I finally lead Ash upstairs into my room, which has been kept exactly as it was when I left. I get a pang of nostalgia when I see the posters on my walls. *Juno* on one wall. *Little Miss Sunshine* on another. A corkboard with a hundred cinema ticket stubs. My school desk still has my landline, and even my first iPhone is sitting in a little cup with various pencils and pens. I pick up a notebook from my bookcase and flick through it, cringing at the seriousness of my ramblings.

"Good God, I have not changed," I say, laughing. "Look at these quotes I've written, all from movies."

I hold up one particularly intricate one, the words delicately sketched with lacy lettering.

"What does it say?" Ash asks. "I can't make it out."

"Life is not a series of coincidences, but rather, it's a myriad of events that culminate in one perfect plan. It's fate."

"Is that like Buddhism or something?" Ash says.

"Nothing that profound. It's the message of the movie *Serendipity*."

Ash looks at me and kind of cough-laughs.

"I loved it," I say.

"I can imagine," he replies, grinning.

"I have believed so hard in romantic destiny since forever," I say. "Don't look at me like that. I'm not ashamed to believe in romantic destiny. All the great romantics do it. Imagine *not* believing in it. Now, there's a life so void of magic I wouldn't even want to be part of it."

I laugh uncomfortably, tossing the notebook on my desk and turning to the room setup. Mum has made Ash a pullout mattress on the floor with her "good linen."

I turn to Ash and ask him if we can leave.

"Leave? Feels like we've only just arrived."

"We've mingled," I say flatly.

"Why?" he asks, putting his overnight bag down on the floor.

He looks at me, and although he doesn't mention the lying about the job and exaggerating the boyfriend, I know he's thinking about it. He's studying me.

"What is it?" he asks.

"I only lie to them because it keeps them off my back," I say, shrugging. "If they think I'm struggling it will be a nightmare."

"We've all embellished shit to our parents," he says, shrugging.

"I wonder sometimes if I've let it go so long there is no way back," I say now, feeling a momentary sting of tears.

"Of course there is. Family is family, Mara. Go have a gin with your mum and take the piss out of your brother. That's how it works."

"I just feel so uncomfortable," I say. "I don't know how to connect with them anymore."

"Effort," he says now. "Your mum seems super nice. She seems kind of nervous of you, to be honest. Like she's walking on eggshells," he says, peeling his T-shirt off and changing it for a fresh one. I feel myself start to tense up at that flash of skin. For a moment, I feel the pull toward him, a desire to be drawn into his arms. A distraction.

"I know," I say, plonking down on the bed, brushing my fringe back out of my eyes. "I revert back into an angsty teenager around her."

"You need to get over it," Ash says, and then he sits on the edge of my bed and touches the thin cotton of my bedspread. "I pretended I was happy to give up studying for years around my parents. It took a long time to build up the courage to tell them the truth. And, you know, they were great. I really think parents just want you to be happy."

"Exactly," I say. "*We just want you to be happy, Mara.*' Only I think their version of happy is living in Corbridge and working at a travel agency and marrying one of Dad's employees. No offense."

"Tell them about the lido that you're working on saving. Tell them about the amazing floating cinema night, and how you made the place more than three grand in one night. All the stuff you're doing is really cool," he says.

I consider it for a moment. But then the thought of a heart-to-heart with my mother fills me with shame and dread.

"No. Please, let's go. Like, let's go for an hour or so; then we can come back."

"Now?"

"Yes, now. Let's go to the dark park."

"Won't they be pissed off?"

"There's plenty of people down there. I've done my bit. I drove all day to be here." I pull off my shoes and toss them under my bed and fish around in my bag for my sneakers.

"Are you sure, sure?" he says. "We've come all this way."

"Now," I say, feeling tears start to come.

"I've got a head torch," he says.

"You've got a head torch?"

"Yes."

"A head torch?"

"Yes."

"Okay, well, let's go."

22

⁓

WE PARK AND walk along a well-worn little pathway toward Hadrian's Wall. "There it is," I whisper, as we can just make out the edges of the ancient stone wall that stretches ahead of us in the near darkness. "Mind your feet."

There is very little sound, except for the gentle breeze rustling some nearby trees that we can't see, and the occasional hoot of a night bird.

"I used to come here badger watching with my dad," I say. "You'd need a little moon, though. We'd come and we'd pitch a tent and stay up all night watching badgers and field mice."

It was one of my purer childhood memories. A time filled with Twix bars and baked beans cold from tins and flasks of hot milky tea.

"Your dad seems really nice," Ash says, turning, his head torch shining right into my face.

"Careful. It's like looking into the sun," I say. "Can you just point it ahead?"

"Sorry," he says, as I rub my eyes and wait for them to readjust.

"You really can't see much of the wall at night."

"Waxing moon," he says, looking at the slither of crescent in the sky, low on the horizon.

"You mean waning," I reply.

"Yes," he replies, with a sort of embarrassed chuckle. "Of course. New moon is in two days."

He turns to me again, this time switching his head torch downward as he looks across into the darkness. Suddenly, he leaps up on top of the stone wall and reaches his hand down to me, heaving me up to join him. I throw down the heavy blanket I'm holding and he stretches it out across the wall.

"So, you know about badger watching," he says, as I sit myself down a little too close to him. "Do you know about the wall?"

"Yes. It was the edge of the Roman Empire. Some say that Hadrian had enough of dealing with the north, so he just built a wall to keep them out. It ran from coast to coast, with little stations along the route. There are a ton of Roman ruins around here. Corbridge town was apparently bustling in its time," I say.

"Why are you whispering?" he says.

"I'm not sure," I reply, speaking normally. "Because it's dark?"

"It's amazing how intact it still is for two thousand years old."

"Used to be much higher, though. Not like *Game of Thrones* the wall high, but a bit higher than this," I say. "Did you know that the *Robin Hood* scene with Kevin Costner and Morgan Freeman was filmed about forty-five minutes in that direction? We could visit tomorrow."

"With a picnic. It's going to be hot tomorrow," Ash says, "like seventy-three degrees hot. That's hot for these parts, right?"

"Fuck off," I say, laughing, "but yes. God, it's literally the worst time to visit for stargazing, though. See how it's not totally dark over there? Like dark purples and midnight blues. We should come back in winter, when the skies are the most clear and dark."

"I'd be up for that," he says.

I hand him the half bottle of vodka I'd stashed in my jacket on the way out the door. "Can you turn that bloody head torch off?"

He flicks a switch and the bright light changes to red. He removes the head torch and lays it down on the wall next to me, and we are bathed in a red glow, which makes everything more visible as our eyes adjust. Ash takes a swig. It's eerie here, but to me it is so familiar. The rustle of the brush. The echoing silences on a still night. I get a flash of my brother and my dad, and those cold nights stargazing and badger watching come rushing back into every sense. The heat of tea in my hands. The orange glow from the fire embers. The long wait for badgers in the field. My dad and my brother with the star map out, fighting over which bright dot in the sky was Jupiter. I would wake up early in the morning, my sleeping bag zipped around me, having fallen asleep before my big brother and my dad. The memory is comforting, and I long suddenly for those days. That feeling of protection and love. I miss it. Deeply.

"We won't be able to drive back if we have too much," he says, expertly tossing the bottle onto the soft grass below us.

"Yes, Officer," I reply, a little flirtatiously, and I feel his gaze turn from me toward the darkness. I try to remind myself not to encourage him, but I cannot stop the pull toward him that I'm feeling. That giddy feeling of being desired, and if I were to admit it, my desire for him.

I breathe slowly out. I *do* desire him.

Ash zips up his jacket and lies along the wall so he's looking up. The top of his head is inches from my thighs, and I do not dare to join him lying down. Every movement close to him feels like an invitation.

"Aren't they wondrous," he says.

"Wondrous?" He can be so earnest.

"Amazing," he corrects himself, and I can almost feel the blush radiating from him.

"They are. Amazing *and* wondrous," I say. "Do you think you'll try to be an astronaut or . . . like, what are the jobs you can do with the degree anyway?"

"I think that spaceship has sailed, Mara. But yeah, I mean, I'm not really thinking past whether I pass or not. The stars. The planets. Dark matter. Black holes. Theoretical and numerical cosmology in the pre- and post-recombination universe. Well, that last bit is if I do a postgrad cosmology course."

"Nerd," I say teasingly.

"Weirdo," he replies.

"It's very inspiring, what you're doing," I say. "It's on my mind, the idea of going back to study."

"You totally should. I know you think it's too late, but why is it? Because you're supposed to know what you want to do with it?" he says. "I want to just do this quietly, on my own, and see if I can do it. Finish it, you know? Maybe I'll just stick the degree on the wall in the toilet and grin every time I walk in there. I like my day job too. I can't see myself giving that up."

I stare up at the stars again.

"Okay, this sky is probably too light to see Andromeda, but I reckon we can still see a lot," he says. "I'll be right back."

He disappears into the darkness and I hear the car boot open, and the sound of something heavy being heaved out. Then I hear his footsteps crunching on the ground as he heads back to me.

"Is that a telescope?"

He laughs. "I can't think what else it could be. I borrowed it," he says, putting a huge tripod down on the ground.

I watch in the red light of the head torch as he sets up the tripod and then carefully lifts a telescope out of its protective casing. The whole thing is about the length and breadth of a trumpet, with a glass end about as large too. He sets it carefully into the tripod and fixes some screws before grinning.

"Eight-inch aperture for a guaranteed view of deep space," he says. "You want to see Polaris?" He presses on his watch, which lights up momentarily. "I think we might just make it."

A few moments later, he whispers, "Mara, come. Look."

I jump down from the wall and I crouch down and look in the viewer.

"Jeez, it's so bright. Amazing," I say. "Polaris? The North Star?"

"Yes," he says. "The guiding light. It holds almost perfectly still while the rest of the sky moves around it in a circle."

"I know," I say, nudging him with my hip. "You do know that someone who follows astrology properly knows about the night sky, right?"

"I'm learning," he says.

"What else can I see? Can you show me Saturn?"

I feel him gently push me aside, and then with expert movements he swings the telescope and moves it around slowly. "Should be around here, but not quite visible."

He pushes it back to me and I gaze through it. I look for the fuzzy plate, but can't make anything out. "Well, it is one-point-four billion kilometers away."

"So, what, like five miles?" I feel his breath on my neck as he laughs. I move my shoulder to try to rid myself of the feeling of tingling that remains where his breath was. He moves forward to adjust something on the lens, and then I feel his arms pressing into my sides. I resist the urge to lean into him. "Did you know there are more stars in the sky than grains of sand on every beach on earth?"

"Carl Sagan," Ash says.

"Yep. It was coming here camping that got me interested in the stars, actually. My dad had a way of explaining it so that everything felt so expansive and so possible. There is something so grounding about feeling yourself on a rock, hurtling through space. So insignificant and yet so significant. So much to think and wonder about."

"I agree," he says, and his hand comes to mine as he moves the telescope gently upward. "Sagittarius, right?"

I peer in and see my constellation. I know it so well, but I've never seen it like this. Ash is even closer now, and I can feel the hairs on my arms standing on end. I'm almost willing him to cross that line.

"Wow, that just makes me want to log on and check my daily horoscope," I say, and I hear a very faint sigh from him. "I'm kidding. Christ. Show me more."

"And that's Hercules," he says, becoming animated, his voice lifting. He's pointing over to the three stars in a row, almost dead center in the night sky.

"We have to come back in winter," he says with wonder. "It's really such a magic spot for stargazing. I wish we had something like this in Broadgate, but it's getting more and more difficult with the light pollution. And there isn't a decent telescope anywhere."

"You should build one. You could be Broadgate's weird star guy."

"I wish," he says. "When I'm finished studying and shot of my student loan, it'll be first thing on my list to get a telescope." He steps back from the telescope and looks up. "You know what? I may not have faith, but this is totally my church."

"It's mine too," I say.

"I just don't know why anyone has to fill in the gaps of life with made-up stories and magic when all of this is right here. Provable. Calculable. Endlessly explorable. And, you know, completely *fucking majestic*. I look up and see all the answers I need."

"I look up and see questions," I say. And then, as I feel the wooziness of the booze and the heat of his body next to me, I find I'm unable to stop pushing him. "Why are you here, Ash? On this trip with me?"

"I said. I had some time. I had some holiday. I needed a break," he says.

"And?" I ask, almost willing him to say that he has feelings about me. I want him too. In this moment, I want him.

"I was worried about you, I suppose."

"Why?" I say, almost egging him on.

"Well, if we're sharing honestly . . ."

"We are," I assure him.

Ash suddenly moves back from me. Like something has occurred to him. Like something has changed. "It's very cold, Mara. We should probably get back soon."

"Is there something wrong?"

"No. Nothing. I just . . ." Ash's voice trails off into the darkness, along with his thoughts.

"I'm glad you came," I say, putting my hand on his shoulder. "You were very kind to come." He stares at the hand on his shoulder. And then at the telescope and then back to me.

Ash turns his head, and in the red glow his eyes look dark. Fierce even. I smile at him and the invitation is enough. He leans in and touches the side of my face with his hand. I feel my knees go weak, and I have to lean back against the wall to steady myself. He closes his eyes and breathes out. Then he leans into me and pauses, his lips hovering just apart from mine. An inch. Then a little less. And then he brushes my mouth with his.

A small moan escapes me, and he kisses me harder. Hungrily.

I let him kiss my neck. I feel the warmth of his lips and the soft touch of his tongue as he trails down until it hits the collar of my jacket. His move is aching. Desperate even, and I revel in the sensation. I lean my head back, a further invitation, and he pushes himself between my legs and runs his hands through my hair, dotting light kisses across my cheek.

"Mara," he says breathlessly. I feel the whisper of my name wrap around me, and I unzip his coat, running my hands up the soft skin under his T-shirt. I feel his muscles flex at my touch. I curl my fingers into his lower back and feel him arch. I feel powerful. Sexy.

"Mara," he says again, and I move my lips to his ear, whispering, "Yes." Ash pulls me closer, pushing himself into me, his hands moving across my chest now, his palms rubbing against my nipples, hard under my jacket. He pulls my jacket open roughly, touches the soft silk of my dress gently at first, and then he searches for a way inside.

His thighs are huge between my legs, and I squeeze mine shut now, another soft moan escaping me. He finds the hem of my skirt and gently moves it up, the silk bunching in his hands, his fingers softly trailing along my thigh.

"Yes," I reply, and before I have time to think, his hand is against my bare skin, inches away from my underwear.

"I adore you," he says.

I feel myself stiffen slightly, a sign Ash takes as a further cue of my pleasure, and he kisses my mouth again, one hand in my hair, tugging back slightly, and the other slowly inching upward again. As he gets closer I feel myself start to question this. It's Ash. My flatmate.

He pulls back, staring into my eyes, looking, I think, for a moment's reassurance. He moves his hand from my thigh now, letting the almost weightless fabric fall. He brings his hand to my cheek and runs a thumb across it. "Still there?" he says.

"Umm . . . yes," I reply, tugging my dress back in place and leaning slightly back.

"I like you," he says.

"I know," I say again. I don't know what else to say, but I want him to stop talking now. He does, briefly, because he kisses me so lightly on the lips and looks down to my hand, which is curled around his.

We stand like that in the darkness a moment longer, and then he whispers, "You don't feel the same, though, do you?"

I do. I really do. But this is not the plan. This is not what I'm supposed to be doing. Joe is so close. He's weeks away. "I have to stick to my plan. I've come so far. I have to see if—"

He groans as if he knows what's coming, and I wish there was another reason I could give him.

"It's just . . . Joe," I say. "I have to see if he comes. I mean, what if he comes and you and I are . . . *something*."

"Joe," he says, and it comes out hard. "Mara, you don't even know him. *Anything* about him. You've never actually met him properly."

"I can't explain it if you don't want to understand," I say, pulling back slightly more, enough now that he does, too, and stands awkwardly in the red light, arms folded. "You weren't there. I saw all the signs one after another. I know he's coming. I have to wait. I have to see this through or . . ."

"Or what?"

"I could miss it. My one and only chance."

"Right. Sure," he says, standing farther back now. He's upset. "You want me to wait?"

"No. I didn't mean that. Shit," I say. "I would never ask that. God no. But, Ash, I can't . . ."

"Okay. Okay. Fine. I get it," he says, waving his hands in front of his face now. "I got this totally wrong," he mutters. "Sorry."

He turns, but there is nowhere to go, except together. I am suddenly in a panic. I feel a taut pull, like a rope between Ash and me is about to snap, and I desperately don't want it to.

"Hey, Ash," I say. "I'm so sorry. I'm really confused. I need to think." He fishes into his coat for the keys.

"Let's go," he says.

23

~~~

WE WANDER BACK in, sheepishly, to find the lights on full and my mother sitting at the kitchen counter with a cup of tea. I wonder how long we were gone. Was it hours? It seemed like hours. And I'm quite drunk, having drowned the tension in the twenty-minute car ride back with vodka as Ash drove in awkward silence.

"Mara. Finally," she says, raising her teacup like it's filled with gin. "You're back at the party."

"Mum, what happened? Where is everyone?"

She turns to me, and I can see her eyes are red, puffy. She's been crying.

"Mum!" I say, rushing forward to her, reaching out my arms, then awkwardly not knowing where to put them when I get there. Hugging my mother is not a natural act for either of us. "What's happened?"

"Nothing's happened; the party is over; everyone has gone. And once again, Mara was nowhere to be found."

I can feel Ash shifting uncomfortably behind me as she speaks.

"Oh, Mum, sorry. We just went for a drive, to see the, um, the dark park, and then we kind of . . . well, the time . . ." I slip my phone out of my pocket and see several missed calls, some from Ben, some from Mum, and the time is nearly midnight. "Fuck," I say quietly.

"Your brother announced they are pregnant. You're going to be an aunt," she said.

"I'm going to be an aunt?" I feel genuinely thrilled at the notion. I look back at Ash and smile, biting my lip. An *auntie*.

"Yes, and it would have been nice for you to be here for that," my mother says. And then she starts crying again, clutching a scrawny tissue to her face, a guttural moan escaping from her. "What did I do, Mara? What did I get so wrong? It feels like you hate me. I can't bear it."

"I don't hate you," I say, shaking my head.

"All I do is worry about you."

I stare at her for a moment. This is the depth of the failure she feels when she sees me.

"I think about you all the time. Are you happy? Do you have friends besides Charlie? Do you have a local pub? Who are your work friends? I don't know anything. I'm not in your life." Her voice cracks again, and I look out the window, ashamed.

"It's not that strange for kids to leave home and go and make their own life, Mum. My friend Charlie has never gone back to North Yorkshire."

"I don't even really know Charlie," my mother says pitifully.

"You look so beautiful tonight, Mara. So radiant. So happy, for the first time in so long, and I'm no part of it."

"Please stop worrying," I say, trying to be light now. Upbeat. Trying to convince her there is nothing going on here. "I'm getting my shit together. I'm making friends," I say, nodding toward Ash, who I think—right now—hates me. My mother doesn't say anything at this, so I continue. "I'm dating."

"Oh, are we talking about this man you met?" my mother says, shooting me a look of cold disbelief. Too worn-out, too upset to play the game of pretending to believe my stories anymore.

"Does she even work at an art gallery?" She addresses this to Ash.

He stands, stunned for a moment, and then looks to me and back to my mum.

"Yes," we both say at the same time. Ash's answer is firm, but mine is strangled, humiliated.

Shamed, my eyes flicker up at her, then at Ash. They are now bonded by me. Not a love of me, but a *knowing* of me.

"Mum, I'm doing well. It's lovely in Broadgate. I'm sorry. I'm really sorry," I say, and I feel the tears coming to me now and I work hard to keep them at bay. I glance back at Ash, who has a look of intense pity on his face, and I look away again. Then at the floor. Should I just tell her how it all went wrong? How I'm so embarrassed and ashamed? How I just want to clear up the last ten years and start again?

Then the sadness turns to anger at myself. A simmering, bubbling anger. A surge of it so strong I want to smash something. I turn, fish a large black garbage bag out of the drawer, and begin to toss things into it. A paper plate. A deflated baby blue balloon, with a hole in it where someone sucked out the helium to the delight of their audience. The crusts of several quiches hidden under a paper cup with some alcohol-soaked soggy fruit festering at the bottom. I clean quickly, angrily. I am doing it as an act of revenge.

"This is why I don't come home! You guys make me feel like such a failure," I say, picking up an empty vodka bottle, surveying it first with the aim to finish the dregs, but they're gone.

Mum flinches as I toss glass bottles in and they clang loudly together—not smashing, I don't want them to smash, but I want to hear the sound that they might. "No one thinks that, Mara. We just want to know you again."

"Mara," Ash says quietly, edging toward me, "maybe a little less ferocious cleaning."

He turns to me, takes the Heineken bottle out of my hand, and places it into a carboard box, stacking them neatly for recycling. Of course he's helping.

I am humiliated. Two worlds have collided in the most embarrassing way. He who desired me can now see the truth.

Mara Williams. *Never enough.* That's what should be on my goddamn Tinder profile.

Mum watches us for a while, and then, her tears dried, she walks past us both and heads upstairs to her room.

An hour later and in almost complete silence, we are done. Ash follows me up the stairs and into my bedroom. I have nothing for him. I want him out of my bedroom and out of my flat.

"You can still sleep on the pullout. If you actually want to."

"Mate," he says, sitting on the edge of the bed, his head in his hands. He's never called me *mate*. "Mara," he whispers.

"Yes?" I say, holding out the wardrobe door so I can change behind it in privacy.

"What just happened?"

"Well. Welcome to me, Ash. Not so attractive now, am I?"

He sighs, not looking up. "Forget that. Just . . . it's fine. Forget it. But I feel . . . bad for you. You missed your brother's baby announcement. You're going to be an auntie. I mean, isn't that great? We came all the way here and had, like, two hours with your family. I feel somehow responsible too."

I pull my pajama top over my head and tug on my bottoms in silence. I don't want to answer him. Then I emerge from behind the door of the wardrobe and look at my face in the mirror. "It's nothing to do with you," I say finally. "I mean, forget it. You're just my flatmate who gave me a ride here, really."

I hear him suck in a sharp breath.

"I need to do all of this on my own. It was dumb to accept your help. Unfair of me," I say. And it was. What was I thinking bringing him up here? I knew that there was something brewing between us. I knew it and I encouraged it. And now I must squash it because Ash is a really fucking nice, good, kind person, and there is no way I should have ever led him on like this.

"Okay, sure," he says, finally looking up at me. "Sure. Let's get some sleep and head back in the morning, then."

"Great."

He pulls his pj's and soap bag out of his backpack and asks where the toilet is. I climb into bed and pretend to be asleep when he returns. I only realize how hard I'm crying when I move my face slightly and feel the damp of the pillow underneath me.

The silence between us is thick and loaded. I lie there, tossing and turning and waiting for my mind to stop racing.

I can hear Ash's breath slow next to me. I listen to it for a moment, in, and out. Slower. Then it disappears almost completely and he's asleep.

24

A RE YOU AWAKE?" I whisper loudly.

I hear him moan. "I am now, Mara."

He rubs his eyes and I enjoy watching the ruggedness of him as he runs his hands through his hair and reaches clumsily for his phone.

"What the hell? It's not even six."

"Let's get up and go, before my mum and dad get up."

"Don't you want to try to make up with your mum? That was pretty intense last night. You might feel better if you guys talk?"

"No need for that," I say quickly. "Shall we go?"

He sighs loudly and sits up, ruffling that hair again and stretching his neck from side to side.

"Okay, well then, let's go," he says without looking at me. He is fishing around now for his watch.

"Ash, I'm sorry about yesterday," I say, as I watch him moving slowly and sleepily, and the weight of how I've treated him sits on me in the sober early morning. "I am the worst. I should have been clearer with you about what you were walking into. My mum is . . ." I look up to the ceiling and take a deep breath. "She is a nice person. I don't know what my problem is with her. I just look at her and I feel like a loser, and like they're all fed up with me."

"She does seem fed up," he concedes wearily.

"I don't know what came first—her believing I'm a failure, or me being a failure."

"She clearly doesn't think you're a failure," he says impatiently. "She clearly doesn't know anything about you or your life to make that assessment. Tell her the truth. Tell her that film school didn't work out, and now you're doing something else."

"I can't," I say, head in my hands. "I can't."

I told them I was going to be so much more, I think, the shame almost crushing me now.

"You can," he says, shrugging.

"It's okay. It's fine. It will be fine. Let's just go, shall we?"

I pull my duvet up and leave a small note on top of my pillow for my mum.

> Mum—I'm sorry. I need to figure some things out and I will give you a call. I know I let you down. I do really love you and miss everyone. I'll call you soon, Mara x

Ash heaves himself slowly out of bed, and within a few minutes we're sneaking out the front door, closing it quietly behind us. I look back over my shoulder and up to my window to the little purple curtains and feel a stinging in my heart.

The drive is mostly silent, and as I watch the gray tones of the M1 motorway sound walls roll past, I fall back into my Joe-shaped dream, the fantasy of his arrival more necessary than ever. I made my choice on that wall last night, and I cannot turn back now. When we hit the ring road just outside London, Ash speaks.

"Hey, I'm sorry again about last night," he says. When I relive it, momentarily, I feel a heat rising in me. Embarrassment but also the lingering feeling of his thighs between mine. His soft, hungry kisses. I close my eyes and try to push the feelings aside.

"It's my fault," I say. "I'm sorry. Can we please forget about it and go back to how things were?"

"Um . . . we can try," he says, shaking his head as if I'm mad. We both know we can't put this back in a box and hide it away. There will have to be some kind of shift now. Would Ash move out? I feel a cold chill at the thought of it.

"Please," I say, as lightly as possible, looking across at him, begging him not to leave me. Not to leave the friendship.

"Okay," he says.

We pull into Broadgate and Ash drives right up to our front door, pulling the car in to stop, but leaving the engine running.

"I need to return the car," he says.

"I realize that was the worst weekend getaway of your life. I really owe you, Ash."

He smiles. "I dunno. I once went to an all-inclusive and got norovirus. I'll see you in a bit."

I laugh, grateful he's eased the tension. Then he turns on the radio and drives off, leaving me standing on the pavement.

I walk to the front door, then try to ignore the chaos of the renovations and make a cup of tea. The house feels hollow without Ash here, but I am grateful for the moment to think.

I curl up on my bed, in my untouched room, and call Charlie back as promised. "Hey!" she says, "thanks for calling. Sorry I've been harassing you a bit."

I sit up slightly. Normally it's me that feels as though I'm harassing her.

"It's no problem, Charlie. Don't feel like that. I've been a bit distracted lately."

"Let's forget it," she replies, little Sophie already wailing in the background. "How was it up at your folks'?"

"Shitty," I reply. "Literally couldn't have gone worse. I'm at my wits' end with everything honestly."

I hear her sigh, and then there is quiet for a moment.

"Everything I do turns to shit," I say now.

"Mara, I can't do this now," she says, and then I hear the crying closer to the phone as I imagine her scooping up Sophie and holding her closer to her chest. The idea of that contact, human contact filled with such warmth and protection, makes me feel like someone has grabbed my heart in their fist and lifted me off the floor.

"What can't you do? You wanted to talk?" I say, confused. "Are you okay?"

"Yeah," she says, "I *did*."

"Was it something urgent? I'm here?"

"I don't know. I don't anymore," she says now.

"What have I done?" I say, and with a huge, dramatic sigh, the weight of the weekend coming down hard on me now, I add, "How have I let you down, Charlie? Tell me all about it."

"Don't be so over-the-top," she says.

"Why not? It's who I am."

"Why are you angry with me, Mara?" she replies.

"I'm not," I say. "You're clearly angry with me."

"You know what? Forget it," she says, and then, for the first time in ten years and for reasons I cannot understand, Charlie hangs up on me.

Part Three

AUGUST

25

T'S A FEW DAYS later, and Lynn is making an impassioned speech at the Broadgate Working Man's Club, a fiercely loyal Labor crowd, most of whom are tanked up on cheap ale and frustrated the racing has been turned down.

"Hurry the fuck up!" shouts one rather inebriated man leaning against the bar with a fistful of pork scratchings. His arm is tattooed from his Rochester City football shirt to his fingers. Skinny. Ferocious.

Lynn is commanding the stage, though. She looks out across the room and holds both her hands up.

"Lads," she says, "I know you don't want to miss the three thirty-five in Cheltenham—and while I'm here I recommend My Lazy Heart; he's showing great speed on these longer courses."

That shuts them up. They all glance down at their slips and double-check the listings in their papers, circling, with blue biros, their new tip from Lynn, Broadgate's independent candidate for council. Lynn turns to me and winks. This is it.

Her maiden speech.

"Ladies and gentlemen, this community was built by people who wanted something special along our stretch of the coast," Lynn begins, "but in the past few years, the elite have taken control of our town and turned a good community—*our* community—into a *commodity.*"

Ooh, this is a good start. I am very proud of my speech; although it is cobbled together from some I found online, there's no way the men will know.

"City boys—and girls—with deep pockets have swooped into this stretch of the Kentish coast, bought seafront properties, converted our oldest pubs into boutique hotels, and ripped the heart and soul out of our town."

There is a boo from one of the round standing-height tables by the stage, and I realize they are agreeing with Lynn. It's working.

"We want progress *without* profit for the few," she says, "the few from bloody London, am I right?"

She is freestyling already. Still, in here, they hate London, so there is even a whoop from the bartender.

"There are plans to sell our lovely lido and turn it into luxury apartments. Our lido, the cornerstone of Broadgate since its construction in the 1930s. If I am elected to the council I will seek funding to restore Broadgate Lido to its former glory, while updating it and making it once again the center of life here in this small town."

No one responds. And for a moment Lynn looks around the room, looks down at her paper and then at me. She tugs on the bottom of her blazer and coughs into the microphone and frowns at the speech in front of her. She glances over at me, and I wave her over.

"Tell them you'll seek funding for this club. Something like an upgrade to the tables or subsidies on parking," I say.

She nods, slides back onstage.

"Look, lads. This town has been run by the same man for nine years. Our local council elections attract less than seventeen percent of the eligible voters, and you know what has improved in Broadgate since then? Nothing. Meanwhile, Margate, with its fancy music festivals and flat white coffee shops, is . . ."

She's lost them again, and the bartender has headed over to the sound desk to turn off her microphone when she blurts out, "And we'll make sure this place has a brand-new seventy-inch flat-screen TV for watching the footy and the races, and I'll make parking free for locals."

Nods of approval. Cheers.

"All right, love, you've said your bit," says a man in a flat cap, who already has the TV remote control lifted.

As Lynn and I crowd around the car in the back lane, preparing for her next rally in the car park outside the garden center, she turns to me and says, "Well, you can see how this works, can't you? You want to do the right thing, but to get votes you have to do these simplistic popular things. It's complicated."

"It is, but I think you just promised them a new TV, and that's okay for now."

"I actually think I want to do this job," she says, sighing. "I love this town."

"I know you do," I reply.

"But do these locals actually want it?"

I shrug. "The floating cinema did so well. Seems to me they

want it; we just need to keep coming up with things they want to want."

"I am quite amazed by your work, Mara," Lynn says, "for someone who didn't seem to give a hoot about anyone a few months ago. You have to get back up and keep going, don't you? Learn from your setbacks. Keep pushing forth!" She holds a fist up to the sky like a freedom fighter.

We stand in silence for a moment, and I glance down at my phone and frown. It's nearly time to get to the next event, but Lynn's words are gnawing at me.

"Well, sure, but it depends on the setback," I say, trying not to think of university and Noah. Have I used all that as an excuse for my own giving up?

"You're not dead, Mara. If there is something you want to do that isn't this, you should chase it," she says. "Don't be like me. I never even asked myself the question of what I wanted to do, never mind giving up on it. Seems so indulgent, really."

I roll my eyes at her and she breaks into a wry smile.

Samira arrives with her arms still full of flyers and plonks the pile down on the bonnet of the car. "All this paper waste." She sighs. "People think I'm trying to make them sign up for a charity or a religion, and I'd just rather not put myself through this anymore."

"Ryan can take over," I say.

"Did you tell her, Lynn?" Samira says, glancing over at Lynn, who purses her lips and folds her arms.

"I told Gerry like you said, and then Gerry fired me," she says.

"What? He can't do that."

"Probably not, but since I'm HR, and also the employee in question, who am I going to complain to? Ryan?"

"Lynn, he can't fire you. That's not right," I say.

"Meh," she says putting her hand on my shoulder, "if we lose this election, we're all out of a job eventually anyway."

We head to the garden center car park and Lynn picks up three mugs of sweet tea, all with milk and two sugars just as she likes them, and we sit on a couple of logs while we wait to see if anyone shows.

"You didn't reply to my message," says Samira, as Lynn becomes distracted by a passing friend and swans off in a self-important flurry of *did you know I'm running for council?*

Samira had sent me a message to see if I was okay, and I felt so grim after speaking with Charlie, I'd ignored it, turned off my phone, and gone to sleep. She touches the edge of her skirt and brushes off some invisible crumbs.

"Are you okay?" she asks.

I look at her and then down to the tea in my hand, and I shrug. "Not really," I say.

"What's going on?" Her eyes are fixed on mine with such an engaged intensity I feel almost compelled to answer.

"I don't know if I should say."

"Yeah?" she says, not pressing me further, but the invitation is absolutely there if I want to take it. She stares out across the rows of baby birch trees in pots and waves away a bee.

"Yeah," I reply. "It's such a long, convoluted story, Samira." I sigh. "You're going to think I'm nuts."

"Too late for that," she says, one eyebrow lifted. She grins.

"Okay, first up, the guy I met in Budapest? I need to tell you the whole story."

"We've got time," Samira says.

So I do. I tell her about the fortune-teller and what she told me, about Josef walking in and how I felt deep in my bones that he was, might be, *the one.* That I was certain he was going to come in a few weeks. I tell her about the things I'm supposed to fix. And about Ash, and the kiss on the wall and how I hurt him. I talk about my own feelings and my confusion. And how I wanted to go back to before, but also to see Josef and then I'd know. And then I tell her about my best friend and how we felt so out of sync and disconnected with each other. Samira listens, without judgment, until I'm finished.

"Well, it's you who decided that the fortune-teller was talking about this Joe guy. It's *you* who decided which are the various things you need to 'fix' because it's what you *want* to believe. How do you know she wasn't talking about Ash?"

I stare ahead at Lynn, who is gesticulating toward the beach and making shapes that I think are meant to be the lido's rounded roof. She's giving this everything.

"Because she described him. She said he was tall—"

"Ash is tall," Samira says. "What else?"

"That he was passionate, and that she saw a lot of people around him. That my meeting with him was imminent. And he came straight in. Right then! It was *Joe.*"

"But didn't you meet Ash the *very next day*?"

"I'd already met Ash once."

"But not properly. You said so yourself. And Ash is surrounded by people—he's one of the most popular guys in the town. My God, Mara, *he* works with his hands. He's a very warm person. Is Joe warm?"

"I'm not sure . . ."

"And you were literally looking for it. If Ash had walked in, it would be him! If Jesus Christ himself had walked in, you'd be sworn off sex and wearing a habit right now."

I shake my head. *No. No. No.* "It's August now, Samira. It's just so close to the time he is meant to come."

"Do you really believe it? Or do you just want to?" she says now, reaching forward and touching my knee. She gives it a little squeeze and I feel my stomach clench at the gesture.

"Both," I say miserably. "I don't know."

"You're a hopeless romantic. With big Aquarius rising energy."

"I *am* Aquarius rising," I say, nodding.

"But this is about love and being loved," she says. "That's what all this is."

I nod again and see that she's motioning to my clothes, my hair. The whole transformation that I've worked on for two months. It's all been about love. It's all it's ever been, really. This idea of romantic love—of *the one*—coming in and giving me a sense of myself in the world. I feel like I've been holding my breath waiting for it to happen.

"Now, about your friend, Charlie? You both need to cut each other some slack. You're just in really different places now."

"Not really; we're both in northeast Kent."

"She's a mother, and married, and you're not. What are you two gonna talk about between feeds and playdates?"

"That's a bit harsh," I say.

"That girl's life is all wrapped up in the day-to-day drudgery of motherhood and you're out looking gorgeous and gaining confidence and starting to shine, and I think that must be hard for her, no? She needs to be around people like her. Doing those vagina squeezes they do and talking about the color of poo."

"I'm gorgeous?" I say, grinning.

"You always were," Samira says, rolling her eyes. "But seriously, it's absolutely okay to drift apart for a bit. You don't have to put any more weight on it than that. You don't have to make a big deal of it. You can just let it drift, with love, and see what happens. You'll find each other again."

"But it's too painful," I say, clutching at my heart. "I can't bear it. I feel so rejected. It's worse than breaking up with a partner. She hung up on me. Hung up!"

"I lost my best friend from high school," she says. "She went to college in London and made a friend there and just didn't have any use for me anymore. Mind you, I had no use for her." At this she laughs. "What, am I going to have endless conversations about cocaine and house parties? I don't even drink. But seriously, we have moved on. She's changed; I've changed. Doesn't need to be a drama."

"You should be a therapist," I say.

"I want to be a stylist, actually."

"You'd be good at that too."

"In this town? Who am I gonna style?" she says, laughing. "Lynn?"

There is a silence now and I ruminate on my friendship with Charlie. We have drifted apart, that is true. Is it terminal? I think about our last interactions, the fact that she is always busy, and now it seems to be me who is. That I am genuinely frustrated by how much time and energy we spend on talking about Sophie. That I have been upset for the last few years with her, on some low level, just for getting on with her life. That the main problem is that I didn't have a network to plug the gaps while she readjusted to a new normal. She knew it, and I wonder if, in a way, she has forced some kind of space because of it. I cringe about the day I told her I was moving near her. The pause on the phone. What must she have thought? What must Alex have thought?

"Am I sort of creepy?" I ask Samira, who is eyeing me with interest, like she's waiting for something to happen.

She laughs a little too long at this and then says, "No. Now that I know you, you're really rather sweet."

I hear my phone ping and look to check it. It's Ash.

> I'm going to be out tonight. Just to let you
> know. Ax

"Is that Ash?" Samira says, grinning and lifting both eyebrows suggestively.

I flush red, recalling a flash of his thighs jammed between mine, and his hungry lips on my neck. I have to bite my lip at the memory. "I do really like him. He's actually one of the kindest, most patient, most generous humans I've ever met. And I fancy him. I admit it. He's tall, dark, and handsome like a mid-century movie star."

Samira smiles. "But?"

"But I have put all this energy into Joe," I say quietly. "Samira. I'm torn here."

"What does your heart tell you?"

As soon as she says it, I picture him.

"I don't know," I lie.

26

A WEEK LATER, I'm lying on my bed, my face cradled in my hands as the final scene of *Pride and Prejudice*—the correct and only version, with Keira Knightley and Tom from *Succession*—finishes in a kiss on the moors, the rising sun bursting between them. I think about the kiss with Ash in the darkness and how I cannot deny I want more. I cannot shake him from my thoughts. It's like someone keeps hitting Play on the same scene from a film, and I have to work hard not to look.

It is a mere two short weeks now until the election, and only three until the last Friday in August, and Project Mara is coming to a giddy climax. I have been to choir group, which was extraordinarily fun—twelve of us singing hilarious arrangements including Wilson Phillips's "Hold On" and Harry Styles's "Watermelon Sugar."

I look in the mirror. I'm wearing a cherry-red top and wide-leg jeans. Birkenstocks. It is a mix of vintage and new. I bought a leather backpack, and on Wednesday, I found an old bicycle for sale, which is now my primary mode of transport around Broadgate. No one wants to buy the old hearse, and I'm thinking of just dumping it at a parts yard at this point.

Out in the lounge, I can hear Ash moving around. We've barely seen each other since we got back from Corbridge last week. Ash has dug in on studying, despite being on summer break. He's been getting ahead for the new semester. There have been no movie nights since we got back.

I switch off the TV and cautiously make my way into our shared kitchen.

"Hey, Mara," he says, seeming to take some effort to look at me. "We're like passing ships at the moment."

He smiles, and I feel a rush of affection for him. His eyes are crinkling, but he looks really tired. Then I see the outfit. Is that a new shirt? I've never seen that shirt.

"What are you wearing?" I ask; then I quickly add, "Are you going out?"

"Thanks," he says, looking at the cuff on his shirt, tugging on it slightly. "I, um, have something to tell you."

"Oh, this can't be good," I say, perching on the edge of the table, folding my arms.

"No, it's not . . ." He stops himself and looks at me, pained.

"Is this about the paint work at the lido?" I ask. "You don't have to do it."

"No, that's fine. The boys are joining me on Wednesday to do the foyer. I also need you to decide on the final color for this room," he says, giving me a stern look. "I know you've narrowed it to three different blues, but just take the plunge, Mara."

"Yes, yes, I will," I say.

"But that's not what I wanted to talk to you about."

He puts down the plate he's cleaning, and I suddenly feel the air come out of me. I glance at the shirt again, and then the clean jeans, and then I look at the back of his head and notice the crisp edges of a fresh haircut.

"I've got a date tonight . . ."

No, don't say it. Don't say it.

"A date with Kate," he says, pulling a face when he hears the ridiculous rhyme.

"Oh," I say, as nonchalantly as I can. "Okay."

It hits me like a sucker punch to the stomach. My eyes hit the floor and then I notice his shoes. His nice, going-out shoes. No. No. No.

"Yes. She contacted me, not long before we went up north. I met her for a coffee after we got back," he says pointedly. "And she wants to try again. And, you know, I miss her." He shrugs.

"I see," I say.

"Yes. So, I thought I'd tell you." He turns back to the dishes now and then stops and puts the dish towel down. I can hear him sigh. He pulls a beer out of the fridge and turns to me, twisting the top off as he does.

I can't bear it. I can't bear the thought of it. I shake my head involuntarily.

"Mara?" he says gently, and I lift my eyes up to his, and when they connect I have to look away immediately. My leg starts to jig up and down. "Is this . . . is it weird for you?"

"It's great. I'm happy for you guys," I say quickly, and I glance up at him again and see a flicker of resignation on his face.

"Okay," he says, putting down his beer and heading to the door.

He pauses before he reaches the door and looks back to me. "I'm sorry."

"Why?" I snap. He and I lock eyes for a moment, and then I see the intensity leave his and a resignation take hold.

"I'm just sorry," he says again.

"Stop saying that," I say. I don't care. I do not care. I'm not in love with him, after all. I'm waiting for Joe. I rejected Ash. Surely if he'd been right for me I would have known it right there on the wall. I made a clear decision, didn't I? Flashes of the kiss start to disorientate me, the real, true feeling of his lips on mine as I jostle with the images of Joe. They are just images, with hope projected onto them. My blood runs cold. It isn't real, this thing with Joe. The kiss with Ash was warm and wet and very real. And Ash is right here.

"Just go, Ash. She's waiting for you," I say, hands to my face, stepping back from him.

I have never moved so fast into the safety of my room as after the door shut behind him.

I'm thrown. I sit back on the bed. Slump, rather. I want to shake him and ask if he's really sure about this. *Really* sure, I mean.

I look down at my phone and hastily pull up Joe's Instagram. I zoom in all my energy to his latest photo. The one of him in Vienna, by the Natural History Museum. Then I stand up, look at myself in the mirror again, and open a bottle of prosecco that has been sitting on the hallway shelf since the floating cinema night. I tear out the cork and pour myself a glass.

And then I start to pace. I look at the paint swabs for a few minutes, staring blankly at them until all the blues look the same. Then I head back to my phone to look at Joe again.

Then I wander to Ash's room and push open the door.

His laptop is closed and his pad ripped clean of his notes. His books are in a carboard box next to his desk. I spin around. His bed is made. He has new bedsheets.

His whole room is tidy, neat. The walls are freshly painted cream, the new window frames fitted, and there's a single dangling cord where the new light fixture should be. I recall the brochure he slid under my bedroom door with the note that he'd *found these nice pine lampshades at a fire damage job and did I want them for the bedrooms?*

I hadn't replied.

His room is transformed. It feels lighter. Clearer. And like he might be thinking of moving out.

I head into the lounge and stand there, feeling like an addict waiting for their next hit. But I have nothing of Joe. Just his photos, and a few videos online. Nothing new. Nothing real. I know every image by heart. I've projected myself into all of them. I'm desperate. I'm tired of waiting. I drink more prosecco.

And then I pick up my phone and open the Skyscanner app and search for flights to Vienna. I fantasize about wandering around those old, cobbled streets with Joe, hand in hand, ducking into little wine bars for a quick drink before the concert. I quickly google Vienna for more accuracy and find that it is more wide streets and bold, handsome buildings than dinky and cobbled streets and wonky roofs, like England. Still, we could walk down those wide streets of the first district, taking in music and art and architecture. I look down at my chic cherry-red blouse with its Peter Pan collar and little cap sleeves and think, *I'm ready.* I know I'm ready.

I have to see him, and I cannot wait another three weeks for him to decide if he's going to show or not.

THE SETUP

I find two flights. One that leaves Stansted in three hours, and the other that leaves at 5 a.m. I click on the outbound 5 a.m. flight. I don't even bother with a return; I just buy it. Then I go into my room, throw some clothes into a bag, and my new silk pajamas, and I head out the front door, clutching my prosecco, and make my way to catch the train to London.

27

~~~~~

AFTER TWO TRAINS and a very expensive minicab, I enter through the gates at Stansted Airport. It's 3 a.m. I begin to feel queasy. Why am I doing this? What am I doing?

I clutch my heart and lick my dry lips.

I don't want to go. I want to go home to my flat. To Ash.

But Ash is out with Kate.

I stand there as a family behind me inch closer to me, passive-aggressively telling me to move forward and close the gap.

Am I doing this? Could I check my star sign quickly to help decide?

I still haven't moved, and it's getting dangerously close to my turn to heave my roller suitcase up onto the conveyor belt and walk through the body scan.

I don't know if I'll see Joe, of course. I could just be taking a spontaneous weekend holiday to Austria for fun. And it would be fun. I could clear my head. Get some perspective on Charlie. Decide how to move forward with Ash. And if it's right, if fate and destiny really are working on this, I might just bump into Joe.

I could come back on Sunday evening and just slide back into work, saying, *Oh, this weekend? I took a spur-of-the-moment trip to Vienna.*

Fuck it. Live, Mara. Live.

28

BEFORE SUNRISE CAME out when I was five years old, around 1995, but I didn't watch it until ten years later, after I rented the sequel, *Before Sunset*. I immediately went back to the store and picked up the original so I could watch them in order. *Before Sunset* is set here in Vienna, in high summer. I imagine Ethan Hawke and Julie Delpy falling in love as they wander these streets, and it feels completely fitting that this is where Joe is now. The question is, will I find him? Will destiny bring us together outside a store, or across from each other at a bar, or reaching for the same gloves in a department store?

It is a strange thing to know a place through film. I expect I would feel the same if my feet ever touched the ground in New York and I gazed up at the towering skyscrapers, ready to take on the world, like so many small-town movie heroines.

Despite my hangover and exhaustion, I feel childlike leaning out of the taxi through the open window, watching the grand yellow buildings roll past me. There is a daring in my heart that wasn't there in Budapest. I am ready for adventure.

My last-minute room reservation is not ready when I arrive, as it's still early—11 a.m.—and so I hit the nearby boutiques, picking up a polka-dot tea dress that I know Samira will love from a woman who speaks very loudly and slowly to me in German despite me waving my hands and explaining, "No Deutch!" what felt like a dozen times.

When I go to the hotel, the man at reception takes one look at me and says, "Please fill in this form," in perfect English.

"Thanks for speaking in English," I say.

"Most people in Vienna speak some English," he replies, smiling. "Third floor, on the far end of the corridor. Breakfast is between six and eleven, and you've paid for a single room, so it's just you, then?"

"Yes, it's just me," I say, putting on a very brave face. "Alone. Party of one. And I'm okay with it."

My room is deep red with gold fittings on the door handles, the lamps, and the frames on the wall. The bed has crisp white sheets under one of those old-fashioned and very well-loved bedspreads. It is tiny but perfectly situated, with a view over the restaurant-lined streets below. I stretch myself out across the bed, exhausted from a night's sleep on an airport floor, and check to see if there's been anything new posted on Joe's Instagram.

Nothing.

I feel that same wave of tiredness again and decide that the very best next step for me is a luxurious hotel bed afternoon nap, and so I roll over and within a few moments I'm fast asleep.

When I wake up it's nearly 4 p.m.

I have a quick shower, pull on my dress and my sandals, slide my little leather cross-body on, and tie a denim jacket around my waist. I blow-dry my hair using a hair dryer so small it takes about fifteen minutes just to do the fringe. I toss the rest of it loosely up and look in the long mirror by the hand-painted floral wardrobe. I look good.

I step out onto the street and pause for a moment, taking in everything. I decide to catch the sun slicing in between the tall terraced buildings and have a drink.

I perch on the edge of the seating area outside a little bar by the main square and order an Aperol Spritz, which I down a little too quickly. Next to me, an old Viennese couple drink—prosecco, for her, and beer, for him. The man is smoking and gesticulating while the woman sits perfectly upright, her hair set, her Dolce and Gabbana sunglasses sporting the most enormous gold emblem on the side.

I smile at the woman, who smiles back warmly and tips her head.

I log on to the Wi-Fi and decide to quickly check my star sign.

> There are times when you have no choice but to charge ahead, alone. This is particularly true of single Sagittarians or those working to complete a difficult project. Be kind to yourself. Not everything resolves in a timely manner.

"Clearly bloody not," I mutter to myself.

When the waiter comes to ask if I'd like another, I shake my head. I need to eat. I suddenly find myself ravenous. I decide to head to Naschmarkt, a famous Viennese food market, for some dinner.

As I navigate the metro using my phone, finding my way easily to the edge of the market, I stop and take stock of the moment. I'm traveling. On my own. And this time, I decided to do it. It was all me. I grin a ridiculous grin. The kind that people passing you on the street notice, and grin back at you.

I take a snap of myself standing outside the Viennese market and send it to the Election group chat.

> Taking a break in sunny Vienna. Back
> Monday xxx

WFT? I HOPE YOU'RE NOT DOING SOMETHING SILLY. WILL DM YOU. And then eight side-eye emojis from Samira.

> **LYNN:** Good for you, Mara.

> **RYAN:** How is it?

I'm hot, sweaty and alone! I say, and then Ryan comes straight back with:

> *Mara's new Tinder bio.

I gift-wrapped that one for you, Ryan ☺, I reply.

I head down the little market, jostling for room as I pass a Turkish stall selling jeweled jellies and vibrant spices. I squeeze through bar-height tables where locals drink Grüner Veltliner and huge pints of lager. I duck and weave as I avoid stalls selling cheap tat, secondhand clothing, more food. Finally, I stop at a little restaurant, find a table outside, and settle in for some food and some people-watching.

I'm at the corner table, right on the market thoroughfare, practically in the line of the busy shoppers. A particularly bombastic trader across the walkway from me is desperately trying to get rid of some roasted nuts, and the lady selling children's novelty lederhosen across from him occasionally shouts for him to shut up. At least I think that's what she's saying.

The waiter comes over and offers me the menu, and then does a whole spiel at me in German, to which I nod and smile along, and then I say, "Danke," in my best German accent.

When he returns with something called a Hugo, which I must have accidently ordered, I point to the thing that says Rindsuppe on the menu and he writes it down and in a flash he's off again.

I sip on the cocktail, which is bubbly and ice-cold and tastes of mint and sparkling wine and cucumber. It's so refreshing in the heat. I take a photo of the tabletop with its red paper tablecloth fastened at the edges with metal clips to stop it from blowing in the breeze. But there is no breeze. The air is hot and thick and I find myself longing for that cooling breeze we get through the bay in Broadgate. And then I think of Ash and wonder where he is. If he came home last night. If he slept with Kate. My mood sinks and I squeeze my eyes shut tight.

I am here for Joe.

My dinner arrives, a clear beef soup with something like ribbons of pancakes floating in it. Still hungry, I finish with a plum dumpling with sweet vanilla cream dessert and another Hugo.

"You're in Vienna alone?" the waiter says, now speaking to me in English, as he prints my bill out at the table.

"Yes," I reply.

"Are you sure I can't get you another Hugo?" he says, with what I think is a mild flirtation. I look up at him, tempted by another. I can feel myself a little tipsy now and on the precipice of wanting to really cut loose.

"I'd better not," I say, handing him my card.

I leave five euros on the table for him and head out onto the street to wave down a taxi back to my hotel. It is nearly 9 p.m., and despite sleeping all day, I am ready for the safety of my hotel room now.

Tomorrow I will see Joe. *Tomorrow.* I want to tell Charlie I'm here.

I'm in Vienna, call when I'm back. X

I feel momentarily proud of myself, and then I check Joe's Instagram, again looking for clues as to where he might be, but still there have been no updates. I close my eyes and picture him and get this strong, visceral feeling that he is here somewhere. And we will come together.

I flick over to Ash's feed. I have been checking it more regularly. There is a photo of Ash and a group of friends standing outside the pub. I do a search in his friends now for Kate and she comes up quickly. I click on her name and go to her feed, and the latest photo is a selfie with Ash and the caption *Ash and Kate 2.0!*

I close the feed quickly, pushing away the feelings of sadness again. And then I roll over and fall into a deep, slightly tipsy sleep.

29

~~~~~~~

I AWAKE BRIGHT AND excited, and the first thing to do is to find a flight back. I search online and find a very late one out tonight—10:55 p.m. It will be a nightmare to get back to Broadgate again, but I push aside the money and the logistics and focus on what's ahead. I have a whole day here, and a million things I could do. I almost don't know where to begin.

Vienna has a couple of must-dos. I can go to see the huge, golden-leaf-covered Gustav Klimt and Schiele exhibition at the Leopold Museum, as recommended by a "24 Hours in Vienna" column and *Time Out*. But there's also the world-famous Vienna Zoo—the oldest zoo in Europe. The zoo is happily situated in the middle of the grounds of the Schönbrunn Palace, a huge estate that happens to be on Joe's Instagram, since it plays host to the summer open-air classical festivals. I could do any of that, or I could go have a huge slice of the very first and original chocolate cake at Hotel Sacher.

THE SETUP

Buoyed by my ability to easily decipher the metro system, and the brilliant accuracy of Google Maps, I decide to go do something for pure pleasure. Pandas for breakfast and chocolate cake for lunch it is.

I pull on a knee-length denim skirt and my trusty Breton top and head out of the hotel, tucking my passport and my wallet into my cross-body bag.

On the Metro I see a message from Charlie.

> You're shining. It's good to see xx

And then one from Samira.

> On the quiet: Lynn and Ryan had a row
> because she saw him drinking beer with
> the opposition. It's Broadgate for gods
> sake. I've slept with my dental hygienist.

I throw my head back and laugh, and then another message comes through right away.

> Enjoy Vienna. Remember your worth.

Samira is top-drawer. A good person. I reply.

> Yes yes yes. I have decided I'm worth not
> one, but two slices of cake. Photo incoming.

I grin to myself and head to the zoo for a whirlwind stop focused entirely on pandas; then I wander through the massive castle estate, getting lost in a labyrinthine maze and ending up in a tiny garden café, where I enjoy a cold glass of white wine, alone. In the morning. I'm either a free-spirited wanderluster or just a garden-variety drunk at this point.

At Café Sacher, I do take two slices of cake, sending Samira two photos, one of me grinning with cake on my fork, and the second of me pulling a queasy face. She sends back three laughing emojis.

As I burst onto the street, I check Joe's Instagram once more. But nothing.

My heart sinks a little. I look across the main square in Vienna's first district, to the huge church, and decide to head over.

Vienna doesn't seem to do modest. Everything here is extra. And this cathedral is no different. I wander around looking at the art, which is lots of people writhing naked and in pain or breast-feeding man-babies. I light a candle for my granny and grandpa. I sit in a pew for a while and try, as I have so many times over my life, to summon some kind of connection to a god. And then I think of Ash.

I pull out my phone and check Joe's feed and I almost leap out of my seat. There is a new photo, posted thirteen minutes ago, and he's location-tagged it at a bar called the Pony. He's standing out-side, cello leaning casually against the brick wall behind him.

And it is less than thirty minutes' walk from here.

I run out of the church, beaming. I stop briefly at the donations box and stuff ten euros in, crossing myself incorrectly as I do.

"*Thank you, God, you fucking beauty!*" I shout, skipping down the main stairs, past a woman who tells her young son to *see the glory God can bring.*

"I promise to give you a bit more thought, God," I say, as I wave the church good-bye and, stopping momentarily to let my Google Maps calibrate and find the direction, I'm off. Off as fast as my legs can carry me.

As soon as I pull up across the street from the Pony and catch my breath, I realize I don't have a plan.

I can't just bowl in there and barrel up to him.

I can't introduce myself as Mara and hope he doesn't think I'm stalking him.

I am, kind of, stalking him.

I *think* I am stalking him.

I call Samira.

"Hi," I say. "Um, I need a reality check."

"Are you stalking him?" she asks, deadpan.

"I think I am," I say. "What do I do?" I've flown to Vienna to try to bump accidently into someone who last saw me when I was a fortune-teller—and he doesn't actually know any of that.

"I think you should go back to the hotel and have a cup of coffee. Are you drunk?"

"I might be. I did go to church. Like not to the notice board but actually inside."

Samira doesn't answer for a moment, and then she says, "Although I want the drama, and, Mara, hear me when I say I *really* want this drama. My advice to you as someone who quite likes you is that you need to go back to the hotel, or to literally anywhere else."

"Hmm," I say, considering her advice.

Then I walk across the road and peer in the window, my heart thumping wildly in my chest. But I cannot see the short sandy hair I'm sure I would recognize. I move to the door and push it open, a gust of cool, air-conditioned air hitting me, the bartender turning to smile at me, welcoming. But the bar is almost completely empty.

"What's going on?" Samira says in my ear.

"He's not there," I say.

Of course he's not. This wasn't the deal. He is supposed to come to me.

30

~~~

A FEW HOURS LATER and I am sitting in the gorgeous little restaurant across from my hotel, attempting to order another wine and Käseknödel soup, followed by a schnitzel and more white wine, and I pull out my phone and see there are several missed messages from Samira.

> Just want to know you're alive and well and
> not in an Austrian prison.

I quickly message her back.

> Yes, all good. I've realized my date with
> destiny is fixed already.

She replies:

> Good. Because we need you back here.
> The billboard went up outside the garden

center and there was a typo. Ryan says the
opposition's family owns the printers.

She sends a shot of the billboard. Pictured is Lynn smiling, arms folded, looking every inch the local politician. Next to her a large circle with a big green tick in it, and underneath the messaging reads: MAKE YOUR VOTE CUNT.

Well, it's certainly persuasive.

I put my phone down and I take in the clear broth, meaty and deep, and possibly a little too warming on this warm summer evening. The schnitzel arrives with buttered boiled potatoes, cranberry jam, and a mountain of rice. The schnitzel is the size of the dinner plate, but it is no match for my appetite, which is insatiable. My phone buzzes again.

All okay? Not seen you at home? Ax

I'm in Vienna.

I watch as the little dots appear as if he's replying. Then they disappear. I slide my phone back into my pocket. I do not want to think about Ash anymore. I don't want to think about Ash and Kate.

A coffee arrives, cream piped high, and I savor every mouthful as I watch the bustle of Vienna pass me by. My mind wanders to Charlie. Charlie somewhere in Margate wrangling Sophie into a bath, or into her sleep suit, and reading her a book she can't yet understand. I imagine her flopping onto the couch, ignoring the washing, and curling up, finally getting some time to herself before she falls asleep next to Alex on the sofa twenty minutes into a film. She often did that, even without a kid. I hope he makes her the peppermint tea with the pig on the label, in that enormous mug. I hope that for her.

I finish my coffee, and feeling suddenly overwhelmed with tiredness, I decide to take a taxi to the station right away. I am done with Vienna. I need to go home.

As I look up and see the sun about to disappear behind the clouds, I wonder: What did I *really* hope for me? Beyond the romance and the whirlwind and the magic. Beyond the thrill, what did I really want for myself?

I wanted the sofa. And the movies. And the laughter. But most of all, I wanted a best friend. I wanted the calm, ordinary security and endless joy of a best friend to love and to love me in return.

I imagine the romance of the classical music, the grand architecture, the art, the history, and think, What good is it all? What good is any of it if you're not with a man who can make a good cup of tea you didn't know you wanted?

31

$\sim\sim$

I CAN'T BELIEVE I ever wondered what Lynn did," I say, hauling the canteen tables back as Samira sets out the mats for Mocha Mamas, one of several things Lynn coordinated around the pool, which I admittedly thought were a waste of time but should probably form part of whatever new plan we have for the lido.

August is proving to be extremely hot. Even the gulls are perched and lazy at high noon; the only real sound is the pulsing of the sea into the cliffs below. Broadgate is alive now, but languidly so. The summer bringing people out of their houses in search of leafy trees to snooze under and pebbly shores from which to dip their toes into the sea. The fish-and-chip shops are bulging with flip-flopped feet and children's naked torsos, and a few little pop-up stalls set up shop along the promenade.

"Lynn *did* do a lot," says Samira, huffing. "Once this is set up, someone needs to go to the coffee cart and get three cappuccinos, two long blacks, one hot chocolate, and a peppermint tea," she reads from a text message from Lynn, anxious we don't let her groups down now that she's left.

"I can get the coffees so you can get back to reception," I say.

Ryan arrives with four ice creams and waves to one of our summer staff sitting high in the lifeguard's chair. The pool is satisfyingly busy today, with plenty of people under thirty too—due in part to the heat, but also the renewed interest in it thanks to the cinema night and the election campaign.

"Lynn's not here," I say, grabbing a chocolate off him, quickly licking the sweet, melting ice cream, which is running down the waffle cone. "Remember?"

"Shit," he says, "I forgot. My granddad was over yesterday moaning about her being gone too. She gifted him a membership here for his eightieth and he only comes here to flirt with her."

"Flirt with Lynn?" I say, laughing.

"I've tried to explain," he says. "He won't be deterred. Me and Nanna have a right laugh about it."

"I've never worked with anyone who turns up with snacks for the whole team as much as you do, Ryan," I say, half listening. "It's very sweet, and appreciated. It's *so* hot today, my God."

"I know, it must be *at least* seventy degrees, Mara, how are you coping?" Ryan says, grinning across at Samira, who laughs coyly back at him. I roll my eyes at her.

"It's eighty-eight, actually, which to a pale northerner is basically a furnace," I reply.

"Can you help me carry some coffees?" I ask him, as Samira heads back to reception with her ice cream.

We arrive at the coffee-to-go cart and join the queue, Ryan next to me, waiting patiently, topless with his knee-length red shorts on.

"Why are you always topless?" I ask, trying not to look at his chest, which admittedly I know every inch of by now.

"So I'm ready in case I need to jump in," he says.

"Explain the Crocs, then?" I say, looking down at them.

"Same reason," he says. "I once tripped over my flip-flops trying to get to someone."

"I see. Have you ever had to *actually* save someone?"

"Oh, plenty. Roger Cummings, the old boy with the mustache? You know him?" he says animatedly. "He slipped and hit his head and fell straight in. And Samira's mum?"

"What about Samira's mum?"

"She had a funny turn in the pool last summer. I think a minor stroke? Anyway, I pulled her out and did CPR on her. You didn't know?"

"I didn't know," I say, the sun rounding a cotton candy white cloud and hitting me right in the face. "You saved her mum?"

"Yeah, I pulled her out. She's lovely, Mrs. Farhat," he says. "It's weird that I've kind of kissed Samira's mum, though," he says, laughing as he kicks the wheel of the coffee stand.

As I place my order, I finally ask the server his name.

"Justin," he replies coolly.

"You make really good coffee, you know that?" I say. "And who makes the pastries?"

"My cousin Barry. He was on the third season of *Bake Off*," he replies, completely deadpan.

"You don't say," I reply, and then suddenly I get a thought. "I don't suppose you'd be interested in coming along to the church next Saturday, would you? For the election polling station, just to, like, offer some refreshments out in the courtyard. There should be a bumper crowd."

"Sure," he says, shrugging. "Whatever. For *Lynn*."

He hands over the two trays of drinks, and Ryan and I each take one back to the lido, and then I see him. Ash, standing in the hall of the entrance talking to Samira. When we push through the double doors, I hear them both laughing, before they swing around and he offers up one of the sweetest smiles I've ever seen.

"Ash," I say, "you're back."

I haven't seen him in days, and my only knowledge of his whereabouts was a few messages saying he was going to be away.

"Ah, yeah, I went to London to do some *things*, ended up staying the week," he says, being careful not to mention he was working, but the implication is clear. "Just needed time to myself."

"Mara thought you were away with Kate," Samira says bluntly, and while I want to be mad at her, I'm kind of glad he needs to respond.

"Oh, no," he says, his face reddening slightly, as I feel mine burning as well. I breathe out. Relieved. At least they aren't at that place yet.

"The Mocha Mamas are already here, so can you drop those down and then come back? Ash's got someone he wants us to meet," Samira says now.

"Oh, sure," I say, looking at Ash, who gives me a wry smile and scratches the back of his shoulder, like he's trying to be nonchalant.

I rush downstairs with Ryan and we drop the coffees on the table behind the ladies and their toddlers, all of them craning their necks and gasping as we arrive.

"Oh, thank you," says a taller lady with braids piled high on her head. "Best coffee on the coast."

"I just love this fresh mint tea," says another, sipping carefully as she sways from side to side, her newborn baby in a sling around her chest.

"So how do you normally do this?" I say. "Do you pay separately, or do you pay all together? I don't have a huge amount of change."

"Pay?" says the braided lady, scrunching her face up.

"Yeah, for the coffee. Sorry, Lynn's not here and I'm not sure how it all works," I say, as apologetically as I can, while trying to wrap this all up and get back upstairs to Ash and his surprise.

"Lynn never normally asks us for money," says the lady now, looking awkwardly to the other ladies in the group. "Sorry, I think we assumed it was part of the program or something? A council thing. I mean, it's the main reason we come, for the good coffee and the view."

"A council thing?" I reply, confused. I don't understand, but I don't want to pry further. It's only twenty quid, and I can speak to Lynn about how she funded it later. "Look, um, never mind. You guys enjoy your session and pop up if you need anything, okay?"

As I make my way up the stairs, I get a strange feeling, as though a fog is lifting. Lynn paid for their coffees *personally*. She must have. I've never seen any receipts, so it's the only explanation. And what was Ryan saying this morning about Lynn buying a membership for his grandfather?

I shake the thoughts out of my head. I'll have to go and look through the books later and try to figure out what I'm missing here. I see Ash standing in reception, this time joined by a slick-looking man in bright white sneakers, jeans, and a black T-shirt.

"Hi," I say, rubbing my fingers on my shorts to remove any ice-cream stickiness before we shake hands.

"Mara, this is my cousin Chris. He's an interior architect," Ash says.

"He can bring all your ideas to life," says Samira.

"Oh," I say, looking at Ash, who grins broadly.

"Nice to finally meet you, Mara," he says, the emphasis on *finally*.

"Hi," I say.

"I asked Chris if he could come down and hear about your ideas for the lido, and maybe you two could work together to come up with something that the folks in the town can visualize? I just thought it could be my way of helping out the cause." He puts his hands into his jeans pockets, and then I see how tired he looks. Drawn around the eyes. I want to ask him how he's doing, but it is not the moment.

"So anyway, you guys should talk," says Ash now.

"Why don't you all go upstairs and sit in the office," says Samira, shooing us through the turnstiles. "Gerry is out," she says to me, and I nod, relieved.

"I don't need to come with you, I'll just be a third wheel," says Ash, nodding at Chris. "Mara can take it from here, I'm sure."

Chris pats Ash on the shoulder. "Great to see you again. It's been a while."

"I owe you," Ash says.

As we head up the stairs, I look back and mouth *thank you* to Ash. He doesn't move. He watches me go. Our eyes are locked, and yet I turn away. And then I keep turning back to look at him, because I know he's watching me.

32

~~~

FRIDAY, A WEEK and one day before the election, and I'm sitting at Happy Hair getting my highlights and my trim and the town gossip from Jackie, who called with a sudden gap in her books a few hours ago. Ryan and Samira are out and about conducting unofficial and probably unhelpful opinion polls in the car park of Tesco. An excuse to hang out, I presume.

"Everyone knows what you guys are doing, but I just think that opposition guy is too strong," Jackie is saying about Lynn's electoral competition. "Did you know he used to be a magician? How are you going to compete with *that?*"

"I'm no election expert," I reply, "but she *seems* to have a groundswell of support."

"Twitter isn't the real world, sweetie," Jackie says, carefully combing my fringe forward.

"I'm not talking about Twitter," I say. "Frankly, I've never seen the Broadgate election mentioned on there. I mean in the *commu-*

nity. Our community." I feel an unfamiliar bloom of pride as I say this last part.

"Well, I'm happy for you. It would be great to save the lido. My Gus loves a swim there, when it's warm enough, between late July and roughly the third week of August."

"We're looking into the logistics of putting solar panels on the roof and heating it," I say. "What do you think of that?"

"I think sign me up, bitch," she replies.

The door opens and Ash is standing there, boilersuit on; as he clocks me, I see the surprise spread across his face.

"Mara?" he says, striding across the room and taking a seat in the spinning chair next to me. I feel an instant rush of warmth when I see him, followed by a wave of sadness. "I didn't know you'd be here." As he says this, he frowns at Jackie. "Jackie told me to come down for a cut."

"Okay, interesting," I say, looking back at Jackie, who has started whistling and playing with the brushes in her color trolley. "My appointment opportunity suddenly came up too."

"Nothing to do with me," Jackie says, like she's not actually in charge of the appointments. "Your friend Samira suggested it." My eyes catch Ash's and we both offer up a shy smile to each other.

"You were away again," I say, looking back from Jackie to Ash.

"I've been at my folks'. I needed space to work and think," he says, the emphasis on *think*. He's looking out the windows to the bay across the street. I haven't spoken to him in any detail about the trip to Vienna or had a chance to thank him properly about Chris because I haven't had time alone with him, just that one solitary moment at the lido when he brought his cousin in. I have no idea what's happening with him and Kate.

Our eyes meet and I quickly look down at my sandals, my

pedicured toes something I was used to now. I wiggle the little blue nails.

"And how's the, um, work going?" I ask Ash, glancing up at Jackie, who I wish would just disappear now. Fancy setting this up and then hanging around to hear everything.

"It's good," he replies.

"And, how is, um . . . the *thinking* going?"

At that moment, Jackie interrupts. "Kate. For God's sake, tell us about Kate," she says impatiently, knocking over a rounded brush as she gesticulates.

Ash glances up at Jackie and then across at me and lets out a laugh as I roll my eyes. Mercifully Jackie finally gets the message.

"You know what, I'm just going to go and make a call, okay? Then you two can talk."

As soon as she leaves, I say, "I've missed you at home. You don't have to stay away."

"I know," he says. "I just felt a bit . . . I just needed space."

"Are you back with Kate?"

"Did you go to Vienna to see that guy?"

"I didn't see him," I say.

Ash seems to perk up a bit at this. But before I have a moment to push him on Kate, Ryan enters the salon. Topless. With two friends in tow, also topless. Followed closely by Samira, who cannot take her eyes off Ryan's chest.

"Great, Samira said you'd be here!" says Ryan.

"Ryan, what's the news?" I say as Jackie is back, covering my hair in a plastic wrap and nodding that I can move over to the sofa.

"Hey, Ash," Ryan says, a single upward jerk of the head in his direction. "Star and Anchor later?"

"Yep," he says, nodding.

I roll my eyes. Is there no social loop that cannot be closed in this fucking town?

"Yes, the polling is not great, I'm afraid," he says, running his fingers down his phone. The two boys behind him grimace. "Lynn is doing very well among under-thirties, obviously, LGBT community also obviously, Marvel Universe fans, very online liberals, renters, and Gen Z's who won't shut up about the nineties."

"Okay," I say, nodding. "So what's the problem?"

"She seems to have lost older, more conservative people," says Ryan.

"Lucky Lynn," says Jackie under her breath.

"They don't know her like they know the other candidate. Not that a single person could name even one of his policies."

"Everybody knows Lynn," I say, folding my arms. "She's involved in almost everything in this bloody town. You can't join a society or a class without her hovering around in the background suggesting you make a badge for it."

"Speaking of which," Ryan says, nodding to one of the other lifeguards, "these arrived today. I thought we could give them out."

He pulls a little tin out of his pocket and opens it. Inside are little badges that read PINS FOR LYNN, with her smiling face. I almost melt into the floor with the sweetness of it. "Ryan, this is amazing," I say, pulling one out and fixing it to my sweater.

"She needed to have a pin," he says, as if it was obvious, and so I hug him, and Jackie flaps about trying to keep my plastic-covered dye away from Ryan's *beautiful natural hair.*

"Nobody knows Lynn as a politician," Ash says, joining us. "You know, like if I point to Lynn across the street, she's the woman who hosts the bingo or whatever, but you don't think, *There goes Lynn, the next Jacinda Ardern."*

"But what can we do? There's, like, seven days until the election," I say.

Until this point, I had thought her popularity would carry her. But that seems very unlikely now. Everyone looks at one another, their faces grim with disappointment. But then I have an idea.

"There is a way," I say. "But we'll need to be busy. I mean, *really* busy for the next week. We need to reach people on the level where they're really going to listen."

Jackie and Ash both look at each other, confused.

"We've got to tap into the strongest force this town has and tell a story so compelling, so real, so illicit, that nobody will be able to resist sharing the details," I say, grinning.

"Gossip!" gasps Jackie.

"Genius," Ash says. "This town could win an Olympic gold medal in gossip."

"Samira, your time has come. We need all you boys too," I say, pointing at the semi-naked lifeguards.

"What's the strategy, though?" says Ash. "You can't just go around telling people she'll make a good councilor."

I swallow. "I have something on Lynn that could help. It's definitely gossip, and it definitely shows her in a good light, but I'm not sure she'll be happy with me."

"Does she want to save the lido?"

"Yes."

"Will whatever the gossip is make her sympathetic? It's not too personal?"

"Yes, and no, not too personal. I don't think."

"Well?" Jackie is standing next to me now.

"Lynn has been messing with the books at the lido."

"What? That's not good," Ash says, recoiling.

"No. No. You don't understand. She's been sneaking money *in*. Not taking it out. Donations. Like, heaps of them. Fake memberships. Real memberships she actually paid for. Overly generous things for the groups, like free coffees for the Mocha Mamas, just so they paid their gold coin entry and kept coming back."

"But why on earth . . . ?"

"I guess she was trying to help. But I found so many irregularities. I thought, at first, Gerry was laundering money, but I was able to trace it back to her due to the timing of the last three deposits. She has been keeping that place afloat."

"My God, that's a good story. Is it true?" Jackie asks, gasping again.

"I mean, I think so?"

"Good God," Samira says, covering her mouth with her hand. "Oh, Lynn. Oh damn, that makes me angry at Gerry, who has been pulling out almost everything she's put in."

"I know," I say.

"We have one week to hit every book club, music class, gym, hiking group, beach yoga, and bingo hall in this town. Everyone needs to work the groups and tell her story. Lynn is the greatest philanthropist this town has ever known, and she's going to use that passion and love to help lift Broadgate up," says Samira.

"I'm not sure," Jackie interrupts. "Is this ethical? Won't she be angry that we've outed her?"

"I think this is a greater-good thing." Ash shrugs. "If she's really doing that, throwing her arms around our community in that way, then it's time we did the same in return."

"Ryan," I say, on a roll, "we need to come up with a strategic plan of attack. We need people everywhere, telling the real story of Lynn. And we need to start at the beating heart of Broadgate's grapevine—you, Jackie."

"I have eighteen appointments this week," she says.

"Excellent."

"I'll help too," Ash says, and our eyes meet fleetingly, and I feel a piercing pang of sadness in my heart.

"You're the best," I say, staring at my toes. "Truly the best."

I head to the coatrack and pull down my handbag. There, in the back zipper, is the tin filled with phone numbers that I'd torn down at the church notice board. Guitar lessons, choir, book groups, belly dancing, and the lady offering Russian language. Dozens of numbers of local Broadgate residents. Hundreds of potential voters.

33

$\sim\sim\sim$

I RUN OUT OF a kundalini yoga class, laughing to myself. I bolt toward the hearse, which has still not sold, and drive down the main street to pick up Samira, who is standing outside the Broadgate youth soccer training ground with a group of mothers surrounding her. She waves to me as I approach, says her good-byes, and runs up and jumps in the car.

"This has been a quite a week," she says.

"I know," I say. "The ladies at that kundalini yoga class were all over it. So were the choir. I couldn't get through to anyone at paint-ball, but I doubt anyone there was old enough to vote."

"It's the fact that everyone kind of knows her, but no one *really* knows her."

"Everyone should know her. She's kind of a superstar."

"Did you speak to your friend, by the way? Charlie?" she asks as the car chugs up the street.

"Not yet. But it's okay. I'm trying not to worry too much. I'm trying to just let it breathe as you suggested."

"And what about Ash?" she says, frowning at me.

"I don't know. He has been avoiding me this week, and I'm not sure . . . ," I say.

"Look, Mara, Ash and Kate are no more. They only really got back together for one date or so, but the word is he wasn't feeling it."

I gasp quietly to myself.

"But I saw a photo on her Instagram," I say meekly.

"Was Kate on Ash's Instagram?"

"No," I say and then: "Are they really not together?"

"No, you dumbass. He likes you. He's crazy about you. I know you like him too. You need to get on with it. You're not still thinking about Joe, are you?"

"Not really," I lie.

We drive down the main street and spot Ryan coming out of the windsurfing kit hire shop. He waves good-bye to the lads and nods in our direction. Job done there. I drop Samira at the fish market on the far end of the pier, and as she slides out the passenger door she grins my way. "Reckon we can get this done, or what?"

"It's possible," I say, looking out the window. I swear I can see more whispered chitchat among the locals than usual. "So you're here until four fifteen, and then?"

"Well, Ash suggested we all go to the Star and Anchor," she says. "Five p.m. But Ryan can't make it, so it would just be us three."

"Well, that would be nice," I say, side-eyeing her.

The rest of the afternoon is a blur of social anxiety and excitement. I tell the story about Lynn, everyone gasps and promises not to tell anyone, and I leave knowing they will tell everyone. With only a week to go until the election, I hope we can all say that we've done enough.

I'm at the pub before Samira, and when I open the door, desperate for a glass of wine or an ice-cold beer, the first person I see is Ash, sitting there at the little table by the bar.

34

HE GRINS AT ME when he sees me, pushing the chair adjacent to him out so I have to sit right there with him. And I'm glad.

"Hey, stranger," says Ash.

"Hi," I say with a smile as I drop my gym bag. "Thanks for helping."

"I like helping you," he says plainly.

I can't answer. I don't know what to say, so I smile weakly. "I like you helping me too."

He smiles back and waves Eddie over—who actually smiles at me and says hello, and then Ash orders me a beer, glancing over at me to confirm he made the right decision. I nod. This is not rude or presumptuous of him; it's attentive. He's always attentive. I thank him.

"I hear you didn't actually get back with Kate."

"No," he says, shaking his head, "it was all a bit silly, really. We'd both moved on. It was one dinner date in the end."

"Really?"

"Yes." He is nervous. I can feel the vibration of his leg moving up and down.

I want to calm him. I reach over and put my hand over his and he looks startled at first and then turns his face to me. He is uneasy. His hand stiffens under mine.

"I get it," I say.

He pulls his hand back and looks at me. "You really didn't see him in Vienna?"

"No," I say, "I couldn't find him. And honestly, I just keep thinking about you."

"Because you couldn't find him?"

"No, because I couldn't bear the thought that I'd lost you."

He nods cautiously.

"I'm not very good at knowing what I want, Ash. I'm not very good at trusting my own feelings. I struggle with it. It's almost like if it's big and unattainable, then it must be love. But if it's real and simple and easy, it can't be."

"Easy can be epic," he says.

"Tell that to all the world's scriptwriters," I say, rolling my eyes. "But you know, there *are* great stories about the love that was there all along. In almost every makeover movie, the girl gets all dressed up and realizes she loves the person who was always there."

"What about in *Moonstruck*?" he says, and I smile.

"That makeover was always about Cher opening herself up to romantic love. It was never about winning over Nicolas Cage," I say, shrugging. "She had him all along."

He pulls his hand back and looks at me intensely, his eyes narrowing in a way that makes my stomach flip.

"Not that I think I have you," I say quickly.

"And yet," he says, staring deeply into my eyes, his face still and serious, "you do."

The last line hangs in the air for a moment, and I swallow a large mouthful of beer. Ash looks at the beer and then at me and then stands up. He picks up my gym bag and with his free hand he grabs mine and pulls me toward the door.

"What's going on?"

"Come," he says.

He pulls me by the hand out of the pub and up onto the promenade, and I let him lead me home. As we near the house, he pulls me closer so we are walking with his arm draped around my shoulders. He tugs me in for a squeeze.

Ash puts the keys in the bowl by the door, and as he flicks on a lamp, I catch my breath. The room is immaculate, the painting finished, all the mess cleared away. The kitchen bench is gleaming from a fresh sanding and oiling.

"Wow. It looks so beautiful," I say, turning back to him. "You finished it?"

"Me and the boys," he says, looking hard into my eyes. "Are you still with me?"

"Yes," I say, nodding.

"Thank the stars," he says, moving toward me, his strong arms outstretched, reaching around me to pull me close.

His first kiss is soft and gentle, and then he stops and smiles at me. He's checking to see I'm certain. The second is deeper and more longing, and a moan escapes my lips. He pulls back again, putting his forehead on mine.

"I think we should . . ." He pauses, and I want to tell him not to worry. That I won't waver. That I'm here.

"You want to take it slowly?" I say, finishing his thought for him as I pull back and look him in his eyes.

"You're not going anywhere, are you?"

"No," I say. "Right now, I just want to be on that sofa, with a film. With you."

"Well, okay then," he says, pushing my fringe back from my eyes with a gentle finger. And then he smiles and reaches down and picks me up in his arms, swiftly and easily. He kisses me again on the mouth and then throws me playfully on the sofa.

"Let me go and get my pick boxes so we can choose a film," I say, about to pull myself up.

"You stay right there," he says. Then he heads into his bedroom, and he comes back out with something behind his back. "I made this before we went up north. And then I never got a chance to share it with you."

"What is it?" I say, my eyes narrowing.

He comes across to the sofa, and when he gets close to me, he gets down on one knee.

"Ash, what the hell?"

He cackles, producing a small box from behind his back. And so I grab a pillow and smash him over the head with it.

"You bastard," I say, snatching the little box from his hand and opening it up.

"It's only got seven films in so far, but they are ones you said you hadn't seen, and a couple I haven't seen."

"It's our little pick box," I say, biting my lip and grinning. I suddenly want to pull him down on me, to have him completely. "This is so sweet, Ash. But why does it have a lettuce leaf stuck to the bottom of it?"

"It was in the bin, briefly," he says, a shy grin on his face.

"Oh, Ash, I'm sorry," I say, grabbing his hand and squeezing it. "I've been such a shit to you."

"You can save yours and Charlie's for you guys," he says. "She'll be back, Mara."

"I had another idea," he says, standing up and flicking the kettle on. Then he turns to me. "What about we have a party next weekend? End of summer. Election is tomorrow. You'll have the results and we can have a wee celebration with your work friends. Thank the boys for the renovations?"

"That's a great idea," I say, grinning. I could do that now. Have a party in my house. With Ash. "Next week though?"

"End of August," he says, his eyes fixed on mine. "I mean, you're not doing anything on the last Friday, are you?"

I smile. "I suppose I no longer have any plans." Joe feels like a surreal dream I left behind in Vienna now, and all I want in the whole world is to be right here, in this flat, with Ash by my side. I watch him as he goes through his methodical tea making, dumping bags in the bin and wandering back toward me.

"Are you sure?" Ash says, sliding them onto the coffee table.

"I'm as sure as I can be," I say, nodding, reaching shyly out to grab his hand in mine.

35

~~~

'M SURPRISED TO see her.

When I open the door she's standing there, with no Sophie. Her hair is pulled back into a grip, and she's wearing her glasses instead of contacts. She looks tired. Ash is in the kitchen and stops pouring his coffee when he sees her.

"Charlie?" I say, looking over her shoulder to see if there is a pram on the street, but she's alone. "Oh my God. How are you?"

"Sophie is with Alex," she says. "I have tried to call you. I wanted to see you." She looks behind me to Ash, who has traded his fresh coffee for his wallet and is heading toward the door.

"Sorry to rush off," he says, smiling at Charlie, then turning to me. "I've got to pick something up from work. I'll leave you two to catch up."

I smile to let him know all is okay.

"Is that Ash?" Charlie asks, as he disappears off down the street.

"Yes, that's him," I say, as lightly as I can.

"Oh, I see," she says, grinning at me, her eyes dancing. "Looks like he's settled right in."

"Come in," I say, waving her into the lounge.

"I'm sorry I've not seen your place yet," she says, looking around the tiny front room. "It's so sweet. Gosh, it looks newly done up. So he did it after all?"

"Yes," I say, spotting the movie pick boxes on the coffee table and cringing. I don't want her to see them.

"It's great, Mara," she says. "I'll be so pleased to picture you here."

I stare at her, realizing we haven't hugged. I go to her now, reaching my arms out. "It's great to see you, Charlie. What a nice surprise."

She pulls me in, tight and hard, before pulling back and looking at me with red, sad eyes.

"Can I have some water?" She sniffs. I hurry to fill her up a glass and motion for her to sit.

"What's going on?" I ask, handing her the drink.

She sighs and then I see her face crack and a couple of tears slowly start to stream down her cheeks.

"I don't know, Mara. It's just that you've totally disappeared," she says, rubbing at her eyes.

"Charlie." I rush over to her and pull her awkwardly into me, rubbing her back. "I haven't disappeared."

"You have," she says. "I really fucking miss you."

My breath catches in my throat. "I miss you too," I say. "I'm sorry, there's been this council election . . ."

"Yeah, and you're sleeping with your flatmate," she says, sniffing.

"Well, not yet," I say, feeling my cheeks redden as my eyes hit the floor.

"He's cute," she says.

"He's great," I reply, smiling.

"What happened to the Austrian? I thought you went to Vienna to see him."

"Joe? Um. Yeah. I think it wasn't really going to ever work out," I say, turning now toward the kitchen, as if to make us tea. I stop at the sink and look ahead at the dirty backsplash and pick up a cloth and start to rub it.

"You were right. He wasn't my destiny, after all that," I say.

"He wasn't? Isn't he due here, like, next week?"

"Yes, he was," I say, rinsing the cloth and hanging it up. "But I was wrong about it all."

I turn around, feeling sheepish.

"Are you angry with me? Have I done something?"

I think about this. I want to be completely honest with Charlie. I need to tell her how I have been feeling.

"I'm not angry with you. I've been a bit hurt maybe," I say, and she looks up, surprised.

"Hurt?"

"Yes. I feel as though *you* disappeared a long time ago."

"I had a fucking baby, Mara," she says, instantly defensive. "Jesus. None of this is easy, you know. None of it. I'm tired, I hate my body, I feel like I'm on one of those spinning things . . . ," she says, motioning her finger in endless circles.

"A hamster wheel?" I suggest.

"Yes, a constant hamster wheel. Up. Baby. Sleep. Baby. Eat. Baby. Baby. Fuck husband reluctantly. Baby. Eat. Sleep. That's it. There is no Charlie."

"I know," I say. "You asked me and I'm just trying to be honest. It's been hard. I've missed you the last three years or so. Even before you moved here. We used to tell each other everything. And now we don't. And you tell Alex instead, I guess. And . . . well, fuck it. It hurts and I know I'm not allowed to be hurt by it, but I am."

"I see," she says, "I get that. I get it. But, Mara, you used to get annoyed with me if I went out on a Friday night without you when we lived together. I could never give you enough."

I grimace. She's right, of course. I can see that now.

"Look. Shall we take a walk down the pier?" I say. "Come on, it's so warm and we can get a coffee or tea or something."

We head out of the house and down toward the promenade. It's sunny and warm and the little beachfront is showing off its full gorgeousness. I watch her smiling at the sea, then the little colored beach huts, and then across to the pool.

"Is that the lido?" She points to the distance.

From here, it looks spectacular, its curved building overhanging and glistening white in the summer sun.

"Hopefully, soon to be the lido with solar-paneled heating and an event space, and a proper organic café."

Charlie laughs, impressed. "The fantasy is real."

"Hi, Mara," says a voice, and I turn to wave at Sanka, who is outside the video store smoking a proper cigarette.

"Don't forget to vote today!" I say, waving back at him.

He gives me a lazy thumbs-up, and Charlie and I cross the zebra crossing and head onto the pebbled beach and across to the little café. I glance down the bay and have a flash of Ash pulling me out of the pub by the hand, and I smile and blush.

"Mara!" a voice booms, and it's Ryan in his red lifeguard shorts waving from the sea, clutching his wakeboard.

"Jesus, do you know everyone?" Charlie says, looking at Ryan with the kind of thirst I haven't seen since our London days.

"He's hot, but he doesn't know what an encyclopedia is."

"Even better," says Charlie, and I laugh, releasing some of the tension as I do. "You've really settled in here."

"Yeah, it's a great place, really. And many of the residents are under sixty," I say.

We push into the café, and I get a knowing nod from Chrissie. As Charlie lowers herself into the chair, I see the bump, and the edge of her maternity jeans. Is she going to mention it? It's just getting weird now—I first suspected she was pregnant two months ago. I hear my phone ping with a message.

"I better just check this," I say. "It's Election Day today, and my team are doing an exit poll by the church. I'm supposed to be there in an hour, actually, but don't worry. I can be late. "

I feel bad saying it because she's come all the way down here, but my priority today is to get through the voting. My mind wanders to the massive to-do list I have on the kitchen countertop, and I fret slightly. What a time for us to try to talk this out.

My phone shows a missed call from Charlie from yesterday, and I cringe slightly when I see it. There are WhatsApp messages on our Election group chat and one from Ash.

I hope you guys are okay. xA

I look up at Charlie and slide my phone into my pocket as we order a coffee and a tea.

"I'm really so sorry, Mara," she says, stirring the coffee with her teaspoon. "There's been so much going on and it's hard to talk about with friends who don't have kids. I feel like a bore."

"It's okay, Charlie," I say, looking at her, offering up my best, warmest smile. "It's not like I'm going to offer the best advice on leaking boobs."

She laughs and then looks out the window, her face hardened.

"There's something I need to tell you," she says, putting both her hands on the table as if she's summoning the courage.

"Okay, but, Charlie, I can see that you're pregnant, honey. Unless you have like a giant cyst or something . . ."

"Gross," she says. "No. I am pregnant, of course, but there's more to it."

She shuffles in her seat, stopping to touch her bump as she does, and then she says, "I've really struggled with Sophie, Mara. Like really. I wasn't exactly happy to be pregnant again. I'm sort of dreading it. I've been seeing a doctor about it."

"Oh, Charlie," I say, cringing in horror at how I'd been that day with her.

"I didn't tell you before the trip to Budapest because all I could imagine was being in the city with you, wandering around, unable to drink, feeling like absolute shit. Just so tired. And so conflicted about all of it."

"I wouldn't have minded," I say, wondering, as I say it, if that is absolutely true. "Well, I might have minded a little," I say lightly.

"But then it felt like every time I tried to get in touch with you, you were busy or away up north or in Vienna, and that's not like you, and I realized we'd split apart somehow. I owe you an explanation."

"It's okay," I say, reaching across the table, holding her hands. "How are you feeling now about it?"

She looks up at me and smiles weakly. "We had the twenty-week scan and everything changed for me. I just saw it and I was like, *yes, girl, you can do this again.*" She cannot hide the love as she says it. "It's a boy."

"I'm so happy that you're happy," I say, and I mean it. "And I'm so sorry I'm not more there for your journey to be a mum. I think about it all the time. It feels so unfair that we can't share the journey together. I don't want to sound dramatic, but sometimes it feels like I'm grieving and you're not."

Charlie smiles at this. "Believe me, there is a lot to mourn for when you become a mother. A lot of it is amazing, but how I long for those days with us together in that little flat."

"So do I," I say, feeling a little tear in my eye.

She sighs. "Mara, you're just . . . look at you."

"The hair?"

"Yes, the hair, but you look so different. I mean in your smile. You seem lighter. Happier. Less"—she pulls a face—"manic?"

"I guess I am," I say. "I've been working hard to try to get out there, and it's been really good. I mean, most of it has anyway. The eyelash extensions were a low moment." I laugh.

"I'm happy for you," she says, but she looks as though she's heartbroken.

"How many close friends do you have, Charlie?"

"I don't know. Including mum friends? Five or six. And my sister?"

"Well, up until a couple of months ago I would have answered one."

I feel the tingle of tears in my eyes as I say it, but I blink them away and continue. "I've been so lonely. I felt rejected. And I know it isn't fair on you, you're just living your life with your husband and your baby."

"I have done my best," she begins to protest. "You know, Alex is rarely home with the new start-up . . . I've been lonely too."

"I know, Charlie. I'm sorry. I relied too much on you. And I was scared to make friends. You were always enough. Until you weren't."

I sigh and look down at my perfectly manicured nails, care of Samira's time and attention and friendship.

"I found it hard to make other friends. It was the risk of rejection I was scared of, but mostly I was scared that when people got too close they would see all these faults in me and run for the hills. I kept myself small. My circle small. It was like the more invisible I was, the better."

"Mara, I really don't think you're invisible," she says.

I put my coffee down. "I know you didn't. Charlie, you were my whole world."

She softens, and she looks down, but not before I can see a tear in her eye.

"I opened my world. I needed to. I opened it beyond you and my bedroom, and I've met some really lovely people."

Charlie pushes her hair back from her face, twisting her wedding ring round in her fingers, and then gazes out the window.

"I'm sorry, I'm not exactly sure what this means for me," she says, looking back at me finally. "Are you breaking up with me? Is that what this is?"

I reach across the table and grab her hand. "No," I say, squeezing it a little. "I'm just saying that you don't need to be *everything* anymore."

But as I say it, I realize that in a grown-up way, we are breaking apart from the friendship that was and moving forward into something new. I am braver now. I *can* make more friends. And I can have Charlie too.

My phone beeps again, and I look down at the WhatsApp notification from Ash.

THE SETUP

Working through your to do list, let me know
if you've done any of it.

Then there is a snap of the list, and a smiley face. I feel warm.

"So, what happened with the cellist?" Charlie is saying now. "You've really, truly put that to bed?"

"Yes," I say, "I think so. I haven't even looked at a photo of him in days, and although I'm very much aware the last Friday in August is *next* Friday, I am also ninety-nine-point-nine percent sure he isn't going to come. That he was never going to come. And I'm having a party on that night even. That's how sure I am. A late kind of flat warming. You should come!"

"Next Friday?" she says, her eyes narrowing.

"Yes . . ." I pause for a moment. "We only decided last night. I would have called you."

"It's okay, Mara," she says, waving the thought away. "You *have* been busy."

"Ash is so great, Charlie. So . . ."

"Sexy? Hot?"

"Is it very unromantic to say it's completely comfortable?"

Charlie laughs. "It's very un-Mara."

She reaches over the table and squeezes both my hands. "I love you," she says. "But why were you in Vienna? I'm a bit confused."

"It was a whole impulsive decision thing when I thought my flatmate was in love with his ex-girlfriend. There's actually a lot to catch you up on," I say, looking down at my phone, "and I've really got to go soon. We've worked so hard, and I need to get to the church and join everyone."

"Can I see of a photo of him?"

"Of Ash?"

"No, the Austrian guy. The reason, I presume, that this make-over happened and the reason you look so damned sophisticated suddenly."

"Sure." I flip my phone over and pull up Instagram and then click on his profile, a new image there catching my eye right away.

It's a photo of Joe, in London. He's looking out toward Tower Bridge. And it's captioned: *A Date with My Destiny.*

"What?" she says.

"Nothing," I say, gawping at my phone.

"Show me!" she says, grabbing at it.

"It nothing, it's just—he's in London. I knew he would be, but look at the caption."

"Oh my God, he is fucking gorgeous. No wonder you fake told him his fortune. I would have done the same."

"I know," I say, frowning. "Read the caption."

"*A date with my destiny?*" she says, before she looks over at me. "Mara. What are you going to do?"

36

I AM SORT OF floating as I wave Charlie off at the train station, trying not to think about Joe.

That caption has upended me. I stop on the sidewalk, and for the first time in a couple of weeks, I pull up my daily horoscope. The first one, in *New York* magazine, says the following:

> Stop and take a breath, Sagittarius. Trust
> yourself and move forward on that project
> you've been working on.

I frown. Which fucking project? Project Mara? Project save the lido? I flick across to Astrology.com and try another:

> You are at a crossroads, Sagittarius, and
> it's time to make a choice.

"Urghhh," I groan as I slide my phone away and shout to the heavens. "Just once, just fucking *one time*, it would be nice for some-one to clearly just tell me what to do! I can't do this on my own."

"Well, lady, you could start by moving so I can get past," says a voice, and I spin around to see an old man on a mobility scooter. I stand there staring at him until he reaches up to his horn and honks a high squeak, like something between a duck quack and a bicycle bell.

"Sorry," I say, as I step aside, and he trundles slowly past.

"Trust your gut," he says, nodding toward me as he rounds the corner toward the beach.

"I don't know what my gut is saying!" I shout after him, waving my fist. "My gut is confused. My gut is a damn liar. My gut is full of shit!"

"Everyone's gut is technically full of shit," says another voice, making me jump.

It's Lynn.

"Are you coming to vote?" she says, smiling warmly at me, "or are you having some kind of crisis?"

I smile at her, my eyes flicking down to the PINS FOR LYNN badge she has in pride of place on her lapel. I want to fall into her soft arms and be patted on the head.

"Sorry, I'm turning into the town madwoman," I say, as she threads her arm through mine and guides me toward the church.

"Turning?" she says, scoffing, and then she squeezes my arm. "Is everything okay, Mara?"

"No," I say. "But this is your day, so don't let me bring you down."

"Your happiness is my happiness," she says.

I resist the urge to call her a classic Libra, but as we approach the gates to the church, I stop in my tracks and pull her in for a hug. "Whatever happens in the election, Lynn, I want to say that I know what you've been doing for the lido, and subsequently for all of us. I'm in absolute awe of your kindness."

Lynn stiffens in my hug but I hold her tight until I feel her relax again.

"Can I ask you something?" I say, as I wave at Samira, who is standing by the main doors, and the guy from the lido coffee cart, who's doing a roaring trade in Election Day coffee. "Do you believe in fate?"

"Yes," she says, without skipping a beat.

"I've always had faith in it. Always. It's been my comfort, really. But I am coming to believe that faith is just trust in something other than myself. And that perhaps I can make my own fate."

Lynn unthreads her arm and smooths down her blue jacket and pants. "How do I look?" she asks.

"You look like a politician," I say.

"Good," she replies, "because I have no idea how to be one, so as long as I look the part."

She turns to leave before stopping and taking a deep breath and looking at me. "If you need someone to tell you what to do, I can do that," she says.

I nod.

"Ha. Sorry, love. You have to figure this out on your own," Lynn says, and then she turns on her boxy, mid-height heels and heads to her people. "Simon Weston! How the devil are you? Helen! You got out of the football, I see. And, Benji, did you really think we wouldn't notice the new Tesla?" she says, as the crowds turn to face her.

It's Ash. I know it. But I can't help the niggling feeling I might be wrong. It's like after a decade of second-guessing myself, I can't truly be sure which decision means I'm following my intuition—my gut. Is the "be careful" voice my intuition, or my fear?

I walk slowly toward the church, knowing that after we cast our votes we're off for a celebration lunch at the Star and Anchor. I feel my heart beating in my chest and an insatiable need for oxygen because my lungs feel like they are being squeezed.

Samira greets me. She's wearing a floating red dress, with a serious blazer over the top, and is conducting what looks like an exit poll by the entrance.

"Well, well, well," she says, "look who has finally emerged out of the love nest."

"How the hell do you know?" I say.

She shrugs. "Don't question it. That grapevine is why our exit poll is looking so very strong." She hands me the clipboard and I am amazed to see Lynn out ahead by at least thirty votes.

"Wow," I say, "we might actually do it."

"You were really the instigator," says Samira, "but, yes, I will take some credit. She has nine hundred and eighty-one Broadgate followers on Instagram now. That's basically over the million mark, if she were in London."

"You've done such an amazing job, Samira," I say.

"Are you okay? You look kind of shell-shocked."

"Yeah, totally fine," I lie.

"Sure, Mara," she says, touching my arm. "Here if you need. By the way, Lynn said to tell you that she donated your car to the church. She said she was very sorry but she had to promise them something and it was just sitting there. And you love your new bike. I mean, you and that fringe with a sourdough in the basket? You can't drive a hearse anymore."

"Fair enough," I say.

I wander to the edge of the churchyard and spot the hearse still there, unsellable, parked under the chestnut tree, covered in bird shit. I wander down to it and slide my hand inside the passenger window and tear the FOR SALE sign off the windscreen. "Bloody car," I say under my breath.

And then I stare at it for a moment and I think about the phone mount in the back seat. I walk to the door and open it, fishing around under the driver's seat and then the passenger's seat until I find it. I look down at the phone mount still in its box.

I owe my mum a call.

37

~~~

AFTER AN HOUR of hand shaking and occasional uncomfortable hugging later, I'm feeling overwhelmed by all the noise and the people and just want to go home for some quiet. I head back to the house and slide into my bedroom—a total catastrophic mess—and stare at it. I didn't fix this room, did I? It's the last thing.

Fix many things and he will reveal himself.

I begin to strip my sheets and fold and put away clothing. I toss old makeup into the bin. Then, I push my bed aside and clear out the months of accumulated shit from underneath it. Plastic bags, clothing tags, hair, my old journal, and a garbage bag with clothes that I'd stored for charity weeks ago.

I am frantic in my clearing, stripping. Everything must go. All of it. My bedroom was the last untouched place—my sanctuary, my quiet space to come and think and be.

I am upset about Joe's Instagram post. It has totally caught me out. I was so sure that I had made the right decision. So convinced that choosing Ash was right and true, and I feel completely shaken.

Red-faced and crying, I hear my bedroom door open.

"Mara?"

It's Ash. He's standing in the doorway, holding shopping bags, which he lets fall immediately.

"What's wrong?"

He moves quickly to me and pulls me close to him, and I stiffen at his embrace. "Is it Charlie? Did you fight?"

"No, it's not Charlie," I say, feeling almost unable to speak. "I'm unraveling. Can we do my room? I mean, can I do it? I need to do it myself."

"What's going on, Mara? What happened?"

"Nothing," I say. I want him to go away. I don't want him to see me like this. I need space, time, isolation. I need only myself right now so I can figure out what is going on.

Ash pulls back and looks at me, holding my arms so he can study my face.

"Do you want me to go and get the paint?"

"Yes," I say.

"You want to do your room now?"

"Yes," I say, nodding. I can't look at him.

"Okay, let me put these groceries away, while you clear your things, and then I'll come and help move the furniture to the middle of the room—"

"I can do it myself," I say. "I just need the paint."

"But you don't have to," he says, and I look at his face. He looks genuinely worried. "I'm here. I can help you."

"I don't want any help," I say. "*I* have to do it."

"Mara, will you look at me?" he says sharply. I feel the shift in tension in the room. I force myself to look him in the eyes.

"Sorry, I just realized with all the people coming, and such a tiny house, I needed to do my room."

"You're lying," he says. "What happened with Charlie?"

"It's not Charlie," I say, feeling immediately defensive.

"What is it, then?"

"I just want my room done before the guests arrive."

After what feels like hours, he finally steps out of the room and picks up the groceries again. "Fine, Mara. I'll drop the paint in later."

38

~~~~~

I GO TO BED alone that night, no films. And the next day, I slip out of the house before Ash wakes. I have filled a backpack with my swimsuit, a brightly colored blue-and-pink beach towel, a book, a flask of tea, and a fully charged phone. I drop the backpack into my bike basket, fix my helmet, and push off down Sandhill Way onto the promenade. It's early, but the sun is already out. As I cycle down the main road, there is barely any traffic and the whole town seems to be asleep.

I have never done the coastal trail, a long, flat, looped path along the north coast of Kent and back inland. It's going to take some time, but I have time today. The election is over, and we are waiting to hear if Lynn has won. The gang is gathering at the Star and Anchor in the early evening to wait for the news. And Ash is in bed. I feel a crushing guilt as it dawns on me that when I told him I knew what I wanted, it turned out my foundation could still be shaken by that photo of Joe.

It feels like an insidious toxin moving through me, the bleed of doubt that that one image was able to seed. I used to joke that deliberation was my kryptonite. That I couldn't even order lunch without crippling indecision. I was the person who preferred, almost to a comical degree, to rely on star signs and serendipity and fate to guide her. And yet, for a sweet, blissful moment, I had gone with my gut and chosen Ash. I had given in to the pull and allowed myself to float, untethered to any kind of permission. It was nothing other than my own feelings pulling me to him. It was freeing.

I turn off a large promenade with sweeping views of the Thames Estuary ahead of me, and onto a small country lane, its thin path curving inland and slightly rising. Alongside me the hedges are glistening with new blackberry growth and the little green buds of the coming berries. It will not be long before the lush green of the birch trees and their teardrop leaves start to fade to yellows and oranges and autumn starts to roll in.

The sun hits me right on the face as I cycle hard to get to the top of a small verge and pull over to slip on my sunglasses. I stop and look back down toward the sea and along the coast to the next village.

As I continue, I think about how my confidence has crashed. How the grasp of doubt has reached for me and found me willing to walk away so easily.

I take a small slope downward toward a bay, nothing but a few cottages dotting the shoreline now. In the distance the wind farms tower and the blue sea glistens. I love it here.

After an hour or so back down along the coastal trail, I find a quiet bench overlooking a shingle bay fixed with timber groins—large wooden walls placed a few meters apart, which act as a defense system against the tides. A structure to prevent the shingle beaches from washing away, essentially.

I cast my eye west, wondering if I should continue in that direction, knowing that at some point I will tire. Then I cast my eye east and wonder if I'm ready to head back to the house. I close my eyes and try to summon my true feelings. What do I want to do?

I want to keep going.

After some tea and a couple of snaps of the view, I jump back on my bike and keep pedaling.

Thoughts of my parents start to flood my mind as I imagine my mother telling me to *be careful* and *did I have enough water* and *am I sure that I will be able to make it all the way back?* I think about how I fought against her as a teenager and told her she was worrying too much. To leave me alone. That I knew what I was doing. But then at some point I didn't.

I think about Noah and my time at university. I have this flash of memory—me walking away from my professor's door, heading back down to the media lab to wait for Noah. I remember being something like shell-shocked. I think about when he came into the room, smiling gently at me. That patronizing tone he adopted. I feel his cold hand as he reached across the table and touched mine and told me that he was going to go ahead and do his idea and I should do my own and that he'd spoken to the professor. I didn't fight back. I didn't say anything. I just nodded along while he told me this bullshit version of events.

Then I remember the awful moment when he hugged me and told me that it would be better this way and that we were holding each other back.

I remember telling myself that he was right. I remember thinking that it was probably a good idea that Noah moved forward with "his" project, even though the idea was mostly mine. I remember thinking that it was probably fair because of the small things he'd suggested we change in the plot. I purposefully rearranged the significance of my own input to justify his cruelty. I even felt sorry for him.

I remember spending the next fortnight stressed to the point that I was feeling physically sick. Like at any moment I might faint or throw up. But everyone else was working toward their final project and they were all saying that too. My classmates were all *stressed out of their minds* and *barely sleeping*. I couldn't think straight, and I panicked. I handed in an unfinished script that was fathoms below what I was capable of.

I joined some others from the class in a celebratory drink when we were done, and that afternoon I went back to the halls and packed up my things. A little drunk, I decided to go and tell Noah good luck. In my mind, as I walked toward his room, I pictured him seeing my face and remembering all the good times and all the laughter and all the film nights. I pictured him pulling me into him and begging for me to come back. And that's when I found that he'd already moved on and into bed with someone else.

I brake suddenly, dismount my bike, and start to gasp for breath. I lay my bike down on the grass next to the path and sit again, trying to slow my breathing. How in the hell had I been so stupid? Why did I not stand up for myself when all this happened? Why didn't I bash down the professor's door and show him my notebook and my drafts and say that it was *my idea*?

I know why now. It was because of this thing inside me that I cannot seem to shake. This distrust in myself.

It crushes me to consider. I had more belief in *him* than I had in myself. I had faith that whatever he was doing or saying *had* to hold more value than what *I* believed to be true. I ignored my anger—my rage—at what had happened because for some deep-seated reason I could not trust my feelings.

I am angry at myself for not standing up and saying *no*.

But I am also sad for the insecure young woman I was.

I know that to some degree I turned out like my mother. She's never traveled. She's never seen the world. She stayed small, kept tight with Dad, despite some of his imperfections. She is easily frightened by change. And in the end, I am living out my life in the same way.

I resent her for it. It's like I'm angry at her for not giving me the tools to be stronger. I longed for a mother who was worldly, adventurous, a trailblazer. And instead I got one who kissed me good night and told me, *"Everything I needed in life was right here. So why go anywhere else?"*

And yet, she helped me pack. She bought me bedsheets and paid my tuition. She put me on the train and told me to *"knock them all dead."* That was the truth of it. As much as she didn't understand why I wanted to go, she supported me every step of the way. I reach into my backpack and pull out my phone.

> Hi Mum. I'm having a flat-warming party on Friday. I know it's late notice, but would you and Dad like to come? XM

I throw my phone back into my bag immediately, too nervous to wait and see if she reads it and when she might reply.

And then I have a good, long, overdue cathartic cry, followed by an emotional recovery snooze in the morning sun.

When I pull myself up and take some tea from my thermos, I

realize I'm ravenous. I decide to follow the signs to Whitstable—a coastal fishing village famous for local oysters.

After an hour or so, I arrive at the bay and make my way to a bright blue oyster shack in the fishing port. Seagulls cackle above me and I'm reminded of my day with Ash when I was brutally attacked by the flying demons, and I laugh. I laugh remembering his face laughing at me.

Little by little, Ash and Samira and Lynn and even Ryan have bashed away at the little protective cover I'd built up. My own internal tidal defense system has begun to be torn down. And I am feeling freer than I ever have.

I lock my bike up on the rails and spend the rest of the day wandering the windy streets of Whitstable. A few hours later, I realize that I'm too tired to get on my bike and cycle back.

I reach into my bag and fish out my phone. There are several missed calls and messages.

First up, Samira: Results are coming soon!!!!!!!!!!!!!!! Where are you?

Then Ash: Hope you're okay, Mara. I'm here if you want to talk.

The missed calls are from Lynn and then Samira. I hit Samira's number and she answers in a few rings.

"Hey, where are you?"

"I rode my bike ride to Whitstable—"

"You what? That's like two hours away on bike," she says.

"It took me three," I say. "My bum is actually numb."

"Why did you bike all the way there, you weirdo?"

"I needed to think," I say.

"Uh-oh."

"What?"

"Mara needing to think means Mara will probably overthink,"

she says. "Do you need a lift back? I can pick you up. Otherwise you'll miss the results coming in."

"That would be *amazing*," I say.

"Okay, well, it's half an hour, so try not to do too much thinking, okay?"

Before she arrives, there is another message. This one from my mother.

> Sorry for the delayed reply. We had to
> figure out the last minute logistics of it. But
> yes, your father and I will come. Wild
> horses, darling. Mum x

Samira and I arrive at the Star and Anchor an hour later. Lynn is at a table with Ryan, her knee jiggling like mad as she stares at her phone.

Ryan spins his finger by his temple when he sees us, indicating that Lynn has gone crazy. We get some rounds in. And we wait.

39

T HE NEXT MORNING, I emerged from my room, hungover, with a sore bum from the bike ride, and I saw Ash sitting on the sofa looking forlorn. He looked up as soon as he heard me.

"Do you want space to think?" he said, right off the bat.

"Yes," I said.

"Do you want to cancel the housewarming party?"

"No," I said.

"Do you want a hug?" he asked then.

I nodded. And he pulled himself up from the sofa and hugged me, and I said, "I'm sorry," into his neck.

Neither of us mentioned Joe.

We knew Lynn had won within about fifteen minutes of wetting our lips on the first pint of the night. The results came in unofficially at first. Lynn knew someone at the office who was pulling together the final figures, and sent Lynn a text message that said:

You've won in a Lynn-slide.

Lynn burst into tears, and we all shared hugs. Ryan and Samira had several hugs, I noticed.

A few of the regulars came over to cheer our success, and Eddie, the world's least interested barman, even offered up a free round.

By about 6 p.m., we heard of a concession speech at the working man's club, and Ryan said Gerry was absolutely fuming. I stumbled back home at around 9 p.m., to find the house empty, much to my relief. It was too much to face Ash after the excitement of the evening.

• • •

OVER THE FOLLOWING days, I went through the final motions of party preparation. I knew how it looked to Ash, the way I kept a distance. It looked like I was hedging my bets by running down the clock in case Joe was coming. But in truth I was trying to unpick the feelings I had. This feeling that Ash was the one I'd waited my whole life to meet, but that I was a fool for walking away from the destiny that I'd believed in for all this time.

We fell back into the routine we had those first few weeks after he moved in. The one where I stayed in my room when I knew he was home, and where he left for work early. When we do see each other, he grabs my hand gently, or rubs my shoulder, and I stiffen at his touch. We discuss practical things about the impending housewarming party. Bills. Where to put the BBQ.

When Friday arrives, Lynn comes down to the lido to discuss next steps. None of us are sure how Gerry is going to react and what is to happen next, so we want to get our ducks in a row. Lynn pulls the end of a party popper as soon as she enters the foyer, defying both her firing and, now, the ban Gerry placed on her entering the building.

"You did it," we all say, cheering again.

"By a Lynn-slide!" says Lynn, shaking her fist to the sky.

"Lynn-slide sounds like a sex move," says Samira, handing her a coffee.

"Well, I'm thrilled," she replies, shrugging. "I've never won anything in my life. Not even a scratch card."

And now that Samira has said it, all I can think of is sex.

"Gerry apparently looked like he might explode," says Ryan.

"Well, there's still a mountain to climb," says Lynn, wandering around the 3-D model of the lido that Ash's cousin delivered here yesterday. "Now the real work begins."

"I love the tiny little people," says Ryan, bending down to inspect the pool. "That's me, isn't it? With the board shorts and the bare chest? Such amazing details in there, Mara. You've thought of everything. I always knew you were thorough, but you're actually totally anal."

"Don't call her anal," says Lynn.

"It's okay. I'm comfortable with anal," I say, shrugging.

"*Comfortable with anal?* Definitely put that in your Tinder bio," Ryan says.

Everyone laughs, and then Samira says, "Mara doesn't need a Tinder profile now, do you, Mara?"

I shift slightly in my seat and look at the ground.

"Oh no, Mara," Samira says now. "You're still together, right? We're going to your party in a few hours."

"Yes," I say. "No. I don't know."

"You literally live together. You'll need to figure it out," says Samira.

I go through the final motions at work, stopping to pick up sausages, beers, and wine on the way home. When I arrive, Ash has already done everything. He got the food, he borrowed glasses from the pub, a trestle table from his parents, tidied the bathroom, and even set up the BBQ on the strip outside our house, which is not strictly legal, he tells me, but he's spoken to the police. Of course.

How is one person so capable? How does anyone cruise into adulthood like this? How could I ever date anyone who never seemed to meet a crease in the fabric of life he couldn't iron out?

I pull on my outfit for the evening: the gorgeous green dress. I look good. Really good, by anyone's measure, but when I see myself in the mirror, everything just feels like a Band-Aid. The new room, the new house, the new clothes, the new hair.

I want to go back to how everything was before I saw that post from Joe.

40

BY 5 P.M., guests start to pour into our flat. Jackie and her boyfriend, Gus, are first. Gus is so handsome I nearly collapse into myself.

"He's taken," says Jackie, pulling him in protectively as she kisses me on the cheek. "You look very nice. Where is the cat?"

"I don't have a cat," I say wearily.

"It's imminent," says Jackie, as she heads toward the kitchen and hugs Ash. Ash always looks so good in his regular jeans and T-shirt combo, but tonight, I notice he's looking particularly good in a threadbare tee and his two-day stubble. I wave at him nervously. What am I doing? What am I going to do?

Ash smiles back at me, and in that smile I see that he knows what I'm thinking about. I hate myself. I *hate* myself.

I take another call from Mum, who is now lost at the turn-off near Faversham, but at least they are nearly here. They will be staying in my freshly painted room, although the idea of being in Ash's bedroom with him feels more and more like a very uncomfortable decision.

"Your father is worried there isn't enough beer. Do we need to stop for crudités? There's an M&S here."

"No, Mum," I say.

Chrissie from the café arrives with armfuls of leftover bread and cakes. She smiles warmly at me and coos at the interiors.

"I picked out the colors, and it was my idea to do the feature wall over there, but it's ninety-nine percent Ash," I say proudly.

"When you say *picked*," Ash says, "you mean pained over it for weeks and then closed your eyes and pointed."

"Sure, but at least I made a decision either way," I say, unable to ignore the subtext of the conversation.

Sanka arrives next and heads straight for the fridge. "You haven't returned *Zoolander*," he snaps. "That was a forty-eight-hour, not a one-week rental."

"Sorry," I say, pulling a face.

By the time Samira and Ryan arrive, there are enough people milling around that I don't need to welcome new arrivals, so I decide to take a moment. I grab a large glass of white wine and hide in the bathroom.

I try my star sign again, sitting on the new toilet.

Buckle up Sagittarius, you're heading into very emotional territory today. The sun slinks into heart-centered Leo, sending your focus toward intimacy. Rather than push your feelings away, sit with them and nurture them. Your heart needs healing and romantic love deepening. The heart will tell you what it wants.

I mean, it could be referring to Ash or Joe. I sit for a moment, on the toilet, underwear down around my ankles, and try to really assess my feelings. There is a radiating, pulsing desire to walk out of here and throw my arms around Ash and never let him go, but what if I'm wrong? What if true happiness—my fate, my destiny—is really coming for me tonight?

I sigh, resigned to question my decision for all eternity. As I emerge from the bathroom I walk almost immediately into Lynn.

"Now, Mara. Let's cut to the skinny-dip. I know you told everyone in Broadgate that I had been slipping money into the accounts at the pool."

"I guess you were going to eventually find out," I say, rather resigned than apologetic.

"That was personal, private information, and you treated it like cheap gossip."

"I'm sorry, Lynn," I say shamefacedly.

"I'm surprised at you," she says, and I finally look up from the floor and lock eyes with her. But she seems amused. "You came here all 'weird and reclusive,' and look at you, gossiping round town like a total pro. You're practically a Broadgater now," she says.

"You're not mad?"

"Of course I'm mad," she replies, "but the fact I can now cockblock the private sale and development of the lido will make it worth every damn heated whisper."

"You're a tiger," I say, impressed.

"Thank you for caring, Mara," she says, her eyes a little glassy. "Thank you for being you."

"Well, thank you too," I say, as she passes me.

I check my phone again. *Am I going to see if Joe is there? Am I going to resist?* There are no further posts on Instagram, nothing to help sway me either way, and so I head into the kitchen, hugging both my builders and thanking them again for such a wonderful job. I slide a cold bottle of white wine out of the fridge and pour another huge glass. May as well get wasted.

Ash sees me from across the room, where he's chatting to one of our lifeguards and a girl I recognize from yoga. We meet eyes and he excuses himself from the group and heads my way.

"Hey," he says. He stands back slightly, touching the bare skin on my arm, leaving a heated pulse so fierce I pull back. "How are you feeling?"

"Low," I say, taking a huge gulp of wine.

I shrug and look up at him, feeling guilt and pressure so thick I can't take it.

"I know what day it is," he says finally.

"You do?" I say, shrugging.

"I knew when we picked the night for the flat warming. I thought it was over."

"So did I," I say.

Ash nods.

"And it is over. I don't want him, I want you, but I can't stop wondering if at the last minute I'm turning my back on what I'm supposed to do."

I turn from Ash, my legs shaky and my heart racing. Then I look back at his face, and I mouth *sorry* to him. I can't deny this. I can't not go. I can't not see Joe for myself. I just can't.

Ash puts his beer down and heads toward his room, and Lee from the art class slides up next to me. "Anyone know who I have to shag for a drink around here?" he says, grinning.

"In the fridge," I say, motioning toward the kitchen. "Sorry, I have to go."

The room is swimming. All around me, new friends, acquaintances, in my very house. I am so torn between the pleasure of it and the pressing, probing claustrophobia of it. I down the last mouthful of my glass of wine and head for the front door. As I spill out onto the street, where one of the builders is grilling Jackie and Gus, who are both literally drooling over him, I turn toward the Star and Anchor.

Then I feel a hand on my arm. It's Samira.

"Where are you going?" she says.

"I . . . ," I reply.

"You're not going to go?" she says, looking over my shoulder. "Where's Ash?"

I don't answer, feeling the heat in my cheeks as she looks at me.

"Don't do this," she says. "You like Ash. Ash is real. Ash is here. Ash knows you."

"Ash doesn't know me," I say. "He knows, like, the first layer or two."

"Mara," she says, folding her arms and smiling, "you're not that complicated."

"Okay, please don't do this. Don't analyze me," I say, raising my hands. "There's nothing you could tell me about myself that will be a shock. I know I'm a mess. I don't need to be told again and again and again and a-fucking-gain."

"I wasn't going to say you're a mess," she says, frowning. "And who are you comparing yourself to anyway? Everyone's a fucking mess."

"Ash isn't," I snap. "You're not."

"Is that what you think?"

"Yes," I say.

"Well. I am in love with Ryan. Have been for three years, and

I've never told him," she says. "I have no savings, no career ambition, my screen time is around six hours a day, and I am scared of heights, spiders, oranges, and older white ladies. I'm a mess. And Ash? He's completely broke, he's come out of a shit engagement three years ago, and the only woman he's seen since then is the same woman who broke his heart, and now you. Ash might seem solid and in control, but he's a mess too. He's insecure, self-conscious, and lonely."

"No, he's not," I protest.

"We all are. Everyone is. Everyone's struggling. Everyone's trying to find happy and grabbing the bits that they can when they can. Everyone's scared. Unsure. Confused. Especially the ones who look like they're not, like Lynn."

"Lynn does seem like she has her shit together."

"Lynn is a machine."

We fall silent for a moment before I feel determined. I cannot not go.

"I just have to see if he's there. I have to know for sure. If he's not there, then I know it's Ash," I say, looking down at my fingers again and spotting a chip in my otherwise perfect red polish.

"If you go, you're choosing Joe," she says, a stiff warning tone in her voice now.

"I just don't know for sure," I reply, sniffing.

"You already know for sure," she says. "I know you do. Stop looking everywhere else for the answers. Trust yourself, Mara."

41

*T*RUST YOURSELF. I curse those words as I hightail it up the street, stopping briefly to look in the inordinately shining chemist window to check my appearance. I look good. I definitely look my best.

Trust myself. When you've been told all your life that your own instincts are wrong, it's impossible to believe you can make a good decision. As I walk to the Star and Anchor, I ruminate over years of insecurity and second-guessing myself.

Should I date this guy? I better check in with Charlie. Charlie not available? Astronomy.com might help. But the one voice whose advice I have never trusted is my own. Isn't this me doing what I think I should do? Isn't this my intuition? I feel a tug on my heart back to Ash again. Or is it that? Is that tug my intuition? And how do I know my intuition is right? Isn't it just another bunch of feelings that are supposed to guide me?

Why is this so hard?

By the time I'm standing outside the Star and Anchor, I stop for a moment and look upward. The sky is completely clear, and I can see the Milky Way fanning above me in all its gloriousness. I briefly consider checking in on my horoscope again. Something, anything, that will tell me the right thing to do. Samira said I shouldn't go, but she's invested in me being here, isn't she? She knows and adores Ash.

I look away from the night sky, my heart aching suddenly.

I do *not* want to go in here.

I want Ash.

The heart will tell you what it wants.

And yet, I put my hand on the cold metal of the door and I close my eyes.

This is it. This is the moment I've been building toward for the last three months. I take a big, deep breath in and contemplate everything that has happened to bring me here to right now. To this decision.

Can I go in? Am I going to see if he's here?

I glance back down the street and I feel a strong pull along the waterfront in the other direction. Or—am I heading to home to him?

Trust your heart. Trust your gut. Trust your intuition.

I shake my head. Which one of these invisible threads in my internal tug-of-war is my heart? Is it the soft and gentle pull home? A strong thread, I note. Strong and solid. Or is it the wild and hopeful yank toward what may or may not be behind this door?

My heart pounds in my chest.

Is he in there?

Did he come?

The wind picks up my skirt, and I will it to blow me in the right direction, to help me make that decision.

And yet pushing this door open, even just to look, would *be* the decision.

And then, as I look up to the clear night sky, I see the fullest full moon and the brightest stars I've ever seen. The night-sky light is trailing down to me, making a path on the damp cobbled road in front of me. It glistens and shimmers silver and beautiful. It is leading me away. I follow its trail and find myself heading back toward Sandhill Way. Back home. To Ash.

I run.

42

WHEN I RETURN to the party, it's heaving, and the first person I see is Mum standing at the BBQ chatting to Jackie.

"Mum!" I shout as I rush back toward her, looking over her shoulder for Ash as I hug her, without stopping to think about whether I should or not. She pulls back and beams at me. I realize I cannot run to find Ash now. I'm going to have to get Mum settled before I find him.

"Where's Dad?" I say breathlessly.

"He's looking for a spot to park," she says. "I'm sorry we're so late, we were hoping to catch the sunset."

"He can park at the church," I say, pulling my phone out of my pocket and calling him right away to let him know. When I'm done, I look back at my mum.

"Thanks for coming," I say.

"Can you show me the house? I told Jackie here I wouldn't go in until you were back. Where have you been anyway?"

"I just went to . . ." I pause for a moment. "Finish something off that I've been working on."

I motion her inside, smiling at Samira as I do, who clutches a hand to her heart in relief as she realizes that I didn't see Joe. I look across at Ryan. Then at Lynn. And then I turn to Mum. "I have no idea where to start, Mum."

"Everything looks very freshly painted," she says, just as my dad arrives rolling two enormous suitcases. I glance down at them, trying not to smile.

"You know your mother. Every single weather or occasion eventuality has been planned for," he says, kissing me on the cheek. "Thanks for the invite, love."

I show them around the kitchen and the living area, and then into my room.

"Gosh, Mara," Mum says, marveling, "everything looks so grown-up."

I open my wardrobe and wave at the hanging contents. "Yes, look, Mum, no black. Well, minimal. Listen, I have to do something really quickly, so why don't you settle and I'll be back. Then I can introduce you to my co-workers, and Ash is here, of course, and get you a drink."

"Go on," my mum says, waving me out of the room.

"I'm sorry, Mum," I say to her, just as I slip out of the room and close the door. She waves at me again, as if it's nothing.

There are people spilling out onto the street in groups, beers everywhere, smokers' circles; somebody is doing the splits on my lounge room floor. It feels like half of Broadgate is here to celebrate our flat warming. I push through the sea of people to find Ash.

I feel complete. This is what balance is all about. I have fixed every major thing in my life I could, and now the one has revealed himself to me. And that one is Ash.

When I can't find him anywhere in the main house, I wander through the little hall to his room, where I find the door closed. I knock on it gently and hear a craggy voice.

"Yes?"

I push open the door and find Ash sitting on the edge of the bed. He looks up at me and smiles weakly.

My heart breaks. I take a deep breath.

"I've been an absolute asshole," I say.

He doesn't reply, just looks sad. "Well, you're back already. I hope that's a good sign."

"I'm sorry I went. It just felt like after everything I should just see," I say.

Ash shrugs. "I know."

"I didn't go in."

"You didn't?"

"I didn't."

"You don't know if he's there or not?"

"I don't."

Someone turns up the stereo and it sounds like a bit of a dance party is underway now, and I look from the door back to Ash, closing it gently.

"Can I tell you something?" I say, leaning back against the door, looking across at him sitting heavy on the end of his bed.

"Sure," he says.

"I'm nervous of this," I say. "Of you. Of us."

"Nervous? Of course," he says, looking up at me. "So am I."

"Really?" I say, trying to smile.

Ash looks sideways to the bed next to him, encouraging me to join him.

"I'm sorry," he says, as I take a seat.

"I'm desperate to figure out how to trust myself," I say, looking down at my hands and feeling tears threatening. "I just have such a low belief that I know what is good for me. For so long, I didn't understand how people can listen to their intuition. Or trust their instincts. Or rely on their gut. It felt unfathomable to me. I feel like my 'instincts' are a constant knot of worry and anxiety."

He nods. "I know."

"And then, behind all that worry, there is a stronger force driving my indecision. It's the fact that I honestly don't know if I deserve this."

Ash puts his arm around my shoulders, pulling me in for a squeeze, and I rest my head on his chest.

"I'm sorry I went to the pub. I'm sorry I did. But I didn't go in because I finally felt, with absolute clarity, that I knew what I wanted."

Ash doesn't say anything, so I continue. "I'm a mess, Ash. But I want this with you. Can you work with that? *Any* of that?"

"I always could," he says. "You make the mistake of thinking you're hiding all of this, but, Mara, you're an open book. You wear everything on your sleeve. It's the nicest thing about you. Kate was such a mystery to me. Everything would be fine and then out of nowhere there would be a list of charges as long as my arm of things I'd done, not done, said, not said, worn, drank. It was exhausting. With you, there is no chance of that. Even when you're lying, it's clear."

"I have been trying to cultivate more mystery, but clearly failing." I laugh, and he does too. "Samira is right. Everyone's a mess."

"That's for sure." He kisses me on the forehead. "When I said I adored you, I really meant it."

"Ash. I adore you too. I really, truly do. This is what I want."

"How do you know?"

"I don't have to try to believe in it," I say, sighing. "I don't have to hope. I don't have to have faith. I don't need to do anything. It just is."

"It is," he agrees.

"I've never felt so sure of anything," I say.

"Well, Mara. To be fair, that wouldn't be hard," he says, smiling now. "Come on. Let's go get a drink."

• • •

WE HEAD OUT into the party, and I try to let everything flow around me. I watch, almost as an onlooker in my own life, as Ash hugs my mother and shakes hands with my dad. I watch as Lynn gets drunk and slightly rowdy, and as Samira and Ryan cozy up on the sofa. I watch as Dad and Ash talk about fixtures and fittings in the hallway and as Mum giggles nervously while Jackie points out each person in the room, their relation to me, and an added tidbit about their lives for our pleasure. I watch as people start to leave, and a few help with the cleanup, stuffing bottles into boxes for recycling and rubbish into big black bags. I watch as Chrissie does the dishes while Mum dries. Someone takes the rubbish, but I don't know who.

I watch as the evening slowly ends and Mum and Dad retire to my bedroom with hugs and promises of breakfast, and Ash and I look shyly at each other as we make our way down the hallway to his room. We giggle as we close his door, and I'm grateful that there is a bathroom between me and my parents. I stand against the back of his closed bedroom door and he leans in to kiss me. He stops just before and looks at me teasingly.

"Are you sure?" he says, leaning in and pinning me against the door with his body.

"Yes," I say, smiling back at him.

"Just in case you try to run," he says, putting an arm either side of me again, kissing my neck once so my whole body melts and I feel my knees sink.

"I won't run," I say.

"Shhh," he says, as he kisses me gently on the mouth.

And then I kiss him. His mouth is strong and hungry, and my body echoes the same urgency. I cannot move fast enough, and yet I want everything to linger.

Ash lifts me up, easily and gracefully, and my legs automatically curl around his waist, and we kiss deeply again. He walks me toward his bed.

"Shhh," I say, "my parents."

I can feel his mouth break into a smile as he kisses me and then pushes me onto the bed, following me down so his full, heavy weight is on top of me.

His eyes take me in, and his mouth is open as he kisses me again, pushing my dress all the way up, exposing my underwear. He moans into the pillow now as his hand trails from my thigh to my breast and he shakes his head, smiling again.

"What?" I say.

"It's the waiting," he says. "It's been kind of overwhelming."

And so now I take over. I reach down and pull off his shirt first, revealing that broad chest and spray of hair, and I unzip my dress and pull it over my head. Then I reach back and unclip my bra and he helps me by grabbing it and tossing it aside.

"Beautiful," he says, kissing me. "Lovable. Worth it."

"Stop it," I reply, blushing now, wanting to cover up.

I can feel the length of him pressing into me, and I feel completely ready for him.

He's stopping again, though, to kiss me, to look at me. He brushes my fringe off my face and runs his hand from my neck across my nipples to the top of my underwear. He doesn't stop and his fingers are between my legs.

"I want you, Ash, I want this," I say in a ragged whisper, gasping as his fingertips find their target.

And that is enough for him. As I feel him inside me I want to cry out, but I bury my face in his neck.

"I always did," he says, kissing me on the ear, moving slowly at first.

I bite my lip and the waves of pleasure overwhelm me as I fade into the bliss of Ash.

●　●　●

THE NEXT MORNING, we lie on his bed. I'm curled up in the sheet and pull Ash down to me.

"This is the best decision I ever made," I say.

He kisses me on the lips and nods. "Agreed," he says. "I am your best decision."

And then as he stands to pull on a fresh T-shirt, I glance up at the calendar on the wall. University starts up for him in a couple of weeks. And then I see in little red pen *Mum's Birthday.* Sweet, I think, that Ash would write these things down so he doesn't forget.

And then I gasp.

Ash spins around at the sound, as he yanks his T-shirt down and looks at me.

"What is it?" he says. "Mara?"

"Your birthday. When is it?" I say. "My God, Ash. I don't even know your star sign."

But instead of feeling panic, the thought makes me laugh, and Ash comes down onto the bed, leaning across me, his arms on either side of me, pinning me in place.

"I'll never tell," he whispers.

Acknowledgments

Hello. Thank you so much for reading my book. I wish I could hug you and tell you personally how much it means.

To me, a book is not your baby, but more like a difficult partner. She is challenging, stubborn, complicated, and omnipresent in your life. She is everywhere you turn. Suffocating one minute, and your greatest joy the next. Then one day she leaves and is no longer yours. Emptiness follows, then an anxious, lonely hope that she finds someone to love her without all your history and baggage. That she brings joy and warmth. That she will make someone smile as they clutch her to their chest.

I hope that person is you.

I want to thank my publishers, Tara and Harriet, for pushing me when it got really hard to get this book across the line. I honestly don't know what I would have done without them. To Katie and Vicky and everyone at Viking from the OG team, I can't *wait* to see you all again.

ACKNOWLEDGMENTS

To my agent, Hattie, who is always on my side, even when I'm a nightmare.

And finally, I want to thank the book blogging and reading community and all my fellow authors who make this often tough and lonely job so rewarding. When I have felt my most alone, you have all been there. You bring the light.

Lots of love, Lizzy. X

The Setup

LIZZY DENT

A Conversation with Lizzy Dent

Discussion Questions

BOOK
ENDS

PUTNAM
— EST. 1838 —

A Conversation with Lizzy Dent

What inspired you to write _The Setup_?

The pandemic. When I was stuck at home in March 2020, I was really feeling lost and lonely and wishing that someone or something could tell me what was coming next. I hated the unknown. I clung to every news article that predicted the way the pandemic would play out. It got me thinking a lot about belief structures and how much peace they must bring for people.

This is your second adult novel. Was the writing process different than for _The Summer Job_? Was anything harder for you? Easier?

This was so hard. I have cried so many tears over this book. Writing was difficult because of the pandemic: struggling with kids, working from home, and just the fear and the unknown of 2020 made it hard to focus. By comparison, my next book has taken three months to write. _The Setup_ took more than a year and a half!

What was your favorite scene to write in the novel?

I love when Mara finds the video store, because honestly, I'd love to own a video store. I hate scrolling through a screen to get a recommendation. Remember when you could go into Blockbuster and a kid named Noah would implore you to watch some black-and-white art-house film and you'd take it out of politeness and then discover a brilliant film like *Frances Ha*? I WANT THAT PLEASE.

Do you see yourself in Mara? Why or why not?

I understand and quite enjoy her obsession with astrology, though I don't relate to it. I do relate to her insecurities about how she looks—wearing black and wanting to disappear. But the thing I relate to most of all is her difficulty in trusting her instincts. I find it very hard to trust myself. I am in constant awe of people who say they know what they want in life and then go for it in this clear and blinkered way.

Mara and Charlie's friendship plays an important role in the novel. Why did you choose to write about the struggles they face at this point in their lives?

Awww. I fell out with a few friends in my thirties and had a few move on and have kids before I did. I wanted to examine that—how friends change and friendships change, and how you can fall out of sync but still love each other.

The concept of fate is mentioned multiple times in *The Setup*, and Mara herself undergoes a reckoning about her decision-making. Do you believe in fate, astrological signs, and the uni-

verse guiding you down a certain path in life? What do you think are the potential pros and cons of this outlook on life?

I don't really believe in fate as such. That said, when I started writing *The Setup*, I didn't really understand why people were into astrology, and by the end of the book, I totally got it. It comes back to those feelings of being lost and having no idea what is going to happen next during the pandemic. I'm not a religious person but there were times when I looked up at the sky and prayed for a god—anything—to comfort me because I was scared. Astrology gives a framework to help you understand yourself, and it's no wonder it's as old and as embedded in the world as it is. It's pretty incredible when you start to learn about it. Some people have God. Some people have tea leaves. Some people have Gwyneth Paltrow. We all just want the same thing: a bit of guidance.

What do you think lies at the core of Ash's character? What do you think is special about his relationship with Mara? Is Ash based on a real person?

Ash embodies my dream of going back to university to do the science degree I always thought I should have done. He's also every nice guy you've ever hung out with and looked back on longingly when you get a little older and think, "I would really have enjoyed growing old with that person." Ash is the best of us.

If you were Mara, would you open the door at the end of the novel?

I would so open the door.

What do you want readers to take away from *The Setup*?

Hopefully a bit of a warm glow.

What's next for you?

My third novel, which feels like my best yet! I used to make TV for a living once upon a time, and it's been fun to revisit that world and see what happens when you write an outrageous, summery romance set in gorgeous London featuring a former child star, a reality-TV bad boy, and a tortoise called Elfie.

Discussion Questions

1. Although Mara feels average in almost every part of her life, she steps out of her comfort zone and impersonates a fortune-teller at the start of the novel. Have you ever stepped out of your comfort zone and done something you never expected? What happened?

2. If you underwent a Project [Insert Your Name Here], what are three things you would reinvent about yourself? They can be as small as "get my nails done more often," or as big as "make new friends."

3. Mara reads Ash a quote from the movie *Serendipity* about life not being a series of coincidences, but events that culminate in one perfect plan—fate. Do you agree or disagree with this statement and why? How do you think this idea applies to Mara's life?

4. What is your astrological sign and do you think it is an accurate depiction of you? Why or why not?

5. What was your favorite scene in the novel and why?

6. Mara's relationship with her family is a complicated one. Have you ever felt disconnected from your family? What was the issue and how was it resolved? If it hasn't been resolved yet, how could it be fixed in the future?

7. Discuss the importance of having a gathering space in a community. Do you have somewhere like that where you live? How has it changed the dynamic of your town? Has it changed your life?

8. In *The Setup*, Mara's friendships in her small town and with her best friend change dramatically. How have your friendships changed as you've entered different phases of your life? Are you happy with your friendships now? Why or why not?

9. Why do you think Ash and Mara have a connection? What do they bring out the most in each other? What was your favorite scene of theirs from the novel?

10. If you were Mara, would you open the door at the end of the novel?

11. Were you surprised and satisfied by the ending?

About the Author

LIZZY DENT (mis)spent her early twenties working in Scotland in hospitality. After years traveling the world making music TV for MTV and Channel 4, and creating digital content for Cartoon Network, the BBC, and ITV, she wrote three young adult novels as Rebecca Denton, which were published in the UK. *The Summer Job* was her debut adult novel. Now in her late thirties, she lives in London, Austria, and New Zealand with her young family.

CONNECT ONLINE

LizzyDent.com

🐦 DentLizzy

📷 Lizzy.Dent